KU-768-783

JAMES PATTERSON

& NANCY ALLEN

JAILHOUSE LAWYER

CENTURY

1 3 5 7 9 10 8 6 4 2

Century
20 Vauxhall Bridge Road
London SW1V 2SA

Century is part of the Penguin Random House group of companies
whose addresses can be found at global.penguinrandomhouse.com

Penguin
Random House
UK

Copyright © James Patterson 2021

James Patterson has asserted his right to be identified as the author of this
Work in accordance with the Copyright, Designs and Patents Act 1988

This is a work of fiction. All characters and descriptions of events are the products of the
author's imagination and any resemblance to actual persons is entirely coincidental

First published in Great Britain by Century in 2021

www.penguin.co.uk

A CIP catalogue record for this book is available from the British Library

ISBN 9781529135770
ISBN 9781529135787 (trade paperback edition)

Printed and bound in Great Britain by Clays Ltd, Elcograf S.p.A.

The authorised representative in the EEA is Penguin Random House Ireland,
Morrison Chambers, 32 Nassau Street, Dublin D02 YH68

Penguin Random House is committed to a sustainable future
for our business, our readers and our planet. This book is made
from Forest Stewardship Council® paper.

MIX
Paper from
responsible sources
FSC
www.fsc.org   FSC® C018179

In memory of Susan Appelquist

CONTENTS

JAILHOUSE
LAWYER

PROLOGUE

I WASN'T PRESENT at the courthouse in Erva, Alabama, on that morning in June, when events unfolded that would suck me into the undertow of Douglas County. But I've talked to the people who were there. I've heard the story from all perspectives.

They all recalled that it was a bright day. The morning sun filled the courtroom with light, making the polished walnut benches and vintage millwork gleam.

The county inmates, garbed in orange scrubs, sat together in the front row of the courtroom gallery, bowing their heads to keep the sun out of their eyes. One young man covered his face with his hands.

The district attorney shifted in his chair to peer through the glass panes in the doors leading into the courtroom rotunda. His unlined face wore an anxious expression.

The court reporter's heels tapped a nervous staccato beat on the tile floor. She turned and whispered to the bailiff, who stood beside the door to the chambers of Judge Wyatt Pickens.

"Well, where is he?" the court reporter said, just as the chamber door opened and Judge Pickens emerged.

The occupants of the courtroom jumped to their feet even

before the bailiff's voice called out, "All rise! The Circuit Court of Douglas County, Alabama, is now in session, Judge Wyatt Pickens presiding."

The judge settled into his seat. He opened the laptop on the bench before briefly examining a stack of manila file folders. "You may be seated."

As the courtroom rustled with the sounds of people shuffling back onto the benches, the judge looked out over the courtroom.

His eyes narrowed. "Where is the public defender?"

No one answered. The inmates in orange exchanged glances but maintained perfect silence. The district attorney tugged at his suit jacket and cleared his throat.

The noise caught the judge's attention. "Mr. Carson? Where is the public defender?"

The young attorney stood and said, "I haven't seen him this morning, Judge."

Judge Pickens turned to the bailiff. "Harold?"

"Well, Judge, I've been here since about 7:30 this morning. Didn't see him in the coffee shop or the lobby."

Judge Pickens sighed. "This is our criminal docket day. We can't proceed without him." He turned to his clerk, a pretty woman hovering near the door to chambers.

"Betsy, if you would, please make a call over to the public defender's office. See if you can raise him."

"Yes, Your Honor." She disappeared through the chambers door.

The silence in the courtroom was broken by a female inmate. "Judge? I seen him this week at the jail." When the judge ignored her contribution, the woman slid back onto her bench.

Betsy reappeared. With an apologetic grimace, she said, "Judge, I just got the answering machine at his office."

"Call his cell phone." The judge's voice was patient, but his face grew ruddy.

"I did, Judge. He didn't pick up." After a pause, she said, "I left a message."

Judge Pickens drummed his fingers on the surface of the bench, the tempo increasing in speed and intensity. Then he stopped and slapped his palm on the wood veneer.

"Harold, you're going to have to head over there and get him."

The bailiff bobbed his head. "Yes, sir, Your Honor."

Outside the courtroom, Harold took the century-old courthouse's marble stairs cautiously, gripping the brass handrail as he descended. He didn't care to take a tumble. The bailiff wasn't a young man, and his prosthetic foot made maneuvering the stairs particularly tricky.

He exited the courthouse and headed across the street to a two-story building that had been converted into the public defender's office. The paint on the door designating Rob Ford public defender of the district was still shiny, as though it hadn't yet had time to dry.

Harold turned the door handle, half expecting the entrance to be locked, but the door opened freely. The reception area was empty.

"Mr. Ford?"

There was no response. When the bailiff stepped inside, the door shut behind him. Harold made a face. It smelled like there was a sewer backup in here, and since the office was county property, Harold made a mental note to tell Judge Pickens so the judge could get the county commission on top of the problem.

As he walked across the reception room, Harold heard the crunch of broken glass under his shoe leather. He looked down and saw a shattered picture frame, facedown on the floor. Bending over with a grunt of effort, he picked up the frame and examined it. It was a family portrait: the public defender, his wife holding an infant, and two young children, a boy and a girl.

The bailiff lifted his head and called out again, "Rob? You in here? The judge is waiting on you."

He set the frame faceup against the wall, then walked a narrow hallway where a closed door bore a plastic nameplate, designating it as the office of Robert Ford, public defender. Harold rapped on the door with two knuckles.

"Rob? We've got a courtroom full of folks waiting across the street."

The smell of sewage was stronger outside the office door. The bailiff's head bobbed as he swallowed. His hand shook when he turned the doorknob.

When he pushed the door open, a low moan escaped his throat. Moving involuntarily, he stepped back into the hallway and turned his head away, burying his nose in his sleeve.

The public defender's body hung by a leather strap tied to an overhead light fixture. On the floor, a wooden office chair lay on its side, near the puddle of excrement under the hanging man's still body.

The bailiff stole another glance, to determine whether there was any chance the man was still alive. One look confirmed it: the gray face, bulging, sightless eyes, limp hands left no doubt.

He pulled the door shut and made his way out of the building with speed that defied his age. Once safely outside, he leaned against the rough stucco exterior of the building and drew deep breaths before pulling his phone from his pocket to call the judge.

As he scraped his shoes on the sidewalk to remove the glass particles, the bailiff muttered to himself: "Here we go again."

CHAPTER I

A HUNDRED MILES away from Douglas County, I hurried into the elevator of a 1970s office tower in downtown Birmingham, Alabama. I checked my reflection in the metal doors, fruitlessly attempting to finger-comb my wind-whipped red hair before the door opened onto the eleventh-floor offices of my workplace, Simon, Shelton, and Associates.

I dropped my briefcase inside my office. The color scheme was beige: paint, paper, carpet, upholstery. Even my wall hangings were strictly business: my license to practice, two diplomas from the University of Alabama, and my framed law review certificate. The last one hung directly across from my desk, where I could see it. Because I'd worked my butt off to obtain it.

The only treasures in my office were some framed pictures, which sat on my desktop, facing me. I had a smiling snapshot of my parents, taken a year before they were killed in a highway collision when I was in college. All of the other frames held photos of my five-year-old son, Andy. The wallpaper on my computer screen displayed my favorite shot, taken this past March, the Saturday before his open-heart surgery, when we toured the Alabama Sports Hall of Fame—a proud Andy sitting beside a

Leabharlanna Fhine Gall

bronze football player, with the statue of Bear Bryant grinning behind him.

I quickly settled down to business, editing an appellate brief that one of the senior partners had handed off to me. It was meticulous work, and I took care to double-check the quotations and citations in the text. The law firm didn't want to look sloppy in the eyes of the Alabama Court of Civil Appeals. If there was an error, I knew exactly which direction the shit would roll.

After an hour, I needed to get up and stretch, so I headed to the employees' refrigerator for a bottle of water. On the way back, I stopped at the employee mailroom, where I saw that almost every mailbox held a single sheet of loose paper. I found mine—under FOSTER, MARTHA—and glanced at the heading as I carried it back to my office. A chill ran through me as I read.

To: All company employees
Re: Changes to company benefits plan

The memo contained only five brief paragraphs. But the message it conveyed was so jarring, I knocked over the water bottle as I read it. The water spilled onto a file folder I kept on the far corner of my desk: the growing stack of Andy's medical bills, coordinated with explanations of my benefits.

My breath hitched as I read on, and phrases jumped out at me:

only able to offer high-deductible policies
$6,000 individual deductible, $12,000 family maximum
out-of-network providers will no longer be covered
family medical leave no longer compensatory

The bottom line read:

Our goal is to mitigate costs associated with our self-insured program.

The memo was signed with a familiar scrawl: Sterling Shelton, the senior partner.

When I read it through to the end, the wave of fury that rolled over me made my vision gray out, blurring the words on the page. But I didn't need to see the printed paragraphs to comprehend the target of the memo: me.

The new policy was clearly aimed at me and my five-year-old son.

I launched out of my chair with the paper in my fist. The senior partner's office was on the floor above mine, but I couldn't wait for the elevator. I took the stairs up two at a time.

Sterling's office sat at the far end of the hallway. I flew down the beige carpet, pausing only to take a breath in front of his closed office door. But I flung the door open without bothering to knock. Shelton looked up, surprised.

Standing in the doorway, I held out the sheet of paper in my shaking hand.

"Got the memo," I said.

CHAPTER 2

SHELTON NODDED AT a chair. "Have a seat, Martha."

"No. Don't think I will." I walked up to his desk, determined to remain on my feet, though my knees trembled. "This is bullshit," I said, partly crumpling the memo in my grip.

"Martha. Sit down."

"I don't want to sit down."

He glanced away, giving a shrug. "Suit yourself."

"So about this new policy," I said. "Don't think I'm fooled. You're aiming this at me and my son, Andy."

My voice had cracked when I'd spoken Andy's name aloud. I cleared my throat, trying to hold it together.

During the pause, Sterling leaned back in his chair—making it easier to maintain eye contact, I assumed—and let loose the cannon.

"Your son cost this law firm a fortune this year alone. It's not sustainable. I have a business to run."

The tone of his voice was more chilling than the words he'd uttered. At that point, I slid into the chair I had refused to occupy, because my knees gave out.

"I'm entitled to my employee benefits. It's one of the reasons I work so hard at my job. I need the health insurance. For Andy."

His eyes shifted to the side, and when he spoke again, his voice was cool, as if we were discussing everyday business. "Our stop-loss is one hundred thousand dollars per insured. Why do you think you're worth that?"

Affronted, I said, "I do great work for this firm, have for the past six years. I'm responsible for all of the legal research and writing—"

He cut me off. "What about your absenteeism? You missed three successive weeks in March."

The statement was so unfair, I saw red. "I worked from the hospital, worked from home."

"This is a law office. You have to be a visible part of the team. The rest of the staff shouldn't be expected to cover for your babysitting."

At that, I nearly choked. "*Babysitting?* My son had open-heart surgery."

Soberly, he nodded. I thought my words had made an impact until he said, "Yes. With the most expensive health-care provider in the region."

Angry tears threatened to erupt; I forced them back through sheer will. "Andy has a rare congenital heart defect. There's only one surgeon in Alabama qualified to perform the procedure he needed."

Shelton cocked his head to one side. "I'm sure that's a weighty problem."

I received the message: it was my problem, not his. I got back to my feet, unable to stomach remaining in the room much longer. "Don't expect me to apologize for my son's heart condition. I've pulled my weight for six years, and you know it. No associate in this firm produces more billable hours."

"That's right. Six years ago, we couldn't tell you were pregnant when you interviewed, and you sure as hell didn't mention it. If I'd known, do you think we'd have hired you?"

I grasped the back of the chair. I knew Sterling Shelton was a cold, hard man, but he'd never revealed himself so baldly. "Oh, my God. What you're saying—it's illegal. This whole conversation— my pregnancy, my family medical leave—you're flouting federal law. Title VII, and the FMLA."

He scoffed. "You have a lot of nerve, Martha, storming in here with your pious attitude while I foot your medical bills. Where's the boy's father in all of this? Do you even know who the father is?"

By that point, I had headed for the door, but now I turned to face him. "You despicable sack of shit."

He actually smiled when I said it, then gave a low whistle. "You're showing your true colors today. I always liked your gumption, but don't think you can aim it at me," he said. "If you don't like the new benefits policy, you know what you can do. Or we can pretend this conversation never happened. But if you ever talk to me like this again, I'll have you escorted off the premises."

I wheeled around, pulling myself up straight. "I'd like to see you try."

Then I escaped, determined to have the last word.

CHAPTER 3

THAT NIGHT, I sat cross-legged on the sofa in my cracker-box apartment in Birmingham, folding our clean clothes. My hands worked on autopilot as my eyes strayed to the crumpled sheet of paper that lay on the coffee table, near the laundry basket.

The five paragraphs printed on the page had turned my world upside down. That and the ugly scene that had followed. I'd retreated to my office afterward and shut myself inside, trying to breathe around the angry ball lodged in my chest. Though I wanted to flee, I couldn't simply walk out; I couldn't jump without a place to land. Because of Andy.

I needed to devise a getaway plan—immediately.

A nudge at my shoulder interrupted my dark thoughts.

Andy's arm, swathed in a layer of toilet paper, reached over the back of the couch. He held a spoon—a sticky one that should have been in the sink with the dirty dishes. In a deeply solemn voice, he said, "It's time to get the brain out."

Twisting around on the sofa, I saw that Andy's upper body was draped in an untidy wrapping of toilet paper. His mummification was already unraveling, leaving a mess on the floor behind him.

"Andy. We talked about this."

He used the sticky spoon to tap a jar of peanut butter clutched to his chest. "We will preserve it in this jar. You'll have to pull my brain out through my nose."

That made me snicker. Forgetting the crumpled memo for a moment, I scrambled off the couch and found the end of his paper trail. As I tried to wind it around my hand, I said, "Now, what did we agree about this mummy thing? You can't waste toilet paper like this. Andy? You hear me, buddy?"

"My name is not Andy. I am King Tut."

A few months ago I'd taken him to an Egyptology exhibit in Atlanta. When the mummies quickly seized his imagination, I was delighted. But that was before he began raiding the toilet paper on a regular basis. He unwound so many rolls, I'd recently had to switch from Charmin to the one-ply store brand: a rough exchange.

Dropping the spoon and jar onto the coffee table, he bent over the laundry basket and commenced digging through the clean clothes.

"Are you looking for your Spider-Man pj's? It is almost bed-time," I said.

He pulled a shirt from the basket. "I don't want to put on pj's. I'm wearing this to bed."

It was a red Kansas City Chiefs jersey. As he pulled it over his head, Andy said, "It's my Pat Mahomes shirt. I want to sleep in it."

I took a moment to straighten the glasses that sat crooked on his nose. "Suit yourself. Time to head to bed."

Behind the lenses of his glasses, two blue smudges made shadows under his eyes. "When do I get to be on a football team?"

"Oh, I don't know. Maybe when you're fifteen."

My lighthearted tone was a ruse to cover the lie. The cardiologist had told me that Andy could never play contact sports. But I wasn't ready to force my five-year-old to face hard truths, not yet.

His bedtime ritual took a while. After he brushed his teeth, we had to take his blood pressure, then he wanted a story, and a rehash of *Goodnight Moon* wouldn't suffice. Forty-five minutes later, I was back on the couch with my laptop open, trawling for job openings.

It was a frustrating quest. Hours passed as, hunched over my keyboard, I searched for prospects. I paused to read a new listing for an associate position in Birmingham, but when I reviewed the job benefits, I exited the page with a huff of disappointment.

When I struck out in Birmingham, I flipped through postings in other judicial districts. I'd hoped to avoid a move to a different community, but I needed to see what was out there. Staring at the screen, I kept up the hunt with dogged determination. When my head began to throb, I almost shut down the computer. But just before I did, a brand-new posting caught my eye: a vacancy announcement in Douglas County, Alabama, for the office of district public defender.

I clicked on it, curious. Alabama didn't have a statewide public defender system. Only the big communities, like Birmingham and Montgomery, hired full-time counsel to represent indigent defendants. Smaller places still used the old judicial appointment system, whereby local judges parceled out cases to local attorneys.

Douglas County wasn't a population center in Alabama, like Birmingham. But the salary posted on the announcement was nearly as high as what junior partners received at Simon, Shelton, and Associates. I sat back, thinking hard.

Serving as a public defender wasn't a cushy occupation. It could be backbreaking work, with caseloads heavier than one attorney could competently handle.

And it would involve a move, venturing into the unknown. I needed to be sure it was worth it. So I scrolled down the page, and when I saw the benefits package they offered, I squawked out loud.

Covering my mouth, I double-checked the website: there it was, in black and white. Unbelievable. The public defender's benefits were identical to those of the district attorney. The county offered a golden government package, one that couldn't be arbitrarily snatched away just because my son required medical treatment.

I had an inspired thought: there might be a way to determine the defender's load in Douglas County. Lots of communities posted mug shots of inmates in the local jail.

I opened a new page on the laptop and searched for the current inhabitants of the Douglas County Jail. When they first popped up, it looked like a collection of the usual suspects. Drug offenses, petty crimes, driving under the influence, burglary, one violent felony. I had almost reached the bottom of the last page when I spied a face I hadn't seen in years.

Jay Bradshaw, a law school classmate from the University of Alabama, stared shell-shocked at the camera. The website said he was incarcerated for "failure to appear." I shook my head, wondering how it was even possible, but the description underneath his picture confirmed it with his height, weight, and date of birth, along with his full name: Jeremiah Lawford Bradshaw.

What is Alabama's Student Most Likely to Succeed doing in jail?

I closed the mug-shot tab and accessed the Douglas County application link, thinking hard.

I decided to go for it. I filled out the application, my hands flying across the keyboard.

After I hit Send, a whisper in the back of my head nagged at me: maybe this was impulsive, too hasty. I was a thirty-one-year-old single mother to a young son with a heart condition, and we'd already had a tough year. Was it foolish to pull up stakes? I had no family support system to lean on, and limited experience in criminal defense. But looking around my small living room, with its dingy carpet and drooping plastic blinds, I bucked up. Andy and I were due for a fresh start.

"Pick me. I need this job," I whispered to the picture of the Douglas County seal on the computer screen. With a glance at Andy's bedroom door, I amended the plea: "*We* need this job."

CHAPTER 4

DOUGLAS COUNTY DETECTIVE Patrick Stanley sorted through an open box of donuts that sat on the late public defender's desk. He selected an iced long john and took a bite as he reclined in the dead attorney's chair and lifted his feet to the desktop.

"Sure you don't want one of these, Clark?" He gave the box a push across the desk, in the direction of a uniformed deputy.

Deputy Clark, sprawled out on the brown vinyl sofa in the corner of the office, shook his head in response to the offer. The deputy tapped on his cell phone with both thumbs. After a moment, he looked up. "Pat, how much longer you reckon we need to hang around here? My partner's asking."

Detective Stanley licked icing from his thumb and forefinger. "Gotta stay a half hour, anyhow. We can leave in thirty minutes, something like that."

Frowning, the deputy returned his attention to the cell phone and commenced tapping on the screen again. The men sat in companionable silence as the detective finished off the pastry and wiped his hands with a paper napkin, then reexamined the contents of the donut box.

The deputy breathed out a sigh as he checked the time on

his phone. "Pat, you think you got enough for us to make a report?"

"Oh, hell yeah." Detective Stanley glanced up at the overhead light fixture. "Just don't forget to collect that too. Bag and tag it, Clark."

Both men focused on the leather belt that dangled from the light fixture. The deputy cleared his throat before asking, "Pat, you really think that lawyer killed himself?"

"I think there's room for doubt. It's possible he had some help." With a shrug, the detective added, "On the other hand, that guy didn't have much backbone. One of those nervous types. Never know what a guy like that will do."

The deputy stood up with a grunt and unfolded a stepladder to retrieve the belt.

Detective Stanley looked back into the donut box and pulled out a chocolate-iced cinnamon roll. He chewed as he watched Deputy Clark, saying, "Don't forget to put on some gloves before you yank that strap off of there." Detective Stanley's head gave an appreciative shake as he added, "Clark, these donuts are mighty fine. You sick or something?"

The deputy glanced around the room. "Tell you the truth, Pat, it's still a little ripe in here. Puts me off my feed."

"You think?" The detective raised his nose and sniffed.

"Yeah. Is it my imagination?"

"Maybe not." The detective dropped the cinnamon roll back into the box, as if it had suddenly lost its appeal. "Probably ought to get the janitorial folks back over here. I hear they've got a replacement coming."

"A new public defender already?"

"Next week, I heard. It's a woman this time." The men exchanged a look, and the detective chuckled.

"Is she married?"

"No husband in the picture. But she's got her a little old kid." The detective shut the lid on the donut box and said, "Let's wrap this up and get on out. I believe you're right. It stinks in here."

CHAPTER 5

EVENTS FLEW BY fast. The Douglas County Commission offered me the job on the spot during my Skype interview, if I could get down there ASAP. I accepted and started packing. So I didn't have time for nerves until Andy and I pulled into the city limits of Erva, Alabama, on a Monday afternoon in June, just one week after I had taken the job. That's when the anxiety hit. My hands grew sweaty on the steering wheel at a four-way stop, and I started to whistle under my breath.

"Mom. You're doing that funny whistle."

I glanced at the rearview mirror. Andy was twisted in his car seat, looking out the window.

"I see a lot of rich houses."

He was spot-on. Erva looked prosperous, with a neighborhood of newly constructed buildings right off the highway.

My voice held a warning note. "Our house is closer to downtown, in an older neighborhood."

But driving to the center of town, I gained confidence. The trees lining the streets made a green canopy as I followed the directions to our rental house. On the sidewalks, kids maneuvered bikes and played in front yards like scenes from 1960s television series. When

I pulled up to our address, and the robotic voice on my phone's GPS announced, "You have arrived at your destination," I had to check twice to be sure it wasn't mistaken.

The rental house was a vintage Craftsman bungalow with brown-brick piers, peeking from behind a huge magnolia tree in glorious bloom. It looked like an ad out of *Southern Living* magazine rather than a humble rental property.

"Mom! There's a fence!"

I craned my neck. Just as Andy had said, a chain-link fence lined the backyard.

"You always say we can't have a dog because we don't have a yard with a fence, but now we do, so we can get one."

I groaned. It was an old argument, replayed many times. Following behind as Andy ran up the front walk, I breathed in the scent of magnolia blossoms. On impulse, I dodged into the yard and broke a bloom off the tree to place it in a bowl of water in the house.

Andy waited impatiently for me to reach the front porch. As the landlord's email had instructed, a key had been left for me on top of the window ledge. Glancing overhead, my face broke into a smile.

The beadboard on the underside of the porch roof had a coat of sky-blue paint. Our new home in Erva was full of surprises. Lovely surprises.

Until we walked into the house.

The landlord had informed me it was partially furnished; it had been home to his grandmother, who had recently passed. I had welcomed the news, because the scanty possessions from our tiny apartment couldn't outfit a house. But as I glanced around the living room, I realized I should've asked him to be more specific about the meaning of "partially furnished."

It was wall-to-wall knickknacks in there.

A curio cabinet loaded with odd vases, figurines, and planters sat beside a faded pink settee. Dusty lady heads, from the 1950s, with closed eyes and pursed lips. A grimy plastic violet planted behind a pair of porcelain praying hands.

"What's that?"

Andy pointed at a Shirley Temple doll that sat on the fireplace mantel. Stepping up to inspect it, I grimaced. Time had shattered the doll's glass eyes and lined her face with a network of cracks.

"It's scary," he said.

"It's fine," I lied, turning the doll's head, so Shirley wouldn't give Andy nightmares.

Hell, she might give me nightmares.

So maybe it wasn't quite a renter's paradise, but it looked solid and well maintained. It had everything we needed: two bedrooms, one and a half baths, and a small kitchen that led to a fenced back-yard, where an old tire hung from the branches of an elm tree.

Andy's footsteps echoed across the hardwood floors. Setting the magnolia blossom by the sink, I called, "Honey, stay inside the house. I'm going to start unloading."

On the street, as I struggled to open the U-Haul cargo trailer, a car pulled up behind me. I ignored it, my hands full trying to maneuver my first load onto a dolly. But when two women emerged and approached me on the sidewalk, I gave them a friendly nod as I jerked the dolly onto my front walk.

I expected them to walk on by, but they followed me. The younger one, a pretty woman in her forties, said, "Miss Foster? Martha?"

Surprised, I paused. "Can I help you?"

She smiled. She and her friend were dressed to the nines in "Junior League casual." She'd obviously taken pains with her coiffure. *Big hair*, I thought. No judgment. Just saying.

Her voice was as bright as a new penny. "I'm Sydney Hancock, this is Diane. We're the welcome wagon."

CHAPTER 6

"THE WELCOME WAGON," I parroted. Because I sure couldn't say what was rocketing through my head.

You've got to be kidding.

Sydney said, "Is this a good time, Martha? Diane said we might be too early. But our kids are at swim team right now, so I thought we should head on over here. Believe me, Martha, you don't want our kids running all over your house. Especially mine. Right, Diane?" She sent her friend a wink and gave a little laugh, revealing teeth that were a startling shade of ultra-white.

Mystified, I said, "We just got here. We're not in great shape for company yet, I'm afraid."

Sydney waved a hand toward her SUV, making the bangles around her wrist jangle. She said, "It's just some things to help you get settled. We have a box in the car. Can we bring it in?" She popped open the back door of her SUV and took out a big cardboard box. "Diane, get over here. You can bring the pie inside."

The other woman finally spoke. "It's gifts from local businesses." She was smiling, too.

Sydney made her way up the front walk. "This is your official welcome to Erva. We're so glad you're here."

Deserting my loaded dolly, I followed her. Diane was at my elbow, toting a peach pie. The crust actually looked homemade.

Sydney stepped over the threshold and deposited the box on the floor. "We don't want to be a bother. We'll let you get settled in. I know they're looking forward to getting you to work at the court-house. I don't know how you do it, but somebody's got to, right?"

Her nonstop chatter made my head spin. "Beg pardon? What's that?"

She grimaced. "Represent those criminals. Yuck. But somebody's got to. That's what my husband says."

Diane handed me the pie plate. "Judge Pickens says he hopes that this time we've got one who'll stick around."

The statement puzzled me. "The last public defender didn't stay in town long?"

Diane's smile faltered. She looked to Sydney.

Moving briskly, Sydney pushed the front screen open. "No. Not long. Diane, we better go pick up the kids."

In a flash, she jogged down the steps and onto the walk. As Diane departed through the door, I followed, still carrying the pie.

"Diane? Why didn't the last defender stay longer?"

Diane halted on the front steps, her brows making a crease above the bridge of her nose. A look of uncertainty flashed across her face. She said, "I hate to be the one to break it to you, but you'll hear it soon enough. Truth is, Rob killed himself."

I almost dropped the pie. As I fumbled to regain my grasp, Diane made her escape. Hurrying toward Sydney's car, she spoke over her shoulder. "So nice to have a fresh face in town. Welcome to Erva!"

CHAPTER 7

WHEN WE PULLED up to Happy Times Day Care the following morning, I liked the exterior. Outside the neat one-story facility, kids were climbing on playground equipment in a securely fenced side yard. A petite woman in her twenties appeared to be keeping a close eye on them, and not one of the children was crying.

When I opened the car door, it looked like my kid would be the unhappy exception. The lenses of Andy's glasses were fogged. In a decided voice, he said, "I'm going to stay with you today, Mom."

When I tried to unfasten his shoulder harness, he clutched the straps together in a tight fist. "If I was King Tut, I wouldn't have to go there."

"But you're not."

He teared up. "Please, Mom. Don't make me go in."

I had to hang tough. If I backed down on the first day, it would be even harder later. Keeping my voice upbeat, I said, "Andy, you have to go inside. I can't take you to work—you know that. And you wouldn't like it, anyway. There's nothing fun to do at a courthouse."

It wasn't working. His fingers clenched tighter, and tears rolled down his face, clinging to the lenses of his glasses. "I don't feel like it. I want to stay with you."

Gently, I removed his eyeglasses and wiped them off with the hem of his T-shirt. And then I played my trump card, one I had kept up my sleeve for a crisis.

"If you'll be brave and go into your new school without making a fuss, we'll get you a pet."

He brightened, but his voice retained a suspicious note. "Today?"

We'd fought the pet battle for over a year, but I had to wave the flag of surrender. I needed to get over to the courthouse, and I didn't want to be late for my first day on the job. So I buckled.

"Today, right after I pick you up in the afternoon. I promise."

When Andy scooted out of the car seat, I exhaled with relief. We hurried into the building, where I met the proprietor, Peg. She welcomed Andy so heartily that he shrank from the attention, looking relieved when she sent him to join two other kids in a play kitchen. After I advised her of his health restrictions, I lingered, keeping him in my sights to make sure all was well.

With a reassuring pat to my shoulder, Peg said, "He'll be fine. You slip on out; they always settle down better after the parents leave. Believe me, I know what I'm talking about."

I pulled an embarrassed face. "You're right," I said, but I wasn't quite ready to depart. "He's really into King Tut, mummies, that kind of thing."

Peg gave me a funny look. "You don't say."

I switched tactics. "And he loves the Kansas City Chiefs. Are any of the kids football fans?"

She smiled at that. It was the right tactic. "Honey, this is Alabama. Everybody's a football fan. It's a state law."

That got a laugh out of me. *It's funny because it's true.*

Peg patted my shoulder again. "You'll be back here to get Andy before you know it." She followed me to the door and wished me a good first day at work. "Lucky you," she said. "I'd like to get to hang around the courthouse all day, just for the view."

I looked back, wondering what she meant. "The view?"

"Mercy, yes. That man could be a movie star." She gave me a conspiratorial wink.

I didn't have the foggiest idea who she was referring to until she added:

"If he wasn't a judge, that is."

CHAPTER 8

I'D APPEARED BEFORE a lot of Alabama judges over the prior six years, so I gave no credence whatsoever to Peg's claim about the stunning "view" at the Douglas County Courthouse. I figured Peg's standards must be low.

When I followed the directions to the courthouse that my iPhone provided, Google Maps almost messed me up. I pulled up to a construction site, where a billboard declared I had arrived at the spot of the new criminal justice facility. PROJECTED COMPLETION: THIS DECEMBER!

A couple of blocks deeper into the center of town, I found the old courthouse, a brooding granite structure that was showing its age. Directly across the street, a two-story building with a stucco facade was clearly marked as the public defender's office.

I hit the courthouse first, so I could show the people in charge of Douglas County that I was a go-getter. *Check this out,* I thought, strutting up the steps with an "I have confidence" attitude.

The signs in the lobby led me straight to Judge Pickens's chambers. I paused to take a breath before I pushed the glass door to enter his clerk's office. In the judge's outer office, a trim woman with a full face of makeup sat behind a tidy desk. She looked up when I entered. "What can I do for you, ma'am?"

Glancing at the nameplate on her desk, which said ELIZABETH MICHAELS, I said, "Ms. Michaels, I'm Martha Foster, the new public defender. I believe Judge Pickens is expecting me."

The clerk's face lit up. "Bless your heart! Martha, you don't know how delighted we are to see you."

She jumped up from her desk and embraced me in a full-body hug. Startled, I stood as stiff as a statue, thinking, *Too much perfume.* When she released me, she ran to the glass door and pulled it open, shouting into the hallway.

"Harold! Get in here! I've got something to show you."

The clerk turned back to me, beaming. "You call me Betsy, Martha. We'll be seeing a lot of each other."

An old man dressed in a baggy suit and wearing thick bifocals stuck his head through the open doorway. "Who's this?"

"Harold, this is Martha. The new public defender." To me, Betsy said, "Where'd you say you're from, honey? Montgomery?"

"Birmingham," I said, surreptitiously bracing myself for another hug. But the bailiff kept a polite distance. He walked with a limp as he entered the office. I understood why when I saw his prosthetic foot.

"You didn't tell me we were getting a redhead this time, Betsy," he said.

"I didn't know. Martha, this is Harold Elmore, Judge Pickens's bailiff. You'll be getting to know Harold real well too."

"Nice to meet you, Harold."

"Mighty glad to have you here in Erva, ma'am. But maybe I shouldn't be so quick to decide—I never knew a redheaded woman who wasn't a firecracker. Guess I better be keeping an eye out when you're in court."

When he and the clerk laughed, I joined in, even though I'd already heard every ginger joke ever written. Many, many times. Still, they were undeniably cordial. I couldn't quite comprehend what I had done to earn such an enthusiastic welcome, but it was a nice surprise.

Betsy bustled to the corner of the office, where a coffee maker sat on a small table behind her desk. "This occasion calls for a cup of coffee. Or do you prefer tea, Martha?"

The bailiff chimed in. "Or I could go downstairs and get you a soda pop. You want something cold, Martha?"

I wanted to take a step back from the excessive hospitality. It felt like another suffocating hug. "No, thanks so much. Y'all are too kind. But I'd best introduce myself to the judge first. He emailed me last week and told me to meet with him this morning."

Betsy set the coffeepot down. With a note of regret, she said, "Well, shoot. He's not in yet."

"Nope. Not yet," the bailiff said.

"Oh. Okay, I'll check back later." There was a moment of awkward silence as I stepped away. Before I opened the door to depart, I said, "I sure appreciate the awesome welcome. Nice to meet you both."

Betsy said again, "You sure I can't pour you a cup of coffee?"

I shook my head. "No, seriously. Since the judge isn't here, I'm going to head over to the county jail this morning. I want to check on an inmate." I was curious to see whether Jay Bradshaw was still incarcerated. I was worried about him.

Betsy's smile dimmed. "Is that right? You know, Martha, if you're planning to go by the jail, you'll probably want to clear it with the judge first."

That stopped me in my tracks. I looked from Betsy to Harold, hoping the bailiff would disagree, but the old man nodded in agreement.

"Why would I do that?" I asked.

Betsy didn't reply immediately. She pinched her lips together with a plaintive expression on her face.

Taking care to keep my tone pleasant, I said, "I can't imagine that anyone would object to the public defender seeing a client at the jail."

She said again, "I'd clear it with Judge Pickens first. That's the way we do things here." Betsy's sunny smile returned. "Wait! I've got something for you."

She opened a side drawer of her desk, pulling out a miniature manila envelope. Holding it out to me, she said, "The key to your office. Did you see the building? Across the street?"

I nodded as I took the envelope. As I walked away, she said, "Come back when you're ready for a coffee break!"

CHAPTER 9

I HAD INTENDED to march directly to the jail, regardless of the clerk's admonition. But clutching the small envelope in my hand, I felt the shape of the metal key inside and reconsidered. Maybe, I thought, I should check out my new workplace first, just to get a feel for the space. I'd never had an office building to myself before. As I looked at the light reflecting off the windows of the public defender's office, they beckoned to me: a new beginning.

I crossed the street, and when the key unlocked the door, my shoulders twitched with a childish thrill. Stepping inside, I took a deep breath and looked around.

My breath turned into a racking cough. The outer office area reeked of chlorine bleach, the fumes making my eyes water. It appeared that an overzealous cleaning crew had sterilized the rooms in advance of my arrival. Propping the door open, I walked around the room—an unfurnished space with a stack of folding chairs leaning against one wall. There was no receptionist's desk, but I'd been prepared for that. The public defender was expected to do her own clerical work in Douglas County.

Walking along the bare walls, I saw nails and hooks jutting out of the drywall, but not a single picture adorned the space. Shrugging it off, I looked on the bright side. The office was a blank canvas. I could fix it up, put my own thumbprint on the place. This was a new day.

A few steps down a hallway brought me to a door that opened into a private office: mine, I gathered. An office chair sat behind a utilitarian metal desk at the far side of the room, with two chairs facing it. The desktop held computer monitors and a keyboard; a stapler lay at a haphazard angle. A brown vinyl couch occupied one corner of the room; in another, a printer sat on a small cabinet. Like the outer room, the walls were bare.

I sat behind my new desk and pulled a metal drawer open, wondering whether I would need to do any housekeeping of my own. But it was empty, not even a stray pen or paper clip rattled in the bottom. When I turned on the computer, it asked me for a password.

"Shit," I muttered, reaching for the landline phone that sat to the right of the keyboard.

I called Betsy, in the judge's office.

She picked up immediately. "Hi, Martha. How's your office?"

"Fine," I said, momentarily startled to hear her call me by my name, but her office phone would have caller ID.

"What can I do for you?" she asked in her chipper voice.

"I'm trying to get on the computer over here at the office, but it's asking me for a password."

"I can't help you with that."

Her reply stumped me. "What do you suggest?"

"You'll need to talk to Judge Pickens about that."

"Okay, I'll do that. You know, Betsy, I was thinking I'd like to consult with one of my predecessors, who held the job before. Someone told me that the former public defender passed away. Is that correct?"

I heard a quick intake of breath. "Yes. It's true." Her whisper tickled my ear through the telephone receiver when she said: "Suicide."

"So tragic. I hate to hear it." I tsked. "How about the defender who held the position before? Can you give me his or her contact information? I don't have a name."

There was a pause before she spoke. "I'm afraid I can't do that."

A flash of irritation buzzed through me. "Why not?"

Her voice lowered. "I don't know if the judge would like it."

She said someone else was ringing in and ended the call abruptly. Sitting behind the desk, I grew increasingly uneasy, and the chemical air was oppressive. I bolted for the exit. As I locked the door behind me and sucked in the fresh summer air, my shoulders drooped.

I'd already reached an unhappy conclusion. I didn't like Judge Pickens. And I hadn't even met him yet.

CHAPTER 10

I STOOD ON the sidewalk, uncertain where to go next.

Betsy's forewarning still echoed in my ears. I was not to visit the county jail without prior approval. But Betsy didn't know me very well. Not at all, in fact.

And that woman was not the boss of me.

I took off for the jail, walking at a brisk pace. It sat on the other side of the street, next to the courthouse, in two structures that had been cobbled together to create a lockup facility. The portion that looked like the original jail had been updated with a formidable addition, which was marked as the main entrance. I entered and walked to a glass-enclosed reception desk.

A uniformed woman with bobbed gray hair sat behind the counter in the enclosed area, chatting with a sheriff's deputy, a slim man in his early thirties. When I approached, they both turned to stare.

"Hi. I'm Martha Foster, the new public defender."

Before I had finished identifying myself, the gray-haired woman enthusiastically clapped her hands. "That's great news. Welcome to Erva, Martha. I'm Sherry Grimes. This is Deputy Clark." Deputy Clark squinted through the glass, inspecting me like a specimen under a microscope. I ignored it.

"I appreciate the welcome, Ms. Grimes. Nice to meet you both. I'm here on business, checking in on Jeremiah Lawford Bradshaw. He's being held on a failure to appear charge."

The woman's expression sobered. She exchanged a glance with the uniformed deputy, who leaned on the counter behind the glass, gripping it with both hands. "Foster, is it? You related to any of the Fosters in Tuscaloosa?"

"Not that I know of."

"I dated a girl from Tuscaloosa. Caroline Foster." One of his eyes twitched, like he was winking at me when he shared the information.

"Yeah, well, it's a common name," I said.

The woman jailer stood abruptly. "How about I get you some coffee, Martha? Clark, watch the desk for a minute while I go to the break room."

She disappeared before I could protest. The deputy slid into her empty chair and continued to scrutinize me. While I waited, a man in plain clothes entered the building and walked into the reception area. Deputy Clark lifted his left hand in a wave, calling: "Hey, Pat." Then the deputy reached under the counter. A buzzer sounded, and the man disappeared through a security door, into the main facility.

I tapped on the glass enclosure. "Beg your pardon—Deputy Clark, is it?"

"Yes, ma'am." In a pleasant voice, he said, "We'd appreciate it if you don't knock on the glass."

"Oh. Sorry. I'll remember that." I shoved my hands into my pockets. "Looks like you're the man with the key to the door, Deputy. I'd certainly appreciate you letting me come on back."

Giving his head a reluctant shake, he said, "Can't do that, ma'am."

My temper started to simmer, but I tried to suppress it. "I just need to confer with the inmate Jeremiah Bradshaw. It will be brief."

"Can't confirm or deny," Deputy Clark said.

I took a step back in confusion. "Excuse me? Can't confirm or deny what?"

"That we have an inmate by that name, incarcerated in our Douglas County facility."

His tone was glib and his face friendly, but I wanted to smack him. Fortunately, the glass partition was a deterrent, or I might have landed in jail that day.

"Deputy, please. His mug shot's on your website. Why are you playing coy with me?"

Sherry Grimes reappeared at last, holding a steaming foam cup. "Got that coffee for you, Martha. Sorry for the wait. I had to make a fresh pot."

She set the cup on the counter and pushed it toward the small opening in the Plexiglas. I ignored it.

My voice rising, I said, "What hoops do I need to jump through, Ms. Grimes? Because there's no legal or logical reason why you would deny the public defender access to inmates in custody. I'm entitled to talk to them, for God's sake. Do you need to see my identification? Check my Alabama State Bar number?"

I could feel the blood rushing into my face, and I suspected I was turning bright red. The jailer and the deputy exchanged glances again as I pulled my driver's license and my Alabama bar card from my bag, then slapped the cards against the glass, where they couldn't fail to see them.

Sherry Grimes looked bewildered. "Why, no, Martha, I don't need to see your ID. What for?"

The young deputy chuckled. With a glance at the cards, he reached out to pick up the foam coffee cup, saying, "If you don't want this, Martha, I'm just going to drink it myself."

The jailer's voice was resigned as she said, "No sense letting it go to waste."

It took me a minute to absorb the obvious: they really weren't going to let me in. "This isn't over," I told the pair before I turned on my heel to make my exit.

Just as I reached the door, the jailer called out to me. "Have a nice day, Martha!"

Her facile tone as she uttered the cliché made my temper boil over. Jerking open the door, I said to them, "Oh, screw you."

Then I stormed out, letting the door bang shut behind me.

CHAPTER 11

I SHOULDN'T HAVE done it. Shouldn't have lost my temper. Shouldn't have cussed at the jail personnel on my first official day on the job. At this rate, I might have the shortest tenure of any public defender in Douglas County history.

But I was still too ticked off to entertain serious regrets, and certainly too steamed to consider turning back for a do-over at the county jail.

So I trotted back up the courthouse steps and followed the signs directing me to the circuit courtroom. When I entered, I was disappointed to see the judge's bench unoccupied.

I roamed around the room, to get a feel for it. Like courtrooms in most historic courthouses, it was a large space, designed for function in a different era, when courtroom activities were a public draw. The benches in the public gallery could seat eighty or more, and ceiling-high windows lined the walls, to provide ventilation in the era before air-conditioning. Ceiling fans whirred overhead, circulating the air.

A woman walked through the door that led to the judge's suite of offices: the court reporter, I deduced when she bent over a transcription device that sat near the witness stand. I trotted down the center aisle to speak to her.

"Ma'am? Are you Judge Pickens's courtroom staff?"

She looked up with a guarded expression, giving me a once-over. I checked her out, too: stiletto heels, manicured nails, and yet another fluffy hairdo reminiscent of the welcome-wagon coiffures. Some salon in Erva obviously specialized in big hair.

"I'm the court reporter, Liza Walther. Don't remember seeing you around here before."

She neither hugged me nor offered coffee. Frankly, it was refreshing.

Once again, I parroted the refrain: "Nice to meet you. I'm Martha Foster, the new public defender. I've been looking all over for Judge Pickens. Is he around?"

She studied her fingernails, painted movie-star red. "He's around. Somewhere."

Frustration ignited sparks under my temper again. "Where might he be? If you had to guess."

"You could try the prosecutor's office." As I turned to go, she added, "No guarantees."

The prosecutor's office sat across the hall from the courtroom. The clerk at the reception desk had another mane of blond hair. When she looked up from her computer screen, I asked, "Have you seen Judge Pickens?"

This county employee was young—early twenties. But she gave me a wary smile that belonged on the face of an older woman. "He was with Mr. Carson earlier this morning."

Doug Carson, I knew, was the Douglas County district attorney. I was getting warmer. "Where do you think I might find them?"

She glanced off to the side, as if she feared she'd be overheard. "I'd try the coffee shop in the basement. Don't tell them I told you."

She gave me a conspiratorial grin, like we shared a secret.

As I headed back to the stairs, I saw a photo composite hanging on the wall next to the Alabama governor's portrait, depicting the elected county officials. Pausing, I lingered to scope out the photos of the men I sought. I spotted the prosecutor first, smiling into the camera like a high school kid. Doug Carson's cherubic young face looked like he hadn't yet lost his baby fat.

When I found Wyatt Pickens, I laughed out loud. The photo looked like a Central Casting leading-man headshot: square jaw, Roman nose, full head of close-cropped hair, arresting eyes. But I'd been fooled by enough profile pictures on Tinder to be skeptical that the judge looked like that in real life.

When I walked into the basement coffee shop and beheld him in the flesh, however, seated beside the boyish prosecutor, the sight was startling enough to give me pause.

Damn, I thought, with a silent nod to day-care Peg. *That* is *one handsome man.*

CHAPTER 12

WHEN I APPROACHED the table where the men sat, the prosecutor looked up at me with a baffled expression, as if he was trying to place me.

Ignoring the younger man, I stopped in front of Judge Pickens and met his eye. Though handshakes were no longer commonplace, I decided that the occasion called for the gesture. Sticking out my hand, I parroted my opening line for the umpteenth time that day. "Your Honor, I'd like to introduce myself. I'm Martha Foster, the—"

He finished the sentence for me. "The new public defender."

My instinct on the handshake was correct; he didn't look askance at my extended hand. He clasped it in a firm grip as he stood and said, "It's about time you showed up."

His statement jarred me momentarily; after all, I'd spent the morning chasing him down. But his smile was warm as he pulled out the chair beside him and invited me to join them.

As I sat, he called to a man behind the counter. "Jeb, bring Ms. Foster a cup of coffee."

It was the third or fourth offer of coffee I had received that morning. But this time I didn't decline. After Jeb set the cup in front of me, Judge Pickens placed a hand on the prosecutor's shoulder.

"Martha, have you had a chance to meet our district attorney, Doug Carson?"

"Not yet. I just came from his office, though."

In a mock-stern voice, the baby-faced DA said, "Did Lindsey tell you where you could run me down? I'm going to get after that girl. She's supposed to keep my whereabouts a secret."

I hesitated, remembering how the young woman had asked me not to reveal that she'd suggested the coffee shop. But when both men laughed, I relaxed. Obviously it was a joke. They had to be kidding.

The judge said, "Are you getting settled in, Martha?"

I swallowed a mouthful of coffee before I could reply. "I've run into a couple of obstacles, actually. The computer in my office requested a password, so I can't use it."

He shook his head. "I meant, whether you're getting settled into Erva. You're renting from Buell Hawley—isn't that right? I heard you're in his grandmama's house."

"Yes, he's my landlord." When I paused, the men looked at me expectantly, waiting for further comment. "It's a nice house—just what we needed."

The prosecutor edged his seat closer to mine. "Buell's a good man. He'll treat you right. He's the sergeant-at-arms in our Rotary group. Have you met yet?"

I turned to the young man. "Just over the phone."

"Well, I'll fix that. We've got our monthly meeting next week. I'll take you as my guest, introduce you around."

I didn't respond immediately, trying to get my head around the prosecutor's invitation. Weren't we supposed to be adversaries? In Birmingham, the DA and the public defender were not chummy.

Judge Pickens laughed. "Look at you, Doug, already trying to get into the defender's good graces. Martha, I think he wants to butter you up so you'll give him some sweet plea bargains."

When both men laughed, I joined in. As the mirth subsided, I said, "Judge, another thing I need to address is access to the inmates in lockup."

There was more to say on the topic, but Jeb appeared at our table with the coffeepot, so I paused while he refilled our cups. As he walked off, the judge leaned toward me with a confiding look. I expected him to make some explanation about his odd jailhouse policy.

"My wife wants to get you over to our house for dinner."

The statement left me dumbfounded. I stammered in confusion. "What? That's—it's so nice of you."

"One of our girls is on the debate team, says she wants to be a lawyer like her old man. My wife was thinking you could tell her about your experience. You know, talk about the practice of law from the female perspective."

At that, he pulled out his phone to show me the wallpaper: a shot of a tall, brown-haired woman standing on the beach with two adolescent girls.

"What do you think?"

Studying his cell phone, I didn't tell him what I was actually thinking: *Thank God there's one woman in Erva, Alabama, without big blond hair.* Instead, I handed back the phone and said, "What a beautiful family. I'd love to meet them sometime. Judge Pickens, your invitation is unbelievably gracious. But I have a five-year-old son, so I don't know how—"

He waved a hand, cutting off my objection. "Bring him. What's the point of having teenage daughters if they can't do some baby-sitting? Can I tell my wife you're willing?"

Frankly, I was astounded. No Birmingham dignitaries or officials had ever invited me into their homes. The short time I'd spent in the coffee shop with the judge had reversed my earlier opinion of him. In retrospect, I felt ashamed that I'd taken a dislike to Judge Pickens without having met him first; it seemed totally unfair. I resolved to remember that and turn over a new leaf: I wouldn't judge people so hastily.

The smile I gave him was genuine. "Yes. Thank you so much. Whenever it's convenient for you."

"Good. That's settled." He pushed his chair back, apparently ready to depart. "I'll have Betsy send you that computer password, Martha. Doug? You heading upstairs? We are burning up the taxpayers' time down here."

Once he was out of the chair, the judge moved fast. I had to trot behind him to catch up. "Judge Pickens? About the jail?"

He paused in the hallway. As he turned to look at me, I thought his expression changed.

"What about the jail? Why do you have business over there already?"

"There's a man in custody I want to see, Jeremiah Bradshaw. I tried to contact him earlier today, but the personnel at the jail refused to give me access."

His brow furrowed. "Were they rude to you? I won't tolerate rudeness."

His jovial mood had disappeared. The swift change was unsettling. Hastily, I said, "They weren't rude, exactly. Just unaccommodating, I'd say. Because they wouldn't let me talk to an inmate. And that's my job, isn't it?"

After a second, the judge's countenance cleared. He nodded, as if the situation was suddenly clear.

"They were just observing security precautions. That's a necessity, in corrections and law enforcement. I'll give them a call, Martha."

I felt a wave of gratitude for his intervention, though an hour prior I'd been righteously indignant. When I spoke, my manner was effusive.

"Thank you, Judge Pickens. Thanks so much for all your help."

"Glad to be of assistance." Before he turned and walked away, he pointed a finger at me. "Don't you forget about dinner, now. I'm holding you to that, Martha."

Watching him walk off, I noticed that he carried himself with an erect posture that hinted at a military background. As he made his way to the stairs, an elderly woman with a walker approached the elevator. The judge crossed the hall to push the button and hold the door open for her, waiting graciously as she progressed slowly into the elevator car. A true Southern gentleman, I thought. Old-school.

But an unrepentant voice in the back of my head wasn't convinced. It whispered: *Watch out*.

CHAPTER 13

ALTHOUGH I LET some hours pass before I returned to the jail, I felt edgy when I again approached the Plexiglas window. Judge Pickens hadn't guaranteed my passage in. But I skipped the pleasantries and wore my tough face, giving Sherry Grimes a glare when I said, "I talked to Judge Pickens this morning."

Before I could elaborate, the buzzer sounded. "Come on back, Martha," the jailer said.

After the security door shut behind me, Sherry Grimes led me through a labyrinth of hallways to the old section of the jail. We paused at the entry to a visitation booth, the old-fashioned kind where visitors talk to inmates on a telephone. The seat on the other side at the security glass was empty.

"I'll get him. We didn't tell him you were coming, didn't know when you'd be back."

While I waited for Jay to appear, I grew apprehensive. Six years had passed since we'd last spoken, and the circumstances for this reunion were not ideal. I was staring at the puke-green paint on the cinder-block wall, mentally rehearsing my opening line, when he appeared. He did a double take as he slid into the seat across from me.

He couldn't have been more taken aback than I was. The words of greeting I'd practiced flew out of my head when I absorbed the changes he had undergone. I searched his face for the guy I had known in law school—the Pied Piper who could talk people into anything, even me. But Jay had aged twelve years since graduation. As pale as death, with prominent cheekbones on his thin face, and strands of silver in his dark hair, pulled back into a ponytail. And his eyes looked haunted.

Jay picked up the phone receiver, as did I. In a terse voice, he said, "Martha Foster. This is a surprise."

After an extended pause, I finally found my voice. "Jay, how are you?"

He laughed, a mirthless sound. "Not great. Pretty shitty, actually. What are you doing here in Erva?"

"I just moved here. I'm the new public defender."

He leaned back in his seat with a look of disbelief. "You've got to be kidding me."

"No, it's true. I just started today."

Jay shook his head. "Of all the self-destructive career moves, I think that takes the prize." And then he laughed again. It had an ugly ring.

He was getting my dander up. Though I hadn't expected a hero's welcome, he clearly felt no gratitude for my presence. "You think?"

"I do." Jay coughed, switching the receiver to his other hand. "You must be insane to take that job. But I guess it was fated."

"What's that supposed to mean?"

"Have you forgotten your law school nickname? Jailhouse Lawyer?"

I hadn't heard that catcall in years. It had come about when I was arrested at a civil rights protest in Selma for getting mouthy with a cop, and was held overnight in the local jail. No charges were filed against me, but I spent that night in lockup listening to the woes of my fellow inmates and dispensing legal advice. When the story made the rounds at law school, someone coined the nickname, and it stuck. It wasn't flattering at the time, and it stung to hear it from Jay.

Maybe if I hadn't worked so hard that day to secure the jailhouse meeting, I wouldn't have snapped. But the fact was, I had moved mountains to sit in that vomit-green cubicle and hold a dirty telephone receiver to my mouth.

"You are criticizing my legal career choices? That's pretty ironic, Jay. Considering that I recently found out through the alumni grapevine that you lost your law license last year. And now you are sitting in jail."

It looked like my blow had connected; a flush reddened his pale complexion. "Ouch. Jesus, Martha. I see you haven't lost your touch."

I gave him an unrepentant shrug.

With a rueful tone, he said, "I should have remembered not to cross you. 'Martha Foster can be your best friend or your worst enemy.' That was the conventional wisdom."

That took some of the fire out of me. Though there may have been a basis for that harsh assessment of my temperament, Jay Bradshaw had always occupied the friend territory. My voice was kinder when I replied. "I was sorry to hear about it, Jay—about the disbarment. You were such a natural, one of the brightest guys I ever knew."

He grimaced. "A natural. Huh. The law always fascinated me. Handling people's money, though? Apparently, I'm not so good at that." His eyes slid to the side. "The drinking didn't help."

I digested the new information. Everyone who holds a law license knows that the surest way to lose it is by mishandling client funds. It's the deadliest professional sin, more unforgivable than sexual misconduct, addiction, or sloppy legal work. At my first firm meeting, Sterling Shelton had shaken his fist at the lawyers assembled in the room and said, "Never. Fuck with. The *money!*"

I sighed into the grimy phone. "Jay, I'm here to help. As your friend and as a lawyer. What's going on here? Why have you been behind bars for weeks on a failure to appear charge?"

He shifted in the seat on the other side of the glass, as if the question made him uneasy. "I made the mistake of getting a speeding ticket while driving through here on my way someplace else. I totally blew it off."

"Why didn't you just pay the ticket?"

"I guess because my life was falling apart, and a traffic ticket in Douglas County wasn't my top priority. Honestly? I forgot about it until I got pulled over in Mobile, and the Douglas County warrant for my failure to appear popped up. Next thing I know, I'm in Erva, wearing orange scrubs."

"But why are you *still* in here?"

He gave a guttural moan. "I need cash. I'm broke. My personal account is overdrawn, and my business account is frozen. They won't let me out unless I pay."

"Have you reached out to your dad?"

"He's not talking to me. Maybe you can help me out, give me a loan?"

The suggestion unsettled me. He knew that it created a dicey ethical situation. And aside from attorney ethics, I was living on a shoestring. "Money? Jay, I can't do that. Let me give you legal assistance. Let's talk about how to resolve this failure to appear charge."

My refusal agitated him. The hand holding the phone began to shake. "If you don't have the money, get in touch with my dad, down in Mobile. Tell him I'm begging this time. Maybe he'll listen to you."

"I can call, but your dad would surely rather talk to you. Shouldn't you give it another try?" Searching his face, I braced for the reaction. I knew there was bad history there. "You're his son."

But instead of anger, his face lined with regret. "We're tapped out. I went to the well one too many times." He rubbed his eyes. "Dad and I used to do battle back in the good old days, before my fall from grace. Remember? It's worse now, believe me."

I recalled Jay's tumultuous relationship with his father in law school. I didn't understand why they could never get along. I'd lost my parents in my late teens and would give anything for a chance to see them again.

I wanted to dig deeper, but just then, my phone alarm pinged. Without checking the phone, I pulled my bag onto my shoulder.

"I'll be back tomorrow, Jay. We can talk about it in the morning."

As I stood up, his voice grew strident. "I thought you said you wanted to help me. Why are you leaving? You said you'd be my attorney."

My alarm pinged again, its message insistent. I shoved the folding chair into place under the counter. "It's time for my son's medication. I have to go."

I heard him say, "Medication? What son?" before I returned the receiver to the cradle. It was a long story. And I didn't have the time to tell it.

CHAPTER 14

THE KIDS AT Happy Times Day Care were scattered across the lawn in the fenced side yard, their voices making a clamor. Peg sat in a lawn chair, supervising. I spied Andy sitting alone by the chain-link fence, pulling up spent dandelions.

I opened the childproof gate, calling out to Andy. When he saw me, he jumped up and sprinted across the grass. I leaned down to hug him, but he clutched my hand and pulled me toward the gate.

He tugged insistently, saying, "Come on, Mom, let's go." I let him tow me along. Peg caught up to us before we made it to the street.

"How'd your first day go, Martha?" She swiped sweat from her forehead. The afternoon heat was fierce.

Andy scrambled into the back seat of the car and struggled to buckle the harness without help. I leaned against the doorframe and said to Peg, "No complaints. Everyone was incredibly friendly."

With her hand, Peg shaded her eyes from the afternoon sun. "You got back here pretty early. I used to watch the last PD's kids. Not anymore, though. They moved away, right after it happened."

"It's a sad story." My phone pinged the medication reminder yet again. Leaning into the car, I grabbed a cold water bottle and unscrewed the cap. "Here, Andy," I said, reaching for my bag on the passenger seat.

When I pulled the medicine box from my bag, Peg got the message. She backed away, saying, "See y'all tomorrow."

Andy ignored her as he swallowed the pills. He was uncharacteristically cooperative, taking his medicine without raising a fuss. He didn't speak at all until we came to a four-way stop, several blocks from the day care.

"How was it today? Did you have any fun?"

"No."

A glance in the rearview mirror showed that he was glowering at me. My shoulders knotted up; it was going to be one of those nights.

"So not a single kid there was fun. Really?"

His voice trembled. "I don't know those kids."

We stopped at a red light. I peeked into the rearview mirror again. No tears yet, but he was blinking hard.

In a bright voice, I said, "Peg seems okay. Did you like her?"

"Peg's mean."

That jarred me. I twisted around in the seat. "Are you messing with me? She was mean to you? What did she do?"

When the light turned green, the car behind me laid on the horn. Andy clapped his hands over his ears. I turned back around, keeping my eyes on the road. "Andy, you need to be straight with me. What did Peg do that was mean? Did she yell at you? Because if she's yelling, I want to know."

He didn't answer immediately. When he did, I almost didn't catch it, because he spoke under his breath, like he was telling a secret.

"She doesn't yell. She whispers."

While I digested the information, Andy added, "Don't worry, Mom. I won't cry at day care anymore. It's against the rules."

That bugged me.

I ruminated over the revelation as I drove to the outskirts of town, to a strip center we had passed the day before. Pulling in front of a big-box pet store anchoring the shopping center, I waited for the reaction. If this couldn't brighten his day, I was out of options.

When Andy saw the big yellow PET HAVEN sign, he lit up. "It's the pet store!"

The tightness in my chest eased. After I freed him from his seat, he jumped out of the car and tore across the parking lot. I chased after him, snatching his hand before he reached the door.

"What do you think you're doing? You know better than to run off like that. You want to get hit by a car?"

He dragged me into the store. I looked around to get my bearings, wrinkling my nose. The animal dander was thick.

"Oh, geez, Andy. The smell in here." I pulled a face.

He looked up, the fluorescent overhead lights reflecting off his glasses.

"I like it. It smells like the jungle."

He freed his hand from my grip and took off down the aisle, tearing past the fish aquariums without giving them a glance. "Where are the dogs?"

I caught up with him, grabbing him by the hand again. "Let's check out the hamsters."

"Hamsters?" He grumbled under his breath as I pulled him over to the small-pet section, where rodents sat listlessly in small enclosures.

Manufacturing enthusiasm, I said, "They're cute, don't you think?"

Andy stepped closer, pointing at one of the creatures. "That looks like a rat."

Revulsion made a shiver run down my spine. "Yeah. We're definitely not getting that."

The small-pet section started giving me the creeps; we were surrounded by gerbils and hamsters, rats and mice. I glanced across the store, searching for inspiration.

I gave his hand a squeeze. "Want to look at the birds?"

"No. Birds aren't friendly. I learned that on a TV show."

He was right. My aunt had kept parakeets when I was a kid.

They made a terrible mess on the carpeted floor. And they never shut up.

We were striking out. Our Pet Haven venture had been poorly planned. In a reasonable tone, I said, "Maybe we should come back another time. We could do some research first, figure out exactly what you want. That would be scientific, right?"

Andy's blue eyes glared through his glasses. "You promised."

A lanky young man wearing a Pet Haven T-shirt sauntered up. "Can I help you find something?" He opened a cage and reached for a white rat. "You want to hold it?"

Andy looked interested, to my dismay. I backed away from the beady-eyed rat, pulling Andy by the shoulder. "No rodents."

The employee shrugged as he restored the rat to his home. "Have you checked out the reptiles? We got some cool geckos. Or maybe I could interest you in a bearded dragon?"

Andy's mouth was set in a stubborn line. "Where are the dogs?"

I shook my head. "Andy, this pet store doesn't sell dogs. They sell fish and hamsters, stuff like that."

"I've wanted a dog my whole life." He sounded like a negotiator when he added, "We have a fence."

The young employee edged up to me. In a confidential tone, he said, "We've got a couple of dogs in the back, actually, available for adoption. The local Humane Society brings them in on weekends. There's two still here that nobody wanted."

Next thing I knew, we were following the guy into the back of the store, where dog kennels sat. Most of them were empty, but the largest kennel held a black-and-tan dog that looked way too much like a rottweiler. I prepared to do battle with my son, because it was more dog than we could handle, without question.

But Andy was drawn to the other kennel, sitting behind the barking rottweiler. It held a midsize spotted mutt of dubious heritage. Andy knelt in front of the cage, talking softly to the dog. The mutt stuck his paw through the wire enclosure. Andy grasped the paw and shook it.

My son looked up at me, his face transfixed with delight. I stepped over to the cage and read the hand-printed tag attached to it.

Homer, good with children, housebroken.

"Mom, this is my dog. We're lucky nobody else took him. He's been waiting for me."

I knelt beside Andy to inspect the dog. With his tongue lolling out, Homer appeared to be smiling at us. Under his bushy brows, one of his eyes was clouded, completely opaque.

"Oh, honey. I don't think this is the dog for you. He's blind."

"Mom, he can see me. I can tell."

The young man spoke up. "He can see out of one eye, I'm pretty sure."

Andy inched nearer to the cage. "You see me, boy, don't you?"

Homer barked in response, then continued to smile at us. I looked to the store employee for support, but he wasn't offering any backup.

I edged closer to Andy and spoke quietly to him. "This dog has been hurt, honey. He lost his eye. Who knows what else is wrong with him? We can come back next week, find a dog for you who's in really good shape, with two good eyes. There will be more dogs next weekend." I looked over at the young man. "The Humane Society will send over more dogs, right?"

The Pet Haven employee nodded to confirm it. But Andy wore a take-no-prisoners expression.

"I wear glasses. I don't have good eyes." He pointed to his chest. "I have a scar. Just like this dog."

The pang in my chest nearly floored me. The message was clear. Apparently, Homer also understood. He stuck his nose through the cage wires, and Andy stroked it, smiling.

Thirty minutes later, we loaded Homer into the car with his adoption papers, a new dog bed, and a jumbo bag of dry food. Then we all headed for home, with Homer's head hanging out the window of the passenger seat.

CHAPTER 15

THE NEXT MORNING, getting out of the house posed a challenge. Homer didn't want us to leave, and Andy didn't want to be separated from Homer. The chorus of my son's protest mingled with the dog's whining. My nerves were frayed.

Our departure was also complicated by the weather forecast, which called for thunderstorms. I had uneasy thoughts about the fate of the landlord's knickknack collection, but I couldn't leave the dog outside in the rain.

Giving the dog a final glance, I said, "Don't tear the house apart."

I made it into the office before the rain commenced. At my desk, I logged into the computer. Betsy had sent me the password the day before, as Judge Pickens had promised. Rob Ford had left a wealth of standardized pleadings that I could adopt for future cases; I appreciated that. But scrolling through the skeletal files, I wondered whether my predecessor had had a personal account I couldn't access. From the information in my possession, it was impossible to get a handle on the status of my caseload.

Pulling on my rain jacket, I darted across the street to the courthouse as a bolt of lightning lit up the gray sky. I was glad to know the one-eyed dog wasn't hovering under the elm tree in my backyard.

Inside the courthouse, I met Doug Carson climbing the marble stairs, with a cup of coffee in hand. He gave me a friendly nod.

"Doug, do you have a minute?"

"Sure thing." As we reached the prosecutor's office, he held the door open. "After you."

When I walked inside, the young clerk looked up from her desk in consternation. Her face cleared when Doug escorted me through the reception vestibule.

"Martha, have you had a chance to meet Lindsey?"

We exchanged a hello. Lindsey's eyes followed me as Doug led the way into his private office.

I looked around as I settled into a leather chair facing him. Compared to my digs across the street, Doug Carson's office was luxurious: upholstered furnishings, glossy wooden desk, matching credenza. Framed certificates, photos, and clippings plastered the wall. In addition to the standard diplomas and law license, Carson had framed his high school debate awards, a photo of his college barbershop quartet, and a gavel he'd used as president of some club or organization. The guy was definitely a joiner. Suppressing a smirk, I focused on the desk. Next to a set of Alabama Revised Statutes sat a silver-framed portrait of a bride holding a bouquet of pink and white peonies.

He caught me looking at the picture. "My wife, Heather."

"Pretty."

Beaming, he nodded as he made a slight adjustment to the position of the frame. "So tell me, Martha. How can I help you?"

"I'm trying to get a handle on the criminal docket. Can you bring me up to date?"

He lifted his coffee cup and stared into it. "You should check your office account."

"I did, but there's not much there. I've been through the file cabinets in the office, too, but the former defender didn't keep complete hard files. Not a fan of paper, I guess."

Doug leaned forward, lowering his voice. "Who knows what was going on in his head. He left a wife and three little kids behind. Can you imagine?"

I made a sympathetic grimace. "Tragic."

"Selfish—that's what I think. But it's water under the bridge." He winked at me. It made me uncomfortable. We were talking about a young man's untimely death.

I shifted in my seat. When I spoke again, my voice was several degrees cooler. "Can you share your court calendar? Provide a copy of criminal cases? Preliminary hearings, cases set for trial, upcoming jury dockets. And the pending misdemeanors. I want to get up to speed. It's not fair to the defendants to slow down the process."

"I can do that." He swiveled in the chair and tapped on his keyboard. "Emailing you the docket right now. But you don't have to worry about prepping for any jury trials."

My cell phone pinged: a new email. But his statement baffled me.

"Why wouldn't I need to worry about jury trials? That's my job, right?"

Patiently, like he was explaining to a neophyte, he said, "Because the only current felony trial settings in Douglas County are bench trials."

"Bench trials? Before Judge Pickens?"

"Exactly. Rob Ford waived jury in all of his felony cases."

Doug Carson's round face was cherubic as he relayed the information. But I felt like I'd landed on Mars.

"Why the hell would Ford do that?"

I didn't state the obvious; as a prosecutor, Carson already knew that judges were more likely to convict than juries. By waiving a jury trial, the dead public defender had hamstrung his clients.

Carson wore a three-piece suit, decked out with an old-fashioned gold pocket watch linked to a chain that ran across his vest. He toyed with the chain while we stared each other down. When he finally spoke, he said, "You'll like your position in Erva, Martha. It's going to be a piece of cake. We don't overwork defenders. We're not like other communities."

"No disrespect to Mr. Ford, but I'll be doing things differently," I said as, outside the window, thunder rumbled. "And I anticipate that my schedule will be full."

With a furrow between his brows, he said, "You think?"

My frustration mounted. "The court has to appoint me to represent any indigent defendant who's charged with a crime who has a possibility of six months' jail time, including misdemeanor offenses. Jesus, Doug, you know that better than I do."

Carson made a dismissive noise. "I routinely waive jail time on misdemeanors."

On the surface, it sounded like good news for the criminal defendants in Douglas County. But it didn't jibe with what I'd already seen. So why was Jay Bradshaw still locked up?

"I talked to a man in custody yesterday who's been held in jail for weeks on a failure to appear charge."

Carson looked startled. "You talked to him?"

"Yeah. Jeremiah Bradshaw. Why is he behind bars if you waive jail time?"

The prosecutor shrugged his shoulders. When he answered, he sounded defensive. "Not familiar with the name, and I can't remember the particulars, offhand. But I assume the guy failed to pay his fine and court costs."

He rose abruptly, pulling the gold watch from his vest. With a glance at the time, he said, "I'm going to have to wrap this up, Martha. Did I mention that Rotary has its luncheon meeting next Thursday? I'm taking you as my guest."

Pocketing the watch, he stepped closer and stood over my chair. I slid from the seat, ready to go. As he turned the knob on the door, he said, "I'll give you a ride to Rotary. It's important for you to meet everyone."

Keeping my voice neutral, I said, "I'll see if I'm free."

A jagged lightning bolt flashed right outside the window, followed immediately by a deafening crash of thunder. The air felt charged, like electricity was making my hair stand on end.

Carson wasn't smiling anymore. "You have to be there. They want to talk to you."

Before I could argue, he shut the door in my face.

CHAPTER 16

MY EXCHANGE WITH the prosecutor left me feeling off-kilter. But despite the weird vibe, the DA's policy on jail time was good news for Jay Bradshaw, and I was eager to discuss it with him.

Bowing my head against the downpour, I descended the courthouse steps and walked to the jail. Rainwater gushed across the concrete, and by the time I entered the county jail, my shoes were saturated. I paused on the vinyl mat inside the foyer, shaking rivulets of water off my jacket. My sodden shoes tracked watery prints across the tile floor as I walked up to the reception window.

An unfamiliar jailer sat behind the glass: a young man whose short-sleeved uniform displayed tattoos on his muscular arms. He watched warily as I approached, his jaw working.

"I'm here to see a man in custody, Jeremiah Bradshaw. I'm his attorney."

Keeping his eyes trained on me, the jailer pulled a stick of chewing gum from his breast pocket and peeled off the silver wrapper. "Can't help you. Sorry." He folded the gum into a square and popped it into his mouth.

Again? Really? Briefly, I closed my eyes and silently counted to ten. When I opened them, the guy was still staring at me, chewing.

Taking a deep breath, I said, "What's the problem? I spoke with my client yesterday afternoon, in the visitation booth. He's expecting me back today."

The jailer looked skeptical.

With mounting frustration, I said, "Is Ms. Grimes around? She can vouch for me."

"She's around."

"Let's get her in here, then. She can clear this up."

The man lifted a phone receiver and pushed a button. "Send Sherry to the front." After a pause, he added, "Some lawyer wants to talk to her."

He dropped the phone in the cradle. I said, "The name is Foster. Martha Foster, the public defender."

He didn't give any indication that my name would open doors. The jailer continued to fix me with a dead-eyed stare.

I was determined not to let him think he had unnerved me. "This is ridiculous. What's your name?"

Tapping the name tag on his chest, he said, "Robertson."

"Mr. Robertson, you know what this is? It's called abuse of power. I won't put up with it."

He didn't reply. When he opened a notebook and bent over the pages, I took a seat in one of the metal folding chairs that lined the wall and stared at the pattern of muddy footprints on the floor.

A digital clock on the wall ticked off the minutes. I waited a quarter of an hour before Sherry Grimes appeared in the glass cubicle. When I saw her, I nearly slid across the floor in my soggy footwear.

"Watch out, Martha," she said. "It's cats and dogs out there. Don't slip."

I grasped the counter for balance. "Ms. Grimes, this guy refused to let me see my client. Please inform him that I'm entitled to enter the jail."

She clicked her tongue regretfully. "I just hate that you ran over here in this weather. Honey, you're soaked to the skin."

Don't call me honey. But I swallowed the sharp retort. "We went through this yesterday, remember? Judge Pickens informed you that I have the right to speak with inmates."

She gave me a rueful smile. "But that was yesterday."

I shook my head. "You can't be serious."

Robertson grinned at me, chewing his gum openmouthed. "I tried to tell her."

Grimes said, "Judge Pickens said you could come on back yesterday. He didn't say anything about today."

I clutched the reception counter with both hands, white-knuckled. "What kind of jail are you running here?"

Before she could respond, an alarm sounded. The muscle-bound jailer bounded out of his chair and ran for the metal security door. Before it closed behind him, I heard sounds of a struggle, someone screeching.

The noise muted when the door clicked shut. Sherry Grimes wheeled away from the door and fixed her eyes on me, her face contrite.

"Sorry," she said.

She didn't elaborate. I couldn't tell whether she was apologizing for the disturbance or for barring my entry. The muffled noises that continued to resound from the jail were frightening.

"What's going on back there?"

She expelled a deep sigh before stepping over to the coffeepot. As she poured, she said, "Some inmates are more difficult than others. You'd know that if you spent any time in law enforcement. Maybe they don't teach it to you in law school." She lifted the pot. "You want some?"

I backed away. "I'm going to talk to Judge Pickens. We're going to resolve this shit, I guarantee it."

I turned so abruptly that my shoes slid in a slick spot I'd left behind. My arms flailed as I slipped and fell face-first on the tile floor.

It took a moment to catch my breath before I could crawl onto my hands and knees. I heard Sherry's voice, ringing with reproach.

"Martha. You're going to have to learn to be more careful."

As I hobbled out of the lobby, I thought I heard the sound of someone pleading for help behind the security door.

CHAPTER 17

SLOGGING UP TO the courtroom in my wet shoes, I paused to peer through the glass panes in the door. It was a relief to see Judge Pickens sitting at the bench. We had vital issues to address, and I was in no mood to chase him all over the courthouse.

When I entered, I took care to close the door noiselessly behind me, because court was in session. Pickens was presiding over a hearing; the counsel tables were occupied by lawyers in suits and ties, with clients seated beside them. One attorney was on his feet, making an argument. I tiptoed in, intending to take a seat and wait my turn to speak. Despite my effort to be unobtrusive, the proceedings came to an abrupt halt.

"Ms. Foster?" Judge Pickens said, eyeing me with shock.

The attorneys at the counsel tables turned to stare at me; one of the clients laughed before she clapped a hand over her mouth.

Looking down, I understood why I'd created a sensation. My wet clothes were plastered to my skin. Beneath the hem of my skirt, my knees were muddy, and dirty water had made tracks down my legs. I'd left the jail in such a huff that I'd failed to clean up before coming to court.

The judge waved me forward. "Ms. Foster, please approach." To the attorney standing at the counsel table, he said, "We'll recess briefly. Give us a minute."

The attorney took his seat, surveying me with curiosity. My shoes made squishing noises as I walked.

When I reached the bench, Pickens squinted his eyes as he scrutinized me. In an undertone, he said, "Are you all right, Martha?"

"Judge Pickens, I apologize. I know I look a sight."

"Yes, ma'am, you do. Have you been in an accident?"

To my chagrin, I felt my face heat up. Wet, dirty, and flushed was not the professional impression I had hoped to create. Which meant that everyone in the room could also see me blushing like a schoolgirl. It's a redhead's curse. "It's just the rain. My shoes got wet, and I had a slip and fall in the lobby at the jail. I'm fine, really."

Some of the tension left his face. "Glad that's all. You should know, Martha, that we have rules about proper courtroom attire. But I'll make an exception for you today."

Was he joking? Though I tried to read his face, I couldn't tell.

He spoke softly. "We can discuss Douglas County courtroom standards tonight, at my house."

A stray drop of water trickled from my hair and ran down the back of my neck, making me shiver. "Tonight? Your house?"

"Yes, my wife, Paula, suggested it this morning. She wants you to come for supper tonight at six o'clock, and bring your little boy. Does that time work for you?"

I was astounded. It had never occurred to me that he'd follow through on the invitation so swiftly. In a voice that sounded pitifully eager, I said, "Yes, that would be wonderful. It's a privilege."

"We're privileged to have you." He edged closer to me and spoke with a teasing lilt in his voice. "By six o'clock, you think you can get yourself cleaned up? I don't want you to give my family a fright."

My laugh sounded like a nervous titter. "Absolutely."

"Paula wants to know if you have any food issues. Allergies, gluten problems, that kind of thing."

"That's so thoughtful. But Andy and I like pretty much anything."

His brown eyes were warm. "Good! I'll let her know."

Behind me, one of the lawyers cleared his throat: a hint, maybe, that our conversation was running long. The judge refused to acknowledge it. He continued, "The whole family is looking forward to meeting you and your boy."

His sincerity completely won me over. I recalled his courtly assistance of the old lady at the elevator the day before. It was no wonder the citizens of Erva held him in such high esteem. "This is such a nice surprise. I can't thank you enough."

"I'll let you get on back to work, then. Betsy will send my home address. We'll see you tonight, Martha."

Nodding, I backed away, so completely under his spell that I'd forgotten my reason for coming into the courtroom. But I regained my senses before I made it to the exit.

"Judge Pickens," I called, hurrying back to the bench, "I have a problem."

His mouth turned down as I skirted the counsel tables. One of the lawyers tossed his pen down, saying, "Really?"

Stopping directly in front of Pickens, I said, "The reason I came into court to speak to you is because I was at the jail this morning, and it happened again. They refused to let me go back to talk to an inmate. I thought that was cleared up yesterday."

"Ms. Foster. Please."

He pointed his black-robed arm in the direction of the counsel tables, occupied by attorneys and their clients. "We're in the middle of a contested hearing."

I glanced over my shoulder, at the people sitting behind me. They were giving me the stink eye. With an apologetic grimace, I said, "Sorry."

I turned back to Pickens. "But, Judge, we discussed this."

He waved me up to the bench. Sotto voce, he said, "If you like, you can go right over to Betsy's office and request an appointment for a conference on this matter. But I'll see you tonight. We can discuss it informally after dinner."

From his manner, it was clear: he wanted me to take the second option. With a smile, he gave me an encouraging nod, making it difficult to argue with him.

My shoulders sagged as I let out a deep breath. "I guess we can talk about it tonight."

His eyes gleamed with approval. "Later, Martha." In a whisper he added, "We'll talk."

After I left the courtroom, I sank onto a wooden bench in the hallway, befuddled. Judge Pickens had given me the royal treatment in his courtroom, despite my woeful appearance.

But I hadn't gained any ground at all. They still would not admit me into the jail. The prosecutor, for all his affability, wanted to manipulate me. And I'd also failed to report the disturbance I'd overheard at the jail. The judge should know what was going on over there.

I had to show them they couldn't push me around. Otherwise, I couldn't do my job. Maybe dinner with Judge Pickens would be a good starting point.

CHAPTER 18

JUDGE PICKENS'S DINING room table was set with gold-rimmed porcelain and crystal glassware. The possibility of disaster set me on edge. I leaned over Andy's dinner plate, cutting his chicken breast into bite-size pieces. When I was done, I whispered, "Use your manners." What I meant was: *For God's sake, try not to break anything*.

Though Pickens had already said grace, his wife and daughters still sat with their hands folded, waiting for some kind of signal. When the judge picked up his fork, they began to eat.

I turned to his wife. "This is so kind of you, Mrs. Pickens, inviting us into your home."

She gave me a cool smile, a bare upturn of the mouth.

I babbled on, gushing. "The table is lovely. And your house is so beautiful. I can't stop looking at the wallpaper in here. It's gorgeous."

Her eyes flickered toward the wall, where a scenic mural of an English garden made a panorama around the room. "It's chinoiserie, imported from England. The paper is original to the house, actually."

I nodded, like I knew what the hell she was talking about.

Because the message was clear. The paper was the genuine article: old, expensive, and classy.

The same description could be applied to the judge's wife. When Andy and I had arrived at the Pickens home at six o'clock, Mrs. Pickens's physical appearance took me by surprise. She didn't have the fluffy blond "look" so widespread in Erva. Paula Pickens stood tall and angular, her face plain, her smooth brown hair pinned back in a simple French knot. She wore no jewelry, other than her wedding ring.

And despite Judge Pickens's claim that the dinner invitation had come from his wife, I could tell she wasn't particularly happy to receive us as guests in her home.

The Pickens daughters, Isabelle and Phoebe, faced me across the dinner table. Isabelle, the elder, was the pretty one, with her father's eyes and a hint of his charm. She was also the high school debater.

Recalling the judge's reason for inviting me, I said, "Isabelle, I hear you're interested in law school. I'd be more than happy to answer any questions you have."

She gave me a blank look, and I decided against inquiring further. Apparently, that was another fib the judge had told.

Isabelle turned to her mother. "Mama, I'm supposed to go by Jenna's house after dinner. We're going to work on our affirmative case for the district competition."

Before Mrs. Pickens had an opportunity to react, the judge spoke up, in a decided voice. "Not tonight, Isabelle. We have company."

Isabelle took the setback with good grace, but her younger sister sent a resentful look across the table at us. Phoebe was the handful, I suspected. She gave off a rebellious vibe.

Andy had said little and eaten less; but he chose that moment to drop a forkful of scalloped potatoes onto the floor. Mortified, I jumped up and squatted beside his chair. The potatoes had landed on a faded Oriental rug; I feared that, like the wallpaper, it was the real deal. After scooping up the potatoes and scrubbing the spot with my napkin, I sheepishly resumed my seat.

Turning to Mrs. Pickens, I whispered, "I'm so sorry about that."

Her face wore a long-suffering expression that made me want to cringe. But the judge chuckled. "No need to apologize. We've raised two youngsters in this house, Martha."

"That's hard to believe. It looks just like a picture out of a magazine, one of those historic home publications."

For the first time since we'd arrived, Paula Pickens gave me a genuine smile, a look of approval. "My great-grandfather built this house in 1890. It was their summerhouse. That's why the screened porches go along the front and side, to catch the breeze from the river."

"I noticed the porches when we drove up. They're absolutely gorgeous. So the family only lived in Erva in the summertime?"

"They spent the balance of the year in Montgomery. He owned the bank, you know."

In those few sentences, Mrs. Pickens had cleared up the mystery. Now I understood why a man with movie-star looks had married Plain Jane. Judge Pickens had "married up," into Southern aristocracy.

I glanced down at the spot Andy's food had left on the rug, wondering whether we had blighted a family heirloom. "I hope we didn't stain your rug, ma'am. It looks like an antique."

"I don't want to hear any more about the rug," said the judge.

Though his language was innocuous, the force with which he spoke charged the air with tension. The only sound in the room was the clink of silver as Phoebe dropped her fork onto her plate.

The silence grew so stifling, I felt compelled to say something. "Judge, you mentioned that we could clear up the situation at the jail tonight."

"Later," he said shortly.

Everyone was looking at me; I felt like an explanation was called for. "I've had considerable trouble with jail personnel since I came to town."

"Martha," he said, so sharply that I froze. In a more civil tone, he continued, "We don't discuss business at the table."

"I beg your pardon." It was embarrassing to be reproved like a misbehaving kid. To cover my discomfort, I pulled a comic face. "It sounds like we're doing a scene from *The Godfather*."

Nobody laughed.

Isabelle folded her napkin into a neat rectangle and set it beside her plate. "May I please be excused?"

Judge Pickens said, "You may, but I'd like you and Phoebe to take Andy out back. Show him the little playhouse in the yard."

Phoebe's face contorted with disbelief. "The old playhouse? We haven't gone near it in ages. There's bugs in there, Dad."

Andy had been quiet throughout the meal. I gave him a nudge. "You afraid of bugs, Andy?"

He looked intrigued. "Not me. I hope there's beetles."

Phoebe acknowledged his presence for the first time since we had arrived. "Why?"

Andy perked up. "The Egyptians really liked beetles. They made jewelry to look like beetles, and they painted them on jars."

The Pickens family stared at him. I volunteered, "Andy is interested in Egyptology."

He stuck his fork in the potatoes. I watched warily, braced for another catastrophe. After swallowing a bite, he said, "The Egyptian sun god had a beetle for a head. It was the dung beetle. Do you know why they call it a dung beetle?"

I knew. I wanted to cover his mouth with my hand.

But Andy was warming to the topic. "They call them dung beetles because they eat poop."

As Isabelle gave her mother a look of horror, Mrs. Pickens inclined her head toward me.

"He is a precocious child, isn't he?" Her gaze focused on Andy. Softly, she murmured, "Wyatt always wanted a son." Her brow wrinkled, as if the judge's wish for male offspring was incomprehensible.

My face heated up. I scooted Andy out of his chair, eager to help him escape. "You go on out with the girls, Andy."

He went willingly enough, slipping his hand into Phoebe's. Phoebe rolled her eyes but didn't protest. After the girls walked Andy out of the dining room, the tension in the room decreased; I breathed easier. Mrs. Pickens seemed more relaxed, too. The presence of a five-year-old in her formal dining room had certainly made *me* nervous.

"How do you like your new job, Martha?" She smiled, as if she really wanted to know.

"So far, it's pretty good." I wondered whether dinner was officially over. I wanted to resolve the jail issue, but I was afraid to break the house rules again.

Judge Pickens said, "Martha has landed in defense attorney paradise. You're in heaven, young lady."

It was a relief to see that his mood had improved. The man tended to be mercurial. My tone was light as I said, "I keep hearing that. So if I'm in heaven, that makes you Saint Peter, I guess?"

Polite laughter rang out at the table—even Mrs. Pickens joined in.

"Saint Peter? Me? I'll have to think about that."

His eyes crinkled with good humor. It gave me the courage to speak up. "It's a pretty accurate metaphor. I have to get past Saint Peter to get into the jail."

The smile dimmed. "All right, Martha, I get the message. Tomorrow I'll make the call."

Mrs. Pickens toyed with her water glass. "Wyatt says he's glad you've come to Erva, Martha. He hopes you'll fit right in." After some more small talk, she dropped the hint that I needed to get my young son to bed. I took the nudge gratefully, glad to see the dinner concluded.

Driving back to our neighborhood, Andy was quiet in the back seat. I gave him a quick glance over my shoulder.

"What did y'all do in the backyard? Did the girls show you that playhouse?"

"No, they didn't show me anything. They sat on swings and looked at their phones."

Although it sounded like normal teen behavior, it bothered me that he'd been banished to the backyard and ignored. I shouldn't have been embarrassed about the dung beetles. I was proud to have such a smart kid. I wished I'd made that plain.

After a moment, Andy interrupted my train of thought. "What's a psycho?"

Taken aback, I said, "Where did you hear that?"

"In the backyard. Phoebe said her dad's a psycho. And she said a bad word. A swear word."

Curious, I prodded him. "Tell me what she said."

"I'm not supposed to say the word."

If Phoebe was cursing at my son, I was determined to find out about it. "You're not in any trouble, hon. I'm just interested to hear what that girl was saying in front of you."

Finally, Andy whispered, "She said her daddy is a psycho asshole."

I didn't know how to respond. What would cause the girl to say such a thing in front of my five-year-old son?

CHAPTER 19

IT WAS JUST past nine o'clock when I presented myself at the reception window of the county jail the next morning. The young guy, Robertson, sat behind the glass again.

"I'm here to see Jeremiah Bradshaw."

My voice was stern, but inside I quaked. Had Pickens made the call yet? He might have changed his mind overnight.

It was a relief when the buzzer sounded. I was in—this time.

As Robertson escorted me through the hallways that led to the visitation booth, he presented a friendly face, as though we hadn't tangled one day prior.

"Nice to see the sun out this morning, isn't it?" he said.

I nodded without comment, not disposed to pretending that he and I were on cordial terms.

The old section of the jail smelled dank, like mildew and dirty socks. I resisted the urge to cover my nose.

As he pulled the door to the visitation booth open with a jerk, Robertson spoke again. "You can call me Jesse, Martha. No need to be so formal. Rob Ford and I were on a first-name basis, back when he used to have your job. That's how we roll here, in Erva."

I gave him a flat look. "I'd like to see my client as soon as possible, Mr. Robertson."

"Sure thing," he said, and the door clanged shut.

While I waited, I proofread the hard copy of a pleading I'd brought in my briefcase. When Jay appeared on the other side of the glass, I looked up, setting the document aside.

He jerked the receiver from the wall and held it to his ear, skewering me with a burning look. The light fixture over his head made the dark circles under his eyes more pronounced.

I lifted the phone. "Jay, are you all right?"

"No, I'm not all right. You said you'd help me, and then you didn't show up yesterday. What happened?"

His anger was unjustified, but it made me defensive. "I *was* here, but they wouldn't let me see you. They keep denying me access. I'm the public defender—it doesn't make sense."

Jay raked his fingers through his hair with a shaking hand. "That's no surprise, actually. This place is insane."

Attempting to provide a boost of optimism, I said, "Well, my access to the jail shouldn't be a problem anymore. I had dinner with Judge Pickens last night, and he promised to clear it up for me."

Jay gave me a blank look. "Are you fucking kidding me? You had dinner with Judge Pickens? Are you *dating* him?"

I pulled myself upright in the metal seat, keeping my back ramrod straight. "What's the matter with you? I was a guest in his home. He introduced me to his wife and family."

Jay tipped back in his chair and started to laugh. It had an ugly ring.

"What's so funny?" I demanded.

"You are. Making friends with that psychopath."

My curt comeback stuck in my throat, unuttered. The judge's own daughter had called him the same thing. It was a disturbing parallel.

Drawing a calming breath, I picked up the legal document and pressed it to the glass so that Jay could see it. Squinting, he leaned in to inspect the page.

"I didn't get to talk to your father, but I prepared this motion on your behalf: a request for a hearing on the failure to appear. It's crazy that you've been sitting in here so long. I hope this will set things in motion."

Jay's eyes moved over the page and he nodded in approval. "Good, that's good, Martha. I appreciate it. But what about money? Did you make any progress on that?"

"Jay, be serious. I can't give you money. It creates a conflict of interest, and that would violate the rules of professional conduct. And I couldn't reach your father. I tried. He didn't get back to me."

His face twisted with frustration. "They won't let me out of here until I give them money. And I've got to get out of this jail before they put me in the chair."

The exaggeration made me want to scoff, but Jay was clearly agitated.

"Why are you being so dramatic?" I said. "Failure to appear isn't a death-penalty offense. Besides, they haven't used the electric chair in Alabama since, what, 2002?"

"I'm not talking about Yellow Mama."

I shuddered at the old nickname for the Alabama electric chair—its moniker, Yellow Mama, came from the coat of bright yellow highway-line paint that had covered it.

"It's not the electric chair I'm worried about," he said as the door to his booth flew open. Jay's mouth clamped shut when Jesse Robertson appeared on the other side of the glass, looming over him. I tried to read the jailer's face, to determine whether he had overheard our discussion.

But if Robertson had been eavesdropping, he didn't let on. In a civil tone, the jailer said, "Sorry to break this up. Bradshaw has to go to court."

"Me?" Jay said, incredulous.

"Jay? Was this scheduled?" I asked him.

I could hear Robertson's answer, despite the glass barrier—the booth wasn't soundproof. He said, "It's the regular criminal docket. Thursday morning at 9:30, just like always."

The jailer stood at the door. Jay filed out, leaving the booth without giving me a backward glance. After the men were gone, I stuffed my paperwork back into my bag, waiting impatiently for my own escort. I was grateful to see Sherry Grimes appear to walk me out.

As I followed her, I said, "There's a criminal docket? This morning?"

"Sure," she said, as friendly as ever. "Didn't anyone tell you?"

My face heated with outrage. I was the goddamned public defender, yet this was the first I'd heard of a regular Thursday criminal docket.

Why was I being kept out of the loop?

CHAPTER 20

I MARCHED INTO court with a determined set to my jaw. People were filtering into the courtroom, with a handful already scattered along the wooden benches. The inmates had not yet been escorted in from the jail.

The bailiff sat at his desk, bent over a magazine. When I approached, he dropped the pen he held and shut the magazine. The cover read *Easy Large-Print Crosswords*.

"Harold, rumor has it you've got a criminal docket in here this morning," I said.

Speaking in a pleasant voice, he said, "Yes, ma'am. We'll be starting up here pretty soon."

He fumbled through some papers strewn across his desk. Plucking a hard copy of the docket that rested underneath a folded newspaper, he handed it to me.

Though I wanted to demand that he explain why I'd had to discover the docket through the grapevine, I held my tongue. The bailiff was not the villain of this drama. However, I seriously wanted to pick a bone with two other individuals: the prosecutor and the judge.

A quick scan of the docket pages showed a long list of charges.

The lengthy document reinforced my original assumption that the Douglas County public defender ought to have plenty of work.

Eyeing the defendants seated in court, I decided to jump right in. Walking up to the man at the end of the aisle closest to me, I introduced myself and asked, "Are you appearing in court today?"

He gave me a suspicious look.

I said, "I don't mean to intrude. I've just been appointed public defender, so I may be in a position to help you out."

He told me that he was present on a first appearance for the charge of driving under the influence, but he had hired a lawyer to represent him and was waiting for her to show.

Moving down the aisle, my eyes lit on a young woman seated in the back of the courtroom. She looked like a likely candidate for my services, dressed in a tattered T-shirt that didn't cover her belly. Her hair had been dyed sky blue at some point in the past, creating a startling contrast with the inches of dark hair growing in from the roots. I slid onto the bench next to her. When I told her that I was the new public defender, the woman's face lit up, revealing a missing tooth.

"I'm awful glad to see you. My name is Abby Zimmerman, and I need your help real bad."

Flipping through the pages of the docket sheet the bailiff had given me, I found her name. "Abigail Zimmerman? Theft of property in the fourth degree, class A misdemeanor?"

She grimaced, shamefaced. "It was a dumb thing to do. My dad kept nagging at me about the hair—I just couldn't stand to hear the bitching anymore. I went to the drugstore and took a box of rinse."

"Hair color?" Taking care, I did not permit my eyes to stray to her Crayola-colored mane.

"Yeah, L'Oréal. I was gonna pay for it, I swear, but it cost more than I thought. I had five bucks on me, but that didn't cover it. So...you know."

"Did they detain you at the store? Call the police?"

She nodded. "Yeah."

"Did you put up a physical fight, anything like that?"

Abby looked over my head and froze. As I turned to see what had distracted her, a hand clapped my shoulder and squeezed it, taking me by surprise.

"What do you think you're doing here?" he said.

Instinctively, I jerked away. Doug Carson tucked his offending hand into the pocket of his suit jacket and took a step back.

"Didn't mean to startle you," he said, sounding apologetic, "but you are wasting your time."

Feeling ruffled, I was short with him. "And why is that?"

"This woman won't be entitled to a public defender. No sense in spinning your wheels back here."

Hungry for a fight, I started to ask Carson to explain himself. But at that moment, Harold beckoned to him. The prosecutor hurried away to the counsel table.

Abby Zimmerman grabbed my arm. "Why won't he let you help me? I need somebody to tell me what to do."

She sounded distraught. I wanted to reassure her, but the courtroom personnel were taking their places. The court reporter was setting up her equipment, and Betsy had taken her spot next to the bench.

"Court's about to begin. We can talk about this later," I said.

"I don't know how long I can wait around. Can I give you my sister's address, just in case? I'm staying with her, since my dad kicked me out. I don't want to go to jail."

I glanced at the front of the courtroom; the bailiff was on his feet. "Hurry," I whispered, turning the docket over to a blank page.

She scrawled on the paper as Harold called out, "All rise!" I barely made it to my seat before Judge Pickens emerged from his chambers.

Covertly, I watched for his reaction to my presence at the defense table. But if he was surprised to see me sitting there, his face didn't give anything away.

When Pickens asked whether we were ready to proceed, Carson rose from his chair and said, "Yes, Your Honor."

Pickens took no notice of me. Standing, I spoke out. "Judge, I think it's important to inform you that this morning's docket came as a surprise to me."

He stared at me, impassive. "Surprise?"

"I wasn't informed in advance. Nobody told me about it."

A moment of silence ticked by before he said, "You're here, aren't you, Ms. Foster? Be seated so we can proceed."

Chastened, I sat. I sent a resentful glare to Doug Carson, but he ignored it.

One by one, the judge began to call up defendants for arraignment on the criminal charges. With a pen poised in my hand, I prepared to receive my new clients.

Judge Pickens said, "*State of Alabama versus DeShawn Jackson.* Is the defendant present?"

A young man stepped forward. When they read the charge against him, one count of reckless endangerment, his hands trembled. I found him on the docket list provided by the bailiff, and underlined the man's name, prepared to receive him as my new client.

Before the ink on the page could dry, Judge Pickens turned to Doug Carson. "Is the state seeking jail time in this case, Mr. Carson?"

"No, Your Honor. The state waives jail time."

"Then Mr. Jackson is not entitled to the appointment of counsel."

The waiver of jail time barred me from becoming involved in the matter. As I struck DeShawn Jackson's name with a stroke of my pen, the judge informed him of his trial setting.

Before he was dismissed, the young man shot an inquiring look at me. I shook my head; Judge Pickens hadn't appointed the public defender to represent him. There was nothing I could do on his behalf.

When the next name was called, I prepared again to gain a client. But when Carson waived jail time, the second man was denied a public defender. Forty minutes dragged by as the court-room emptied out. Repeatedly during the process, I looked over at Carson with a challenge in my expression, awaiting some kind of explanation. He refused to acknowledge me.

By midmorning, with the courtroom benches nearly vacant, most names on my copy of the docket sheet were scratched out. And I didn't have a single client.

CHAPTER 21

ABBY ZIMMERMAN WAS the last defendant to be called forward. As she passed by my table on her way to the bench, she tucked a blue hank of her hair behind her ear and shot me a pathetic look.

The wordless plea prodded me from my seat. "Your Honor, may I approach the bench?"

Judge Pickens swiveled in his chair and beckoned me with a wave of his hand. Doug Carson bustled up to the bench with a bemused expression, mouthing at me: *What?*

Without apology, I faced Judge Pickens and addressed the elephant in the room. "Your Honor, I don't understand why none of the individuals appearing in court today are entitled to a public defender."

Pickens's mouth twitched. "Have you been paying attention, Ms. Foster?"

"I have. Mr. Carson has charged a roomful of citizens with criminal offenses, and I don't represent any of them."

"Did you hear Mr. Carson waive jail time for those individuals?"

"I did, Your Honor."

"Are you familiar with the case law regarding the rights of indigents to counsel in criminal cases?"

"Yes, of course."

"You recall *Gideon v. Wainwright?* I should hope you'd be familiar with *Alabama v. Shelton.*"

Like an echo chamber, Doug Carson chimed in. "I'd hope so."

A chunk of resentment felt like it was wedged behind my rib cage. "Yes."

"Then why are we having this conversation? If you know the answer to your own question, why are you wasting the court's time, Ms. Foster?"

The shutdown was so abrupt, it was mortifying. Tempted to make a sharp comeback, I locked my jaw to stifle an imprudent reply.

Carson took advantage of my silence. "I'm filing a felony charge this week, Your Honor, in a drug case. If the defendant can demonstrate that he lacks the funds to hire a lawyer, the court might appoint Ms. Foster to represent him."

Pickens focused on the prosecutor. "Are you instructing me how to rule on appointments, sir?"

Carson backed away a step. "No. Beg your pardon, Judge Pickens. I meant no disrespect to the court."

Pickens turned back to me. Expelling a deep sigh, he whispered, "Step closer, ma'am."

Apprehensive, I inched up to the bench, afraid that the judge would snap at me. But when he spoke, he was affable.

"Ms. Foster, look out that window." He inclined his head.

Following his direction, I gazed out one of the high windows that provided a view of the courthouse lawn. There was nothing to see but grass, and cars passing on the street nearby.

"Wouldn't you say it's a beautiful day outside?" he asked.

I nodded, without comment. Where was he heading with this?

"I have a recommendation. You should leave the courthouse and spend the day with your son."

My face must have expressed disbelief, because he bent closer to me, speaking even more softly.

"When I met your boy last night, I noticed that he's frail, and very pale. Your son needs sunlight and exercise."

I wondered: should I explain about Andy's heart condition, his recent surgery? But this felt hideously intrusive, totally out of line.

He continued. "We have a fine swimming pool at the city park. Big old slides, three diving boards. I want you to check it out, take your boy for a swim."

The judge paused, watching me with an expectant face. When I glanced over at the prosecutor, it was clear that Doug Carson was glued to the exchange. He shrugged and nodded, signaling his agreement that I should depart, take the rest of the day off.

"No. I can't."

A telltale muscle made Pickens's eyelid twitch. "You can't?"

"There's going to be a hearing on Jeremiah Bradshaw's incarceration. I have to be here for it."

The judge leaned back in his chair, creating distance between us. In a cool tone, he said, "I see. You may be seated."

Hurrying back to the counsel table, I wondered whether my intervention would be a help or a hindrance to Jay. It was tough to read the judge; after the bench conference, he didn't make eye contact with me as the court business resumed. When the courtroom emptied out, he turned to the bailiff and said, "We're ready for the inmates, Harold."

CHAPTER 22

THE BAILIFF DISAPPEARED through a doorway that led to a holding cell. When he returned, he ushered in a short string of prisoners who all wore the faded orange scrubs of the Douglas County Jail. Jay was third in line. The bailiff led them to the jury box and supervised as they settled into their seats. It was a relief to see that none of the inmates wore restraints. At least Jay wasn't suffering the indignity of metal shackles.

The judge called Carson forward, murmuring something in his ear that I couldn't make out. The prosecutor then turned to the jury box and said, "*State versus Jeremiah Bradshaw.*"

I met Jay at the bench. Before Doug Carson could speak, I launched in.

"Your Honor, Mr. Bradshaw has been incarcerated for over three weeks on a charge of failure to appear. His original charge in Douglas County was a traffic offense, speeding twenty-five miles per hour over the posted speed limit, for which he was fined fifty dollars and court costs."

Judge Pickens said, "Have you formally entered an appearance in this matter?"

I flushed. "No, Judge. Mr. Bradshaw is a personal acquaintance."

He turned his attention to Jay. "Mr. Bradshaw, did you retain Ms. Foster prior to her tenure as county defender?"

Jay's voice was hoarse when he spoke. "Ms. Foster is appearing as a courtesy, Your Honor. We went to law school together."

Pickens raised his brow with surprise, but he didn't delve further. Turning to the prosecutor, he asked, "Is this the defendant's first appearance on the failure to appear?"

"Yes, Judge. We've been backed up. Really busy, as you are well aware."

The pitch of my voice raised with outrage. "A first appearance? After three weeks? That is insupportable. Your Honor, I demand his immediate release."

The judge made a show of inspecting the docket sheet. "Your statements hold little weight, Ms. Foster, since I don't see any record of your entry as counsel in this case. But regardless, Mr. Bradshaw can't be released, because he hasn't paid his costs."

Jay spoke up on his own behalf. "What is the amount, Your Honor?"

Pickens glanced down at the file again. "One thousand two hundred forty-eight dollars."

I gasped audibly. "That's impossible."

Carson said, "That's the figure my file shows, Judge."

I turned to Jay for support. He shook his head, with a lost look. Astounded, I wondered whether everyone had lost their minds.

I knew Pickens wanted me to back off, but an important point had to be made, on the record. "Your Honor, Alabama law limits penalties for nonpayment of costs, and limits the amounts that can be assessed. This is improper and unenforceable." My voice was firm.

But the judge smiled at me. "We have our own system in Douglas County."

CHAPTER 23

JAY CLEARED HIS throat. I turned expectantly, waiting for him to counter the judge's outlandish pronouncement. But nothing came out; he didn't utter a word.

Since Jay wouldn't speak up in his own defense, I did. At this point, I sounded strident. "Douglas County has to follow Alabama state law."

In an amiable voice, the judge said, "Douglas County charges a board bill fee as part of the court costs. And this defendant hasn't satisfied it. With his current incarceration, it is increasing by the day. He's been a guest of the county for three weeks prior to today—is that about right?"

At my side, Jay nodded wordlessly. The judge said, "I'll take that as an answer in the affirmative. If he doesn't satisfy his obligation, and remains for yet another week—"

And then the judge paused, turning to Doug Carson with an inquiring shake of his head. "What will that bring the new total to, Mr. Carson?"

The prosecutor's pen scratched frantically across his file folder. "One thousand six hundred seventy-two dollars. Approximately."

My throat was so dry I made a croaking sound. "What's that for? I don't understand."

"His room and board," the prosecutor said.

A jolt of fury ran through me. "Unbelievable!" I thundered. "This isn't just or fair!"

Pickens's face reddened. "Do you think it's fair for the people of this county to pay for the food that criminals eat and the clothes on their backs? The utility bill to keep them in air-conditioned comfort in the heat of summer? Why should law-abiding people have to pay for that?"

"That's what's not fair," Carson said, with a sanctimonious lift of his chin.

"Mr. Bradshaw, do you have the funds to pay your costs today?" The judge cut a glance in Jay's direction.

Jay bowed his head. "No," he said, his voice low.

Pickens exhaled, tapping a pen on the manila file before him. After a long pause, he said, "As an accommodation, to demonstrate goodwill to Ms. Foster, our new county employee, we will set up a payment schedule for Mr. Bradshaw. One hundred dollars a month in four weekly payments, until your obligation is satisfied in full. This is Thursday, so I'll schedule your first rehearing on Tuesday of next week. Your initial twenty-five-dollar payment will be made at the hearing on Tuesday. Is that clear, Mr. Bradshaw? Payment commences next Tuesday."

Jay raised his head. His throat moved as he swallowed. "Your Honor, does this mean I'll be released today?"

"Yes, Mr. Bradshaw. But I'm setting a hearing for you, next Tuesday at 9:30 in the morning. You will appear and make payment of twenty-five dollars toward your costs in accordance with the new schedule."

"Thank you, Your Honor."

Pickens's voice grew stern and hard. "If you don't show up next week with your payment, we'll have to issue a warrant for your arrest. Again."

The judge tossed the file to the side before adding: "Don't try to run, Mr. Bradshaw. If you do, we'll find you."

CHAPTER 24

"SO DO YOU think you can get him off?"

The question came from the mother of a flesh-and-blood client I had acquired in court that morning: one of the inmates arraigned after Jay's appearance.

Despite Judge Pickens's urging, I didn't take the day off. By stubbornly remaining in court, I managed to score one appointment. My new client was being held in jail. He had no money to make bond. But he had a devoted mother who had begged to meet with me at my office. I was glad to accommodate her since I had the whole afternoon free.

Jeanette Barker sat across from my desk in the public defender's office, tearing at her cuticles. "Will Shane have to do time?"

"Making a prediction at this point would be premature, Ms. Barker. When the prosecutor opens his file to me, I'll be able to assess the case."

I had talked to her son at the jail earlier that afternoon. The police had caught him in the act of burglarizing his ex-wife's apartment while she was at work. When the police searched him after his arrest, he had their son's prescription bottle of Adderall in his pocket. No judgment, on my end; a public defender serves all clients, regardless of guilt or innocence. But the wealth of damning evidence made it unlikely that Shane would walk away from the incident.

Nonetheless, my client's mother was insistent. "It's not like they were strangers. She called him to come over all the time, wanting him to fix something that was broken or watch the kids. Maybe you can get them to knock it down to a misdemeanor. Or maybe drop one of the charges."

"We'll see. Too early to say right now."

I was ready to wrap up the meeting when I heard the unexpected sound of the front door creaking open and shut. I pushed back my chair and stood. "Shane is lucky to have your encouragement and support, Ms. Barker. You'll visit him at the jail, won't you?"

She began to tear up. Ducking her head away from me, she nodded. "Sure. If they'll let me."

I came around the desk and said to Ms. Barker, "We'll stay in touch."

I walked her down the hallway into the reception area, stopping short when I saw who was seated there, on a folding chair against the wall. A backpack sat on the floor beside his chair.

Jay Bradshaw and I locked eyes, but neither of us spoke until the door shut behind Ms. Barker.

Once we were alone, I broke the silence, saying, "Good. They let you out."

"Yeah. Finally." He slumped in the chair, resting his head against the wall. "Until I made it out onto the street, I worried it was a cruel joke, that they would somehow drag me back to the cell." He raked his hair back with his fingers. "Can I have a drink of water?"

"Sure. There's a bathroom right in the hall."

He rose from the chair with an effort and loped across the room. His clothes hung loose on him; he must have lost weight during his three weeks in lockup. I heard the faucet run in the restroom. When he returned, his hair was wet, slicked away from his face, and his shirt had been tucked into his pants.

He laughed, looking chagrined. "No wonder people avoided me on the street. I look pretty scary."

It was true, but I didn't want to make him more self-conscious. When he smiled at me, I saw the ghost of my old friend. "I've been walking around. Trying to figure out what to do. My car is still impounded. I've got no money, nowhere to go. My landlord in Mobile initiated eviction proceedings weeks ago, so he's probably disposed of my stuff by now. I had to work up the nerve to come to your office."

The late-afternoon sun slanted through the blinds while we sat on the folding chairs. I was turning over a proposition in my head, trying to calculate the wisdom of it, and the possible fallout. Staring at my hands folded tightly in my lap, I spoke the words out loud. "You can stay at my place for a while."

Jay's foot had been tapping on the floor, but when I made the offer, he stilled. "Really? You sure you mean that?"

Am I? Some doubts seized me, and I hastened to address them. "We need an understanding. I have a son, and our lifestyle is very quiet. You'll have to respect that in my house. No drinking, no drugs, period. No guests, no irregular hours. Can you commit to that? It's a deal breaker."

He didn't respond, so I nudged him with my elbow. "Well, can you?"

"Yes."

"Okay, then. We don't have a spare bedroom, but I've got an old sleeping bag. You can crash on my couch."

He looked at me, shamefaced. "I shouldn't let you do this."

His reluctance made me more determined. "I'm just returning a favor. Remember when I got into a huge fight with the editor of the law review? I was going to quit. You talked me out of it, smoothed everything over. You always had my back."

It was true, though it had been years since I'd thought of the good turns Jay had done for me.

He shook his head, despondent. "It's not the same thing."

"Sure it is. One friend lending a hand to another."

My mind was made up. I pulled the keys out of my pocket.

"We'll lock up in here, then I'm taking you home."

CHAPTER 25

"BUT WHO IS this man staying in our house?"

Andy hung back as we walked up to the front porch. I tugged at his hand to hurry him along, my other hand holding a scorching-hot pizza box.

"I already told you—he's an old friend of mine. We're giving him a place to stay for a little while."

"For how long?"

I couldn't respond, because I didn't know the answer to his question. Exactly how long *was* "a little while"? Checking out Andy's stony face, I worried that I hadn't thought the situation through.

When we walked into the living room, Andy's mouth tightened at the sight of Jay and Homer cozied up together on the pink velvet settee. Jay's hand idly scratched behind the dog's ears.

"That's my dog," Andy said, with a catch in his voice.

I hacked a nervous cough. "The dog's supposed to stay off the furniture, Jay."

He gave Homer a gentle shove, and the dog obligingly hopped down to the floor and walked up to Andy. "Sorry about that. I don't think the dog's aware of the policy. He was snoozing up here when I got out of the shower."

I was relieved to see that after a shower and shave, and dressed in clean clothes, Jay looked more like himself. "Andy, this is Jay, the friend I was telling you about."

"Hi, Andy. Nice dog you've got there."

Andy knelt and put a possessive arm around Homer. Burying his face in the dog's neck, he didn't respond.

I didn't try to force a polite exchange. This wasn't dinner at Judge Pickens's house.

"Anybody up for a picnic? We can eat pizza in the backyard, on paper plates. And I won't have to wash dishes tonight."

Nobody spoke. *Oh, Lord,* I thought. I turned my back and walked through the kitchen with the pizza box, grabbing paper plates and napkins from the counter. I stood at the back door, waiting for them to follow. When no one appeared, I called, "Homer!"

The dog ran into the kitchen, smiling at me. I held the door open for him, grateful for the cooperation. Andy and Jay followed a moment later.

"I got your favorite, Andy. Pepperoni."

"My favorite is cheese."

That was a bold-faced lie, but I let it pass. We sat on the grass, juggling paper plates on our laps, while I struggled to figure a way to break the ice. But while Andy hadn't immediately taken a shine to Jay, the dog was not so aloof. Homer edged up and put a paw on Jay's leg.

"Hey, Homer." Jay studied the dog's face. I remembered that Jay's father was a veterinarian, and Jay had always had a way with animals.

Andy said, "My dog's not blind."

"You're right. Check this out." Jay peeled a piece of pepperoni off his slice and held it up. "Homer, sit."

Enthusiastic, Homer sat, wagging his tail. Jay tossed the circle of meat into the air and Homer caught it neatly in his mouth. Jay laughed out loud. "There you go. Good dog."

Andy was wide-eyed. "How did you teach him to do that?"

"I didn't teach him. He already knew. Homer's a smart guy."

Andy pulled a glob of meat from his pizza. "Show me how."

Ten minutes later, Andy's paper plate lay in the grass, forgotten, while he and Jay threw sticks across the yard for the dog to retrieve. I took a seat on the back steps. Homer eventually tired of chasing after sticks, and lay in the grass, with his tongue hanging out. I overheard Andy say to Jay, "Have you ever heard of King Tut?"

Jay turned to me with a quizzical glance. Hiding my smile, I lifted my shoulders in a shrug as Andy launched into his favorite topic. I relaxed on the concrete step, enjoying the hot summer evening. From the corner where our house sat, I could see lamps light up the windows of the house next door, and the moving images of a television screen. A girl on a bicycle rode past us, lifting her hand in a wave. Waving back, I thought, *Erva really is a friendly place.*

Then a sedan with tinted windows turned the corner, driving slowly by our house. I couldn't see the driver, but I stood, trying to check out the make of the car. As I walked toward the fence, the car picked up speed and raced off, moving far too fast for a residential neighborhood.

I caught a glimpse of the license plate, though; it was a sheriff's department vehicle. An unmarked police car.

CHAPTER 26

THE NEXT MORNING, I exited the courthouse and jaywalked across the street to the public defender's building. I'd left Jay sitting inside my office earlier that morning.

When I walked in, he was in the same spot on the faux leather sofa, frowning at the screen of my cell phone.

"Any luck?" I asked.

"I'm still on hold." He gave me an anxious look. "You need the phone back?"

In all honesty, I felt naked without my phone. But the service on his cell phone had been cut off, and I didn't feel right letting him use the public defender's landline, which was paid for with taxpayer money.

And Jay needed to talk with his bank in Mobile, to see whether they would permit him to activate overdraft protection. It was imperative that he manage to scrape together some money before his first scheduled payment of court costs came due. Judge Pickens had made that very clear.

I pulled two file folders from my briefcase and tossed them onto my desk. Jay gave me an inquiring look.

"Anything much going on at the courthouse?" he asked.

"Not for me, there isn't." I would have said more, but a voice came through the speaker on my cell phone.

"Please continue to hold. Your call is important to us."

Jay groaned. "I've been on hold for over twenty minutes." Sighing, he rubbed his face. "I almost forgot. Someone's looking for you, Martha."

I dropped into my chair. "Who?"

"A woman named Zimmerman. She stopped by the office and asked for you, about half an hour ago."

I recalled the name. "I met her at the courthouse yesterday. Blue hair, right?"

Jay frowned, shaking his head. "No. Black hair. She left a note for you; I put it on your desk."

On the corner of my desktop I found a folded strip of paper that looked like a crumpled grocery receipt. I picked it up and inspected it. It was a receipt from a Dollar General store; a hand-written message had been scrawled on the back of the receipt with a green felt-tip pen.

Abby's in jail. Needs your help. Thanks, Molly Zimmerman,
- *807 N. Travis St., 205815976*

The note puzzled me. Abby had walked freely out of court a day prior. I pulled open my desk drawer to hunt for the stapled docket sheet I had given Abby Zimmerman to use as a notepad. Pulling it out, I flipped through the pages to find the handwritten message she had left for me. It gave the same address on North Travis Street. Molly must be the sister Abby had told me she was living with.

"Well, shit," I muttered.

With my phone in hand, Jay rose from the vinyl sofa and walked over to the desk. "What's up?"

I smoothed the wrinkles from the dollar-store receipt. "The note is from the sister of a woman I talked to in court. It says she's in jail, but that doesn't make sense. I heard the prosecutor waive jail time. Maybe they picked her up on something new?"

Jay started to speak, then looked away, shaking his head.

"What?" I said.

"Who knows? There's weird shit going on in Erva. You ought to talk to the woman's sister."

I picked up the landline phone and entered the number written on the back of the sales receipt. When I couldn't get through, I swore—spouting words I couldn't use in my home. "The phone number is a digit short. I don't have her damned phone contact."

"So? You've got her address."

"That's a pain in the ass," I said. "What am I, everybody's babysitter?"

As soon as I spoke those words, I wanted to recall them. Jay set my cell phone down on the desktop, as if it burned his fingers. Neither of us spoke for a moment.

"You haven't been a public defender for very long," he said. "I'm sure the problems of poor people are a burden to bear." His voice was cool, and he didn't make eye contact with me.

I shoved the grubby note from Abby's sister into my briefcase and pulled out my keys. I had plenty of free time to drive to her house. It wouldn't hurt to see if I could run Molly Zimmerman down and learn what she had to say.

Before I left, I hesitated in the hallway. On impulse, I said, "I'm going to go ahead and lock the door behind me. Hope that's okay with you."

Looking up, he nodded. "Sounds like a good idea."

There was a tendril of paranoia unfurling in my brain. As I walked outside and turned the key, I wasn't sure just who I wanted to lock out. But it felt like the smart thing to do.

CHAPTER 27

THE ADDRESS ON Travis Street was in the north end of town. The bedraggled neighborhood bore little resemblance to the areas of Erva that Andy and I had encountered so far, with their new construction and bustling building projects.

And although the houses on North Travis weren't much older than the bungalow we had rented near the downtown area, the difference in upkeep was shocking. Many yards were littered with rusty appliances and broken furniture. Sagging front porches looked as though a gust of wind could flatten them. Windows were shaded by torn canvas awnings, and an attached one-car garage was shielded by a black plastic tarp where the door should be.

The Zimmerman home was covered in buckling aluminum siding, overtaken by a coating of greenish mold. As I walked to the front door, a bright touch made an unlikely appearance: a clay pot of purple petunias sitting in a patch of sunlight on the porch.

There was no ring when I pressed the doorbell, so I knocked on the frame of the screen door. After a couple of moments, I heard a voice shouting inside the house.

"Mom! Somebody's outside!"

"Well, go see what they want."

A stocky little girl wearing basketball shorts and a faded pink T-shirt sidled up to the door and peered through the screen.

"What do you want?"

"I'm looking for Molly Zimmerman. Is she here?"

The child wore a suspicious look. "Who wants to know?"

"I'm Martha Foster. Molly was looking for me this morning. She left this address at my office."

The girl ran off, calling, "Mom! She says you've been looking for her."

Footsteps sounded inside the house; through the screen, I could see a woman emerge from the back, walking toward me. She held a dish towel in her hand.

When she reached the door, I said, "I'm looking for Molly Zimmerman, Abby Zimmerman's sister. Molly left a note for me at the public defender's office."

Initially, the woman's face had puckered with distrust, but when I introduced myself, her countenance cleared. She pushed the screen door and held it open. "Come on in. I'm Molly."

As I followed her into the house, she said, "It's hot as Hades in here—sorry about that. Our window unit broke last week, and the landlord won't do anything about it."

She wasn't exaggerating. The heat inside the house was stifling.

The girl appeared in a doorway. "I'm hungry."

"Get your little brother and take him on down to the school for lunch. It's close to time." Turning to face me, Molly said, "Their school has a summer lunch program. It helps out, you know?"

"That's great." I was glad to hear that Erva provided free lunches in the summer; it was a crucial service for low-income families. She waved her dish towel at a sprung sofa. When I sat, I sank so low I had to clutch the arm to keep my balance.

The girl reappeared with a little boy in tow who looked about Andy's age. He ducked behind his sister and hid from me when I smiled at him.

"After you eat, you hang around the playground for a while. Watch your brother on the swings—don't let anybody push him off." Molly glanced at me. "Some of the kids around here are just plain mean."

I nodded, sympathetic. "I hear you. I have a son going into kindergarten in the fall."

"Is that right?" The screen door slammed as the children left the house. She shouted after them. "Make sure he eats something!"

When Molly joined me on the sofa, I pulled a legal pad out of my briefcase. "Tell me what's going on with Abby."

Shaking her head, Molly sighed. "She's in jail. I said that on the note, didn't I?"

"You did. But Abby was charged with petty theft, a misdemeanor, and the prosecutor waived jail time. So please explain for me: why is she in jail?"

The woman's face contorted with distress. "They made her come back later, to talk to the judge, and he got really mad at her, so he put her in jail."

Molly gave no hint that she was trying to misrepresent the facts; her face was open, her tone sincere. But the story she told made no sense.

"When did this happen?"

"Yesterday, the day she had to show up for stealing from the store."

"You're talking about the theft of the hair dye?" Because the logical explanation would be that they'd apprehended Abby committing a different crime.

"Yeah, that. The box of L'Oréal. And then when she left court, a deputy caught up to her and said she had to go back later because Judge Pickens wanted to see her. So she went back to the courtroom around four o'clock. And the judge said he wanted to know what she was talking to you for."

I gaped at her. "To me?"

"Yeah, you. The judge said he seen you all had been talking together in the courtroom and he wanted to know why."

I was blown away by the story, but I tried to remain cool. I said, "Where did you hear about this?"

"From Abby, when she called from the jail."

Sweat dampened my hairline and trickled down my face. The heat in the room was almost unbearable. "What happened in the courtroom?"

"The judge got mad and put her in jail."

"But why?"

"Abby wouldn't tell him what you and her was saying. She said it made him awful mad. She told me on the phone that she thought what she said with a lawyer was supposed to be a secret."

"This is crazy."

Molly twisted the damp dish towel in her hands. "I'm just telling you what I know. Abby said he told the bailiff to take her to jail. And she said, was she going to jail for the L'Oréal? But he said no."

I repeated it. "He said no."

Molly dropped her voice to a whisper, even though we were alone in the house. "He said it was because of her bad attitude." She leaned back against the broken couch, pressing her lips together in misery.

"What else did she say to the judge?"

"She told me she didn't say anything else, but he said he didn't like the look she gave him."

Confused, I said, "But what was the basis for locking her up? Did he hold her in contempt?"

She lifted her shoulders in a helpless shrug. "All I know is he didn't like her attitude. That's what she said on the phone."

"Have you been over to the jail to see her, since you talked by phone?"

Molly Zimmerman gave a slow blink. "Are you kidding?" She leaned so close, I could feel the heat of her breath on my face as she whispered: "They don't let nobody into that jail. They don't want people to see what goes on in there."

CHAPTER 28

WALKING UP TO the security glass with a determined set to my jaw, I had a feeling of déjà vu. The lobby of the county jail was becoming my second home.

I gave the woman at the desk a grim smile. "Hey, Sherry. I hear you're holding Abigail Zimmerman."

Sherry Grimes regarded me with a look of dread. "That's right, Martha."

"What's the charge?"

Sherry tapped the keyboard. Staring at the monitor, she said, "Contempt of court."

"Civil or criminal?"

Sherry squinted at the screen for a moment before turning back to me. "Doesn't say."

I hoisted my bag onto my shoulder. "I need to talk to her. Let me come on back."

I walked to the security door and waited, but Sherry made no move to grant me entry. With a grimace, she called out, "There's nothing in the system about Abigail Zimmerman having an attorney yet. You know, Martha, the judge says you can't just run over here anytime you get the notion."

I stepped back to the security glass, and we engaged in a staring contest. Sherry Grimes looked away first.

"Sherry, anyone who's being held on criminal contempt is entitled to counsel under the Sixth Amendment. That is a constitutional guarantee. If the Douglas County Jail denies Abigail Zimmerman her rights, you're going to end up in court. And it won't be in front of Judge Pickens either."

My tough talk had a visible effect; I could see the indecision as she waged an internal battle. When the buzzer finally blared, she said, "If there's trouble over this, it's going to fall on you, not me."

"Great. Fine," I snapped.

Once I came into the main facility, Sherry pushed ahead of me to lead the way, but it wasn't necessary. I was already familiar with the path that led to the old section of the Douglas County Jail and could probably find the visitation booths blindfolded.

As we rounded a corner, I said, "Sherry, those booths really aren't conducive to attorney-client communication. Does the jail have an interview room where I can meet with defendants? Someplace with a table, where we don't have to use that old phone?"

"Nope." Coming to a stop at the booth, she pulled the door open. When I stepped inside, it shut behind me with an angry clang.

While I waited for Abby to appear, I pulled out a packet of hand-sanitizing wipes from my bag. I was still scrubbing at the grimy phone receiver when Abby entered and sat down on the other side of the booth.

Her right arm shook as she lifted the receiver. With her free hand, she rubbed at her eyes. They were red and puffy.

Through the phone, her voice was a hoarse whisper. "How'd you get in here?"

"Your sister told me you were in jail. What happened, Abby? The jailer says you're being held for contempt."

Abby hunkered down, pressing the phone close to her mouth. With a whimper, she said, "I shouldn't have done it."

Her voice through the receiver was barely audible. "Abby, you need to speak up. I can't hear you."

Twisting toward the door, she peered around, as if she feared that she was being watched. With the phone still pressed against her mouth, she said, "I shouldn't have sassed the judge. It's my own fault."

"What did you do? Did you make a scene? Shout and curse at him, throw things? Something like that?"

Emphatically, she shook her head in denial. "No! It was that I wouldn't tell him what he wanted to know, so *he* shouted at *me*."

"In open court?"

"In the courtroom, yeah. He was awful scary when he hollered. Then he said I gave him a look he didn't like."

Tears ran down her face, and she wiped them off with the back of her hand. I watched, trying to absorb the tale.

"That's it? Just a look?" I was doubtful. I'd never heard of a judge taking action for contempt without legitimate cause.

She bowed her head; the blue hair fell across her face. "It's my own fault, like I said. I should have known better. Everybody knows Pickens don't play."

The booth was heating up. I reached overhead and pressed my hand against the vent. To my consternation, hot air blew through. Why was the heat running in the month of June?

Abby turned around again and peeked out into the hallway through the glass panel. She said, "They'll be coming for me soon. Will you go talk to my sister? Tell Molly she's got to get some money together somehow."

"To make bail?"

"No, for the board bill. Now that I'm in jail, I got to pay to get out of here. Everybody knows that."

Only a day prior, I would have thought that her statement was preposterous. But I had learned a lot about Douglas County justice in the past twenty-four hours. I knew that Jay was on the hook for a staggeringly high board bill. On its face, it seemed patently illegal, but I'd never encountered the issue in my years in Birmingham.

It occurred to me that we were going at the problem backward; instead of hunting down money to pay the bill, I should be launching an attack against it. I resolved to initiate legal research on the inflated court costs that very day, and to set Jay to the task as well. I was pondering grounds to oppose the practice when Abby spoke again, her voice urgent in my ear.

"Don't let Molly tell you she doesn't have the money. She's got to get her hands on it some way, or they're going to give me the chair."

Having visited Molly Zimmerman's home an hour prior, I was skeptical about the woman's ability to scrape any money together. But I was struck by the phrase Abby had used, regarding the chair. Jay had also referred to it when he was in lockup. And they weren't referring to Yellow Mama.

"Abby, what's 'the chair'? What are you talking about?"

She broke into great gasping sobs, her eyes growing wide with panic. Through the receiver, her voice cracked. "You don't understand because you just moved here. They don't let on at first. Don't tell anyone it was me that told."

She dropped the phone onto the counter, covering her face with both hands. And though I knocked on the glass, she refused to pick it back up; she hunched over the counter, her shoulders shaking. Until the jailer reappeared, I sat in the hot cubicle and watched Abby Zimmerman weep.

CHAPTER 29

WHEN I ENTERED the small basement courthouse coffee shop that afternoon, Judge Pickens sat at the corner table, pouring milk into a coffee mug. The judge wasn't alone; a ruddy-faced plainclothes policeman sat beside him. The cop lounged in his chair, his feet stretching across the aisle.

The screen door banged shut behind me as I stood in the entryway, deciding how best to approach the judge. The man behind the counter was busily scraping the grill, but he looked over at me and said, "You want something, ma'am? The grill's closed for the day, but I'm still selling hot and cold drinks."

I was about to refuse, but it occurred to me that if I ordered something, I could act like my encounter with the judge was a coincidence. He'd probably respond more favorably if he thought I wasn't hunting him down. Sidling up to the counter, I looked at the soda dispenser.

"I'll take a Diet Coke, please."

While the proprietor filled a plastic cup, I caught the judge's eye. Pickens watched as I paid for the soda. When I picked up the cup and approached his table, he looked away from me and murmured to his companion, saying something I couldn't hear.

Wearing a tight smile, I stepped around the cop's outstretched feet to stand beside the judge.

"Afternoon, Judge Pickens." With an effort, I managed to keep my voice pleasant.

Pickens lifted the spoon from his mug and took a sip of coffee before he responded. "Hello, Martha. Have you met Detective Stanley?"

"I don't believe so," I said. When the detective met my eye, he covered his mouth, as if he was hiding a reaction. Instinctively, my guard went up.

The detective dropped his hand onto the table. "How's the defense business going? Keeping lots of criminals on the street?"

I glanced away. His barbs didn't merit a response, and I didn't offer one. Instead, I focused on Pickens.

"I'm glad I ran into you, Judge. I'd like to talk to you about an item of business, when you have a minute."

Pickens and the detective exchanged a look. The unspoken communication riled me. They were playing an insiders' game, walling me out without uttering a word.

Detective Stanley drained the remaining coffee in his mug. Rising from his seat, he said, "I guess I'll head on back to the office, Judge."

Pickens nodded. "Don't forget what we talked about."

"No, sir. I won't."

Before the detective departed, he waved his hand at his chair in an extravagant gesture, inviting me to take it. As he walked off, I stood beside the chair, waiting for the judge to ask me to join him. When he didn't, I grew edgy. There's an etiquette involved in these power games, but I hadn't yet learned the Douglas County rule book.

The hell with it, I thought. I grabbed the chair and sat, scooting my feet under the table.

"Judge, a woman is being held at the county jail: Abigail Zimmerman."

He gave me a flat look of disinterest. "That doesn't involve you."

"I believe it does."

"It's none of your business. You haven't been appointed in that matter. Why you are hounding the jailhouse staff to see people you don't represent is beyond me, ma'am."

He picked up the metal cream pitcher and added a drop of milk to his mug. While he stirred it with the spoon, he stared into the mug, as if it required close attention.

I refused to be put off. In an urgent whisper, I said, "If Abigail is being held in jail for criminal contempt, I should be involved. She has right to counsel. And I'm certain she can't afford to hire a lawyer."

At that, he looked up. His eyes pierced mine; a shudder ran across my shoulders. But my voice didn't betray my discomfort. "Judge, I want to be appointed in her case. I'm requesting it." After a moment, I added, "Please."

His face broke into a grin. The sight was unsettling. He said, "You're getting ahead of yourself, Martha. There's such a thing as process. You want to demand judicial action in here? We are sitting in a coffee shop, not a court of law."

Shaking his head, Pickens began to laugh. I edged back in my chair, trying to physically distance myself. I wanted to choose my words carefully, but he went on before I had the chance to speak up. "You're a sight, young woman, and that's the honest truth. So eager. Like a dog after a bone."

The screen door banged again; it gave me a nervous start. A glance revealed a familiar figure standing at the counter: Sydney Hancock, the woman from the welcome wagon. She chirped out an order for a large iced tea. With the plastic cup in hand, she walked over to our table.

In a voice as bright as sunshine, she said, "Judge Pickens, this is a pleasure! Can I join you?" Without taking any notice of my presence, she cocked her head with a flirtatious tilt and batted her eyes at him.

Good God, I thought. *Can she be any more obvious?*

The judge reached for her elbow. Giving it a squeeze, he said, "Find another table, Ms. Hancock. I'll come on over in just a minute. Ms. Foster and I need to wrap something up."

She walked off, tossing a curious glance my way. Pickens's gaze followed her. I had to clear my throat to get his attention. A person would have to be clueless to miss the dynamic between Pickens and Sydney.

When he faced me, his expression had softened—a change caused by Sydney's arrival, I deduced. "I'm glad you came to see me, Martha, because we need to talk. I have a pressing concern."

Puzzled, I nodded. I hoped that he was having a change of heart, that he intended to appoint me in the contempt case.

He waved me closer; I leaned in toward him. Lowering his voice, he said, "Why are you permitting an indigent criminal to stay in your home?"

I jerked backward in my seat, as if he'd slapped me. "I beg your pardon?"

"I'm shocked by your behavior. It's improper, totally unprofessional."

My head was reeling. Why, I wondered, was it any of his business who I shared a house with? I didn't need to ponder how Pickens knew that Jay was staying with me. The image of the unmarked sheriff's vehicle cruising my house flashed through my mind. It hadn't been a coincidence. Detective Stanley might have been the man behind the wheel. It would explain his combative attitude.

My blood was rising. I could feel the heat wash up my neck. "I told you, Judge. Jay Bradshaw isn't a stranger to me. We were close friends in law school. I've known him for years."

He had the temerity to smirk at me. "Close friends? How close?"

Jay and I had never been as cozy as the judge might be with the welcome wagon—but I knew better than to say the words aloud. Instead, I said, "My personal relationships are not open for discussion."

His lips thinned. Perhaps both of us were trying to rein in our tempers. After a tense moment, though, he relaxed. He spoke to me in a paternal fashion, as if trying to offer friendly advice.

"That talk about old friends won't placate your landlord, Martha. The neighborhood you moved into is zoned for single family dwellings. That's why I assumed the man was your roommate, rather than your tenant."

Though I wanted to demand whether the judge was trying to bully me, I held my tongue. It took a huge effort—and when I didn't bite, he pushed further.

He shook his head with a phony show of regret. "I'd hate to see you kicked out of that beautiful house, with the nice elementary school nearby. Most of the rentals on the other side of town are rough." He'd emphasized the last word, rolling the r. "You probably haven't seen the north side of Erva; maybe you should check it out."

I'd seen the north side just that morning. He was dangling Molly Zimmerman's neighborhood as a threat.

But Judge Pickens didn't know who he was dealing with. His method of coercion made me dig my heels in.

"Jay Bradshaw is a guest in my home. If the landlord prohibits guests, that's news to me. So if you don't mind, I'll pick my own friends, Judge. Speaking with all due respect, of course."

The alarm on my phone chimed: time to get Andy. I grappled with the phone in the depths of my bag, trying to snooze it. When the chimes stopped sounding, the judge surveyed me with an inquiring look.

"An important appointment?"

I flushed. "It's Andy. I have to pick him up at day care."

As I stood, I debated whether it would be wise to let the judge know why the reminder was imperative: that it was time for his medicine. But Pickens's offensive comments about my personal life made me hesitate to confide in him.

I was still mulling it over when the judge spoke up. "I worry about Andy."

The words gave me a jolt. His voice was somber as he continued.

"Because I wonder whether having a criminal living under the roof with your son is in the best interests of the child. Do you know what I mean?"

Oh, I knew. The language he'd used—"best interests of the child"—was standard in cases for termination of parental rights.

My throat closed up. I tried to swallow, but my mouth was too dry. The judge didn't give me a chance to speak, anyway. Pickens wanted the last word.

"Sometimes a mother has to choose, between her child and a misguided... friendship. I don't think you're stupid, Martha."

He finished off the coffee in his mug and moved to a seat at the table where Sydney awaited him. His veiled threat rattled me so thoroughly that I couldn't think of the correct response until I'd left the coffee shop and stormed halfway down the hall.

I'd never buckled to bullies, and I didn't intend to start at the age of thirty-one. I wanted to let Judge Pickens know that I was no pushover. Maybe, I thought, I should go back to the coffee shop and tell him so, right in front of the welcoming committee.

But the phone in my pocket chimed again.

CHAPTER 30

THE KIDS AT Happy Times Day Care sat in a big cluster in the grass, playing a raucous game of Duck, Duck, Goose. I couldn't find Andy in the circle. As I searched for him, I began to grow anxious. Peg's assistant left the game and trotted up to me.

"Andy's not out here," she said. "He's inside, with Peg."

My alarm went off. Reaching into my pocket, I snoozed it again. "Is he okay?"

The kids in the side yard were shrieking. She turned to check the noise before she answered my question.

"I don't know. Maybe he was hot, didn't feel like playing in the sun. He's not in a time-out." After a pause, she added, in a doubtful voice, "I don't think so, anyway."

Feeling uneasy, I left her and hurried inside. After standing in the afternoon sun, it took a moment for my eyes to adjust to the gloom. All of the lights were off in the darkened room, and the plastic blinds were pulled shut.

When my vision cleared, I found Andy. He was huddled in a ball, sitting on a square of carpet in the far corner of the room. Walking to him, I said, "Andy? You feeling okay, baby?"

At the sound of my voice, he lifted his head, then launched off the carpet and ran to me. When I picked him up, he clutched my neck and held on tight, saying, "I want to go home."

I was concerned. His unhappiness with the new day-care arrangement was ballooning.

"Everything okay?" Peg asked, her sudden appearance at my side startling me.

Andy tightened his hold on my neck. I placed a reassuring hand on his back.

"I don't know—is it? Why was Andy alone in here?"

"He wasn't alone. I was sitting right over there."

Her hand reached out to rustle Andy's hair. He cringed away from her touch. In a small voice, he said, "I want to go home."

Peg let out a rueful laugh. "Andy's having a moody day, I guess. Happens to all of us sometimes. You'll feel better tomorrow, won't you, buddy?"

He buried his head in my shoulder. Peg nudged me, rolling her eyes. Her manner grated on me. Like Andy, I wanted to beat a hasty path out of there. But it was important to determine the magnitude of the problem before I left.

Working hard to avoid an accusatory tone, I asked, "Why wasn't Andy outside with the other kids?"

"I thought he looked a little under the weather. So I kept him in."

That gave me something new to worry about. His forehead was glued to my shoulder, but I pressed my hand to his cheek. He didn't feel feverish.

"So Andy's not in trouble, right? Not in a time-out or anything like that?"

"Trouble? Gosh, no." Peg strolled to a nearby table, where she began to gather up a handful of scattered Crayola markers. As she dropped them into a plastic box, she sent me a bland smile.

I wanted more assurances, but the alarm went off again. With a hasty good-bye, I set Andy down and walked him out to the car. The afternoon temperature had heated up the interior of the car, but Andy clambered into the back seat, insisting we leave.

Before we drove off, I blasted the AC to cool us down. Talking over the noise hissing through the vents, I asked Andy whether anything had gone wrong at day care.

"Can't we go home now? I want to get home. I need to see my dog."

I put the car in drive, as eager to get home as Andy. After a couple of miles, I checked the speedometer and saw my foot was too heavy on the accelerator.

As I slowed down, he said again, "Mom, I want to go home."

"We'll be there in a minute."

"I mean back to our old home, in Birmingham. We can go back to the apartment and take Homer with us."

I didn't respond immediately. It took a minute to run through the objections that crowded into my head, to choose one that would be most persuasive to a five-year-old.

But I decided to level with him. "We can't go back, hon. I don't have a job there. And someone else has probably moved into our apartment by now."

After that, there was silence in the back seat. I let it drag along, thinking that Andy might need a quiet minute to come to grips with the fact that Erva was home to us now.

But his growing unhappiness bothered me. When we were a block from the house, I tried again to urge him to talk.

"Why were you so upset when I came to pick you up?"

His voice had a quaver. "I'm worried about Homer."

"Why on earth, Andy? He's fine. You just saw him this morning."

There was a pause before he said, "I heard Peg whispering today."

I shot a glance at the rearview mirror. My son was dead serious; his pinched mouth was evidence of that.

"What? Whispering about what?"

"Whispering about us."

He leaned forward as far as the harness of the car seat would permit and said, in a voice of utter certainty:

"Mom. We got to get out of here."

CHAPTER 31

AFTER SUPPER, JAY set my laptop on the kitchen table to get a head start on our legal research while I cleaned up the kitchen. As soon as I washed the last dish, I joined him at the table.

"Well? Have you found anything?"

Hunched over the laptop, his eyes remained fixed on the screen. "It's not just happening in Douglas County, Alabama. There are incidents cropping up in other states, too. Some people are calling it the twenty-first-century debtors' prison."

"Exactly! But debtors' prisons were abolished in the US two hundred years ago. How are they getting away with this?"

Jay tapped the keyboard. "I found a precedent, but it's out of state. A public defender sued on behalf of clients in Missouri, and the Supreme Court of Missouri said counties can't treat board bills as court costs and lock people up for nonpayment."

My spirits soared. "That's good, right? We can use that."

Jay shook his head regretfully. "The decision was based on the court's interpretation of Missouri statutes."

I crossed my arms atop the table. "And Pickens will say that the Missouri Supreme Court can't tell him what to do or how to run his courtroom in Alabama."

Jay's hands returned to the keyboard. He glanced up. "Here's something. The ACLU has come out against it."

Tipping my chair back on two legs, I groaned. "Pickens isn't going to care about that. Pretty sure he's not a big fan of the ACLU."

"I'll keep looking."

Frustrated, I picked up my phone to assist in the research. "Is there any federal guidance on this? Didn't the Obama administration come out against it after the protests in Ferguson?"

"Yeah. They issued a letter advising against debtors' prisons in 2016."

"Good. That's something we can cite. We'll rely on the advisory guidance."

"Sessions revoked the letter when he was attorney general."

"Well, shit."

I didn't think Andy could hear me over the television, but his voice called out from the living room. "Mom! Language!"

I grimaced as I rose from my seat and sneaked a glance into the living room. Andy sat cross-legged in front of the television, with Homer at his side. "My bad," I said, swinging the kitchen door shut.

Returning to the table, I asked, "Did you notice how wound up Andy was when we got home tonight?"

"Not really. But you're the parent." Jay cleared his throat before he said, "It's really none of my business, you can tell me to butt out, but is his dad in the picture?"

I didn't answer right away. I went to the sink, rinsed out the dish-rag, and carefully hung it over the faucet while I debated whether I felt inclined to share the details.

I returned to the kitchen table and sat. "In the picture? No. He ran like a scalded cat." The recollection wasn't pleasant—but having begun, I couldn't stop. "We were pretty serious, had talked about marriage, but the pregnancy wasn't planned. We took precautions. It happens sometimes."

Though he didn't pry, I didn't take Jay through my complications with birth control pills; it wasn't the point of the tale.

"When they discovered Andy's heart defect, he wanted me to terminate the pregnancy."

When tears stung my eyes, it took me by surprise. I blinked them back, mortified. I hadn't wasted any tears over Andy's father in years.

"Ah. I see." Jay's face was solemn.

"You think? You'd almost have to be in my shoes." My voice was sharper than I'd intended. With a conscious effort, I spoke more softly. "Sorry, Jay. There's no reason to snap at you. There was never any doubt in my mind as to what I would do. His natural father just couldn't see it."

There was an uncomfortable silence between us. When the dog barked in the other room, I was grateful for the noise. While waiting for Homer's barking to subside, I decided there was no benefit to dragging up the rest of the story, to explain that some people just weren't cut out to parent a child with health issues. As it turned out, Andy's father was one of those people.

I wanted to change the topic back to business. "Jay, I talked to the Zimmerman woman at the jail. It's an action for contempt."

"Criminal contempt? Rule 33?"

"Yeah. Do you have any experience with that? If her version of the facts is correct, she wasn't actually disruptive."

The dog was still barking. Jay shook his head. "Say it again? Can't hear you."

Homer's barking grew louder, more ferocious. From the kitchen, I had to raise my voice to be heard.

"Andy! What's up with that dog?"

Jay was out of his chair, headed for the living room. When I followed, I saw Homer up on the pink sofa, barking out the window. Andy stood nearby, his hands covering his ears and his face a picture of misery.

"Mom, make him stop!"

Jay joined the dog at the window, staring out into the evening dusk, while I knelt beside Andy. "Did something happen? What in the world is that dog doing?"

The incessant barking made it difficult to hear Andy's voice, but it sounded like he said, "Homer didn't like it when the police car came."

That set off an alarm in my head. I ran to the front door, flung it open, and peered through the screen. A black-and-white patrol car sat directly in front of my house, behind the branches of the magnolia tree.

The sight of the patrol car sent a rush of adrenaline through me. I shoved the screen so hard, it left an imprint on my palm. I shook my hand to ease the sting as I stepped onto the front porch.

Jay came up behind me. In a warning voice, he asked, "What are you going to do?"

I needed a moment to think. But as I stood on the porch, trying to process the situation, Homer's distress became infectious. Dogs yelped all along the street, and the clamor of barking created an uproar. Faces appeared in windows, and a man in one of the houses shouted for quiet.

I held the screen door shut as Homer jumped against it. "Jay, shut the dog inside, please."

While Jay dragged the dog away, Andy appeared and tried to follow me out onto the porch, calling in a voice of distress, "Mom?"

It took an effort to keep my voice calm. "Everybody inside, okay? Homer is making the whole neighborhood crazy."

Before Jay closed the solid oak front door, he asked, "Martha, do you know what you're doing?"

With an assurance I didn't feel, I said, "I'm fine. Everything's fine. It's probably nothing. Just a car on patrol, maybe a neighborhood watch."

But I knew it wasn't a friendly lookout. As I walked down the steps toward the police car, I was blinded when a spotlight focused on me. I stumbled down the front walk, covering my face with my arm to shield my eyes from the glare.

By the time I reached the patrol car, I was agitated as hell. I

Leabharlanna Fhine Gall

knocked on the passenger window as I tried to rub the spots from my eyes.

The window rolled down. I could make out the figure of a man seated on the passenger side of the front seat, but my vision wasn't clear enough to identify him.

"Officer, is there a problem?" I said, my voice sounding a trifle shaken.

The driver of the car, a man in uniform, replied, "You tell us. Is there?"

The insolent response sharpened my senses. I bent down to peer into the car. At that point, I recognized both men. The uniformed driver was young Deputy Clark, whom I had encountered at the jail. In the passenger seat was Detective Stanley, from the courthouse coffee shop.

"Detective, what's going on?"

"Nothing much. We received a complaint tonight. Just checking it out."

The detective's smarmy grin fueled my ire. This was harassment, plain and simple. They were trying to intimidate me—again. I stepped back from the window.

"Stay as long as you like. And I hope this doesn't disappoint you. But I don't scare too easy."

The detective's smile disappeared. He shifted in the seat, turning to face the deputy.

"Hey, Clark. Isn't that what the last defender said?"

I froze, staring at the two men. The detective reached out and tapped the dashboard, saying to the deputy, "Let's go."

The deputy gunned the engine and sped off down the street.

CHAPTER 32

THE TENSE EXCHANGE with the police on Friday night set me on edge. I wondered what other unhappy surprises were in store. But we spent a relatively uneventful weekend, unpacking the last of our boxes and exploring the neighborhood. Jay and Andy gave Homer a bath, and cleaned up the bathroom afterward, relieving me of two messy jobs. The sun was so bright on Sunday that I took Andy to the pool in the town's park. Splashing in the shallow end with him was a tonic. I blocked out the burdens of the prior week while we played together.

But on Monday morning, I huddled over the keyboard at my office desk, churning out suggestions in support of a motion on behalf of Abby Zimmerman. Jay sat in the chair across from me with a volume of the *Southern Reporter* in his lap, poring over a case from the Alabama Supreme Court.

My hands paused, with fingers spread over the keys. "Well? Anything I can use?"

His hair fell across his face as he shook his head. "I got nothing. It's a constructive contempt case, the failure to comply with a judge's order in a civil lawsuit."

Thinking aloud, I mused, "That's not on point. This wasn't

constructive contempt. Pickens will claim he was exercising his judicial power of direct contempt under Rule 33."

Jay made a noise articulating his disgust. "You should allege that his action wasn't justified. He can't lock someone up just because he doesn't like the look on her face."

I squinted at the words on the monitor, tapping the keys to correct a typo. "That's one of the points in my motion, but I'm afraid to rely too heavily on it. Check out the definitions under 33.1. The rule defines direct contempt as disorderly or insolent behavior in open court."

"I've been in that courtroom before. We were all as scared as rabbits. No one has the nerve to be disorderly, ever."

I pulled my eyes away from the screen and met Jay's gaze. His mouth was set in a hard line, and his jaw twitched. I said, "Insolent. We can anticipate that's what Pickens will lean on. He'll say she gave him an insolent look, or exhibited behavior in open court that falls into that category. So he held her in contempt."

"He didn't give her notice. Hasn't provided a hearing yet—I'd stake my life on that."

My shoulders lifted with a defensive shrug. "Under the rules, he can dispose of it summarily, if it happened in open court."

Jay slammed the law book shut and tossed it onto my desk. I had to reach out to keep it from falling to the floor. In a ragged voice, he said, "This is bullshit."

I glanced over at the corner of the room where Andy sat, sorting through a bag of plastic dinosaurs. He had apparently tuned us out.

"I know it is—but, Jay, hear me out. Pickens is totally out of line on this, even if he can claim that a disrespectful look constitutes contempt of court. Assume that he claims Abby committed a direct contempt in open court, within his presence, and that her action somehow screwed with his dignity on the bench. He's required by law to make a record, prepare an order in which he gives the grounds for his finding. Gotta be in writing and signed by the judge." I paused momentarily, to hit the Print button. "He didn't. I checked online this morning. It's not there."

The printer made a preliminary groan. Jay left his chair and walked over to the machine. As it churned out the pages, he picked them up and scanned through them. When he finished, he looked up. "And so?"

"And so he's got to let her out. I'm heading straight over there to take this up."

My suit jacket was draped over the back of my chair. As I shrugged into it, I said, "Do you mind watching Andy while I'm gone? It shouldn't be long."

Andy had sorted the toys into two lines, separating the carnivores from the herbivores, it appeared. I'd let him play hooky from day care. Over breakfast that morning, he had begged to come to the office with me, solemnly promising that he wouldn't do anything to distract me. He had barely made a peep all morning, as if to prove it. I hadn't required much convincing about the change of routine. After the spooky incident on Friday night, I wanted to keep him close.

Jay handed me the printed pages. "Hey, Andy. Okay if I hang with you while your mom goes across the street to the courthouse?"

Andy nodded, intent on his prehistoric menagerie. "Okay," he said as he picked up a T. rex and attacked a smaller plastic beast with it.

I swiftly proofread the document, then scrawled my name across the signature line.

"I'm heading out," I said. "Andy, be good."

Jay followed me to my office door. "Any special instructions? Like if he gets hungry, or bored?"

"He'll be okay." Jay looked slightly uncertain. I hesitated, wondering whether I'd made the right call. "You want me to take him to day care? I can run him over there before I head to court."

"No, we'll wait for you here. Don't worry about us." He smiled at me. "Knock 'em dead."

I nodded, feeling a trifle cocky. "It's gonna be a good day. I'll set that woman free and be back in time for lunch."

"It's like we always said. You're the famous Jailhouse Lawyer."

I rolled my eyes at him. But now I kinda liked the sound of the old law school moniker. It felt like a good fit. As I paused in the hallway to fasten a button on my jacket, I heard the front door open and fought a surge of impatience—I was determined to head to Pickens's courtroom without delay, and I didn't want any interruptions.

My momentary pique was shaken by a woman's voice, crying: "Ms. Foster!"

Stepping into the reception area, I saw Molly Zimmerman standing in the open doorway, her mouth agape and her face swollen from crying. When she struggled to speak, she made inarticulate keening noises.

Still clutching my briefcase, I took her by the hand and led her to a chair. As she collapsed onto the seat, I sank down beside her. I waited as Molly composed herself, feeling mounting dread. When she spoke, my stomach lurched.

"Abby's dead. They called me from the jail." Her voice rose as she repeated the words. "Abby's dead!"

I dropped my briefcase, letting it fall to the floor. The papers inside couldn't set Abby free after all.

CHAPTER 33

I DROVE MOLLY Zimmerman to the coroner's office. She was so distraught, in such a state of shock and grief, it would be callous to send her off alone. And my morning schedule had been radically altered. I no longer had any reason to rush over to the courthouse.

The small gray cinder-block building marked DOUGLAS COUNTY MEDICAL EXAMINER was only a few blocks from my office. I parked in an empty spot directly in front of the entrance.

After I turned off the ignition, Molly snatched my hand and squeezed it in a desperate grip. "When they take me back to see her body, promise you'll go with me. Please. I can't do it alone."

Inwardly, I quailed at the request. This was a first for me. The legal work I'd done back in Birmingham hadn't prepared me for Molly's raw agony. I had no experience viewing corpses freshly delivered to a coroner's facility.

With an effort, I hid my uneasiness. I patted her wrist with my free hand and said in a firm voice, "Molly, I'm here to support you."

As we made our way to the door, Molly stumbled on the curb. I had to grab her elbow to keep her from falling. Once we entered, the loud whir of air-conditioning buzzed in my ears, so noisy it was difficult to catch Molly's whispered plea.

It sounded like she said: "Don't leave me alone with them."

Keeping a firm grip on her arm, I ushered Molly to the reception window, where a woman dressed in nurses' scrubs sat behind the desk. She watched us with a somber face as we approached.

"What can I do for y'all?" she asked.

I glanced at Molly, who commenced weeping when she tried to respond. She couldn't get the words out, so I spoke for her.

"This is Molly Zimmerman. She received a call informing her that her sister, Abigail, died in the county jail."

The woman in scrubs focused on Molly. "Are you next of kin to the deceased?"

Molly's face crumpled as she nodded. The woman in scrubs then turned to me, scrutinizing me with undisguised curiosity.

"And you are?"

"Martha Foster. County public defender." I raised my brow. "Your name?" She wore no name tag, and her desk didn't have a nameplate.

"Doreen." I was about to demand a surname when she pushed her chair away from the desk. "The doctor's still back in the morgue, with the body. Ms. Zimmerman, you can come with me."

Instead of following Doreen, Molly backed up a step. The woman's mouth tightened with impatience.

"You'll need to come on back. Understand? They want you to identify the body."

Molly clutched at my sleeve. In a choking voice, she said, "The lawyer can come with me, can't she?"

Doreen gave me a flat look. "Are you kin, ma'am?" Her tone bordered on insolence. Clearly she knew I wasn't a relative.

"I'd like to accompany Ms. Zimmerman. I met with Abigail at the jail last Friday." The recollection gave me an involuntary shudder, thinking how Abby Zimmerman had still been alive three days prior. "I'm here to support the family."

"Can't do that—it's not policy," Doreen said, adding, "Sorry."

She didn't sound the least bit sorry, but I had no power to force my way into the morgue. Turning to Molly, I said, "I'll wait for you right here. Go see your sister, and when you're done, I'll take you home. Okay?"

Reluctantly, Molly released my sleeve and followed as Doreen led her through the door. After they departed, I circled the reception area, thinking about the work I had done earlier that morning, drafting a motion to release Abby from jail. The inevitable question haunted me: why hadn't I done it on Friday? If I had prepared the motion and taken it up in court before Pickens, rather than trying to appeal to him in the coffee shop, Abby might have been released Friday afternoon.

If I had done things differently, maybe she wouldn't be lying on a slab in the morgue.

Reeling with remorse, I grew anxious to know the cause of Abby's death. She was far too young to drop dead of natural causes; Abby had appeared to be somewhere in the vicinity of my own age. And if she'd had a preexisting condition, it had not been evident when I talked to her.

When Doreen returned to her desk, I ran up to the window before she had a chance to sit down. "Doreen, has the coroner made a determination as to cause of death? What is his finding?"

Glancing away, she picked up a cell phone and rubbed the screen. While she tapped in a passcode, she said, "That's county business, ma'am."

I had to fight to keep irritation from my voice. It felt like the woman was messing with me, and I didn't take kindly to that. "And I'm a part of the county's legal structure."

Doreen didn't look up. From my angle, it appeared that she was checking her recent text messages. "What did you say your name was again?" she said.

"Foster. Martha Ann Foster." A devious ploy occurred to me, and the words spun out without time to consider. "Judge Pickens assured me that everyone in the Douglas County pipeline would be more than happy to cooperate with me. He wants me to stay in my position for a long time."

He *had* said something to that effect. Just not lately.

I'd gotten her attention. Doreen looked up from the cell phone.

In a confiding tone, I said, "I'd hate to have to tell the judge that the staff at the coroner's office has been rude to me. If there's one thing Judge Pickens doesn't tolerate, it's rudeness."

Now, that was a direct quote, straight from the horse's mouth, and the woman undoubtedly recognized it. Doreen set her phone down. Her eyes shifted.

With an effort, I held my tongue and waited for her to speak. Finally, she exhaled, as if she'd been holding her breath.

"Well, you'll hear about it before long anyway, since you work for the county. There might be a press release later today. Pulmonary embolism."

She didn't elaborate, but I was familiar with the diagnosis; a coworker's father had died when a blood clot went to his lung. I wanted to ask for more detail. But at that moment, Molly burst through the door, her hand covering her mouth.

She made her way directly to me and said, "We need to go, right now."

Molly grasped the sleeve of my jacket, and I let her drag me through the door. Once we were safely inside the car, I looked at her with concern.

"Are you all right, Molly? I know what a difficult thing it is, to see a loved one who has passed away."

She began to shake so violently, I anticipated that she would break down, that her grief would overtake her. But she clutched the dashboard for support, cleared her voice, and spoke.

"They killed her."

Initially, I was struck dumb and didn't know how to respond. After grasping for the proper reply, I said, "Did the medical examiner talk to you, explain his findings? I was told that Abby died of a pulmonary embolism. That can happen when a blood clot in the leg—"

Molly cut me off. "You know what I saw on her legs? Marks, deep marks all around her ankles. She had them on her wrists, too. I know where those marks come from."

Her voice rose to a pitch that bordered on hysteria. "They put my sister in the Pickens chair. I'd swear it on the Bible: Abby must have died in the chair."

CHAPTER 34

PIECING TOGETHER THE gist of Molly's accusations, I concluded that the Douglas County Jail utilized a restraint chair.

I had heard of restraint chairs before. In a criminal law class, a guest speaker from the Alabama Department of Corrections had explained that restraint chairs were used when inmates became violent or delusional, due to mental illness or intoxication. He had claimed the chairs were designed to prevent inmates from posing a danger to themselves or others. As I sat in the safety of a university lecture hall years ago, the man's explanation had sounded entirely sensible to me. And I hadn't thought about the chair since then. It was merely a notation in my crim law notes.

But after I dropped Molly Zimmerman at her home, I kept envisioning the picture of the chair that the class speaker from the ADOC had shown us in his PowerPoint presentation: the rigid shape, the handcuffs bolted to unforgiving metal arms, the ankle restraints at the foothold.

I decided to see if there was a basis for Molly's claim. The DA's office felt like a good starting point; Doug Carson would almost certainly be apprised of the circumstances behind the death of an inmate in county custody. Whether he would be willing to share the details with me was more difficult to predict.

Nonetheless, I dashed up the marble steps, catching sight of Carson as he left his office and made his way to the courtroom, bearing an armload of file folders.

"Doug! You got a minute?" I called out, but he didn't turn around. He proceeded into court as if he hadn't heard me. I trotted up to the door and peered through the glass, seeing Pickens sitting in his judicial robe and Carson standing at the bench. Their heads were bent together, in some kind of deep discussion. If court was in session, I couldn't interrupt; so I intended to slip onto a bench at the back of the room. I was prepared to wait him out, because I was anxious to hear an explanation for Abby's demise.

As I made my way to a seat, the bailiff turned his head my way. He sat at his desk near the front of the courtroom, and when he caught sight of me, he did a double take. I saw him cast an apprehensive glance in the direction of the bench as he rose from his chair.

His prosthetic foot made him limp as he hurried up the aisle toward me. When he reached the door, he placed one hand on the knob and beckoned to me with the other. When I didn't move, he grimaced and jerked his head in the direction of the hall.

Curious, I left my seat and followed him through the doorway. He pushed the door firmly shut before he spoke. In a harsh whisper, he said, "Martha, you're not supposed to be here."

Behind his thick bifocals, his eyes were anxious.

I gawked at him, wondering what had possessed him to make such a statement. We both knew that court proceedings were a matter of public record.

"Harold, I need to talk to the prosecutor. But I won't disturb the court proceedings. I'll just wait in there until he has a minute free."

Harold backed up against the door, barring my access. "You need to move along, Martha. Go on back to your office for a spell. Please."

The words had been spoken as a plea rather than a command. My suspicions aroused, I was determined to see what was going on in the courtroom. But when I tried to peer through the glass, Harold sidestepped to block my view.

With an effort, I kept a civil tone. "What are they taking up in there? I didn't receive notice of any criminal cases."

"These aren't your cases. Please, Ms. Foster, you need to get on out. Now."

Harold's impassioned whisper was drowned out by Judge Pickens bellowing inside the courtroom, "Where's my bailiff?"

Harold wheeled around and scurried back through the door. I followed, sliding onto the seat nearest the aisle. Pickens was glaring at the bailiff as he made his way to the bench. "Harold, you need to be available to escort people to the county jail."

The judge turned to face a man standing before him, in front of the bench. "Mr. Jenkins, I told you two weeks ago that this would be your last chance."

Edging forward on my wooden seat, I scrutinized Mr. Jenkins, a man with unshorn graying hair, dressed in cast-off clothing. His name wasn't familiar, so I used my phone to run a quick check of my current caseload. Jenkins didn't appear in any of my files.

The man said, "Judge, I haven't been able to get work. I want to pay, I really do, I just don't have it."

Doug Carson crossed his arms over his chest. In a priggish tone, he said, "Jenkins refused to make payment at the last three hearings, Judge. It doesn't appear that he's taking his obligation to pay the costs seriously."

Pickens nodded soberly. Toying with a fountain pen, he cleared his throat and said, "Let the record reflect that Mr. Jenkins has willfully failed to comply with the ruling of this court and is remanded to custody for his failure to comply with the terms of his release."

He pointed the pen in the direction of the bailiff's desk. "Harold?"

With a nod, Harold rose, pulling the handcuffs from his belt as he approached Jenkins. As Harold cuffed his hands behind him, Jenkins said, "Please, Judge, give me one more chance."

Pickens behaved as if he hadn't heard. Nodding to the prosecutor, he said, "Next case, Doug."

As Harold ferried the Jenkins man out of court, Carson stepped over to his counsel table and flipped open a file.

"The next hearing is in the case of *State v. Hobson,* Your Honor."

A young man rose and headed to the front of the courtroom. This time I didn't bother to check my short list of case names. I was confident that Hobson wasn't among them.

As the young man neared the bench, he spoke in a shaking voice. "I'd like a chance to explain, Judge, why I can't pay the whole thing today."

I didn't give him the opportunity to continue. Jumping to my feet, I charged down the aisle at a near run. My voice echoed across the room as I called out. "Objection, Your Honor! That man who was taken away by the bailiff—why was he incarcerated without counsel? And why are criminal cases being heard in my absence?"

Doug Carson swung around, staring at me like my fiery red hair was literally aflame. And frankly, I was so mad, it might have been in danger of spontaneously combusting. He said, "What are you doing?"

I passed right by the prosecutor without acknowledging him. "Your Honor, this is highly irregular. Are these hearings related to payments of your Douglas County board bills? Because I want to inform the court that I oppose your practice of jailing individuals for nonpayment of those bills. I strenuously oppose it, Your Honor."

Doug Carson began to babble. "Judge, I didn't notify her of today's proceedings. It wasn't me, I swear."

Judge Pickens lifted his hand. Carson clamped his mouth shut.

I said, "Your Honor, the prosecutor is right about that. He didn't notify me, and neither did anyone else. And I want to state on the record—"

Liza, the court reporter, looked up in alarm. She hadn't been recording the proceedings. Swiftly, she began to transcribe the exchange. But she froze when the judge spoke.

Pickens looked directly at me and said: "Stop. Right now."

The judge hadn't raised his voice. But something about his demeanor was so forbidding, I had to fight the urge to back away from him. His features no longer resembled a cinema star. He looked like a movie villain.

When Pickens spoke again, he conveyed so much suppressed fury that I felt like I was witnessing Dr. Jekyll transform into Mr. Hyde.

"Young woman, I want you out of this courtroom immediately."

I started to protest. That's when he got loud.

He said, "If you dare to speak one more word—just one—you'll regret it."

His eyes were genuinely scary to behold, but I didn't look away until he said, "You need to learn your proper place in Douglas County."

CHAPTER 35

HE KICKED ME out of court.

To be precise, Pickens stood up and waved his black-garbed arm, pointing to the door. He uttered only one word.

"Out."

Standing in the courtroom, the scene felt otherworldly, like I had wandered into a different century, an earlier era in which a lowly serf could be arbitrarily banished. Making my way to the door on autopilot, it didn't occur to me to resist. Not at that moment, anyway.

But as I walked out of the courthouse, the fear and humiliation faded, replaced by a surge of white-hot fury.

I tore down the steps and across the street. I wanted to find Jay, to tell him what had transpired. We needed to put our heads together, to plot a strategy. It was high time to launch my resistance against Wyatt Pickens.

Flush with determination, I shot through the entrance to the PD's office and slammed the door shut with such force that it shook the frame. With the door safely shut behind me, I called out: "Jay! You're not gonna believe what Pickens just did!"

My voice bounced off the walls. No one responded. The reception area was empty, the restroom door ajar. When I checked my office, the law books had been reshelved. Andy's dinosaurs were still in the corner of the room, but they had been stuffed back into the bag where we stored them.

A scrap of paper lay on my desk. I leaned over it and read:

Andy got hungry, so I took him over to day care. Too far for him to walk, but he can ride my shoulders. Heading back to your house after I drop him off. Hope that's okay.

I wadded up the paper and tossed it into the trash can, feeling disturbed and unsettled by the message. The thought of Andy left under Peg's wing made me uneasy. I wished I had been more forthcoming about the day-care situation when I'd talked to Jay the prior evening. But we'd had other issues to address—like the weird police surveillance in front of my house—and it had slipped my mind.

Nursing a spike of resentment, I grabbed my keys and snatched the bag of toys off the floor. Why would Jay assume he could hand my son off to someone else when he'd agreed to care for him? The note he'd left didn't set out sufficient reason to change the plan without consulting me. Clearly I should have told Jay that Andy could only go to day care in the event of an emergency. I hopped into the car, determined to set Andy free from Happy Times Day Care.

Maybe I was driving too fast. It's possible I was rattled by the courtroom confrontation, compounded by the discovery that Andy wasn't where I had left him. An overdose of adrenaline could make my foot heavy on the gas pedal.

My car was just within sight of the day care when I saw a patrol car in my rearview mirror, lights on and the siren wailing. Muttering some choice cuss words, I nursed the faint hope that I wasn't the cop's target. But when I pulled to the curb across from Peg's side yard, the police car pulled in right behind me.

"Shit, shit, shit," I whispered as the uniformed officer emerged from his patrol car and strolled up to my vehicle.

I rolled down the window, relieved to see that the young man striding up to my car wasn't Deputy Clark. This guy was younger, his forehead still spotted with adolescent acne.

"Hello, Officer," I said, keeping my manner upbeat.

"Do you know how fast you were going?"

I hesitated for a second, debating the best way to answer. "I don't think I was speeding."

"You don't?" The cop wore sunglasses with dark lenses; I couldn't see his eyes, and it was hard to read his expression. So the next question caught me off guard.

"Have you been drinking?"

My breath caught in my throat. "What?"

"Are you under the influence of alcohol or drugs? Or on some kind of medication?"

"Absolutely not." I dropped the friendly facade. Sucking up to a teenage cop required more patience than I could muster, after the day I had endured.

He peered into the car, checking out the front and back seats as if he expected to find open beer bottles and a smoking blunt. When he didn't spot anything more suspicious than a couple of McDonald's bags, he straightened up and pulled a pen from his pocket.

"You were driving erratically, crossed the center line."

Thinking that my day couldn't possibly get any worse, I sounded snappish as I said, "I certainly did not. You're mistaken about that."

It was the wrong thing to say.

He ordered me out of the car, directly in front of the day-care facility, and began a battery of field sobriety tests.

"Stand with your heels and toes together, hands at your sides."

I glanced over at the windows of Happy Times, wondering whether anyone was looking.

He held up the pen. "Follow the top of my pen with your eyes. Don't move your head."

He waved the pen from side to side, up and down: the Horizontal Gaze Nystagmus Test. As I obeyed the instructions, I nursed the hope that one test would suffice. But although I passed the test, the kid looked unimpressed.

Pointing at the center line of the street, he said, "Take nine heel-to-toe steps on the line, turn, and take nine steps back."

I had worn high heels that day, because I had intended to appear in court and wanted the extra inches of height. High heels are not the best shoe choice for the walk-and-turn test, but I managed the steps without stumbling.

I tried for a winning smile. "Officer, I apologize for sounding abrupt earlier. Haven't we done enough here? To clear up the issue?"

He took a step back and crossed his arms on his chest, without acknowledging the plea. "I want you to lift one leg six inches off the ground and start counting out loud like this—one thousand one, one thousand two, one thousand three—until I tell you to stop."

Standing in the street beside the patrol car, I'd just begun counting when kids started pouring out of the day care into the side yard. They didn't make a run for the swing set or the climbing equipment, not with a real police car putting on a show for them just across the street. They herded up to the chain-link fence, fighting for the best position to view the excitement.

My count had just reached one thousand ten when I heard a savvy kid shout: "It's a drunk driver!"

Several numbers later, Andy's voice shrieked out, louder than the others. "Mom!"

The damned cop made me count all the way to twenty-five—far longer than the standard test, in my legal defense experience. By the time he finally permitted me to set my leg down, my whole body was trembling. But I wasn't wobbling due to physical exertion.

It was because my son was screaming, and shaking the fence like he thought he could tear it down.

CHAPTER 36

THE COP GAVE me a ticket. Not for DUI, of course; they couldn't have made a case against me on the charge. And the ticket wasn't for speeding either, so I suspected his radar gun showed that I hadn't been much outside the speed limit. He wrote it for failure to exercise care, crossing the center line. It would be my word against his.

By the time I had the ticket in hand and the youthful cop had driven off, the day-care kids had been shepherded back inside. As I walked through the front door of Happy Times, my appearance made quite a sensation.

"It's Andy's mom! She's the drunk driver!"

Peg was waiting for me right beside the entrance, holding Andy by his upper arm. When she released him, he clutched my jacket, burying his face in my stomach.

My face burned with chagrin as I backed through the door with Andy glued to me. "Sorry about all the drama, Peg. The cop thought I was speeding or something. Did you get a look at that kid? I can't believe he's old enough to make it into the police academy."

Peg followed us out the door and down the concrete walk. Andy looked up at me and wailed, "What was the policeman doing to you? Was it the one who was at our house last night?"

His voice carried, and Peg clearly overheard the questions; I could see it in her stony countenance. She waited with her arms folded while I buckled Andy into the back seat. When I turned around, she said, "Martha, it might be best if you look for other childcare options."

I shut the door, to keep the conversation from Andy's ears. "Because I got a traffic ticket? Peg—are you serious?"

She wouldn't meet my eye. "I have a reputation to uphold. People want their children kept in a certain environment, with other responsible, respectable families. This is a business; it's how I make my living."

I jerked the ticket from my pocket and held it out, so she could inspect it. "It's just a minor traffic infraction, for careless driving. That's not a crime involving moral turpitude. People get traffic tickets every day."

She backed away, refusing to even glance at the ticket in my hand. "It's not just the ticket, Martha. I don't want any trouble."

My arm dropped as I shook my head, dumbfounded. "What?"

"I'm licensed by the county. I can't afford to lose that license."

She wheeled around and hurried up the front walk. I wanted to shout at her retreating figure, to hurl a comeback that my son didn't like her damned day care anyway.

But I stuffed the ticket into my pocket, got into my car, and drove off.

It took seven minutes to get home, and those minutes were spent explaining the circumstances of the traffic stop to Andy. He wasn't easy to convince, so I even passed the citation back to him, to prove the veracity of my story. He couldn't read the ticket, but I hoped that holding it in his hands would make the incident less frightening.

The ploy appeared to work. By the time we reached the house, Andy had stopped crying.

I spotted Jay in the backyard, sitting in the grass with Homer stretched out beside him. When we got out of the car, Jay jumped up, calling out to me.

Andy ran through the gate, heading straight for Homer, but Jay caught him just before he reached the dog. He said something to Andy that I couldn't make out, and Andy ran into the house through the back door.

As I shut the gate, Jay walked up to me, shaking his head. I was glad Andy was safely inside, because I was ready to unload. When Jay was within earshot, I said, "You aren't going to believe the shit that's happened today."

He took me by the hand, pulling me toward the dog. "I'm worried about Homer."

Jay knelt down in the grass beside the dog and stroked his head. Homer lay unmoving in the grass with his eyes shut.

"Did something happen to him? Did he get out of the yard, get hit by a car?"

Jay's hand kept smoothing the fur on the dog's head. "I think it's poison."

CHAPTER 37

I TOOK AN involuntary step away from Jay, to distance myself from the newest source of bad news. A thought nagged in my head: *I can't handle another crisis right now.* But I suppressed it. Hoping to hear that he was just speculating, I asked, "Why do you think that?"

"He's been having seizures."

My heart sank. "Seizures? Are you sure?" I knelt beside Homer in the grass and ran my hand down his back.

"I've seen it before. I worked for my dad in the summers." He glanced over at me. "I don't know if you remember, but my father—"

"Is a veterinarian," I said, finishing the sentence. I fumbled for my phone. "So I should get him to a vet?"

"Yeah. He should be seen today, as soon as possible."

I ran a search on my phone: three vets had listings in Erva. I called all three of them and struck out. The first office told me the vet was out of town. The second one was too busy to see him. The third vet answered with a recording, telling me to leave a name and number.

While I was on the phone leaving frantic messages, Andy ran out, holding an old bedroom slipper that Homer liked to chew. Jay sat Andy down, telling him to place the slipper where Homer could smell it. While Andy held the dog's paw, Jay explained that Homer wasn't feeling well.

"How'd he get sick?"

"Something he ate," Jay said, catching my eye.

Watching the dog's chest rise and fall, my anxiety increased. Even to my untrained eye, Homer's panting looked heavy and labored. When he began to shake, I grasped Jay's arm.

"What are we going to do? I can't get a vet to see him."

Jay lifted one of the dog's eyelids—looking for what, I hadn't a clue. "Do you have hydrogen peroxide?" he asked.

"Sure." I had a bottle in the bathroom.

"Bring it to me, okay?"

I raced into the house and was back in the yard in a flash. Handing over the brown plastic bottle, I said, "What are you going to do?"

"Induce vomiting." He jerked his head in Andy's direction, and I tugged at my son's wrist.

"Andy, you need to run on inside. You don't want to see Homer throw up."

Andy needed no further persuasion. He jumped up and ran for the house. Once Andy was safely out of the way, I also took an apprehensive step away from Jay and Homer. Though I was willing to help, I wasn't eager to see him vomit either.

"Will this fix him up? If you make him throw up whatever he ate?" I hoped the solution would be that simple.

"I'll have to give him activated charcoal."

My brow furrowed in confusion. "I don't have that, whatever it is. Never heard of it."

Jay was unscrewing the brown bottle of hydrogen peroxide. "I have activated charcoal in my backpack."

"I'll bring it out," I said, relieved to have a reason to escape the yard. Jay's backpack sat in the corner of the living room, next to the rolled-up sleeping bag he used at night. There was no time to ponder why Jay kept charcoal among his small trove of worldly possessions. I grabbed the backpack by one strap and headed through the kitchen, with Andy at my heels.

"What's the matter with my dog?"

I turned, lifting his chin so that he would meet my eye. "He's sick, hon. Something he ate. Jay's going to give him medicine."

"Why don't you take him to the doctor?"

I couldn't take time to explain. I ruffled Andy's hair and told him to stay put before I dashed back into the yard with the backpack. Homer was upchucking. The vomit looked like coffee grounds.

Andy stood on the other side of the screen door, looking pale and shouting Homer's name. His hands were clenched into fists at his sides; I could see that he was terrified. In an accusatory voice, he said, "Homer needs a doctor!"

I returned to him inside and bent to take his hands in mine. "Jay's dad is a vet, and he taught Jay to take care of animals. So he knows what to do for Homer. It's going to be all right."

I hoped it was the truth.

I sat at the kitchen table with Andy on my lap. While we waited. I tried to tell a story to distract him, but he shook his head and buried it in my chest.

So we sat in silence, the minutes dragging by. I checked my phone repeatedly, hoping for a return call from a local vet, but the ringtone didn't sound. After what felt like an eternity, Jay walked in with his backpack and headed to the kitchen sink.

While he scrubbed his hands and arms, Andy asked in a plaintive voice, "How's Homer?"

"Better. I think." Jay turned his head and gave me an uncertain shrug as Andy scrambled off my lap.

Andy said, "I'm gonna go see him."

I caught him before he opened the back door. "Homer needs to rest. I'm going to make us a sandwich. How about PB&J? How does that sound?"

He cast a worried look at the door before he relented. "I guess."

While Andy ate the sandwich, I followed Jay into the living room. "What did you do for him?"

"Made him vomit, then administered the charcoal."

"What is that?"

"The activated charcoal? It can absorb poison."

Rather than providing illumination, his brief answers left me more confused. "So that's something you just carry around with you? Poison antidotes? For dogs?"

Jay zipped up the backpack and shoved it back into the corner. "People take it sometimes. For hangovers."

That statement gave me pause. I didn't like the implication. As far as I could tell, Jay hadn't consumed any alcohol since he'd been in my house. When I'd offered up my home as a temporary shelter, I'd made it clear that I wouldn't tolerate it. If he still intended to indulge a drinking problem, he wouldn't do it under my roof. I had a five-year-old son to protect.

His next question jerked me out of my uneasy thoughts. "Martha, have you set any rat poison around? In the house or out in the yard?"

"Are you kidding? I live with a small child. Do you think I'd leave poison lying around?"

My voice had sounded loud and angry. Jay raised his hands in a defensive gesture. "Hey, it's just a thought. Maybe the owner left it around the house. Otherwise . . ." He paused, avoiding my eye.

I needed to hear him complete the thought. "Otherwise?" I prompted.

"Otherwise, it was intentional rather than accidental. And that's pretty damned creepy. Why would someone want to kill your dog?"

As the significance sank in, I strode up to the front room window and peered out onto the street. My eyes screened the block for signs of suspicious activity, as if I'd find a dog killer lurking nearby. But there was nothing to set off an alarm. A lazy breeze made the leaves rustle in the afternoon sun as a young woman pushed a baby stroller down the sidewalk. Some kids' voices could be heard, a couple of houses down. An old Buick sedan drove slowly past my house, an old woman clutching the steering wheel.

Turning away from the window, I sank onto the pink sofa, feeling like my legs had given out. Jay sat on the edge of the coffee table, facing me.

"Well, Martha? Why would someone want to kill your dog?"

My head began to pound. I rubbed my forehead, but it didn't help. "I guess somebody in Erva doesn't like me."

He gave me a rueful smile. "You're not alone."

He was right about that. Ignoring the throb in my head, I said, "Let's talk about something else."

"Okay. Like what?"

The pain increased; I was tempted to run to the bathroom for a dose of Advil. But I stayed put and answered his question.

"Restraint chairs."

CHAPTER 38

JAY LOWERED HIS voice. "Restraint chairs in general? Or the one at the Douglas County Jail?"

"Either. Both."

The head pain forgotten, I scooted forward on the sofa cushion, eager to hear what Jay knew about the chair. But my phone rang before he could answer. It was one of the veterinarians, returning my call. I hastily answered and explained my concerns about the dog.

Jay and I delayed our conversation as we bundled Homer into the car, and the four of us rushed across town to meet the vet at her office. While Jay relayed his observations, she gave Homer a thorough exam. She was impressed by Jay's handling of the situation.

"Will he be okay?" I asked, casting an anxious eye at Andy, who had insisted on joining us in the small examination room.

"I think so, thanks to your friend's speedy reaction. Take him home, make him comfortable, and keep an eye on him. If you have any problems, call me back."

She cut her eyes to Andy before giving me a significant look. "I'd make sure there's no rodenticide in any corners of the house. It has a pleasant taste, kind of sweet." The vet rubbed Homer behind the ears. "You're a lucky guy, Homer."

When we returned home, I dragged Homer's dog bed into the living room and covered it with a tattered quilt while Jay searched the house for rat poison. Homer settled onto the quilt, with Andy beside him, talking softly to the dog. I hoped Homer would fully recover, for all our sakes.

As Jay walked into the living room, I said, "Well? Did you find anything?"

He shook his head. Though I wasn't happy to think my house was contaminated with toxic substances, it was more worrisome that someone in town would intentionally poison my dog. With a burst of nervous energy, I jumped up and paced the room. The old Shirley Temple doll on the fireplace mantel caught my eye; someone had turned her cracked face back around. I twisted it so that we had a view of the doll's bedraggled ringlets. I didn't like the look in her shattered glass eyes; I needed to tell Andy to leave the doll alone. I was surprised he could reach it, even standing on a chair.

But Andy was sitting cross-legged by the dog, whispering as he stroked his fur. I didn't have the heart to fuss at him, not right then.

Jay took a seat on the pink couch and gestured for me to join him. "You want to talk? About the Douglas County Jail?"

Nodding, I joined him on the couch. "Do you remember that guest speaker from ADOC, who came to our crim law class? He said that the chairs were a legitimate tool, that they were necessary for inmates' safety."

Jay plucked a tuft of Homer's hair from his shirtsleeve. "Any tool can be abused. Depends on who's using it." He reached out to drop the fur into a waste basket that sat under the side table.

"Did they ever put you in the restraint chair?"

"No. But they threatened it, anytime somebody acted out. And the very mention of it made all of the inmates quiet down." He bent close to my ear. "I think we were not just worried about the chair itself but what the jailers could do while we were cuffed to the chair."

In a whisper, worried that Andy might overhear, I asked, "Do they really call it the Pickens chair?"

He nodded. "Yes, ma'am. It's an open secret. Though once I heard a jailer refer to it as the 'Be sweet' chair. Whatever it's called—no one wants to protest or complain too loudly. Because they're afraid they'll end up sitting in it."

With a shudder, I glanced over at Andy. We couldn't continue the conversation while he was in the room. "Andy, how's Homer? Sleeping?"

"I think so."

"You want my iPad? It's on my bedside table. I'll let you play a game on it, as long as you play it in there."

He cheered up immediately—using my iPad was a rare treat because I didn't often share it. When he ran off to get the device, I told Jay, "Molly thinks her sister Abby died in the chair. The body had marks on the wrists and ankles. And Abby died of a pulmonary embolism, the coroner's office said."

"Blood clot?" Jay said.

Homer began to whimper. Jay immediately left the couch. While he tended to the dog, I pulled out my laptop and set it on the coffee table. I had not been searching for long before I struck gold. I peered down at Jay, who was still bent over the dog. "How's Homer? Is he better?"

"Seems like it." Jay gave him a final pat and returned to the couch, sitting beside me to look at the computer screen. "What did you find?"

"A lawsuit in federal court, brought under Section 1983 of the Civil Rights Act, in which someone sued the government and its employees for abusing their authority in violation of his constitutional rights. A guy sued the jail for injuries suffered in a restraint chair. But I only found the pleadings. I guess the case is still pending." I scrolled down the search results. "I'm finding lots of articles about restraint chair abuses, though. This one says they kept a guy restrained in the chair for five days. Jesus! Five whole days?" I shook my head in shock and disbelief.

And that's when I had a eureka moment. "Oh, Lord, do you think Abby was restrained long enough for a clot to form?"

Jay's eyes remained on the screen, scanning the page. "What?"

"Remember the professor at UA who developed a blood clot in his leg during a long international flight? He had to be hospitalized when they landed. They said he was lucky, that it could have killed him."

"Yeah, but he was old, wasn't he? Seems like I remember that."

"But still. Lack of movement is a circumstance that can cause pulmonary embolism."

I jumped up and paced the floor, thinking aloud, eager to bounce ideas off Jay.

"If using the chair is such a frequent practice in the jail in Erva that even Abby's sister made reference to it, it's got to be common knowledge, right? If they're abusing it, maybe someone has sued."

"Why don't we see if a lawsuit has been filed against Douglas County Jail, or the sheriff, or the judge?"

Back on the couch, we did the search together but came up empty.

"Too bad I can't ask the prior PD," I said, deflated. "But that's not a possibility, obviously."

Our eyes met. He said, "Dead men tell no tales, huh?"

Andy's voice called to me from the other room. "Mom! The iPad quit working, right in the middle of my game."

I pulled a charger out of my briefcase. "Coming," I said.

By the time I returned to the living room, Jay had overtaken my spot in front of the laptop. He looked at me with a conspiratorial grin of satisfaction.

"Look who I found on LinkedIn."

I checked out the page, which showed a smiling headshot of a lawyer in his thirties, in private practice in Tuscaloosa. He didn't look familiar. Puzzled, I asked, "Do we know him?"

"No, but I bet Judge Pickens does." Jay used the mouse to point out an item on the guy's bio: public defender, Douglas County, Alabama. It didn't provide a start or end date.

Jubilant, I hugged Jay's neck. When our eyes met, I said, "I believe I'll give him a call."

"I think you should," he agreed.

It didn't take long to find the man's contact information in the Alabama State Bar directory. Pulling out my cell phone, I tapped in the numbers and put the phone on speaker. Both of us stared at the phone as it lay on the table. Unconsciously, I crossed my fingers for luck. When a man answered, Jay shot me a triumphant look.

"May I speak to Mr. Keaton?" I said, my voice strenuously pleasant.

"This is Paul Keaton. Who's calling?"

Jay and I shared a fist bump across the table. "Mr. Keaton, this is Martha Foster. I'm an attorney in Alabama, and I was recently hired as public defender of Douglas County."

"Douglas County? Alabama?"

"Yes. I know that you held this same position in the past, and I want to talk to you about some concerns..."

I never had the opportunity to finish that sentence. My phone said the call had ended.

Jay scooted closer as I stared at the screen of my silent cell phone. "What the hell? He hung up?"

I nodded, my eyes trained on the phone.

"Well, call him back."

Oh, I tried to call back. I dialed the number a dozen times.

Mr. Keaton did not pick up.

CHAPTER 39

THE NEXT MORNING was a red-letter day on the calendar: it was the day Jay's first payment hearing was set in court. My office was crowded; the entire household occupied it. Jay sat at my desk, his hands flying across the keyboard. Andy was curled up on the couch with Homer—we were relieved to see that the dog's condition had improved overnight, but I was afraid to leave him behind at the house. I sat in a client chair across from Jay, scanning a legal case opinion on my laptop.

Explosive sounds from Andy's video game set my nerves on edge. "Hon, you gotta turn the volume down or I'm taking the iPad away."

He looked up with a wounded expression. "It's not even that loud."

"Are you going to mind me?"

Andy must have heard a warning note in my voice because the game was quickly muted. Breathing out in relief, I shifted the laptop on my knees and resumed my reading.

Across the desk, Jay broke into a wide grin and stretched his arms over his head as the printer groaned into action. He hopped out of the chair and grabbed the pages, sorting through them. Approaching me, he held out the document.

"You want to read it? You ready?"

"Sure."

He seemed ebullient as he handed it off to me. Strolling around the office, he picked up a discarded sheet of paper from the floor, wadded it into a ball, and aimed it at the wastebasket. "Score! Two points," he crowed, shooting a teasing glance my way. I didn't respond; my head was buried in the pages, digesting them.

He sat on the edge of the desk and waited.

When I flipped over the last page, I looked up. "This is great," I said, meaning it. His legal work was stellar. It was tragic that losing his license meant he couldn't utilize his skill to practice law.

"Ain't it, though?" His high spirits had a contagious effect, and my confidence surged.

"Okay. I'm going to e-file this motion to retax costs in your case, Jay," I said, "then I'll run over to court."

He took a breath. "You sure I shouldn't be there for the hearing? To appear in person with you? Pickens was pretty specific about wanting to see me back in court."

I lifted my shoulders in a shrug. "You need to find a foxhole, Jay. I'm pretty sure this filing will light Pickens's fuse, and you don't want to be around when that happens." I was worried that seeing Jay might inflame the judge's ire when Pickens understood what we were attempting to do. "I'm not going to e-file until the last minute, so the clerk probably won't get around to posting it before he calls up the case. I'll have the element of surprise."

Taking Judge Pickens by surprise wasn't necessarily a safe tactic. But it was how I'd decided to play it.

I went on. "I'll supply the paper copies, then make an oral argument in support of our position: that the court costs are a violation of Alabama law."

I was fully prepared to launch into a strong defense of the motion. In addition to citing Alabama procedural rules, I would raise points identical to those in the Missouri debtors' prison case. I'd read over the Missouri court opinion multiple times—if necessary, I could quote the Missouri Supreme Court language word for word.

Jay was running both hands through his hair. "And we know

what the judge will do next. He'll overrule the motion. And lose his shit, probably. Scream at you from the bench, most likely."

I was prepared, to the extent it was possible to gird oneself for a torrent of verbal abuse.

But there was no avoiding the confrontation. We needed to obtain an adverse ruling from Pickens in order to move forward.

"And after he overrules the motion, we can appeal," I said, my manner businesslike. I didn't want to give way to drama, not with Andy in the room.

Jay stood and walked over to the copy machine, where he proceeded to duplicate the motion. "It's a plan. Get it out of Pickens's sticky hands and into a higher Alabama state court."

I slid the papers Jay handed me into my briefcase, then called over to Andy, promising him that I'd be back soon. He paused his game long enough to look up and smile at me.

Jay walked me down the hall and out to the front door. When I turned the knob, my hand was slick with sweat. But I tried to disguise my nerves by adopting a cocky attitude.

"Okay! Off I go, to beard the lion in his den."

Jay took me by surprise, seizing me in a bear hug, then putting a supportive hand on my shoulder. "You are going to knock them dead, Martha. Pickens will never know what hit him."

It was an encouraging sentiment. But as soon as I shut the door behind me, my knees felt shaky.

"Buck up," I said in a stern whisper as I crossed the street and made my way to the courthouse. In truth, I didn't need Jay to act as a cheerleader, because I had a secret weapon tucked inside my pocket: two crisp tens and a five-dollar bill.

It was always wise to have a plan B. If Pickens flipped out, I would simply make the damned payment for Jay's court cost installment and let the judge schedule another payment rehearing.

My hand slid into my pocket and clutched the currency like a good-luck charm.

So long as I paid the fee, I had nothing to fear.

CHAPTER 40

THE MOTIONS WERE duly filed. Making my way to the circuit courtroom, I moved like a reluctant grade school kid dragging her feet en route to the principal's office. But when I shut the courtroom door behind me, I stood up straight and squared my shoulders. Every lawyer has to counterfeit the brave face sometimes. I knew how to fake it.

The bench was empty, but all the other players were in place: Pickens's clerk, the court reporter, Harold at the bailiff's post. Doug Carson sat at his counsel table, toying with his laptop. Pickens would emerge soon, I reckoned.

Walking briskly, I made my way to Pickens's clerk.

"Betsy, I'm here on the Jay Bradshaw case. I'd like to call up a motion that's just been filed. Can you put that hearing at the top of the list for me?"

I gave her a chummy grin, like it was nothing out of the ordinary — just a matter of one friend asking another for a small favor.

She didn't meet my eye. "Judge Pickens controls his own calendar. You'll have to ask him."

That wasn't the response I had hoped for. My smile faded and my voice had an edge when I said, "But this is the day for the payment review hearing on Bradshaw—"

Betsy didn't wait for the rest of my pitch. "So ask him. He'll be out here any minute."

Turning on my heel, I stepped over to the prosecutor.

He looked up in surprise. "What are you doing here?"

"I want to argue a motion in the Bradshaw case." I pulled a hard copy from my briefcase and dropped it beside his laptop. "How about letting this one go first? Then I can go back to my office and get out of your hair."

He picked up the stapled document gingerly, as if it might singe his fingers. "What is this? What are you trying to do?"

Just then, the door to chambers opened, banging against the wall. The noise made me take a step back. Harold rose, declaring the court to be in session. Pickens took his place at the bench, and we waited for him to invite us to be seated.

While the rest of the attendants returned to their seats, I stepped up to the bench.

"If it please the court, I'd like to take up the payment review hearing in *State v. Jeremiah Bradshaw*."

The judge squinted his eyes, inclining his ear my way, as if he mistrusted his hearing.

"You want to take it up, Ms. Foster? Why?"

"I've entered my appearance on behalf of Mr. Bradshaw."

Pickens sorted through the files on the bench and pulled one out. "I don't see a formal entry of appearance on the docket sheet."

"I just e-filed it this morning. I have a spare copy, a hard copy, for your file, Your Honor." I took a step toward him, extending the entry of appearance, along with a copy of the new motion Jay and I had prepared.

As he took it from my hand, Pickens's eyes searched the courtroom. "Where is Mr. Bradshaw?"

"I'm appearing on his behalf."

Lowering his head, Pickens fixed his eyes on mine, sending a chill to my toes. "He sent you in his stead? Rather than obeying my order and personally appearing with his periodic payment?"

He picked up a pen with a deliberate hand. "Betsy, we'll be issuing a warrant for Mr. Bradshaw."

"No!" I dug the cash from my pocket; plan B had just moved up to plan A. "Your Honor, please. I have the money that you ordered Mr. Bradshaw to pay, right here."

The fresh bills crumpled in my hand as I extended them to Pickens. At the sight of the currency, he recoiled.

"Do you think this is how it's done, Ms. Foster? Tossing cash on the court bench? I don't handle money."

Hastily, Betsy rose from her chair and beckoned to me. "Martha!"

She placed the cash in a zippered bank bag and scrawled out a receipt form. After she handed a copy of the receipt to me, Pickens's voice assaulted my ear.

"What is the meaning of this?"

My head jerked in his direction. He held up my motion to retax costs; I could see it dangling from his hand. I lifted my chin. This was the opportunity I had sought.

"I'd like to take that up now, Your Honor. Thank you."

I glanced at the prosecution table, half expecting Doug Carson to jump out of his chair and object. But he was silent, shrinking into his seat and burying his face in a file folder.

With Carson's focus elsewhere, I seized the moment. "Judge, on behalf of Mr. Bradshaw, I contest this court's practice of threatening defendants in criminal cases with jail time for failing to pay the jail board bills assessed by Douglas County."

Pickens didn't speak. My adrenaline was pumping, providing the fighting spirit I needed. I went on.

"There is out-of-state precedent, persuasive precedent, for my motion. In Missouri, the public defender filed identical motions in two cases where courts were assessing jail board bills, exactly like those you have initiated here in Alabama."

I was on a roll. The words began to flow seamlessly.

"And in 2019, the Missouri Supreme Court ruled that the circuit courts erred in taxing board bills as court costs. In that opinion, they also ruled that the failure to pay a board bill debt cannot result in another incarceration. Judge Pickens, you can't send people to jail for failing to pay a board bill. Finally, the Supreme Court ruled that board bill payment review hearings, like the one I'm appearing in right now, are illegal. The courts cannot legally require defendants to repeatedly appear to account for those debts, so it follows that the court is not justified in issuing arrest warrants for a failure to appear."

During my argument, Judge Pickens's face had turned a bright shade of pink. He said, "Are we in Missouri?"

My heart was pounding so hard, I wondered whether he could hear it. "The facts of those cases provide a perfect parallel to the instant cause of action. It's an identical case, Your Honor. *State of Missouri v. Richey* and *State of Missouri v. Wright* are directly on point. Did I mention that it was a unanimous opinion of the court?"

He acted as if he could not hear me. "Last time I checked, this was an Alabama courtroom. And the Supreme Court of Missouri is not in charge here."

I shifted arguments. "But the Alabama rules of criminal procedure apply, Your Honor, without question. And Rule 26.11 specifically says: 'In no case shall an indigent defendant be incarcerated for inability to pay a fine or court costs or restitution.'"

Though I was wound up in my advocacy, I observed that his face was now scarlet. "I don't think I understand how that applies to the instant situation," he said.

I let a tinge of moral indignation creep into my voice. "It's an equal protection issue, obviously. The United States Supreme Court ruled in *Tate v. Short* that it's a denial of equal protection to let people with money get off by paying a fine but making penniless people be incarcerated simply because they cannot afford to pay."

The judge opened his mouth to speak, but I was on a roll, and I forged on.

"I'm pretty sure Alabama judges have to follow the rulings of the United States Supreme Court, Judge. And the Equal Protection

Clause of the United States Constitution applies in Douglas County, Alabama, just like it applies everywhere else in the US, despite evidence to the contrary."

His complexion had darkened to a deep crimson hue. Looking back, I should have taken note of that.

Snapping my mouth shut, I stood tall and waited for him to overrule my motion. We needed the adverse ruling on the record so I could appeal it, just like the public defender in the Missouri cases had done.

Pickens's voice came out in a strangled whisper, as if his throat was constricted.

"You dare to stand before me and insult me to my face."

My jaw dropped slightly in surprise. It took a moment to recover. "Your Honor, I'm making a legal point."

"You have mounted a personal attack on my character and cast aspersions that offend the dignity of this court. I'm holding you in contempt—because contempt of court is all that you have demonstrated today." His head whipped around. "Harold!" he shouted.

I watched in shock as the old bailiff limped toward me, pulling the handcuffs from his belt.

CHAPTER 41

I WAS IN a state of shock. As Harold cuffed me and escorted me through the narrow tunnel that led directly from the courthouse lobby to the county jail, two thoughts drummed in my head: *I don't believe it. This can't be happening.*

I must have spoken the words aloud at some point, because Harold's voice rumbled mournfully as he clasped my arm firmly above the elbow.

"You can't say I didn't try to warn you, young lady. I told you, but you just wouldn't listen."

The feeling of unreality persisted as I stood and turned for the mug shot, and while my fingers were pressed onto an ink pad and then rolled onto the fingerprint card. It wasn't until Sherry Grimes placed the folded stack of faded orange scrubs in my arms and ordered me to don them that the cloud in my brain began to lift. I shook my head in an effort to clear it.

"You can't be serious," I said.

Her mouth tightened into a grim line. She waited for several seconds before she repeated the command. "Put them on. Then fold up your things and set them on this chair here. We'll bag them up and log them in with that briefcase of yours, that Harold carried over for you."

"This is preposterous. Judge Pickens will come to his senses, Sherry. He has to."

Sherry turned her back and walked to the door. Without looking at me, she said, "I'll give you three minutes. If you're not dressed by then, I'll have to call for assistance. We can get you into those scrubs without your cooperation. But you won't enjoy it."

She exited, pulling the door shut behind her. With shaking hands, I undressed and jerked the scrubs on. I was still folding my business clothes when she returned.

I rolled my suit jacket into a ball and tossed it on top of the pile of clothes. "Sherry, I can't stay in here. My son is across the street, at the public defender's office."

She stood by the open door. "Follow me. I'll take you to the women's pod."

My knees threatened to buckle. I feared they wouldn't support me, that I'd collapse in the hall.

"I can't go anywhere until I make a phone call. Please, Sherry, you have to listen. I need to call my office, to talk about my son."

Jay's cell phone hadn't been reconnected, but he would pick up the public defender's landline at the office if I made a call from my cell phone. Whether he'd pick up a call from the county jail was less likely. But when they granted me a phone call, I had to use it to reach Jay. Dialing my old firm in Birmingham wasn't a consideration. We had parted on bad terms.

My voice cracked as I said, "Please, Sherry, you have to help me. I need my cell phone. It's in the briefcase. I'm entitled to make a call—you know that."

"Come on with me. No stalling," she said, her voice flat.

I trailed along behind her, sending up a prayer that she would be reasonable and let me make the call. But as I followed her through the maze of hallways, my desperation mounted. When I tried again to reason with her, my voice sounded breathy, like I had been running hard. "My son, Andy, is five. Did I ever tell you that? Only five years old. He takes medication for his heart."

She didn't slow down, didn't respond. I went on, babbling. "He's so little, small for his age. And he says he wants to play football, but he can't, his doctor said. His doctor told me no contact sports, not even when he gets older."

Sherry stopped abruptly. I almost bumped into her. Unlocking a security door, she pointed inside. "In you go."

I fell back a step, shaking my head. "Phone call."

Sherry sighed. "You know I've got a Taser. I shouldn't have to use it on a smart girl like you."

The threat worked. I walked into the women's section on wooden feet. The voice in my head renewed the chant, and it pounded repeatedly in my brain: *This can't be happening.*

The women's pod was in the new section of the jail. The pod was designed with a common area in the center, furnished with picnic-table seating and supervised by a control station where two jailers sat. Two levels of jail cells surrounded the open area on all four sides.

My arrival caught the interest of two inmates sitting at a plastic picnic table. The older one, a woman with grizzled hair, eyed me sympathetically. She waved me over, saying, "Bless your heart. Come on over here, baby. Sit down before you fall down."

Automatically, I obeyed, sliding onto the bench beside her. Squeezing my hands together on the tabletop, I pleaded for information in a voice that shook.

"Is there a phone in here? A pay phone, maybe? I have to make a call."

She raised a brow in surprise. "There's no phone in the pod. The phone is out by the big visitation room. We only get to use it on weekends. And you got to call collect."

A younger woman sat across from me at the picnic table. Shaking her head in disgust, she said, "A phone inside here? Don't she know nothing?"

My voice grew shrill. "I have to make a call. I have a little boy."

The older woman shifted on the bench, casting an uneasy look over at the control station where the jailers sat. "We all do. Everybody in here got somebody outside, baby. You'll have to wait your turn."

"It won't wait." My voice hit a higher note. I couldn't control it.

My shrill plea had caught the attention of a woman sitting at another table nearby. After scrutinizing me, she lunged off the bench and shouted, "I don't believe it. Is that the goddamn public defender?"

"Whoa!" One of the jailers swiveled his chair to face us. "Watch the language."

Immediately, the inmate sat back down, but she pointed a finger directly at me. "Yes, sir, Mr. Robertson, sorry about that. But just look there. Isn't it the public defender? What is she doing here?"

The jailer rose from his padded office chair. Jesse Robertson approached me like a big cat, looking me up and down, while his jaw worked on a wad of chewing gum. A broad grin lit up his face.

"Well, I'll be doggone. It sure enough is." Raising his voice, Robertson announced, "You bunch of skanks got y'all a genuine jailhouse lawyer in here."

CHAPTER 42

AFTER ROBERTSON IDENTIFIED me, inmates from all corners of the pod flocked to the table where I sat.

"No shit," one of them said. "Shake my damn head. Got her locked up just like the rest of us."

The girl who had spoken was so young, she looked like she should be housed in juvenile detention rather than a county jail. But she had a world-weary air that belied her childlike appearance.

She said, "Girl, you must have pissed somebody off."

That line got a rousing laugh from her fellow inmates.

The gray-haired woman reached out to put her hand on top of mine. The gesture gave me a trace of comfort. "Baby, what are you in for?"

Woodenly, I repeated the punch line: "I must have pissed somebody off."

Some laughter followed my statement, but it was patchy and faded quickly.

The young girl shoved her way onto the bench directly across from me. In an eager manner, she said, "Well, I'm glad you're in here. I need somebody to give me good advice. They are holding me on a felony assault charge, and I'm innocent."

Robertson, the gum-chewing jailer, shouted from the monitoring station. "Oh, yeah, no doubt about that. Every one of these bitches is innocent. Ain't never done nothing, no way."

The girl shot an irritated look in his direction. When his jeering ceased, she turned to me and launched into her legal woes. Though I pretended to listen, even nodding when she paused for breath, her volley of words washed over me without my registering them.

Sitting across from her, my mind whirled with my own crisis. I had no emotional or mental prowess to spare for hers. After Robertson had branded me a jailhouse lawyer, I recalled my brief exposure to jail years ago, when I had originally earned the nickname. Back then, I had been a cocky young student with an attitude, proud to be arrested for a worthy cause. It had been a badge of distinction, one I had worn with pride. On that occasion, I had encouraged the inmates to confide in me and ask questions. In return, I'd doled out advice with a sense of confidence entirely out of proportion with the bare-bones legal knowledge I had possessed at that point in my education. It had seemed like a noble adventure: I carried the torch for justice as I waited nine or ten hours before being released on my own recognizance for a charge that was never prosecuted.

But this was no Disney version of incarceration. The stakes were dangerously high. As the inmate's voice droned on, panic built up, expanding in my chest. I wanted to clap my hands over my ears, to drown out her words. Her problems were not my focus. I had to get out. My son needed me.

I felt like all of the oxygen was being sucked out of the air. I needed some space so I could think clearly and breathe. Just as I stood to flee the picnic table, the security door opened.

It was Sherry Grimes. "Martha Foster," she called out. Her grim, unfriendly manner bore no resemblance to the sprightly greeting she had offered when we first met at the jail, only a week prior. Nonetheless, I tore away from the table and ran to her, thinking: *Pickens must have changed his mind. Please, God, get me out of here.*

I stopped at the door, holding my breath, hoping for the words *You can go on home now.*

Instead, she clasped a handcuff on my wrist. "You've got a visitor."

It wasn't what I had hoped for, but I followed her down the hall, like a well-trained dog. "Who's the visitor?" I asked.

It could not possibly be anyone but Jay, and that set me to worrying. If Jay was at the county jail, where was Andy? Andy couldn't see me like this, wearing prison garb and shackles. The trauma would be horrific.

Sherry didn't answer the question, so I puzzled over it silently as we walked the labyrinth that took me to the old section of the jail. She released me from the cuffs right before opening the lock to access the visitation booth.

"I'll be back in fifteen minutes."

Walking into the booth, I didn't know what to expect. Sherry shut the door behind me. I heard the key turning the lock as I looked through the glass and saw my visitor.

If I had placed a bet on Jay, I would have lost my money. The man clutching the dirty telephone receiver on the other side of the glass was Doug Carson.

CHAPTER 43

WHEN I FACED Carson on the opposite side of the security window, he didn't look me in the eye. He stared at my faded orange jailhouse scrubs, his eyes widening.

I grabbed the phone receiver and spoke into it. "Looks like you noticed my new outfit, Doug. This is way beyond absurd. This is insanity. When am I getting out of here?"

His round face puckered, but he didn't answer. My voice sounded ragged as I repeated the question.

"Damn it, Doug. When will I be released? I can't stay in here."

Reaching into his suit jacket, he pulled a folded linen handkerchief from an inside pocket and proceeded to meticulously wipe the surface of the phone in his hand. I recalled that I had taken a similar precaution the week before, when sitting on his side of the glass. It felt like it was a lifetime ago.

When he returned the phone to his ear, he said, "Pickens is furious."

"Yeah, I'm aware of that. How long will this last—how much penance will I have to do? Because I'm telling you, I can't stay in here for long."

With his free hand, he refolded the handkerchief and poked it back into the pocket. "Judge Pickens feels that you offended the dignity of his court."

My pulse pounded in my head like a drum. "How did I do that?"

"The things you said in court, about Alabama disregarding the right to equal protection under the law. He felt like you were aiming the accusation directly at him. He found that insulting."

"It was a legal argument! I was invoking the Constitution. Does he want an apology? If so, take me straight over there, right now. I'll tell him that I regret hurting his feelings."

I could say the words to Pickens with complete sincerity. I did regret it. Stoking his ire had led me to this frightening position.

Carson's lips pressed together in a straight line. "I don't think an apology will be sufficient."

I switched the receiver to my other ear and rubbed my damp palm on the fabric of the orange scrubs. "Then what does he want, for God's sake?"

Through the glass, Carson looked thoughtful. "Pretty sure he wants you to withdraw the motion."

That's when the bizarre situation came into sharp focus: this wasn't just a judicial temper tantrum. This was blackmail.

I gazed at Carson through the window, searching his face for a hint of shame or remorse. Placing me behind bars hadn't been Doug Carson's decision, but as the messenger for Pickens's ultimatum, he was part of the dirty process.

I tried to sound reasonable, like we were holding an ordinary discussion between two lawyers, without the element of jailhouse duress. "But the judge can overrule the motion if he doesn't like it. Pickens has total discretion. All of the power in this situation is in his hands."

"No, he doesn't want to do it that way. He thinks it would be better if you just withdrew it."

My voice became slightly unsteady. "That would be malpractice on my part. It would be an unprofessional breach of duty to my client. I cannot commit malpractice."

Doug rolled his eyes. "Well, maybe you should have thought of that before you struck a match and started a fire."

As I struggled to compose a fitting retort, he pulled the gold pocket watch from his vest and checked it. "I guess we're done here. I gotta go."

Panic bounced through me like a pinball machine. "Doug. What time is it?"

"Time for me to go." He pushed his chair back and stood.

I also rose from my seat. Pressing my hands to the window, I entreated him. "Doug, my little boy, he takes meds for his heart. He has to take the medicine at five o'clock every day."

Doug ignored me. He rapped on the door inside his booth, signaling his intention to depart.

The pitch of my voice rose. "Doug, they haven't let me make a call." When he didn't respond, I began to pound on the glass with the side of my fist. In response to the pounding, he gave me a nervous side-eye and began knocking on his door a second time.

Shouting now, I cried, "Andy has to have his meds! What time is it?"

Instead of answering, he continued rapping on the frame of the door, calling out to the jailhouse staff. My frustration spiked. I picked up the plastic phone receiver and used it to beat on the glass, screaming now. "You have to help me! What about my son?"

When the door to his booth finally opened up, Doug Carson scooted through it like a scared cat, without a backward look.

CHAPTER 44

SHORTLY AFTER DOUG fled the booth, I heard the metallic click of the lock. Sherry Grimes eased the door open and stared at me through the crack.

"Have you lost your mind?" she asked.

I still had the phone receiver clutched tightly in my right hand. It took a moment to relax the grip of my frozen fingers. As I set it down on the counter, I took a breath, to calm myself. Turning to face Sherry, I said, "I want to see the judge."

Opening the door all the way, Sherry shouldered in front of me and snatched the phone off the counter. "Merciful heavens, what's this here?"

Keeping my voice steady required a tremendous effort. "Doug Carson says that Judge Pickens wants to hear from me. Take me back to court. Immediately."

The judge needed to hear about Andy. Pickens had met him before, in his own home; he knew what a little guy my son was. Surely he'd rethink this drastic, unjust step. He would release me if I reminded him what was at stake here. The judge wouldn't risk my son's health just because he bore me a personal grudge.

"Just look at this."

Sherry's face was the picture of righteous indignation as she snatched up the telephone receiver and held it in front of my eyes. "You broke it."

It was true. A long, jagged crack ran the length of the plastic handle. In my agitation, I had hit the window harder than I realized.

"It's a phone. You can replace it."

"This is county property. You've destroyed it, on purpose." She jerked the coiled cord from the base on the wall, unplugging it. Her expression had grown ferocious. I backpedaled, hoping to make peace. I needed to placate Sherry because she was my ticket to the courtroom.

"You're right, Sherry, it's my responsibility. I'll replace it. Submit an invoice. I'll take care of it today, right after I see Judge Pickens."

Deputy Clark appeared in the open doorway. Grasping the doorframe on either side, he leaned into the booth and asked, "Everything okay in here?"

"It's not okay." Sherry held up the cracked phone. "Just look what she's gone and done."

He raised his brow and whistled through his teeth. "How'd she do that?"

"Pounding on the window. Scared the prosecutor out of his wits."

The accusation was ludicrous. "That's ridiculous," I said in a choked voice.

Deputy Clark looked at me with a challenge in his gaze and said to Sherry, "You ready to take her to the SHU? I can give you some assistance."

I automatically backed away. "The SHU? Solitary confinement? What the hell is going on here? You will take me to Judge Pickens. *Now*."

The deputy again addressed his remarks to Sherry while keeping his eyes trained on me. "Jesse said the inmates recognized her in the pod, came buzzing around. So we're thinking the SHU is the best place to put her." A grin spread across his face. "For her own protection."

I took another step back, literally backing my way into a corner. But I spoke without a waver this time.

"I have rights, and I know exactly what they are. I'm entitled to counsel. I haven't even had the opportunity to make a phone call."

Sherry Grimes snorted. "Phone call? You're not getting anywhere near a phone. Look how she treats our telephones, Deputy."

She held out the cracked receiver, and Clark flicked it with a finger. Shaking his head with a show of regret, he said, "Seems like this woman is out of control."

"Yes, sir," Sherry agreed.

Clark snapped a cuff onto my wrist. He moved so fast, I hadn't anticipated it. He asked Sherry, "Is the chair occupied right now?"

That was a mistake. He should have cuffed both wrists before he asked about the chair.

CHAPTER 45

IT WAS A gut reaction.

There was no rational decision-making process that led me to lash out at the deputy. It was pure impulse that caused me to twist around, using my free hand to shove Clark's chest. My resistance took him by surprise; I saw it flash in his eyes right before I kneed him in the groin. Releasing my arm, he fell to the floor and curled into a fetal position.

And then I tried to run for the door in an idiotic, fruitless attempt to get away from them. Sherry blocked the doorway as I launched my body through it, and we both landed on the dirty tile floor of the hallway, with our legs tangled together. Clawing at the tile, I tried to scramble away.

But I didn't stand a chance, of course. It was two against one; Deputy Clark recovered sufficiently to join the fray. My impetuous attempt to flee ended with his knee in my back, pinning me to the floor.

Cursing, he jerked my arms together behind me, cuffing the second wrist so tightly it felt like my bone might snap.

"We need assistance," he shouted at Sherry. "Tell them to bring leg shackles."

The fight-or-flight reaction receded from my system, replaced by horror as I realized what I had done. I had assaulted an officer and attempted to escape from custody. The scenario had gone far beyond Judge Pickens's phony contempt action or the vandalism of a jailhouse telephone. They could bring felony charges against me for my crazed response in the visitation booth.

Turning my head to the side, I said, "Deputy, I'm sorry. I don't know what came over me."

In response, the knee in my back bore down with increased pressure. I heard footsteps in the corridor, running toward us. Someone grabbed my legs, and I heard the rattle of metal as they shackled my ankles together.

Over the gabble of voices, Sherry's shrill words rang out.

"I knew she was trouble! You ought to see what she did to the phone. Clark, tell Fields about that phone."

"Shut up about the goddamn phone," Clark said as he and another officer hoisted me off the floor, clutching me under my arms. The movement was so abrupt, I couldn't get my footing. They dragged me down the hall as I tried to get my feet to work properly.

Gasping for breath, I said, "I'll cooperate, I promise. Just give me a second. Let me walk, okay?"

They didn't slow down. Deputy Fields, who was assisting Clark, was considerably taller than both of us, and the height difference kept me off-balance. I stumbled along, trying to match their pace but moving as if my feet no longer knew how to function.

We turned a corner and arrived at a doorway. The officers halted, and I managed to get my feet safely underneath me and stand erect. Sherry hurried past us to unlock the door. She stepped inside and held the door open. When I beheld the restraint chair in the center of the room, I froze. They had to drag me inside.

The ugly metal contraption dominated the room. It sat on a black metal base, with a high, narrow back and a flat seat. Handcuffs were strapped to the ends of its two long arms. Identical sets of cuffs dangled from a black metal footrest, elevated several inches off the floor.

They removed my handcuffs. I didn't fight when they pushed me over to the chair and shoved me onto the seat. Thick belts of woven polyester were strapped around my waist and shoulders before they secured my arms on each side and cuffed my wrists to the chair.

"Don't you dare kick," Clark said as he bent down to remove the leg restraints so he could replace them with the cuffs attached to the footrest.

"I won't," I whispered.

The tall officer named Fields lifted one of my wrists and assessed the grip of the metal circling it. Sounding uncertain, he said, "Not too tight, Clark."

Deputy Clark made an inarticulate noise of disgust, and Sherry sidled up. "She's okay," she said, craning her neck to watch the process.

Deputy Fields cleared his throat. "We don't want any more trouble this week. Just not too tight—that's all I'm saying."

"She's as healthy as a horse," Clark replied, adding, "the bitch."

Sherry said, "Nobody could have expected anything like that other gal. It's not anybody's fault."

I knew "that other gal" they were talking about was Abby Zimmerman. I kept my eyes on Fields. He might be an ally. After checking both wrists, his brow puckered, and he shoved his hands deep into his pockets. "Could have diabetes. There's that, too."

"This girl doesn't have the sugar diabetes," Sherry said.

"How do you know?"

"I can tell by looking. I'll bet you a hundred dollars."

Clark stood, looking resentful. "Sherry, you ain't got a hundred dollars." Narrowing his eyes at me, he asked, "You got diabetes?"

I almost claimed that I did. And considered telling them that blood clots were a family tendency.

But I stopped myself. A blood test would disprove the statement, and I was already in deep trouble.

"Deputy Clark, my son was born with a heart defect; he had surgery just this year. He's five years old and takes medication for it. I have to get to him and give him his meds."

Clark turned his back to me. "Hear that? She's fine," he said to the other officer.

I struggled to remain calm, but it was impossible. "Please, I'm begging you. Someone has to take care of my son."

Sherry stepped up to the restraint chair and said, "Quit going on about that. Judge Pickens has already made arrangements for your boy."

I really lost it then. I fought against the chair, thrashing my head against the back, fruitlessly trying to escape, though my limbs and body were inexorably constrained. Incapable of speech, I wailed with grief, weeping with a frenzy I had never known before.

When I stopped to suck in a breath, Sherry said, "Cut that out, or you'll end up with a bag over your head."

CHAPTER 46

MY BAWLING CONTINUED despite Sherry's threat. It wasn't something I could control. When the deputies left the room, the tall officer lingered outside the door. I could see his profile through a glass panel that revealed a thin slice of the hallway. It looked like he was waiting for Sherry to join them, and after she exited and shut the door behind her, he said something to her. I couldn't hear what it was. Maybe he had saved me from the bag.

Alone in the room, I hung my head and sobbed, tears raining down onto the legs of my scrubs. My nose ran, too, with a vengeance. When I managed to rein in my hysteria, the snot continued to flow. I wanted to wipe it from my face. With my hands cuffed to the chair, I craned my neck to rub my nose against my shoulder, but I couldn't reach it.

On the wall to my left, a digital clock hung over a corkboard. Initially, I was relieved to see the clock because I finally had the ability to tell the time. When I first looked, it read 1:34 p.m.

Staring at the red numbers, I wondered whether I could trust the clock's accuracy. Maybe my perception of time was off, but it seemed incomprehensible that all my misfortunes had taken place within a few short hours. Jay's hearing had been set at

9:30 in the morning, and it felt like an eternity had passed since then.

I counted off sixty seconds, to be sure. The timepiece was working, it seemed.

And that meant that, wherever Andy was, there was still time for his medication schedule to be met. Pickens had made it clear that he didn't approve of Jay, so Peg was the most likely candidate to care for Andy in my absence. At least she knew about Andy's heart condition.

While I worried about Andy, my eye began to itch. Reflexively, I tried to lift my hand to scratch it. The reminder of my immobility sent a wave of panic through me, making my muscles tense up. A throb deep inside my calf scared me; if I didn't relax, my muscles might cramp. With an effort, I slowed my breathing, trying to remember the principles I had learned in childbirth class. *I can handle this*, I thought. Closing my eyes, I repeated my breathing exercise, focusing on that one thought. *I can handle this.*

The intentional breathing restored a measure of self-control. When I opened my eyes, I turned my head to check the time on the digital clock.

It was 1:57 p.m. Only twenty-three minutes had passed.

I didn't know how long I could stand it.

A time log on white paper was thumbtacked to the center of the corkboard. A pen dangled from a binder clip attached to the log. My eyesight was 20/20—still sharp despite a lifetime of reading. If I squinted, I could just make out the print at the top of the sheet of paper: CHAIR OBSERVATION RECORD.

That brought a token of relief. They couldn't leave me here indefinitely. The jail had a policy, which included keeping a log. The jailers would have to comply with it. At some point someone would check on me.

A muscle twitched—in my thigh this time. I resumed the deep-breathing exercise. And I watched the clock.

By the time Sherry walked back through the door, 143 minutes had passed and I had suffered two painful charley horses in my right calf.

I started talking the moment she entered the room. "Did you tell the judge what I said, about Andy? My son has to have his medicine at five o'clock."

"Everything's fine." Sherry smirked at me. "How's it going in here?"

"My muscles are cramping up. I need to get out of this chair, to move."

"Is that right?" She walked up to the corkboard, picked up the pen, and scrawled on the white sheet of paper. When she walked away, I saw what she had written.

4:21 p.m. OK. SG.

Sherry headed back to the door. When she put her hand on the knob, I spoke in a rush.

"Sherry. I have to go to the bathroom."

The statement wasn't a ruse to get out of the chair. It had been hours since I'd had the opportunity to go. Sherry pivoted to face me.

"Sorry, can't help you. We're shorthanded. I don't have anyone to assist me right now. They've got me working a double shift because of you."

"All I'm asking is to go to the toilet," I said, incredulous. "You don't need assistance to take me to the bathroom."

"The last time I escorted you someplace, you knocked me flat. Maybe you forgot. But I haven't."

She was serious.

In a louder voice, I said, "I need to use the bathroom, and I need water. What is the Douglas County policy on treatment of individuals restrained in this chair? You can't subject me to this mistreatment."

"You need to relieve yourself? Go right ahead." She waggled her fingers at me. "See you later."

The panic returned when she pulled the door shut behind her. Taking a deep breath, I squeezed my legs together and said out loud, "I can hold it. She'll be back."

Facing the clock, I tried to distract myself from the discomfort by giving myself a stern lecture, a mental talking-to.

Sitting in this chair isn't so terrible. I'm tough enough to do this. I've been through labor, given birth to a baby. I watched them wheel my child into surgery, and I waited for hours to hear the outcome. This is not the worst thing I have ever endured. I can handle this.

I can handle this.

CHAPTER 47

I HANDLED IT. Until I couldn't handle it any longer.

Incontinence was the first physical breakdown. I managed to hold on to my bladder for thirty-three more minutes. I knew because I counted them.

When I wet myself, it initially brought a measure of relief. The relief was temporary, followed by shame, discomfort, and fear. The involuntary release soaked my clothes and ran off the seat, puddling on the floor around the chair. As I listened to the urine stream hit the tile floor, I wondered how the jailhouse staff would react when they saw it. I panicked, afraid they would think I had done it intentionally, just to rile them.

I had plenty of time to ruminate about it while waiting for someone to appear. My clothes grew cold and sodden, sticking to my skin. I tried to shift my position on the flat seat of the chair, but it was impossible.

When Sherry finally reappeared, I didn't bother to check the clock to see how long it had been. I spoke before the door shut behind her, defending myself, like a wayward child.

"I told you I had to go."

She stared at the wet floor, her mouth twisting with disgust. "I can't believe you. You are just as filthy as the rest of them."

My voice rose with a mournful pitch. "I couldn't help it."

She pulled a radio off her belt. "Janitorial detail in the discipline room."

A garble of static sounded in response. I couldn't make out the reply, but Sherry must have understood it. She said, "Not me. Just send some inmate trustees in if you get the chance."

Steering clear of the chair, she scribbled a new note on the time log.

As she wrote, she asked, "You need a drink?"

"Yes," I gasped. "Please."

Shaking her head in clear disapproval, she walked to a sink on the opposite side of the room and picked up a plastic bottle.

"I don't know why I'm even doing this. You will just have an excuse to make another mess on the floor later."

My eyes focused greedily on the water tap as the bottle filled. I was parched, my mouth dry. When the bottle was full, she turned off the tap and approached the chair.

I said, "Thank you, Sherry. I'm so thirsty." I sounded like a medieval beggar, groveling for a crumb. Dehydration had the power to strip away pride.

She paused a distance from the chair, right outside the puddle of urine.

"I'm not stepping in that mess. I'll smell it on my shoes all night."

I swallowed involuntarily, anticipating the drink of water. My fingers flexed in a vain attempt to grab the bottle.

"I'm sorry, Sherry. I'll clean it up if you'll let me out."

She snorted. "Yeah, right." Her eyes studied the bottle, as if making a mental calculation. "Okay, open wide."

I didn't follow. "What?"

"Open your mouth so I can squirt it in."

"Sherry, just release one of my wrists. I want to hold it myself."

"Nope."

She aimed the bottle at me and squeezed. It squirted across my face; I turned my head away to keep it out of my eyes.

Her brow furrowed. "Do you want this or not?"

Gingerly, she walked to the side of the chair, standing on tiptoe in the urine. Grasping my hair, she pulled my head back and shoved the bottle into my mouth, tipping it up and squeezing the liquid so fast, I couldn't chug it down. I gagged as the flow of water choked me.

When she pulled the empty bottle out of my mouth, I retched and coughed, trying to catch my breath. It felt like I was drowning, and I heaved until I vomited the water onto the front of my scrubs, along with bile and the contents of my stomach.

Staring as the odorous mucus dribbled down my orange top, I gasped for breath. The sense of unreality returned. This was a nightmare, something from a tortured night's sleep. It couldn't really be happening.

Sherry had backed away from me when the vomiting began, her face contorted with revulsion. As she walked to the sink, she skidded on the floor and had to grab the counter to keep from falling.

"Blast!" she shouted. The vanilla curse sounded far more obscene than any string of four-letter words. "That's it. I've had it with you."

She opened a cabinet under the sink and pulled out a roll of gray fabric. When she shook it out, I saw that it was a blanket.

She wiped the bottom of her shoes on the blanket before she advanced on me. She stopped with her feet safely on the dry tile, but close enough to the chair to fling the blanket over my head.

I couldn't see her leave, but I knew she was gone when I heard the door slam shut.

CHAPTER 48

WITHOUT THE CLOCK, I didn't know how much time passed before my muscles seized in my upper and lower extremities: calves, thighs, arms, shoulders. Even my feet and buttocks cramped up.

When the pain became intolerable, I started screaming. At first, I begged: for mercy, for help, for rescue. When words failed me, I simply shrieked. I couldn't help it.

Eventually, the physical agony reached a level that knocked me out. I don't think I slept, not exactly. But I zoned in and out. When unconsciousness overtook me, it was a blessing. But whenever I regained consciousness, I felt confused and disoriented. And then I would remember where I was.

It felt like an eternity passed as I suffered in the chair, soaked in urine and bile, breathing in my own stench under the stifling blanket. Eventually, the door creaked open. I was dimly aware of voices as footsteps approached.

The blanket was ripped off my head. Blinded by the sudden light, I ducked my chin, closing my eyes to the brightness.

A man said, "Jesus, she's a mess."

I recognized Deputy Clark's voice in response. "At least she's quieted down. She was shouting her fool head off when Sherry clocked out last night."

Lifting my head, I peeked through one bleary eye. Deputy Clark and Detective Stanley stood a safe distance from the chair, regarding me with open curiosity.

Clark observed, "She smells worse than a goat. We had a guy hallucinating on drugs, sat in the chair for three days. She stinks almost as bad as he did."

My throat was raw, but I croaked out: "Help."

They exchanged a look. The detective held a file folder in his hand. He opened it and glanced down at the contents before he spoke.

"Judge Pickens asked me to check on you. See how you're feeling today."

I did not recognize my own voice when I answered. "Whatever he wants. I'll do whatever he wants."

"Good. He'll be glad to hear that." A pen protruded from the detective's shirt pocket. He reached for it, saying, "I've got some paperwork for you to sign here."

Deputy Clark grimaced, then cleared his throat. "She probably can't sign her name, not right now. And you don't want to get the release sticky with what all she's got all over herself."

Nodding in agreement, Stanley pocketed the pen. "Get her cleaned up. Think she can walk?"

"Nah. I'll call for a couple of inmate trustees to bring the wheelchair."

"Where are you taking her? The SHU?"

Clark scratched his jaw. "We'll send her back to the women's pod. That way we can let them clean the mess off her. The county doesn't pay none of us enough for that job." He wrinkled his nose with distaste.

I watched the door anxiously, waiting for the trustees to appear. When they arrived, pushing the wheelchair before them, their eyes darted away from me, as if the sight of me was daunting. I guessed it was.

It was Clark's job to unlock the cuffs. He groused as he did it, complaining about the stench and the muck. When the inmates transferred me from the restraint chair to the wheelchair, the movement of my rusty joints made me cry out in anguish.

My screech quieted to a whimper as they wheeled me through the jail. People we encountered in the hallways hurried to get out of our way, turning in the opposite direction, dodging into doorways. I closed my eyes because I didn't want to witness their reactions.

When the hallway was clear, the man pushing my chair spoke in a low voice. "You are going to be all right. You made it—it's over." After a pause, he added, in a doubtful voice, "For now."

The last two words haunted me. I was out of the chair—but what my future held, I couldn't begin to predict.

When the door to the women's pod opened, the inmates were seated at the picnic tables, eating lunch. At the sight of me, they froze, some with their plastic spoons held aloft.

A young girl broke the silence. Dropping the plastic spoon onto her tray, she said, "Damn! Just lost my appetite."

CHAPTER 49

IT WAS PAST four in the afternoon when they released me. The process was delayed by my cleanup and recovery.

The jailer assigned two women to take me to the showers. I was fortunate that one of them was the gray-haired woman who had shown compassion the previous day.

Before they removed my clothing, I begged for water. She filled a plastic cup for me, but my hands shook so violently, the water splashed out of the cup when I tried to drink. The older woman— her name was Monique, she told me—refilled the cup and held it to my mouth.

"Don't gulp it down all at once, baby. You sip it, all right?"

I obeyed, taking swallows one at a time. She nodded with approval, saying, "That's the way."

The kindness in her voice made me weep as I drank from the cup.

After the shower, they required me to remain in the pod until they were satisfied that I could walk without assistance. And when I finally demonstrated the ability to walk steadily, there was another delay while I waited for the return of the clothes I had worn into the jail the day prior.

Before I dressed, they provided jail-issue underwear, since my own were at the bottom of a trash can in the latrine.

When the jailer, Jesse Robertson, tossed the nylon undergarments onto the picnic table, he said, "Don't worry about getting these back to us. We'll add it to your board bill."

He laughed at his own joke, opening his mouth so wide I could see a white nugget of chewing gum lodged on his molar.

Detective Stanley presided over the final checkout procedures at the jailhouse exit. He opened the file folder I had seen him carry into the discipline room that morning. I scanned the sheaf of papers it contained. One of the documents was a liability waiver, in which I agreed to hold the county and its personnel harmless for my treatment inside the county jail. Essentially, it was a promise that I wouldn't sue.

I scrawled my name across the signature line without comment, keeping my expression impassive. But inside my head, I thought: *This will never hold up. See you in court, Douglas County.*

The detective sorted through the paperwork as a uniformed jail employee handed me a plastic bag that held my briefcase. I checked the contents: files, papers, wallet, pens. And I rummaged through the briefcase a second time.

"Where's my cell phone?"

The jailer, an old guy I didn't recognize, shrugged. Fortunately, I hadn't seen Sherry Grimes around all day.

I told him, "I had a cell phone in the briefcase when the bailiff brought me over to the jail yesterday. It's not in here."

The jailer said, "I don't know anything about a phone. I was off duty yesterday. This was the only bag for you in the property locker."

A flush heated my neck as I pondered what I should do. Detective Stanley interrupted my thoughts.

"We have a form somewhere for missing property. You want me to go look for it? Might take a while—can't say how long."

That clinched it. "I'll check back later," I said. I couldn't tolerate another minute in the Douglas County Jail. I needed to get out, to find Andy.

Walking outside, I breathed in the hot summer air, grateful to be free. Heading directly to the courthouse, I bypassed the elevator and ran up the marble staircase, determined to find out where my son was being kept.

The circuit courtroom was dark. I sidestepped over to Betsy's office. When I opened the door, her eyes widened at the sight of me, but she recovered quickly.

Pasting on a bright smile, she said, "Afternoon, Martha. Can I get you some coffee?" Ignoring the bizarre offer of hospitality, I cut straight to the point. "Where's the judge?"

"He's not in. He'll be in court tomorrow at nine o'clock." She hesitated before adding, "Looks like you've got something set. Judge penciled you in on the docket, at nine."

I reached across her desk and picked up the telephone.

"I need you to get me an outside line, Betsy. Please. I have to call Child Protective Services."

She rolled her chair away from the desk, distancing herself from me. "No one is there to answer. They close at 4:30. You'll just get the machine. You know, telling you to leave a message. Or if it's an emergency, the recording instructs you to call the sheriff."

It was an emergency. But the sheriff's office was the last place I would turn to for help.

Carefully, I returned the phone to its cradle. I did not want to make the error of abusing county property again. Pulling my shoulders straight, I looked the clerk in the eye.

"Betsy. Where is my son?"

She bent down and picked up her purse. I heard keys jingle as she fumbled inside it. "Judge Pickens will be here tomorrow, bright and early. He'll clear everything up, I'm sure." She stood, shouldering her bag. "Time for me to lock up. I'll see you in the morning, Martha."

Tears of frustration stung my eyes. I was desperate to learn Andy's whereabouts. Stepping outside the office, I lingered as Betsy shook out her keys and turned the deadbolt in the door. I was about to plead for information when I heard Harold approach.

"Hey there, Martha."

He took me by the elbow, firmly pulling me away from the door.

"Glad to see you. I've been worried about you, young lady."

I turned to Harold, searching his face for a hint of understanding. "Harold, I have to find my little boy."

He patted my arm in a clumsy attempt at comfort. "Nothing to be done about that, not until tomorrow. You go home and get some rest. Come back tomorrow morning, and everything will be all right."

"Where is he, Harold?" My voice broke. "Where is Andy?"

"I'll see you tomorrow. Everything's going to be fine."

The old man sounded sincere. Behind the bifocals, his eyes looked glassy; perhaps he was also fighting back tears. But Harold's reassurances were not sufficient to appease me.

I intended to find Andy, if I had to drive up and down every street in Erva.

Unearthing my own key fob, I left the courthouse and hurried down the stone steps. When I paused on the sidewalk across from my office, I stopped abruptly.

I had parked my car directly in front of the public defender's office on Wednesday morning. But it wasn't there anymore. The parking spot was empty.

CHAPTER 50

SO AS IT turned out, I had to call the sheriff's office after all.

I used the landline in my office. When a woman at the Douglas County sheriff's office picked up, I said, "This is Martha Foster at the public defender's office. I parked my car, a red 2012 Ford Focus sedan, in front of the office yesterday morning. The car is missing."

"Are you calling to report a theft of a motor vehicle?"

I hesitated, uncertain how to frame my response.

"I'm not sure what has happened to it. Is it possible that the car was towed? I'm not aware of any parking restrictions near the court-house, but the car would have been left on the street overnight."

"What did you say your name was?"

Squeezing my eyes shut, I managed to keep a pleasant tone of voice. "Foster. Martha Foster."

She put me on hold. A recorded voice droned in my ear, advising me of a long litany of options I could choose to seek assistance from the sheriff's office. To report a crime, press 1. To check a pending investigation, press 2. If I knew the extension of the individual I wanted to call, submit a three-digit code. For an emergency, hang up and dial 911.

The voice stopped abruptly when the woman picked back up. "The car is here, at the sheriff's office."

I exhaled with relief; this was far easier than I had expected. "Thank goodness."

"It's been impounded."

"I beg your pardon? What did you say?"

"It has been impounded. On suspicion of drug possession."

"That's preposterous." A pulse began to throb in my temple.

"You'll need to communicate with the Detective Division, but it is closed for the day. Do you want to leave a message for Detective Stanley?"

I hung up the landline. What I wanted to say to Detective Stanley would get me in deeper trouble.

My next call went to Happy Times Day Care. No one answered that phone. So I set out on foot.

It was a long, hot walk to the day care with the late-afternoon sun beating down on my head and back. I wondered how Jay could have made it, with Andy riding on his shoulders. By the time I reached the front walk, Peg was outside the front door, locking up.

When she caught sight of me, Peg did a double take. I must have looked frightening. Turning her back on me, she thrust the keys back into the lock, opened the door, and scooted inside. When I saw that she intended to disappear and evade me, I ran for the door, crying out to her.

"Peg! I have to talk to you!"

Panting, I reached the entrance, tugging on the screen door. She had locked it.

"Don't shut me out, Peg, please. I'm begging you."

My words had erupted in a rush. I could see Peg through the screen, with her hand on the front door, ready to shut it in my face. But she relented.

"You need to go home, Martha. I can't help you."

I was breathing so hard, spots appeared in front of my eyes. I clutched the doorframe to keep from fainting.

"Where is he, Peg? Do you have him?"

"He's not here."

"Where, then? Have you heard anything, maybe about a temporary placement? Who has my son?"

For a moment, it looked like she might tell me what she knew. I could see it in her face. But then she changed her mind, shaking her head. "I don't have him. That's all I can tell you." Before she shut the door, she repeated her earlier words: the statement that had been flung at me all afternoon. "I can't help you."

When I heard her turn the lock, I collapsed onto my knees. Turning to face the street, I sat on the doormat of Happy Times for long minutes as I tried to devise some strategy, but it felt like my head wouldn't work. It seemed that there was no place I could turn. Peg was the latest in a long line of people who would not assist me.

Eventually, I struggled to my feet and hobbled home. When I neared the house, a faint hope surged up. Jay and I would put our heads together, plot a way to battle the corruption of that rotten town. It would be an immense comfort to have the support of a friend.

When I stepped into the house, I shouted his name, moving from the front room to the kitchen. My voice bounced off the walls of the empty house.

I sat down at the kitchen table, dropping the briefcase onto the floor. Hanging my head, I began to cry again.

A sound took me by surprise: the clacking noise made by the doggie door when Homer squeezed through the opening in the back. Barking out a greeting, he bounded over to the kitchen table and stopped beside my chair.

I got down on the tile floor and hugged him, burying my face in his fur. When I lifted my head, I fancied there was sympathy in his gaze.

"Don't you worry, Homer," I whispered, scratching him behind the ears. "We're getting Andy back. I'll bring him home tomorrow. I promise."

Maybe I was losing my mind, but that dog looked like he'd understood every word I'd said.

CHAPTER 51

AFTER I FED and watered Homer, I forced myself to open the kitchen cabinet. Though I wasn't hungry, I had to eat something to remain on my feet. Staring at the cans of Campbell's soup on the shelf made my shoulders sag with fatigue as I thought about the energy it would require to dump the contents into a pan, add water, and heat it up.

Instead, I pulled out the Jif jar: the simplest solution. But when I smeared the peanut butter across a slice of bread, the aroma wafting out of the jar struck like a physical blow, making me miss Andy so much, I bent over the counter and wailed.

I shuffled into the living room with the sandwich in hand. Sinking down onto the pink sofa, I stretched out across it and ate the sandwich. Homer settled down on the floor beside me, sniffing the bread with polite interest. I shared a couple of bites with him, just for the sake of companionship.

After I'd eaten, I fell into a sodden, dreamless sleep on the sofa. The setting sun still slanted through the windows when my eyes closed. But when I awoke, it was dark outside. I struggled to sit up, looking around to get my bearings. Homer lay beside the sofa, snoring softly.

While I tried to twist the kinks out of my back from my nap on the hard settee, I heard a rustling noise coming from one of the bedrooms. I shook my head to clear it, wondering whether I was dreaming.

But it was followed by the unmistakable sound of feet hitting a hardwood floor. My chest tightened, and my heartbeat skittered. There was an intruder in the house.

Frantic, I looked around the living room, and my eyes lit on an ancient set of fireplace tools. Rising carefully from the couch, I tip-toed over to the fireplace and grabbed the poker. It felt heavy and substantial in my hands—a vintage product, not a flimsy modern reproduction.

Homer stirred. From the dim light coming in the window, I saw the dog sit up, smiling at me. The sight was maddening. How had I managed to adopt a mutt too sweet tempered to serve as a guard dog?

In a bare whisper, I said, "Go get him, Homer!" As I waved my arm and pointed, he wagged his tail but remained in the spot beside the sofa.

Footsteps made their way softly down the hallway. I saw the shadow of the intruder as he crept into the living room.

When he entered, I raised the poker, swinging it like a baseball bat as I shouted, "Get out of my house!"

My swing was powerful, and the poker made an impact. It swept a quantity of old lady figurines off the mantel and onto the floor. Over the sound of smashing porcelain, I heard Jay's urgent whisper.

"Martha! It's me!"

My grip on the poker relaxed. My arms dropped, and the heavy iron point hit the floor. I watched as Homer trotted up to Jay.

Along with the blissful sense of relief, a welcome realization washed over me.

Jay hadn't deserted me.

I'm not alone.

CHAPTER 52

I SWITCHED ON the overhead light. Jay stood just inside the living room doorway, patting the dog's head.

"I didn't mean to scare you," he said. "I don't have a key, and I needed to feed Homer. Last night, I came after dark and found that the lock on one of your bedroom windows isn't secure. It's stuck— it won't catch. That's how I got in."

On a normal day, it would have distressed me to hear that my bedroom was open to any burglar who possessed sufficient determination to discover the broken lock. But it wasn't a normal day.

With a flicker of hope, I said, "Please, *please* tell me you know where Andy is."

He shook his head. "Martha, I don't. I'm so sorry."

The spark fizzled. Wearily, I turned back to point at the floor, where shards of porcelain were scattered.

"Don't let Homer over here. I'll sweep this up before someone steps in it."

After retrieving the broom and dustpan from the kitchen, I inspected the damage I'd done. A collection of colonial figurines lay on the floor, in pieces, their china heads and arms scattered across the fireplace tiles. They looked like Humpty Dumpty after the fall; I couldn't glue them back together. I swept them up and dumped the contents of the dustpan into the trash.

Back in the living room, the Shirley Temple doll had also landed on the floor, where it lay facedown. But Shirley had fared better than the china figurines. Her arms and legs were intact. Bending over to inspect the doll, it appeared that her bedraggled wig had come loose. When I picked up the doll, the cap of ringlets fell off into my hand.

Under the wig, I saw a black button attached to the back of her bald head. Barely bigger than an M&M, the button was the size of my fingertip. It held a tiny round metal screen. Like you'd find on a microphone.

"What are you looking at?" Jay said.

I put a finger to my lips, to hush him. He walked over and squatted down beside me. When our eyes met, he lifted his brow in disbelief.

Someone had planted a bug, right on my living room mantel.

I wanted to smash the device, along with the doll's cracked head. But I hesitated. Better to shut the doll away from our voices instead of letting my listeners think that I had caught on to the surveillance gadget.

The bungalow was small, but the house had a basement, a creepy old cellar with a row of shelves lining one wall. Cautiously, I made my way down the rickety stairs and set Shirley on one of the cobwebby shelves, and then tossed the wig beside her. She sat with her legs outstretched, looking even spookier with her newly bald head.

Back up the stairs, I pulled the door firmly shut behind me, satisfied that the doll would not overhear and transmit any conversations from the dusty basement.

Jay waited for me at the kitchen table. "So they've been bugging you, listening to you all this time?"

"God, who knows?" I dropped onto the chair beside him. "I feel like I've walked onto the set of a horror movie, but the camera won't stop rolling."

Jay reached for my hand. I clasped his in a tight grip, grateful for the contact.

"When did they take Andy?" I asked.

Jay released my hand. "They took Andy from the office, shortly before noon. A man and a woman showed up, no warning at all."

"Were they with the Department of Human Resources? Office of Child Protective Services?"

He lifted his shoulders in an apologetic shrug. "They wouldn't give me any information."

Envisioning it, my heart seized in my chest. "They just snatched him?"

It was worse than I thought. Andy must have been terrified. My head dropped, and I shut my eyes, absorbing the information. Jay reached for my hand again.

"All they would tell me was that you were being processed at the jail. After they took him, I ran to the courthouse to find out what was going on. I caught the bailiff in the hallway, coming back from the jail."

"Harold," I whispered.

"Yeah, the old dude. He said you'd been held in contempt, and when I tried to go into the courtroom, he stopped me. Said the judge would lock me up if I made 'a ruckus.' That's a quote."

Withdrawing my hand, I dropped it into my lap. It felt like it weighed twenty pounds. When I looked up at Jay, his face was remorseful.

"I should have done more. But it didn't make sense to have both of us locked up. So I went back to the office and called my father. Collect," he hastened to add.

That revelation shook me out of my funk. "You talked to your father?"

"Yeah, he accepted the charges. I was sweating that—didn't figure he would. He told me I had exactly three minutes, so I talked fast." Jay cracked a rueful smile. "Dad always liked you."

A dry laugh bubbled out of my throat. "Yeah, I'm a real winner. Just look how my life has turned out."

"Well, we mended fences—for the moment, anyway. He wired money to my account, so I'm no longer totally destitute. I wanted to post bond for you, but you were never formally charged. I rented a car, got a new phone, so I'll be less of a burden."

Pulling an iPhone from his pocket, he held it out. I experienced a throb of jealousy at the sight. Not having my own phone made me feel off-kilter and unconnected.

"If you've got a phone and a ride, you're in better shape than I am."

Setting the phone on the table, he said, "I've been working on a legal theory to support a case against the county, for that woman who died."

"Abby Zimmerman."

"Yeah. Seems like the family should sue for wrongful death, make a claim that Douglas County is abusing the restraint chair. What do you think?"

When Jay invoked the Pickens chair, a sick chill gave me the shakes, like I was fighting a fever. "You're right."

"You remember the hitching-post case? I looked it up today, reread the opinion."

"*Hope v. Pelzer*," I said, keeping my voice low, even though the eavesdropping doll was nowhere near. "The Supreme Court ruled that using a hitching post in an Alabama prison violated the Eighth Amendment. Refresh my recollection of the facts."

"They cuffed the inmate to a hitching post, above shoulder height. The guards said they did it because he'd been disruptive. They made him stand in the sun like that for seven hours, didn't give him bathroom breaks, barely provided water. Taunted him and humiliated him."

"Only seven hours," I murmured. Jay gave me a strange look, but I ignored it as the case law came back to me in a rush. I could almost see the words of the US Supreme Court opinion on a page inside my head. "The Supreme Court also said the prison guards didn't have qualified immunity from a civil rights lawsuit, that they could be sued for damages in that case."

"That's right! Do you think we can make the same argument against Douglas County for their abuse of the restraint chair?"

The shakes stopped. "Oh, hell yeah."

An icy sense of determination settled over me. Abby Zimmerman's death would be avenged. And I would have my day in court, too. I would wreak justice against every sadistic player in Erva, Alabama, who had participated in my torment.

But first I had to get Andy back.

CHAPTER 53

JAY DROPPED ME off at the office at sunrise the next morning, long before the courthouse regulars were stirring. I had another unhappy surprise when I discovered that my internet had been disconnected. Despite my best efforts, I couldn't fix it. While I struggled with the computer, I kept an eye on the clock. I wouldn't dream of being late to court.

When I approached the courtroom at eight forty-five for my nine o'clock setting, I saw through the glass in the door that the benches were nearly empty. My heart sank. I had cherished the hope that Child Protective Services personnel might be present, with Andy.

When I pulled the door open, though, I spotted them. Andy sat in the jury box. No DHR workers accompanied him, though. He sat beside Sydney Hancock, the welcome-wagon lady. Her chair in the box was pulled close to Andy's, and she had her arm in an iron grip around his shoulders.

I broke into a run, darting through the courthouse benches like a clumsy deer. In my eagerness to reach him, I smashed my thumb as I threw open the gate that separated the gallery, but I hardly felt it.

He saw me sprint toward him. "Mommy!"

Andy fought Sydney's grasp, but she held him fast. I hopped into the jury box and tore him from her arms, clutching him in a tight hug.

"Mommy!" he repeated. He hadn't called me Mommy since he was a toddler. Andy started to cry as my arms tightened around him. He looked up. "Where did you go?"

Looking down at his woebegone face, I observed that the blue circles shadowing his eyes were darker than usual. My heart twisted at the sight.

"It's okay, baby. I'm here, hon."

The courtroom staff filtered in, stealing glances at us. In a vain attempt to behave as if nothing was out of the ordinary, I sat down on one of the chairs and smoothed Andy's hair. It was neatly combed, but I did it anyway, just for the sheer joy of touching him.

"Why didn't you come get me?"

Sydney tried to pull him away, but we didn't budge. I shot her a look, and she backed off. In a sunny voice, she said, "I told Andy you were busy. But I said your mom would be back soon, didn't I, silly?"

He bowed his head. Putting a hand on my right wrist, he said, "What happened? Did you get hurt?"

His fingers ran over a purple bruise circling my wrist. I tugged down the cuff of my jacket to conceal it. I had a matching bruise on the other wrist, and around both ankles. Jay had photographed them with his phone before I left the house that morning.

I gave Sydney another challenging gaze. "Has Andy been receiving his medicine?"

I knew the truth, because I'd found his prescriptions sitting undisturbed in the medicine cabinet last night. Sydney took a breath, with the air of someone who has rehearsed an excuse in advance. I reached into my bag for the pill bottles, but before I could remove the childproof caps, Harold tapped my shoulder.

"Judge is putting on his robe, Martha. You'd best get over to the counsel table."

"In a second. Andy needs his meds."

Harold grabbed my shoulder and shook it. "You'll have to do that after. Go on and sit in your spot now."

His eyes bored into mine, sending a message. Nodding, I shoved the bottles back into the bag and tried to stand, but Andy grabbed my arm.

"No! Don't leave!"

I shushed him, kissing the top of his head. Under normal circumstances, he would hate a public display, but this day was the exception. "I'm going to sit right over there at that table, see? I'll be right there. I'm not going anywhere."

I hoped it wasn't a lie.

Sydney chirped. "We'll watch. Mommy is doing lawyer business. Isn't that fun?"

Reluctantly, he let me go. I barely made it to the table before the door opened and Harold called, "All rise!"

When the courtroom settled, Judge Pickens opened a manila file folder sitting directly at the center of the bench. Without looking up, he said, "*State v. Jeremiah Lawford Bradshaw.* Is there any announcement to be made in this matter?"

I rose. The sight of Pickens sent my adrenaline into overdrive. I wanted to streak over to the bench and pummel him, headbutt him, strangle him with his own necktie.

But my voice didn't give me away. I said, "The defense withdraws defendant's motion to retax costs, filed in this cause two days ago."

I sat. Made no speeches, offered no explanation.

Pickens broke into a wide smile. "The record shall so reflect. Thank you, Ms. Foster."

He turned to face the jury box. In a cordial manner, he said, "I'm delighted to see that we have special visitors in court today. Mrs. Hancock, who's this fine young man who has escorted you to my courtroom this morning?"

I clenched my hands into fists under the counsel table. My

injured thumb started to throb; it echoed my heartbeat as I waited to see what Pickens would do next.

Sydney beamed at Pickens. "Your Honor, this little guy is Andy Foster."

"That's right. I thought he looked familiar. Mr. Foster visited my home a while back. He is a renowned Egyptologist. How are you today, Andy?"

Andy looked terrified and didn't answer.

Sydney piped up. "He's good."

"Well, that's fine. Mrs. Hancock, it is no longer necessary for Andy to be your overnight guest. Thank you so very much for your gracious hospitality. I know I speak for myself and for Ms. Foster when I say how much we appreciate your kindness to this young member of our community."

I didn't hear her reply. My brain was overwhelmed, focused on Pickens. Because I could read between the lines. This had not been an official placement through the appropriate channels of Child Protective Services. He had done it without statutory authority, simply snatched my child and lodged him with his welcome-wagon stooge. There would be no official record of his action.

Sydney led Andy out of the jury box and walked him up to the bench, holding on to his hand. I struggled out of my chair, trying to suppress the instinct to reach out and grab him away from her.

From the bench, Pickens said, "Mrs. Hancock, will I see you at the meeting today?"

"Yes, sir, Judge Pickens. I wouldn't miss it for anything."

Doug Carson had been huddled behind his own counsel table throughout this process. But at that point he hopped out of his chair and strode over to me. "Hey, that's right. Hope you haven't forgotten, Martha. We have a lunch date today."

I looked at his cherubic face in frank disbelief. "What are you talking about?"

His complexion turned pink, but he retained his pretense of good humor. "I'm taking you to Rotary at noon. Remember? You're my guest. I'll drive you there."

Scooting past him, I made my way over to Andy. When Sydney released his hand, my son launched at me and threw his arms around my waist.

Judge Pickens said, "Do you have any further items for the court's attention this morning, Ms. Foster?"

I shook my head. "No, Your Honor." I needed to get out of that courtroom with my son and administer his meds.

"Then we'll see you at noon, ma'am. At Rotary."

Placing a protective hand on Andy's head, I said, "That's very kind, but—"

He cut me off. "My daughters will babysit your son while you attend the meeting. I've already made the arrangements. Doug, can you drop the boy at my house on the way to the meeting?"

"You bet, Judge. No problem."

By some miracle, my frozen face managed to form a smile as I realized Pickens intended to keep me totally in his power. I was his puppet, and he could pull the strings by maintaining control over Andy.

"Why, thank you, Judge. You are so kind."

My voice didn't even crack.

I looked down, focusing on the top of Andy's head, as my plight swirled around me. I was trapped, entirely at Judge Pickens's mercy. He had manipulated my legal work. He and his minions could bug my house, poison my dog, throw me in jail. He would snatch my son away again if it suited his purposes.

And then it came to me. I knew what I needed to do.

CHAPTER 54

THE LAST PLACE in the world I wanted to be was at the Erva Rotary meeting.

The meeting was held at the Erva Community Center, in an all-purpose room that doubled as a basketball court. A cold luncheon was served, cafeteria style: submarine sandwiches with potato chips and a fruit cup. I passed on the sandwich. I had little appetite for it, and moreover, I had even less inclination to break bread with the community leaders of Douglas County, Alabama.

I sat in silence beside Doug Carson at a round table near the back of the room. He concentrated on his sandwich. I watched the clock that hung overhead by a basketball hoop.

While other people chatted, the minutes dragged by. It was a relief when the meeting officially began. After we stood for the Pledge of Allegiance, my landlord, Buell Hawley, took the podium as sergeant-at-arms. He had a dual role, as master of ceremonies and comic relief. He called out certain members by name, ribbing them for their recent appearances in the local newspaper and issuing "fines" to be paid into the club treasury.

"And I'm going to have to issue another five-dollar fine to

our member Dean Paulson. I read last week that his construction company got the contract for the new jail addition."

The crowd applauded as a slim, white-haired man walked up to drop a five-dollar bill into a basket at the head table. I checked the clock again. It was only 12:30.

My landlord was just warming up. "Now, ladies and gentlemen, you won't believe this last fine I'm about to announce. Y'all are going to think I've got a lot of nerve. But I believe we need to levy a five-dollar fine against the man who is largely responsible for the prosperity we have seen at the county level."

A voice in the crowd shouted out: "I'll second that!"

Hawley continued. "It wasn't always like it is now. We've had hard times before, here in Douglas County. But you know what? Our County Commission isn't walking around wearing a barrel these days—no, sir. Who do we have to thank for that? It's today's program speaker, the Honorable Wyatt Pickens."

The room erupted in enthusiastic, noisy applause.

Pickens stood, waving to the crowd. To my right, Detective Stanley left his seat at a nearby table and headed toward me. Ignoring the detective, I kept my eyes fixed on Pickens as he walked to the front of the room, pausing to shake hands with smiling members of his fan base. But Stanley stopped directly beside my chair. He leaned over my shoulder and whispered into my ear.

I could smell salami on his hot breath as he spoke. "The sheriff says you can have your car back. Looks like they took it by mistake."

Surprised by the news, I met his eye.

He said, "Turns out they had your vehicle mixed up with another car of the same make. You can pick it up whenever you're ready."

He slid a business card onto the table. Stapled to the card was a sheriff's office property tag. It was for my car, a 2012 Ford Focus, Alabama license plate number 14A85K3.

I looked up. "And my phone? Do you have that, too?"

He didn't answer the question. But before he walked away, Stanley whispered, "Sounds like you've been behaving yourself." He patted my back as he added, "Glad to see you looking better."

My face flushed with fury as he stepped back to his own table. His remark that it sounded like I was behaving myself—what did it mean? Was it a reference to bugged conversations at my home? I fumed, too angry to tune in to Pickens's opening remarks.

But as the judge continued with his oration, I began to pay attention. And as I listened, it dawned on me that Pickens was good. Dangerously good. An effective speaker, pushing all the buttons for his audience. His words flowed seamlessly, conveyed with a sincerity that sounded completely heartfelt. And when he smiled, it was dazzling—unless you knew what he was really like.

"Ladies and gentlemen, 'law and order' isn't just an empty phrase to me. It is my passion. In fact, it's no exaggeration when I tell you that it is my life's calling. To effectively ensure law and order in Douglas County, we need the necessary tools. Tools like our new courts facility, which will be completed on time and on budget. The county owes that to its law-abiding citizens. When I look at the plans for this new facility, I can hardly believe my eyes. It will be a showplace that will make all the other counties in the state of Alabama pea green with envy. It's going to be so spectacular, I may not want to leave at the end of the workday. My wife will be pretty darned suspicious."

He paused for a laugh, and he got one.

"And after the new courthouse is open for business, the commission will get to work on another tool to maintain and uphold law and order: the new and bigger jail facility for Douglas County. My fellow Rotarians, this isn't a luxury for our community, it is a necessity. We need to keep up with the inmate population. Because in Douglas County, I don't believe in a slap on the wrist. That is not my idea of true justice. As your circuit judge, I will strictly enforce the Alabama criminal code, and that is a promise."

It was his closing line, and they loved it. As he stepped away from the podium, the Rotarians in the room jumped to their feet to give him a standing ovation. Only one person in the midst was slow to rise. I wondered whether he too had experienced the dark side of the judge's temper. Pickens waved to the crowd as someone shouted: "Governor! Governor!"

Others took up the chant. Soon, the room shook with it. Pickens smiled, lifting his eyes to the ceiling and placing his hand over his heart.

I didn't clap. I was too busy thinking, *Just wait until I bring you down.*

With all the commotion in the room, I didn't figure anyone would notice my lack of enthusiasm. But I was wrong about that. Harold was standing at the back door, not far from my table.

He was watching me.

CHAPTER 55

I ASKED DOUG to drop me at the sheriff's office after the Rotary meeting. Back behind the wheel of my own car, I crept through the streets of Erva, glancing down at the speedometer to ensure I stayed under the speed limit. At every stop sign, I checked the rearview mirror, expecting to see a patrol car on my tail.

But no one followed me. Traffic was light as people milled around town, pulling into strip centers and wheeling grocery carts through parking lots.

When I pulled into the long driveway leading to the Pickens's house, I braced myself for a confrontation. For all I knew, the judge had designs to keep Andy yet again. I didn't know what to expect anymore.

Edgy, I waited for someone to answer the doorbell. When no one responded to the first ring, I pressed the button again, hard, and then pounded on the door. I could hear the bell chimes sounding inside the house.

I was about to lay on the bell again when the door cracked open.

"Oh, it's you." Paula Pickens pulled open the door wide enough for me to enter. "I thought surely someone else would get the door. I was resting."

She wore a summer bathrobe. I could see a nightgown underneath it before she pulled the robe around her and tightened the sash. As I stepped inside, I kept my voice brisk. "So sorry to disturb you. I'll just pick up Andy and we'll get out of your hair."

Absently, she said, "I wonder what they did with him."

It sent a shiver of alarm through me. As I followed Mrs. Pickens down the hallway, I peered into the rooms we passed, searching for a glimpse of him. She raised her voice to be heard over the sound of a vacuum cleaner in the living room.

"My housekeeper is here today. I told Phoebe to take him outside. So he wouldn't be underfoot, you see."

As she led me through the house, I grew more uneasy, anxious to see that Andy was all right. My impatience spiked when we came to the kitchen and she stopped at the sink to pour a glass of water. A prescription bottle sat on the windowsill over the sink. She struggled for a moment with the childproof cap.

Before she popped the pill into her mouth, she said, "I take medicine for a health condition."

Though it was impolite to look, I glanced at the prescription label. Alprazolam, 0.5 milligram tablets. I couldn't begrudge her the dose of tranquility. She had to live with the monster.

We wandered out onto the porch. Andy sat on the swing set by the playhouse. He was alone; the Pickens's daughters were nowhere in sight. I called to him, waving.

As he ran to us, Mrs. Pickens said, "He's a nice boy. Almost pretty enough to be a girl. Is his father handsome?"

Startled by the question, I nodded.

She said wearily, "Beauty is such an overrated quality in a man."

Andy ran up the porch steps. Grabbing my hand, he said, "I'm ready to go, Mom."

I squeezed his hand. It felt hot—he shouldn't have been out in the hot June sun.

I said, "I need to get this guy home. Mrs. Pickens, thank you so much for watching him."

"Mom, no one was watching me."

I put an arm around his shoulder and pulled him close to my side. Andy was right, but it was academic at that point. "Mrs. Pickens, I want to pay your daughters for their time."

"No, no, no. Absolutely not. Good heavens, I don't even know where those girls have gone. Come on, I'll walk you out."

We followed her out, moving at a snail's pace. I wished she would speed up, but although she had not welcomed our presence, Mrs. Pickens seemed to be in no hurry to see us depart. She walked all the way out to the driveway and stood by my car as I buckled Andy into his seat.

As I fastened the shoulder straps, she observed, "Car seats have changed since my girls were little, haven't they? Children! They are an enormous responsibility. Not a burden, of course—I don't mean that." She paused, her brow wrinkling in thought. "The last public defender had children. Three, I think. What was his name, do you recall?"

At that point, she had my full attention. "Ford, I believe. That's the name I've seen on the docket sheet."

"That's right, Robert Ford. His wife was very sweet. She had one of those awful first names, though. Opal? It's so unfortunate when parents name a child after an inanimate object. For the life of me, I cannot imagine why they do it."

I slid into the driver's seat and buckled up, eager to go. But Paula Pickens lingered, with her hand on the car door, blocking my closing of it.

"Your son is a nice little fellow, not terribly boisterous." Looking off into the distance, she murmured, "The problem with children: it puts you at their mercy." She leaned down and spoke to Andy through the open door. "Good-bye, young man. Be a good boy."

As my hands clutched the steering wheel, the sleeves of my jacket fell back just far enough to reveal the bruises around both wrists. I caught her staring at them.

With a sigh, she said, "It's not too late."

Then she slammed the door shut and stepped away from the car. She didn't turn and wave as she walked back to the house.

CHAPTER 56

THE SUMMER DAYS in Alabama are long at the end of June. The sun doesn't set until eight o'clock.

I made sure I left the back door unlocked for Jay while I lay beside Andy in his narrow bed, listening to his regular breathing as he slept. His blood pressure reading had been frighteningly high when I took it earlier in the day. By bedtime, though, it was closer to normal—normal for Andy, that is. Watching his chest rise and fall, I counted his respirations. They were under thirty-four per minute, which was reassuring.

I heard footsteps in the hallway, followed by a whisper.

"Martha? It's me."

I rose from the bed, taking care not to disturb my son, and tip-toed out. I met Jay in the living room, where Homer occupied the couch. He lifted his head and barked a greeting.

"Homer, that's not your bed," I said, giving him a shove. I brushed stray hair from the pink velvet before I sat. "Okay, have a seat. I've got some tales to tell. I'm dying to hear what you think."

But Jay remained on his feet, surveying the array of vintage vases and figurines. In a hushed voice, he said, "Maybe not in here."

Surprised, I said, "Really? The doll is still locked up tight."

He lifted the praying hands planter and peered inside. "I'd feel more comfortable if we could talk someplace that isn't wall-to-wall crap. This place feels like a minefield."

His statement gave me pause. Every room in the house was occupied by my landlord's property, his furnishings and decor.

"The only space in the house that's empty is the basement. And I put the doll down there."

"I'll bring it back up. Give me a minute."

I stood by the basement door while he retrieved the Shirley doll and returned her to the fireplace mantel. After locking the back door, I followed Jay down the basement steps.

Turning, he aimed his iPhone flashlight at me. "Shut the door behind you."

"No, I want to keep it open, so I can hear Andy if he wakes up."

He walked around the basement, shining the phone into the corners of the unlit space. I sat on the bottom step and watched.

"Jay, you want to turn on the overhead light? There's a bulb with a string hanging from it, right in the center of the room."

"I don't think so. Someone might see it. For all we know, you're still under surveillance." He joined me, sitting on the concrete floor at the bottom of the wooden stairway. "This should be okay. We'll just keep our voices down."

Jay swiped the screen of his phone, extinguishing the lamp. His face was barely visible from the light that filtered down through the kitchen. The old cellar was spooky in the near darkness, but he was right. It was our best bet for privacy.

"How did it go today?" he asked.

I hugged my knees, resting my chin on them. "No disasters. After I withdrew the motion, Pickens acted like we were best friends. He handed Andy over to me, thank God."

"And then what?"

My voice rose, despite Jay's admonition. "Then he said I had to go to a Rotary meeting. And he arranged for Andy to stay at his house. When I picked him up, Mrs. Pickens talked in riddles, like she was trying to give me a warning." My shoulders shook with an involuntary shudder. "I feel like I've been transported to bizarro land. Jesus."

"How is Andy?"

"Better. He's better. His vitals are good."

Invoking my son's name gave me the irresistible urge to go check on him, to ensure that he was safely asleep in his bed. I stood up. "I'll be right back."

When I returned, Jay was tapping on his phone with his thumbs. Without looking up, he said, "So I've been thinking. The federal lawsuit is definitely the way to go. Are you licensed to practice in federal court? If not, we're going to need help. Because I'm not licensed to practice anywhere, obviously."

I stared into the darkness of the cellar, weighing the statement. "We're going to have to get help, regardless of how we proceed. Because Pickens has me totally under his control as long as I'm in Douglas County."

Jay looked up from the phone. "So you have to get out."

"Yep."

He was quiet for a minute, studying me. "When?"

"Soon. There are a couple of things that I need to do before I leave."

I had worked through it in my head. But I knew that every day I remained involved a gamble. I might set Pickens off, be locked up in jail again.

Jay interrupted my thoughts. "Should you get in touch with your old law firm? The place you worked in Birmingham—would they help?"

"Oh, hell no." I didn't even have to consider my answer. "They wouldn't take on Wyatt Pickens. Shoot, they might side with him. He's their kind of guy."

"Okay, that settles it. Then I'm heading to Montgomery tonight."

I was surprised to hear it. "What for?"

"That's where the Southern Poverty Law Center has its office. I want to be there when the door opens tomorrow, to talk to them about a Section 1983 civil rights suit. This kind of lawsuit is their specialty. They've sued the Alabama Department of Corrections over prison conditions and abuses. And the SPLC won't be afraid of Pickens. They've taken on an Alabama Supreme Court justice before."

"Jay, here's the thing." I scooted closer, dropping my voice as if Shirley Temple still sat on the dusty shelf overhead. "A federal lawsuit will take too long. It could drag out forever. And it won't necessarily give me what I need."

Jay stared at me with a dubious expression. "What is that? What do you need?"

"Wyatt Pickens's head on a platter."

My mind was made up. But I needed to proceed carefully.

"I'm bringing an ethics complaint to the Judicial Inquiry Commission. I'm going to get Pickens kicked off the bench."

For a moment, it seemed that Jay was struck dumb. At length, he spoke. "Are you out of your mind?"

CHAPTER 57

SITTING IN THE courtroom the next morning, I took care to present the right demeanor. I tried to look chastened, like a sinner who had been taken to task and learned her lesson.

For starters, I changed up my courtroom attire. No suit jacket or pants for me that day. I had settled on a mint-green linen dress that I'd worn to a wedding the prior summer. The dress had a demure cut, with a high neck and a hemline that covered my knees. It did not, however, cover my wrists or ankles. The dark rings of bruises inflicted by the restraint chair were changing color, from purple to blue. They stood out in striking contrast on my freckled arms as I sat with my hands folded on top of the counsel table.

Despite my serene appearance, my mind was in a tumult. My top concern was Andy's welfare. After a phone call with Peg, she'd enthusiastically agreed to take Andy back. Her turnaround was astounding, if not precisely reassuring. Upon our arrival at Happy Times, Peg gave Andy a hero's welcome, acting as if the conflicts of the recent past had never happened. He didn't want to go—no surprise. And moreover, I didn't want to leave him there. But it was necessary. Jay was off to Montgomery, and where else could I turn? I certainly wouldn't call the Pickens girls for babysitting services.

Judge Pickens was running late. As citizens hunched listlessly on the benches in the gallery, the courtroom staff chatted and laughed. Liza, the court reporter, pulled out a bottle of red polish and touched up her nails while she talked to Betsy. I was surprised at her audacity.

Harold put a stop to it. Frowning with disapproval, he limped over to the women. "Liza, don't let Judge catch you at that. You'll have the courtroom smelling like a dang beauty shop."

A shadow of uneasiness crossed her face as she tucked the bottle back into her bag, while vigorously fanning her free hand to dry it. When Judge Pickens emerged minutes later, Liza hid her hands behind her back.

Without any preliminaries, the judge began to call cases. The first case named was *State v. Woods.*

A woman hurried up to the bench, clutching a money order.

Pickens said, "Ms. Woods, are you prepared to make your payment on costs today?"

"Yes, sir. Twenty dollars." She held up the money order, as proof.

"See the clerk. Next hearing set a week from this date." He pulled up the next file. *"State v. Barrett."*

It was his debtors' prison docket. One by one, he called them forward to demand their weekly payment and set the next appearance.

The sixth case called was *State v. Comey.* A bony man in his late thirties stepped forward, literally shaking in his boots.

"Judge, I've been sick. I can't work if I'm sick, and if I don't work, I don't get paid."

Until that moment, Pickens had appeared to be in good humor. When Comey offered an excuse in lieu of payment, Pickens pierced the man with a glare. "There's an old saying, Mr. Comey. I expect you're familiar with it. 'If you can't do the time . . .' You know the rest."

The judge called for Harold, who hurried to the bench with the handcuffs. As he passed my table, Harold cut his eyes at me—looking for my reaction, possibly.

But I didn't give anything away. Didn't want to give them the satisfaction. I sat silently at the table, with my face trained in a bland expression as I gripped my pen. When Harold marched off with the unfortunate debtor, I kept my eyes on my yellow legal pad, where I added the defendant's name and the court's action to my list. And I scrawled notes to myself, over and over, in handwriting that was illegible to anyone but me.

When Pickens called out my name, it was so unexpected that I dropped the pen.

"Ms. Foster, please approach."

I obeyed instantly. Doug Carson also scurried up, stopping in his tracks when Pickens gave him a dubious look.

"Did I ask for you, Mr. Carson?"

Carson pivoted and returned to his seat.

I stood a safe distance from the bench, but he waved me closer. In an undertone, he said, "I hope it's not out of order to tell you that the dress you are wearing today is lovely. Very pretty, in fact."

I thought: *He's a psychopath. Absolutely off the charts.*

But I smiled up at him. "That's such a nice compliment, Your Honor. Thank you."

He made a show of sorting through files. "The Jeremiah Bradshaw rehearing isn't on today's docket. When is it set?"

"Gosh, Judge—next week, I think? I've lost track of the days."

I lifted my hand to rub my forehead in confusion, so that he could get a close view of the blue circle around my wrist.

"I expect him to appear in person at the hearing. It troubled me when he wasn't present at the last one."

"Yes, Judge."

"Will there be any announcement in the case?"

I looked perplexed. "He'll make his payment—twenty-five dollars. I guess he'll announce that."

"That's fine. You may be seated." I turned, but before I could leave, he stopped me. "By the way, did you enjoy the Rotary meeting?"

Wide-eyed, I said, "Great speech, Judge Pickens. Wow. Incredible."

That appeared to satisfy him, and he let me return to the counsel table.

I wished Jay could've overheard the exchange. He'd never believe it otherwise. If Jay could see me in court today, he'd be certain that I'd lost my mind.

Turning to a fresh page on the legal pad, I picked up the pen again. While Pickens called the next case, I scrawled: *I'm going to destroy you. I will rip that robe off your back.*

When I read what I had written, I looked up at Judge Pickens and smiled.

CHAPTER 58

I HAD BROUGHT Andy and Homer into my bedroom that night. Andy lay under the covers of my bed, sleeping fitfully. Homer watched as I tugged on the window, trying to shove open the sash.

The window held. Jay had nailed it shut for me before he left the night before, but I kept testing it, to reassure myself that we were secure inside the bungalow. As secure as we could be, anyway, under the circumstances.

A phone hummed in my pocket. It was not my cell phone; the cell remained somewhere in the possession of the miscreants at the county jail. This was a burner phone I had acquired at a convenience store after I'd picked up Andy from day care. Only one person was privy to the number.

I picked up. "Hi, Jay."

"Martha. How are you doing?"

I pulled the window shade down before I answered. "Doing okay."

It was an overstatement. The fury that had fueled me in court had drained away by nightfall, leaving me tired and depressed. But I wanted to present a brave front.

"What about Andy? Is his blood pressure back to normal?"

"Yeah, pretty close."

"And what about day care? Was he okay over there today?"

My eyes pricked with tears. I blinked them back, embarrassed by the reaction. It was just so nice to hear someone expressing sincere concern.

"Thanks for asking, Jay. I only left him there during the court docket and picked him up before noon. He was jittery when I arrived, but he settled down. He's sleeping now."

I stepped over to the bed to check. Andy's eyes were closed, his mouth slightly open with the steady breathing of his sleep. My hand reached out to stroke his hair, but I stopped myself, lest I disturb him. Crossing to Homer, I sat on the floor next to the dog bed.

I spoke softly into the phone. "What's happening in Montgomery?"

His voice sounded upbeat. "I made some contacts today. Progress."

My dark mood lifted slightly. "Fill me in. Did you get to talk to anyone at SPLC?"

"I had to wait a while for them to see me. But I've garnered some interest there. They said Pickens was already on their radar."

A thrill of excitement shot up my spine. "Really? No kidding."

"Yeah, they've heard rumblings about inmate mistreatment in Douglas County. They weren't familiar with the board bills, but they had heard about the restraint chair abuses. And got an anonymous call from one of the former public defenders some time back."

"So they knew about it, but they haven't done anything?" That sounded discouraging.

"No one was willing to go on record before. Now that they have a solid lead, the SPLC is interested in following up on Abby Zimmerman's death. And they want you to get Molly Zimmerman on board."

It was a reasonable demand. But I hadn't talked to Molly since I'd gotten a taste of the restraint chair.

"I can certainly try." It was hard to predict what she would say. Her testimony could be important in my ethics complaint against Pickens, too. But she might be too intimidated to take a stand against the public officials in Erva.

"I'll try to run Molly down, first thing tomorrow. What else? Did you make it over to the ACLU office?"

"They don't take walk-ins. I'll have to make an appointment. But I talked to a reporter."

Jay sounded so upbeat, so encouraged, that it was becoming infectious. Eagerly, I asked, "*The Birmingham News*?"

"No, I couldn't raise anyone there. But a young guy at the *Montgomery Advertiser* is interested."

That deflated me. Birmingham had the largest circulation in the state. The Montgomery newspaper was down the list in readership.

Jay must have read my mind. "Martha, it's the leading news source in central Alabama. And they read it at the capitol. The reporter wants to talk to you. Can you write this down?"

"Give me a second." The room was almost completely dark; I couldn't see to write, even if I had a pen in hand. Jogging into the kitchen, I tore off a paper towel and grabbed one of Andy's markers. "Okay, I'm ready."

It felt like I was talking to the Jay I used to know, back in law school. His voice maintained that note of confidence when he said, "So you will get Molly Zimmerman on board, plus you're gonna astound the journalist with your account of the jailhouse experience. He'll have visions of a Pulitzer Prize when you're done with him."

At that, I laughed—couldn't help it. "You're good medicine, Jay. I was feeling pretty down before you called."

His tone changed, adding a note of concern. "Any new danger?"

I sidled over to the kitchen window, which gave me a partial view of the street. "I can't shake the feeling that I'm being watched. That they are just waiting for me to make a misstep, and the trap will snap shut."

"Keep hanging tough, Martha. I've got your back. When are you leaving town? Have you decided?"

I left the kitchen, suspicious that even the plates and cutlery had ears. Walking down the hallway, I said, "Soon."

After we ended the call, I tried not to disturb Andy when I crawled into the bed, but he lifted a hand to rub his eyes.

"Where did you go, Mom?"

"I was on the phone, honey. With Jay."

He rolled onto his side, facing the wall. In a sleepy voice, he said, "I want Jay to come back." After a beat, he added, "Homer misses him."

Without responding directly, I tucked the covers around my son with a murmured: "Sweet dreams." It was best not to make too many promises these days. Especially when it came to Jay Bradshaw.

I wouldn't want Homer to be disappointed.

CHAPTER 59

ANDY AND I stood at Molly Zimmerman's front door the next morning. When I knocked, no one appeared. But the front door was open, so I called through the screen.

"Molly? Hello? Is anyone home?"

The curtain shifted behind the front window. A small boy's face peered through the glass but instantly disappeared. Encouraged, I rapped on the doorframe again. This time I raised my voice to a shout.

"Molly, it's Martha Foster! I need to talk to you!"

She emerged from the back of the house. As Molly padded barefoot to the door, I pasted a bright smile on my face. Andy tried to slip behind me, but I kept his hand in a firm grip.

She scrutinized me through the screen without inviting us inside. "So it is you. Bobby said it was the woman lawyer, but I figured he had to be wrong."

"It's me!" I kept smiling.

"Huh. I heard you was locked up."

That wiped the grin off my face. "Where did you hear that?"

"Word gets around." Squinting, she craned her neck and checked out the street behind us. Then she gave the screen a tug and opened the door. "Come on in."

Pulling on Andy's hand, I crossed the threshold. "I brought my son with me—hope that's okay. Ms. Zimmerman, this is Andy."

Shy, Andy ducked his head. But when I nudged him, he whispered, "Hi."

Molly waved an arm at the small boy hiding behind the far end of the sofa. We could see the top of his head peeking over the arm of the couch.

"Get on over here, Bobby."

The head disappeared.

She sighed. "Martha, you want me to send the boys on out back?"

The front room was stuffy, already warmer than the temperature outside. I saw the broken window air-conditioning unit, still in the same condition. The landlord was obviously in no hurry to replace it.

"Let's all go out back. How about that? It's a beautiful day."

Molly shrugged. When we headed through the kitchen, her son left his spot by the sofa, tagging behind us at a safe distance. Molly opened a screen door to the backyard. Bobby shot past us, scooting down the back steps. We stepped outside and watched him scramble up into the branches of an ancient ginkgo tree at the far corner of the yard.

Andy gave me a bemused look through his glasses. I bent to straighten them, whispering, "Go ask Bobby what his favorite dinosaur is."

He ambled off in the general direction of the tree. Molly sat down on the top step with a sigh.

"I expect you're here about Abby."

I crouched on the next step down, where the concrete had crumbled with time; it made an uncomfortable perch. "That's right. I heard from some lawyers in Montgomery who are concerned about her treatment by the county jail. They want to help."

Molly gave me a mystified look. "Too late to help her now."

Hastily, I continued. "We can't bring Abby back, of course. But it's not too late to make Douglas County pay for their actions, for how they contributed to Abby's death. And to keep it from happening again, to someone else. Have you made final arrangements? For the funeral?"

"Too late for that too."

My face flushed with impatience. I didn't want to hear Molly's forlorn discouragement. With an effort, I kept my manner upbeat. "It's not too late for the courts to correct the injustice."

Molly rolled her eyes. "I'm trying to answer your question if you'll just listen. It's too late for a funeral. They burned her up."

I gaped at her. "No."

With a huff, she rose and disappeared inside the house. I tried to get my head around the disclosure. It was a setback I had not anticipated. We needed an autopsy by an independent examiner. I didn't trust the local coroner to be forthcoming with all the facts. I had come to Molly's house with the intent of persuading her to make an official request, and to exhume the body, if necessary.

When the screen swung open again, she emerged with a letter in hand.

"Here," she said, holding it out. "Read it for yourself."

The paper was on Douglas County letterhead. Shading my eyes with my hand, I began to read.

Abigail Jo Zimmerman meets eligibility requirements for indigent burial by Douglas County, Alabama. Douglas County has legal authority and obligation to undertake necessary burial expenses. Under Section 38-8-2 of the Alabama Code, all counties are charged with burial of unclaimed or indigent bodies at county expense.

Bodies are cremated prior to burial unless prohibited by religious affiliation.

The date set for cremation had already passed, three days prior. With a grimace, Molly shook her head. "I couldn't stop it. The letter went to our dad. See there?" She pointed to his name on the correspondence, at a different address in Erva.

"He got it the same day they did the cremation. Maybe he could have done something, but he didn't think to try. Dad said Abby never cared nothing about religion, so it didn't make any difference anyway."

Of course it did make a difference, in hindsight. Our evidence had been reduced to ash.

I shook it off, still determined to proceed. "We'll go ahead with this anyway. Molly, it's important that we wage this fight. We can do something about Pickens. But I am going to need your help."

She looked frightened and confused. "Me? How can I help?"

"You will have to testify at a hearing. Maybe file a lawsuit, saying that they violated your sister's rights by putting her in the chair."

Molly bowed her head. In a low voice, she said, "Who is going to listen to me? I ain't nobody."

"We will join our voices together," I said. "They put me in the chair too, Molly. But maybe you already heard that."

Our eyes locked for a long time, it seemed. Finally, she nodded.

"We'll back each other up," I said.

Squeezing her eyes tightly shut, Molly groaned out loud, clutching the concrete riser for support. When I placed my hand over hers, she opened her eyes.

I needed to hear her say it aloud. "Will you help me?"

"I guess I can try. Can't guarantee anybody will credit a word I say, though."

The hard knot that had formed in my chest loosened slightly. We sat together for half an hour while I took Molly's statement. We walked through the events leading to Abby's imprisonment, what she had told her sister, her death, what Molly had seen, and what the county employees had told her afterward. I scribbled notes while we talked, as my burner phone didn't have the recording bells and whistles of an iPhone.

I was feeling more positive when I rounded Andy up and drove away from Molly's house. Two witnesses were better than one: that was a fact. But I knew I needed a backup for Molly, because she could easily back out. I had to locate a third witness; fortunately, Mrs. Pickens had given me a lead. And I knew exactly where to start looking. *Opal Ford.* My conversation with Mrs. Pickens had planted a seed. It was time to contact the late public defender's wife. She shouldn't be too hard to find.

Seemed like everyone in the state of Alabama had a Facebook account.

CHAPTER 60

"WHATCHA DOING?"

Andy stood in the bedroom doorway, holding a big book against his chest. I'd been wrapping the Shirley Temple doll up inside a worn bath towel—making it easier to carry up and down the stairs, and with the added advantage of not having to see the doll's unsettling glass eyes as they opened and shut during transport. My paranoia regarding bugging devices had spiked, and I shuttled the doll around when I needed to use the basement for confidential calls.

Moving quickly, I shut the eavesdropping doll inside the bedroom and changed the subject, asking Andy what book he had.

He held it up—it was one we had purchased at the museum in Atlanta, full of glossy pictures of Egyptian treasures. "I want you to read to me."

Ordinarily, I couldn't resist a request like that one. Snuggling up together over a book sounded like a slice of heaven. But I had an opportunity I could not postpone.

"I can't read it right this minute. I have to make a phone call, for work. An important phone call."

"But we haven't gotten to read together in ages."

"Why don't you sit down with Homer and look at the pictures? Then we can read it, just as soon as I'm done."

At the mention of his name, Homer trotted up, wagging his tail.

"See? Homer wants to read the book."

Andy looked doubtful. "You know dogs can't read, Mom."

"Homer is very intelligent." I took the book and set it down on the floor, opening it to reveal a glossy picture of King Tut's tomb. Homer did not appear particularly interested, but when Andy settled on the floor beside the dog and pointed out the sarcophagus on the page, the dog rolled onto his side and listened politely.

Clutching my phone, I descended into the basement and sat at the bottom of the stairs. I entered Opal Ford's number and whispered a prayer as I hit Send.

"This is Opal," she answered on the second ring.

I exhaled in relief. "Opal, it's Martha Foster. Thanks so much for responding to my DM and agreeing to talk with me."

There was silence on the other end of the line, but I could hear noise in the background.

I spoke quickly. "I'm so sorry for your loss, Opal."

In a tentative voice, she said, "Thanks. How long will this take? Because I have three kids, and I'm going to have to get them ready for bed pretty soon."

If I lost this chance, I might not get another. "I totally get that. I've got a little boy myself. But this is really important. I told you in my message that Douglas County hired me to replace your late husband, Robert. I've only been in Erva a couple of weeks, but my experience has not been what I expected. There have been some very disturbing things going on here." I paused, hoping she would take the bait.

After a moment of silence, she said, "Like what?"

I murmured into the phone. "Oh, wow. Where to begin?" I was buying time, trying to feel her out, to determine just how much I should reveal. At that point, it was uncertain whether Opal was friend or foe. So I proceeded delicately.

"The defense work, for one thing. There seems to be an expectation that the public defender should not handle cases with the ordinary amount of vigor. Does that sound familiar?"

I could hear her sigh. "Yeah. Yeah, it does."

"Did Robert mention experiencing pressure from certain people in the legal community?" I was still trying to tiptoe.

She said, "He was under a lot of pressure, as a matter of fact. Who is pressuring you?"

I realized it was time to tell the truth and shame the devil.

"It comes from a number of directions. But principally, it's the circuit judge. Pickens." Just speaking his name aloud made my throat tighten, my nose burn.

Maybe she was experiencing the same reaction on her end of the call. Because she said, "That son of a bitch is evil—you know that, right?"

Buoyed by the breakthrough, I scooted around and rested my back against the rough plaster wall. "Opal, I know that for a fact. I swear to God."

"We weren't in Erva that long. Less than six months, actually." She dropped her voice. "They broke Rob down quickly."

I propped my feet against the rickety banister. "How? How did they do it? What did they do to him?"

"Different things. Bribery at first, flattery. Made us think we'd landed in paradise."

My heart began to race. The story she told was familiar.

She went on, her voice gaining strength. "Yeah, they sucker you in at first. Then it gets ugly."

Opal did not come across as a shrinking violet. She sounded tough and was clearly angry. My hopes started to rise.

"Opal, things have turned seriously ugly here already. Did your husband ever tell you about the board bill incarcerations? Or mention the restraint chair in the county jail?"

There was background noise from her end of the call. I heard a child's wail. Opal called out, "I'll be there in a second!"

Then she spoke into the phone, in a hushed voice.

"What do you want from me?"

She wanted to end the conversation. I could tell I was running out of time. "I'm going to file an ethics complaint against Pickens. Take him up before the Judicial Inquiry Commission. I need your help."

Her voice grew sharp. "You realize my situation? I've got a full plate here. I'm a widowed single mother to three kids who just lost their dad, and I'm living back at home with my elderly parents."

I was not too proud to beg. "This is so important, Opal. Pickens has to be stopped. He's destroying lives—literally. I can't do it alone. I need testimony, have to provide witnesses."

"Yeah? Well, I buried my witness. We haven't even paid the funeral bill yet."

I began to speak in a rush, telling her that I understood her circumstances, that I was a single mom, too. We walked in the same shoes; we had to stand together.

No sound came from her end.

I pulled the phone from my ear and looked at the screen. The call had ended while I was still talking. Opal Ford had cut me off.

I banged the back of my head against the plaster, hard enough to raise a knot on my scalp. I'd had her on the line, and I'd blown it.

Back upstairs, I sat in the kitchen and swiped the iPad again. Studying Opal's Facebook page, I looked at her posts. Erva didn't appear in a single photo. Scrolling back, I found family pictures, holiday stuff, Halloween costumes. When I went back two years, I struck gold: Opal at her ten-year high school reunion in Auburn, Alabama.

Opal was an Auburn Tiger, living back home with Mom and Dad. She was hiding in plain sight. Piece of cake.

Staring at her smiling face in the reunion picture, I shook my head, thinking: *Opal, you don't know how persistent I can be. Especially when the stakes are so high.*

CHAPTER 61

I DIDN'T BOTHER Opal again that week, because I was occupied with more immediate concerns. Three days after Opal cut me off, I was back in Pickens's courtroom.

It was time to put the wheels in motion.

I sat at the counsel table with my laptop open in front of me. Jay was seated in the spectators' gallery with Andy at his side, in the row closest to the door. He had chosen the spot intentionally, in the event he needed to make a quick getaway. Before we'd entered the courthouse, I had handed Andy over to him.

In an undertone, I said, "If anything happens—"

He completed my sentence. "I take Andy, we head straight to Mobile. Dad's on board—I told you that. We'll be fine."

He had sounded like he believed it. I tried to take comfort in that. I'd executed a power of attorney, which granted Jay and his dad the right to care for Andy and obtain medical care for him if it came to that. It was strange to think that the best people to provide for Andy's protection were Jay and his estranged father. But I was low on options, and if they locked me up and came for Andy again, I trusted the Bradshaws wouldn't give him up without a hell of a fight.

Sitting in court, I wanted to turn and look at my son, but I resisted, lest I draw undue attention to him.

Shifting in my seat, I surveyed the opposite side of the courtroom, where I spotted a bearded man balancing a small notepad on his knee. I recognized his picture from the *Montgomery Advertiser* web page.

When he looked up, I caught his eye. He nodded, almost imperceptibly.

Harold entered the courtroom, hurrying up to his desk. At the precise moment when he called "All rise!" I hit the button on my laptop to e-file my documents. While I stood, I kept my eyes on the computer screen, to be certain the system had received them.

"Be seated."

Wary, I lifted my eyes. Pickens's voice had a definite edge. I was not the only one who had noticed. Doug Carson began to shrink into his chair. The court reporter dropped a roll of paper onto the floor and scrambled to retrieve it. As Pickens took his place at the bench, it felt like the atmosphere in the room had changed, that the air crackled with tension.

"Ms. Foster. Approach the bench."

Though the room was cool, I started to sweat. As I walked toward him, he fixed his eyes on me with a predator's gaze.

I kept my voice steady. "Yes, Your Honor?"

He spoke quietly, for my ears alone.

"Is there anything you want to tell me?"

The danger was palpable. My mind whirled with possibilities. Pickens couldn't know about the motions I had filed only moments ago. And he shouldn't know about the Judicial Inquiry Commission, which I'd only filed with last night.

When I didn't respond, he said, "A friend in Montgomery says you've filed a complaint against me."

This was my worst-case scenario. I knew he would receive notice of the judicial ethics complaint. But word shouldn't have reached him yet. I braced myself, unable to predict what he might do next. Andy's face flashed in my mind's eye. Maybe, I thought, Jay should grab him and leave right then, while they still had a chance to get out.

When Judge Pickens snorted and began chuckling, I couldn't believe it. He leaned across the bench and whispered, "Please, Ms. Foster! Don't throw me in that briar patch!"

And then he laughed out loud, shaking his head. That broke the spell.

I returned to the counsel table. Sinking into my chair, I had to stifle the urge to run.

Because I caught his meaning.

Clearly Judge Pickens was not worried in the least about my complaint to the Judicial Inquiry Commission. He obviously had allies on the board, which explained how he already knew about it: someone had picked up a phone that very morning and informed him on the down-low, before the official notice had time to go out.

I tried to remain cool, avoid panic. I had an important mission, and I couldn't depart before it was accomplished. Pulling two hard files from the paperwork on the table, I stood and said, "Your Honor, I have an announcement."

Doug Carson's head jerked toward me, wearing an expression of trepidation. But Pickens propped his jaw on his fist, as if I bored him.

"And what is that, Ms. Foster?"

I plucked out the documents that I had e-filed in *State v. Bradshaw* and *State v. Tummons*. A long list of criminal defendants had turned me down flat before I encountered Tommy Ray Tummons, a local drunk who had grown sufficiently weary of his board bill obligation to agree to the motion. Privately, I suspected he might have been half lit when he signed on.

"Your Honor, I have filed motions to retax costs in two cases pending before this court: *State v. Bradshaw* and *State v. Tummons*. We are taking this action on the basis that the imposition of the board bill fee is illegal and creates a debtors' prison in Alabama, in violation of state and federal law."

Pickens's face grew stormy. "You withdrew the motion, just last week."

I was keenly aware that the last time I'd filed this motion he'd sent me to jail. I barreled on, pretending that I wasn't scared out of my wits. "Moreover, Your Honor, in light of the fact that you made reference to the recent complaint I filed against you with the Alabama Judicial Inquiry Commission, I wish to disqualify you in these cases. I'm hereby requesting a change of judge."

Briskly, I gathered my paperwork together, dropping copies onto the prosecution table on my way to the bench.

I held up the signed papers, waiting for Pickens to take them from my shaking hand. But he made no move to receive them.

He said, "You intend to disqualify me? Is that right?"

"Yes. Your Honor." I set the motions onto the bench and took a step backward.

"You've got it turned around, Ms. Foster. I talked to the County Commission this morning. They are terminating your employment, effective immediately."

My breath caught. "Upon what grounds?"

"Ineffective assistance of counsel. Now gather your things and get out."

I ran to the counsel table. While I shoved my belongings into my briefcase, Jay grabbed Andy and bailed from the courtroom. From the corner of my eye, I saw Harold at the bailiff's desk, rolling his eyes in the direction of the door. I didn't need the signal. Grabbing the briefcase, I tore out of the courtroom and ran for the exit, taking the marble stairs two at a time.

I had made it out the door and down the courthouse steps when a voice called my name. Glancing over my shoulder, I saw the Montgomery journalist. He caught up to me, panting.

"Will you give me an exclusive?"

"Yeah," I said, trotting to my car at a fast pace. It was parked across the street.

"Where can we talk? Your office?"

I was more than willing to spill for the journalist. Court actions and lawsuits move slowly; I was ready to appeal to the court of public opinion.

I jerked my car door open. It was filled with a hodgepodge of boxes that contained our worldly goods. Anything that didn't fit in my vehicle or the trunk of Jay's car had been left behind. Before court, I had moved Andy's car seat to Jay's rental car, as part of the getaway plan. The two of them would be heading south on the highway by now, Homer riding shotgun.

As I slid behind the wheel, I said, "I'll tell you anything you want to know. But right now, I'm getting the hell out of Douglas County."

I revved the engine and tore off down the street, headed for the highway.

NOVEMBER — FIVE MONTHS LATER

CHAPTER 62

TEARING THE ROBE off an Alabama judge isn't easy.

It was a tough battle. It began with the complaint that I filed in June with the Judicial Inquiry Commission. The commission assessed the complaint against Pickens and filed a charge against him, alleging that he violated judicial ethics.

That doesn't happen very often. And it likely would not have happened to Judge Pickens if I had been the lone voice raising an accusation. But I had Molly, backing my complaint with her claim regarding Pickens's treatment of her sister. And ultimately, after weeks of effort and unabashed begging, Opal Ford relented and joined us. We tried to bring Paul Keaton—the prior defender I'd located in June—on board too, but he was afraid of the fallout.

The fact that three citizens had joined together—the county public defender, the widow of the deceased prior defender, and the bereaved sister of an inmate who had died in custody—tipped the scales in our favor.

The Judicial Inquiry Commission filed the ethics charge against Pickens in the Court of the Judiciary, a nine-member body made up of judges, lawyers, and laypeople. The second stage of the process would be a public hearing before that nine-person court, where Pickens would be placed on trial for judicial misconduct.

While the process moved toward our public trial in Montgomery, I marked time. My life had experienced a reversal. I was no longer the benevolent friend who provided a spot on my couch to Jay Bradshaw. In the months leading up to trial, Jay, Andy, Homer, and I were all crashing at Dr. Bradshaw's house in Mobile—living in a boomer parent's spare rooms, like so many millennials in the twenty-first century. I couldn't even offer to pay rent. Every penny I had went to pay for health insurance under COBRA.

But we were safe in Mobile, and Andy and I were together. When the school year started, he entered kindergarten. And while I awaited the day of reckoning, I kept an eagle eye on my goal: taking down Judge Wyatt Pickens.

At last, the November trial date arrived. The case would be tried in the Alabama Judicial Building in Montgomery, a huge stone structure that houses the Supreme Court and Courts of Criminal and Civil Appeals. On the first morning of the trial, Jay took off in his car before sunrise, heading to Erva to transport Molly Zimmerman to court. Her car wasn't reliable, and we wanted to be certain she appeared on time.

I arrived at the Judicial Building an hour early. Before entering the building, I paused for a moment to gird myself for battle, leaning against one of the tall limestone columns for support. Inside, I walked up the staircase to the third floor, where the Supreme Court sits. Our case would be heard in that courtroom, beneath the great dome. At the top of the stairs, I had a sinking feeling when I saw Pickens's legal team huddled in the hallway.

His lawyers were formidable: two partners of the leading law firm in the city, joined by two prominent members of the criminal bar. I knew one of the criminal attorneys, Emma Hale, by reputation. She specialized in the defense of high-profile criminals with deep pockets. Hale gave me an icy glare as I walked up to the courtroom and tugged on the door.

"It's locked," she said. Which was obvious to me at that point.

I didn't want to hang out in the hallway with Team Pickens, so I wandered off to the women's room. I hoped it would offer sanctuary.

But once inside the restroom, I heard a woman retching in one of the stalls. It sounded like she was losing her breakfast.

She opened the stall door, hanging on to it for support. It was our lawyer, Addison Holmes, the woman making the case against Pickens on behalf of the Judicial Inquiry Commission. Averting her eyes, she turned on the faucet and cupped her hands under the water. As she rinsed out her mouth, I offered moral support.

"You know, the head litigator at my old firm in Birmingham always said he threw up before every jury trial, even after twenty years in the profession," I reassured her. "It's just one of those things, no matter how many times you've tried cases."

She gripped the sides of the porcelain sink. In a low voice, she said, "I've never done it before."

"Thrown up before a trial? It's really common, believe me."

Our eyes met in the mirror over the sink. Her complexion was a faint shade of green. Splashes of water spotted her ivory blouse. "I've never tried one of these cases before. This is the first hearing I have handled before the Court of the Judiciary. Most complaints against judges get dismissed. We usually don't even investigate."

"So how did you get assigned to prosecute Pickens at this hearing?"

"I pulled the short straw."

The door flew open, hitting the wall with a bang. Opal Ford stepped inside, shut the door, and pressed her back against it. "Pickens is out there. I almost ran straight into him."

Addison gagged and clapped a hand over her mouth. "I'm going to throw up again," she said, running for the stall.

As I listened to her, my own stomach knotted. I had a sick feeling, too.

CHAPTER 63

UNTIL THAT DAY, I had never set foot inside the room where the Supreme Court of Alabama conducted business. My one appearance in appellate court had been before the Court of Civil Appeals, one floor down. And I hadn't occupied a seat at the counsel table on that occasion. I'd been third chair for higher-ups at the law firm, basically acting as a water carrier.

As spectators filtered into the lofty courtroom, I struggled to compose myself. Douglas County had turned out in full force to support Judge Pickens. Isabelle and Phoebe, the judge's daughters, sat directly behind him, though I didn't spot Paula, his wife. I saw my former landlord there, with a delegation of Rotarians. Harold and the court reporter sat behind them, along with Sydney and Diane from the welcome wagon. Even Peg had arrived, leaving the kids at Happy Times Day Care to her assistant. It was the nightmare version of a reunion: I was surrounded by familiar faces, but they were all enemies.

On our side, Opal and I sat two rows behind Addison. Earlier, I had spotted the bearded journalist, sitting alone in the upper gallery. When Jay arrived with Molly Zimmerman, they would have their pick of seats on our side of the room.

The whole scene felt surreal as the proceedings commenced. But the sound of my name being called jerked me abruptly to reality as I walked forward. The nine members of the Court of the Judiciary sat side by side at a long, curved mahogany bench ordinarily occupied by the Supreme Court of Alabama. My eyes swept down the row, assessing them. It seemed that Judge Pickens had a jury of his peers; they were mostly male, mostly white.

My right hand shook as I recited the oath. When I took the witness chair in a separate station below the far right of the bench, I folded my hands in my lap, out of sight.

"Please state your name."

"Martha Foster."

Addison stood at a lectern in the center of the room. When she picked up her legal pad, her hands were unsteady. "Please state your education and background."

"I received my Juris Doctor from the University of Alabama School of Law, graduating magna cum laude. I've been a member of the Alabama State Bar for seven years. Until June, I was employed in private practice in Birmingham."

My heart was racing. I had never been in a witness stand before, hadn't appreciated how frightening it could be. But I needed to project confidence. I took a moment to correct my posture, praying for calm.

Addison said, "What occurred in June of this year?"

"In June I accepted the position of public defender for Douglas County, Alabama. I moved to Erva, the county seat, with my five-year-old son. I was employed in that capacity for approximately two and a half weeks."

One of the commissioners held up a hand. "Excuse me? Did you say two weeks?"

He was one of the attorneys on the court, a portly man in his fifties. His brow was wrinkled, as if he doubted his own hearing.

"Yes, sir. Sixteen days in June of this year."

He gave his head a shake. I read the body language; he thought my two-week experience was not of a duration to make a convincing case against a circuit judge. We might have already lost that vote. And we needed a unanimous court to strike Pickens off the bench.

Addison said, "Describe your duties as public defender of Douglas County, Alabama."

"My position in Douglas County involved appearing in court before Judge Wyatt Pickens. In my numerous encounters with Judge Pickens, both inside court and extrajudicial contacts, he violated the Canons of Judicial Ethics by acting without integrity—"

One of Pickens's silver-haired lawyers rose to his feet. "Objection!"

I turned to the court, to await the ruling. One of the robed judges said, "Ms. Foster, you are making conclusions. That invades the province of this court. Please confine your testimony to statements of fact."

He was right, and I felt a flush of embarrassment at my misstep.

"I beg your pardon, Your Honor. During my time in Douglas County, I personally observed Judge Pickens engage in practices that were alarming to me. In criminal cases, he regularly incarcerated defendants for their inability to pay court costs and fees, in violation of Alabama rules."

An elderly man spoke: another judge. "The rule permits incarceration for willful failure to pay."

Shifting in my chair, I turned his way. "These were indigent defendants. And Judge Pickens never conducted a hearing to determine that the failure to pay was willful, that the defendant had the ability to pay but refused to do so. He dragged them back to court for cost hearings on a weekly or monthly basis. And if they didn't have the means to pay, cash in hand, he locked them up."

Some of the members of the court exchanged glances. I took that as a sign of encouragement. "Rule 26.11 also limits the period of nonpayment incarceration. Judge Pickens ignored that, too. But the most terrifying aspect was the fact that those poor defendants will never be relieved of their court cost obligations. Because Douglas

County is assessing board bills. Every time the defendants are incarcerated, they are billed by the county for the privilege of going to jail. When I opposed the practice, Judge Pickens defended it, claiming that the taxpayers shouldn't be obliged to pay for inmates' room and board. These board bills can create thousands of dollars in liability."

A layman on the court said, "Is that your only problem with Judge Pickens? You don't like his court costs?"

Was that Pickens's crony? I knew he had friends on the court. If I didn't up my game, I would be lucky to get out of there alive.

I turned to Addison, who took the cue. "What else did you observe, if anything?"

"Judge Pickens is a willing participant in jailhouse practices that violate the Eighth Amendment prohibition against cruel and unusual punishment."

The old judge stopped me again. His voice was firm. "Legal conclusions again, Ms. Foster."

I nodded. Again, I had forgotten which side of the witness stand I occupied.

Addison prompted me. "Please continue, Ms. Foster."

"On more than one occasion Judge Pickens lost his temper in court. In an irrational fit of anger, he found individuals in his courtroom to be in contempt, without just cause. When the individuals were incarcerated for contempt, they were subjected to confinement in a restraint chair used for discipline in the Douglas County Jail. The repeated use of the restraint chair in Douglas County causes physical and mental injury and is a form of torture. It can be fatal."

After I had made that statement, I paused to draw breath. The courtroom was silent while I sat, collecting myself. The layman, the one I suspected to be Pickens's inside man, opened his mouth to speak but shut it again, frowning.

Addison was looking better. Her skin tone had returned to a normal hue.

"How do you know this to be true? What is the source of your information?"

She had teed up the lead-in I'd scripted myself.

"I know about the restraint chair from personal experience."

And then I described it for them, the whole hideous story. I didn't leave out a single sordid detail.

CHAPTER 64

"NO FURTHER QUESTIONS," Addison said, taking her seat at the counsel table.

I remained in my seat. My time in the witness chair wasn't over. Pickens's attorneys had the right to cross-examine me.

Bracing myself, I focused on the senior attorney of Team Pickens, expecting the silver-haired King of the Alabama Bar to wage the attack. When Emma Hale pushed back her chair, it took me by surprise.

As she approached the witness stand, she reminded me of a cat stalking her prey—if cats wore stiletto heels and a string of pearls. But the gleam in her eye made it clear she was coming for me. Sending the woman on Pickens's team to cross-examine was a tactical advantage—no matter how relentlessly she bullied me, no one could accuse the Pickens team of misogyny.

"Ms. Hale, you may begin," the senior judge said.

She launched the attack with the first question.

"Ms. Foster, where are you currently employed?"

The flush returned to my face, even though the question wasn't unexpected. I had suggested to Addison that we should suck the poison on my employment status during my direct testimony, that it would be better to bring it up before the defense did, but Addison had disagreed.

"I don't currently have full-time employment. I've been doing some substitute teaching at Mobile public schools."

"No, no, no, I'll rephrase the question. Where are you currently employed in your capacity as an attorney at law, licensed by the state of Alabama?"

My face was hot. "I am not employed in that capacity. Not at this time."

At her counsel table, Addison's head was bowed over her legal pad. It looked like she was doodling, drawing arrows on the paper with her pen. I was determined to keep Pickens out of my line of vision, so I checked out Opal Ford. She sat two rows behind Addison, in the spectators' section. When we made eye contact, Opal's eyes darted away.

"Ms. Foster?"

The attorney's voice was sharp. I jerked my attention back to her. In a level voice, I replied, "Yes, Ms. Hale?"

"Would it be accurate to say that no one in the state of Alabama wants to hire you?"

That was a low blow, a dirty shot. She was starting to make me simmer. But I didn't permit it to show.

"My recent experience has shown that law firms are reluctant to make an offer of employment while the judicial complaint process is pending."

It was the plain truth. With a rueful expression, I turned and examined the faces on the long bench of the court. The one woman seated at the bench nodded in agreement. That was progress.

"It's a yes or no question, Ms. Foster, and you are under oath. Isn't it true that no lawyer, law firm, or agency wants to hire you to practice law?"

I kept my voice matter of fact. "Not at this time."

"And just to be clear, you were fired from your employment

in Douglas County, on the grounds of ineffective assistance of counsel—isn't that correct?"

Without hesitation, I responded, "That's what I was told."

The defense attorney gave a satisfied nod of her head. She flipped a page on the legal pad she held. Apparently, it was time for a different attack.

The next question was not one I had anticipated.

"Ms. Foster, when you lived in the city of Erva, were you ever pulled over for DUI?"

I almost stammered out my answer. "I have never been arrested for DUI. Never."

"That's not the question. In Erva, were you pulled over for DUI?"

It was so deceptive, such a patently unfair trick, that my carefully professional demeanor was shaken. "When I lived in Erva, I never had a drink. Not even in the privacy of my own home. I never purchased liquor. I'm a mother—"

"That's not responsive. I'll repeat the question. When you lived in Erva, were you ever pulled over on suspicion of DUI?"

In the spectators' gallery, Peg hunched her shoulders, bowing her head. When I saw the movement, I wondered: was that why she was present? To testify, in the event that I denied it?

I sat up straight. "There was an occasion when an officer claimed I had crossed the center line. He pulled me over for that."

"In the middle of the day? In front of a day-care center, right?"

There it was: the setup. My eyes scoured the room. The young officer who had written the traffic ticket wasn't present. In fact, no law-enforcement personnel sat in the Pickens cheering section. I didn't see any employees of the county jail, either. So they could raise suspicions against me without the possibility of resolution.

I said, "It was in front of a day-care center."

"And the officer required you to perform a series of drunk driving tests, correct? In front of the children?"

My breath was coming fast. "He did. And afterward, he wrote a ticket for careless driving. The matter is still pending."

I had refused to pay the fine because I wasn't guilty of the charge. The matter had been continued, in light of the judicial complaint.

The defense lawyer flipped to another page on her pad. "This dramatic tale you told, about your experience in the Douglas County Jail. Wow. It sounds like a Lifetime movie."

She paused, wearing a smirk on her face.

"Is that a question?" My voice was back under control again.

"The nasty tale you shared about the time you spent in jail— where is your documentary evidence to prove that it actually occurred?"

I turned, addressing the nine people at the bench. "I provided photographic evidence of contusions caused by the restraints they used to confine me to the chair. The court has seen those exhibits, during my direct examination."

Waving a dismissive hand, Ms. Hale said, "Yeah, we saw a picture of a bruise, didn't we? I'm inquiring about documentary evidence. You haven't provided the court with any records to back up your wild allegations—isn't that true?"

I met her gaze, head-on. "We subpoenaed the records. Douglas County claimed there aren't any. The evidence was destroyed, obviously."

She raised her hand. "The 'alleged' evidence, you mean."

I couldn't suppress the defensive note in my voice. "There were records. The jail has a log posted in the discipline room, an observation log for the use of the restraint chair. I saw a jail employee make a notation on the log when I was cuffed to the chair. I personally witnessed the employee writing on that log the county now claims they can't locate."

Ms. Hale gave her head a shake, as if confused. "What is the name of the individual who supposedly wrote on the log?"

"Grimes. Sherry Grimes."

Ms. Hale pivoted, looking around the courtroom, as if to hunt for the witness. "Is she here today? Will she be testifying in support of your story?"

Of course she wouldn't. Sherry Grimes wasn't going to support us, though Jay had tried to talk to her, months prior. She'd made her position clear.

When I didn't answer, Ms. Hale went on. "I assume she's not here because she denies it?"

I was trying to frame a civil answer when she spoke again. "So! Ms. Foster, who's going to play you in the movie?"

Dumbfounded, I said, "What?"

"This tale you've concocted—it sounds like you created it for the screen. Will you be portrayed by Amy Adams? She has your hair color, I guess. Or maybe Jennifer Lawrence? Who do you see up there, in your fondest hopes?"

Addison started to rise from her chair, thank God. She needed to object, to shield me from this ridiculous and offensive line of questioning. But the chief judge put a halt to it before Addison could protest.

"You are not required to answer that, Ms. Foster. Don't badger the witness, Ms. Hale."

I turned to the bench with a look of gratitude. That's when I saw that one of the members of the court was shaking with suppressed laughter.

He thinks this is funny?

When I turned back around, I caught sight of Opal, just before she slipped through the door and left the courtroom.

CHAPTER 65

I DIDN'T THINK the cross-examination would ever end. But when it finally did, they called a fifteen-minute recess. I tore out of the room, hunting for Opal, who hadn't returned to the courtroom. She wasn't seated in the hallway, so I checked the women's restroom. Every stall was empty.

Leaning against the wall, I pulled out my phone, praying to see a message from Opal. Her text was at the top of the screen.

It read:

> If I get up there, they're going to attack me just like they attacked you. And they'll demean Robert, insult his memory. I can't face it. Sorry.

My heart palpitated with an uneven rhythm, skipping beats. *I'm having a heart attack,* I thought, though I knew it was more likely a panic attack.

Directly under Opal's message, I had another new text. It was from Jay.

> I'm around the corner, at The Cat and the Fiddle.

"Finally," I whispered, grateful to learn they were nearby. Molly was probably suffering from the courtroom version of stage fright. Pocketing the phone, I charged out of the bathroom. Heads turned as I ran for the staircase, nearly tripping on the steps. I needed to collar Jay and get Molly into the hearing, stat.

The Cat and the Fiddle was a local bar and grill, a haunt for lawyers, legislators, and state employees. I pulled open the door and stepped into the restaurant. The tables were set up for lunch traffic, but it was early, just past eleven o'clock. Only one table was occupied, by a group of four people in business attire.

Frantic, I headed to the bar to ask where the restrooms were located. I suspected that Molly might be hiding inside a stall, like Addison had. The bartender was busy, wiping out glassware.

That's when I spotted Jay.

He sat on a high stool, huddled over the bar. When I called out, he turned his head toward me.

"Jay! Where's Molly? She's up next." I pointed at the door. "We've got to move fast. We're in recess."

He didn't jump to attention. In fact, he didn't move at all. A dark suspicion crawled up my spine as I strode up to him.

"Jay. Where is Molly?"

"She's in Erva. She wouldn't come with me."

His hands were wrapped around a lowball glass that contained a couple of ice cubes submerged in an inch of brown spirits. He raised the glass and drained it.

My pitch rose into falsetto when I said, "Are you drinking?"

He nodded his head slowly, as if I had posed a deep philosophical question. "I am. Actually, I'm about half drunk. And I intend to get all the way there before I leave."

The bartender was giving us the side-eye, but I didn't care. Clutching Jay's shoulder in a desperate grip, I twisted the fabric of his shirt in my fist.

"What's the matter with you? We have to be back at the hearing. The recess is almost over."

Jay lifted the glass, signaling the bartender. The guy poured another bourbon on the rocks, and Jay took a sip before he spoke.

"I had one job. Deliver Molly Zimmerman to the hearing."

I checked the time on my phone. It said I had exactly four minutes to get back to the hearing.

Jay repeated himself. He held up one finger, with an exaggerated histrionic gesture. "One simple task. Deliver Molly to the hearing. I blew it. I'm a failure, just like my dad always said." He raised the glass. "Looks like it's all on you and Opal. The two of you will have to carry the ball."

"Opal bailed before testifying."

In response to that news, he took a big swallow from the glass, squeezing his eyes shut with a grimace. After he swallowed, he whooped and said, "I've missed that burn."

I stepped back, looking at his slumped posture over the wooden bar. The plea came out before I could stop it. "What am I going to do?"

"You're asking me?"

Numb, I nodded.

He turned away from me. Facing the bar, he spoke to my reflection in the mirror behind the bar. "You can't count on me when the chips are down. I'm not reliable. But I'm really good company. You want to join me?"

The casual manner in which he had conveyed his betrayal stunned me into momentary silence.

He waved a hand at the bartender. "I need a drink for my friend."

A drink? A hot wave of fury engulfed me, restoring my voice. "I have one minute to get back."

I spun away from him, but Jay caught my hand.

"Martha, it's over. Sometimes the only thing to do is throw in the towel. And reach for sweet oblivion."

CHAPTER 66

SPRINTING BACK TO Dexter Avenue, I felt like I was headed for oblivion, but it wasn't sweet. It was bitter.

As I rode the elevator to the third floor, I watched the time on my phone: seven minutes late. I expected the hallway outside the courtroom to be empty when the elevator doors opened; everyone would be back inside the courtroom, listening to Addison Holmes throw in the towel, just as Jay had suggested. My testimony alone wasn't enough to convince the court to unseat a circuit judge.

When I stepped out of the elevator, I looked around in confusion. The hallway was packed. The sound of voices buzzed in my ears.

A hand clutched my shoulder—Addison, looking wild-eyed.

"What's going on? Where are they?" she demanded. "I had to ask the court to extend the recess. I can't find Opal Ford or Molly Zimmerman. They're not anywhere around, and Jay won't answer his phone."

I wrenched my shoulder out of her grasp. "Jay said Molly refused to come with him this morning. She won't be testifying at the hearing."

Addison literally wrung her hands. "What happened to Opal? She was in court this morning—we both talked to her."

"Opal left during cross-examination. She texted me. She said she changed her mind."

Addison looked stricken. "I don't believe it."

There was nothing to be gained by arguing the point. I pulled up the text and handed my phone over to her. As she stared at the screen, Addison's head started to shake.

"What am I supposed to do? We don't have any supporting witnesses? Just you and nothing else?" Her voice rose. "That's not enough. Do I withdraw the complaint?"

Over Addison's shoulder, I saw Pickens standing nearby, easily within earshot of our exchange.

"Lower your voice," I told her.

But she was already backing away from me. "I'm calling some other people on the commission. I need someone else to weigh in on this."

Addison ran off, leaving me alone in the hallway. Pickens watched her go, then turned his head my way. I looked for an avenue of escape, but there was no place to hide in the crowded hallway. I was cornered.

Pickens approached, a false expression of concern on his face. "The young commissioner sounds disturbed."

I didn't shrink from him, not at that point. It took a monumental effort, but I stood my ground.

He inched closer to me. "My gut tells me Addison Holmes is distraught because her case has fallen apart. I've seen that reaction before, in my years on the bench."

Pickens broke into a smile that didn't extend to his eyes. "The commission is about to lose their case against me. I'll walk out of here in triumph, my good name cleared. You know, a more generous man might decide to be forgiving, in the aftermath of victory."

I still didn't speak. But I backed away from him a step, to distance myself from those eyes and that smile.

"I confess, I'm not that man. I'll ruin you, Ms. Foster. You're going to lose your law license. I'm talking to my lawyers about a defamation suit against you, too. And I wouldn't be surprised if the Department of Human Resources receives calls accusing you of neglecting your boy."

The final threat broke my brave facade. I struggled to protest, but the words came out too strangled for speech.

Harold had been lurking nearby. He stepped up and appeared at Pickens's elbow. "Judge, I believe your lawyer is looking for you."

Pickens backed away, giving me room to breathe. "Thank you, Harold. Ms. Foster and I are done here anyway."

As Pickens made his way through the bodies clustered in the hall, I collapsed against the wall for support. I was seized by the urge to run away, to leave the Judicial Building, grab my son, and flee.

Summoning my strength, I tried to bolt, but Harold blocked me. "Martha, I believe I'd like to testify."

I shoved him, blindly seeking to escape. "Tell Pickens's legal team. Just get out of my way."

"Martha, you're not hearing me. I don't want to testify for the judge. I'm ready to testify against him."

CHAPTER 67

IT COULD HAVE been a trick. A ploy or a ruse, concocted by Team Pickens.

When Harold and I approached Addison, she was hesitant. Even after Harold revealed what the substance of his testimony would be, Addison wasn't sure she believed in Harold's sincerity.

She pulled me aside. "Can we trust him, Martha? The man works for Douglas County. He's been sitting right behind Pickens throughout the hearing, with the judge's other followers."

I stole a look at Harold. He pulled a plastic comb from his pocket and ran it through his thinning hair with a hand that trembled so violently, the comb fell to the floor. Bending over to get it, he had to struggle to maintain his balance.

I was torn, too. But I put on a brave face. "Harold is all we've got."

Addison looked over her shoulder at his hunched figure. Turning back to me, she said, "I need time! To prep him, take a statement, check out his story. Oh, God, I wish someone would take my call."

She hit a button on her phone but got no answer.

Her face twisted with an anxious grimace. "He's a wild card."

I couldn't deny it. But I was warming to the idea. "Let's play it."

"No lawyer in her right mind puts a witness on the stand without knowing exactly what he will say. You know that."

It's true. But I wasn't in my right mind at that point.

"Put him on. What is there to lose?"

"Besides this hearing? How about my reputation?"

The hallway emptied as people returned to the courtroom. We stood outside the door as the judges took the bench. Harold lingered behind us, waiting.

Addison took a deep breath. Our eyes met. It was now or never.

I followed her into court, with Harold bringing up the rear. When Addison called him to the witness stand, I stumbled into a seat, because my knees had turned to water.

As Harold limped up to the witness stand, I saw the shock reverberate at Pickens's counsel table. His lawyers huddled together, whispering in frenzied consultation. Only Pickens remained unruffled. I saw him in profile, as stoic as a marble statue. When the silver-haired lawyer tried to protest in his ear, Pickens raised his shoulders in an elegant shrug. And then he replied to his attorney. I couldn't hear the words, but it looked like he said, "It will be fine."

Harold raised his hand to take the oath. When he sat, he tugged at the jacket of his baggy gray suit, fastening the middle button of his coat.

Addison said, "State your name."

"Harold Lloyd Elmore."

"And what is your occupation?"

"I'm the bailiff of the Circuit Court of Douglas County, Alabama."

"How long have you served in that position?"

"Eighteen years. I was Judge Minor's bailiff for seven years. Wait, that's not right." Harold shook his head, as if he needed to clear it. "It was eleven years for Minor. When Wyatt Pickens took over after Judge Minor died, Pickens kept me on. That's been about seven years now."

He was nervous, already making errors in answers to the simple questions. The palms of my hands began to sweat.

"As bailiff in Douglas County's Circuit Court, what have you observed regarding Judge Pickens's handling of criminal cases?"

Harold shifted in the chair as his eyes flitted over to the defense table, like a scared kid checking out the school bully on the playground. "Over time, Judge Pickens started cranking up his court costs."

"Objection." The head lawyer stood, then paused, as if he was considering the grounds for the objection.

The chief judge didn't wait. "Overruled."

After the lawyer sat, Addison said, "What did you observe regarding costs?"

"They went sky-high. Because the judge decided to add on room and board for jail time, adding on those 'board bills.' Problem with that, most people in the county jail don't have that kind of money. So Judge would have them come back every week, to pay it over time. It increased the county coffers. Everyone in the county thought it was a fine idea."

Harold gripped the arms of his chair, as if he needed support. His voice was stronger when he said: "Everyone, that is, except the people who had to pay. It bothered me to see the judge using poor folks like a doggone cash machine."

Addison said, "How did Judge Pickens enforce payment of the court costs?"

"Folks paid or they went to jail. And once they were in jail, there was always the chance they would be put in the restraint chair." His voice dropped as he added: "People got to calling it the Pickens chair."

"Objection, hearsay."

"Sustained."

Addison gave Harold a reassuring nod. "What are you referring to when you say 'restraint chair'?"

His right hand clenched compulsively. "It's a chair in the discipline room of the county jail where inmates can be confined."

"Please describe the restraint chair and its function in the county jail."

Harold squirmed in his seat again, adjusting his position and extending his leg, as if attempting to find a more comfortable position.

"It's a big metal chair with four sets of handcuffs. Straps, too, made from the same material as seat belts in a car. A person gets strapped in a sitting position, with their ankles and wrists cuffed down, so they can't move at all. It's supposed to be used for inmates who are out of their head, from drugs or whatever. If they are restrained, the person who's out of control can't hurt a jailer or hurt themselves."

His description was consistent with my testimony: a good thing—we reinforced each other.

"To the best of your knowledge, under what circumstances are people placed in the restraint chair at the Douglas County Jail?"

Harold sighed, shaking his head. "Well, everyone knows Judge Pickens has a temper."

"Objection! Nonresponsive."

"Sustained."

Addison gave the court a nod and then turned her gaze back to Harold. Taking Harold's cue, she revised the next question. "In your experience, what did you observe regarding Judge Pickens's demeanor at the bench?"

Harold sneaked an apprehensive glance toward Pickens before he answered. "In court, Judge Pickens is prone to lose his temper. It doesn't happen every day—I'm not saying that. In fact, you never can predict when he'll blow his top. But when he does, Judge Pickens throws people in jail."

"Who? What people are you referring to, who get sent to jail?"

"Criminal defendants mostly. But I've seen him send lawyers, too, mostly in criminal cases. That's why Douglas County had to hire a full-time public defender some years back. Members of the local bar got skittish about accepting any criminal appointments."

"Did the judge ever send any court personnel to jail?"

I glanced over at Pickens. He leaned forward in his chair, his jaw locked. Though I couldn't see the look he fixed on Harold, I could imagine it.

Harold caught Pickens's glare. It rendered him mute. Long seconds ticked by. I edged forward on my seat, praying that he wouldn't cower under the judge's wrath.

Clearing his throat, Harold finally broke the silence. His voice shook when he said, "He put me in jail, a couple of years ago."

I heard whispers from the spectators' section behind Pickens. Twisting in my seat, I studied the faces of his supporters, searching to see whether Harold's revelation had shocked them. I didn't detect any surprise.

They already knew.

"Mr. Elmore, what circumstances led to your incarceration by Judge Pickens?"

He took a moment, gazing up at the dome overhead before he answered.

"The judge had been giving one of the public defenders a terrible time, a young fella who didn't know how to handle his clients too well. I thought somebody needed to say something, so I spoke up, told Judge Pickens he was crossing the line. I thought the judge would listen to me, we've known each other so long."

"What happened then?"

Harold bowed his head. "Judge Pickens called the sheriff's office. Had a detective take me over to the jail, because the judge said I'd been disrespectful to the court and needed a taste of discipline."

Harold sounded ashamed, as though the tale reflected poorly on him, rather than his tormentor. But listening to him, I could see the scenario just as clearly as if I'd been present that day, and it fired my ire to even greater heights. I was furious—angry for Harold, and for myself, and for all of the hapless victims of Pickens's abuse.

Harold continued. "When he strapped me into the chair, Detective Stanley shackled my feet, but he left my hands free. Stanley said he felt bad about having to do it to me. Me and Stanley, we've been in the Elks together for years. Rotary, too."

"How long did you remain in the chair?"

Harold looked up at the dome again, calculating the time. "Kept me there overnight. Fourteen, fifteen hours, I'd say. They come in real early the next morning, said Judge told them to let me out."

"What happened when you were released from the chair?"

He started to speak and then paused, shaking his head mournfully before he continued. "Well, there was a problem. You see, I'm diabetic, have been for years. I got the neuropathy, too. And by the time they took that cuff off my right foot, it had swelled up something terrible. I couldn't walk on it. A deputy had to take me home. When I got there, I could barely get my shoe off. Once I got it off, there was a big ulcer on that foot. It came on overnight, while I was in the chair."

"How do you know it developed while you were restrained in the chair?"

"Didn't have it before then. And I wasn't surprised to see it the next day. Because I had terrible pain while shackled up overnight, shooting pains going down that leg. It was something fierce." He shuddered.

"And then what happened?"

"It got infected—the ulcer. Diabetic ulcers are tricky, you know. There were complications—they had to amputate. That's when I got this."

Harold hoisted up his leg, extending his prosthetic foot for the benefit of the court.

Staring at the prosthetic device that protruded from the baggy leg of his trousers, my eyes pricked in warning. When the tears ran down, I wiped my eyes to scrutinize the horrified faces of the Court of the Judiciary. None of the nine were unaffected. Even the layman I had suspected of being Pickens's inside man rose from his chair to get a better look.

Addison said, "In the past year, do you have knowledge or information that Martha Foster was also subjected to that chair?"

Harold's face creased with deep lines of regret. "I was the one who took her over to the jail when Judge Pickens said she was in contempt, when all the lady did was plead her case to the court. And I saw her come back from the jail the afternoon of the next day, with those marks around her wrists and ankles. She looked a sight, I'll tell you." Harold closed his eyes as he repeated, his voice hoarse, "She looked a sight."

He fumbled in his pocket for a handkerchief, shook it out, and blew his nose into it.

Addison said, "Did you observe anything else on that occasion?"

"I don't know how to describe it any better. But when I saw her that day, I thought, *It's gone too doggone far*. Just the week before, I saw Judge Pickens send a gal to jail because he didn't like the look on her face. And then, putting Martha in the chair for being public defender...And the young defender before her, things got so bad, he hung himself."

I heard gasps in the courtroom before Pickens's lawyer jolted out of his chair. "Objection, hearsay!"

Before the court could rule, Harold grasped the arms of his chair and spoke directly to the lawyer. "It's not hearsay. I'm the one that found him, hanging by his neck in the public defender's office."

Harold looked up at the bench, addressing the judges of the court.

"He's gone too far. It's time to put a stop to it."

CHAPTER 68

ADDISON FOUND US out in the hallway, where Harold and I stood together in an empty circle of space. No one ventured near us after the conclusion of the evidence.

After Harold's testimony, the Pickens legal team called a string of his friends and neighbors to testify that he was a wonderful judge, a credit to the community, a peaceable man. They kept the courtroom staff off the stand. Following a frenzied consultation conducted in whispers at the counsel table, they rested— without calling Pickens to testify on his own behalf. It would be fascinating to learn the reason why. Did the prospect of submitting to cross-examination hurt his pride? Or were his attorneys afraid he would blow a fuse during testimony and injure his chances? I would never know.

When Addison joined us in the hallway, she spoke in a whisper, even though no one dared to come close enough to overhear. "They are about to announce the decision."

Harold nodded soberly. But I froze, too frightened to offer any reaction.

Addison inclined her head toward the courtroom. "Do you want to sit up front?"

Harold gave a thoughtful frown, looking down. "I believe I'll stand in the back. By the door."

"Me too," I said.

When Harold and I took our places along the back wall of the courtroom, I gazed into the upper gallery of the court. The balcony was no longer empty. A number of journalists had joined the bearded reporter from the local paper. I wondered how word had gotten out.

I was glad I'd followed Harold's suggestion. Stationed at the door, I could escape from the building unimpeded no matter what the verdict. After the close of evidence, I felt that the tide had turned in our favor. But it was impossible to know.

The room hushed as the nine judges of the Court of the Judiciary entered the courtroom and took their seats. My eyes darted frantically down the bench as I studied their faces, attempting to get a read on the decision.

The chief judge waited for the other eight judges to settle into place before proceeding. As I waited for the judgment, my heart palpitated. When my vision started to gray out, I gave my head a vigorous shake, sternly counseling myself: *No passing out now, Martha. It's the moment of truth.*

Nonetheless, the moment felt dreamlike as the judge held up a sheet of paper and began to speak.

"All members of this court, after serious consideration of the evidence and testimony presented at this trial, find by clear and convincing evidence that Wyatt Pickens, while in his role as circuit judge of Douglas County, Alabama, did willfully and publicly violate Canons 1, 2, and 3 of the Alabama Canons of Judicial Ethics." He paused, taking a deep breath before continuing. "Finding no other viable alternatives, this court hereby orders that Judge Wyatt Pickens be removed from his position as circuit judge of Douglas County, Alabama. This court is now adjourned."

I was afraid to trust my ears until Addison turned around and caught my eye, looking exuberant. That's when I let myself believe it.

It was over. It was over, and we had won. *We won.* We had beaten Wyatt Pickens. Bliss washed over me in a giddy wave. Harold began to slide down the wall. I grabbed his arm and pulled it over my shoulder, struggling to hold him upright.

"Harold!" I said in an urgent whisper. "Harold. You okay?"

Behind his bifocals, he blinked. "Yep."

"Harold. Did you hear the chief judge? Do you know what this means?" I was exultant.

Drawing a deep breath, he nodded. In a whisper, he said, "We'd better scoot on out of here."

While the court marched away from the bench, there was rustling among the Pickens supporters. I heard indignant whispers. That's when Harold and I made our exit. He was unsteady on his feet. I continued to prop him up, and we proceeded slowly to the elevator as people surged out of the courtroom.

Harold and I were the last to exit the elevator on the main floor. He still leaned on me for support. "I'm parked over in a handicapped spot. Awful sorry to trouble you, but I'm still a little light-headed."

"I'll help you to your car," I said.

It took a while to reach the front of the building. The press had set up microphones on the steps; journalists milled around, talking while they waited for the press conference. As we skirted the cluster of reporters and spectators, Pickens took a spot in front of the cameras.

I refused to look in his direction, but I couldn't escape his voice.

"This ruling today is a miscarriage of justice. When I took the bench, I swore an oath. Every day I served as judge in Douglas County, I upheld my sacred oath and did my duty to the citizens of this state. I have been unjustly accused, and today's decision is in clear disregard of truth and righteousness, because I have done what I was sworn to do."

Our progress along the pavement was excruciatingly slow. Harold was breathing hard. His prosthetic foot caught in a crack on the sidewalk, making both of us stumble. We were still on the outskirts of the crowd when Pickens called out.

"Two people are responsible for this cruel injustice I have suffered, and I see them, trying to scurry away like rats. When they lied on the stand, bearing false witness against me, they violated one of the Ten Commandments that formerly sat in a marble monument inside the building behind me. Those sacred words have been forcibly removed from the Alabama Judicial Building, but they still govern all of mankind."

Heads turned our way. I ignored them as I tried to keep Harold moving, but Pickens wasn't done with us. He raised a hand to the heavens.

"'False witnesses did rise up; they laid to my charge things that I knew not.'"

Pointing a finger of accusation at us, he quoted another passage.

"'A false witness shall not be unpunished, and he that speaketh lies shall not escape.'"

Harold froze, looking up at Pickens. I followed his gaze. Pickens stood on the steps with the limestone columns behind him, like an idealized Hollywood version of a fire-and-brimstone preacher. Confronted by the figure on high with his bizarre biblical threats, my victory high started to fizzle.

A reporter turned a camera on us, while another thrust a microphone in my face. "Do you have a comment?"

My biblical knowledge wasn't as extensive as Pickens's, but a verse popped into my head: the one about "an eye for an eye." It gave me my parting shot.

"Wyatt Pickens is fortunate that he's being judged on Alabama judicial canons. Because by Old Testament standards, Pickens should be walking on one foot."

The reporter grinned. I'd just given him the sound bite he needed. My spirits rose again with the realization that I had aided the goal of "justice for all" in Alabama.

I linked arms with Harold, and we resumed our march. We didn't cut an elegant figure as Harold leaned on me and we proceeded clumsily to his handicapped parking spot. In retrospect, we probably made a comical pair.

But as victory laps go, it was glorious.

CHAPTER 69

IN DECEMBER, WE had a spell of hot weather in Alabama. The day I drove through downtown Erva was unseasonably warm, with highs projected in the mid-80s.

That early afternoon, the holiday decorations were on full display, and old-fashioned tinsel garlands were suspended overhead from the streetlamps. I hadn't ventured back to Douglas County since Pickens's removal was announced and an interim judge was appointed. Aside from the silver and gold holiday garb, things looked unchanged, until I parked my car near the courthouse. The window of the public defender's office had a new name painted on the glass; he'd started the job a few weeks prior.

It was a short walk to my destination. This time, I had no trouble gaining access to the interior of the Douglas County Jail. Harold and I had agreed to meet inside the discipline room.

After I took the photos, we stood side by side, staring at the chair. Harold asked, "You got all the pictures you need, Martha?"

"I think so." To be doubly certain, I walked slowly around the chair, making a video. Once I'd come full circle, I pressed the button to turn off the camera.

I gave Harold a grateful look. "Thanks for the heads-up, Harold."

His face was solemn. "Well. When I heard they were getting rid of it, it struck me. You might need to get a last look at the dang thing."

He didn't add *to obtain evidence for your trial*. But the thought hung in the air between us, unspoken. My 1983 civil rights suit had been filed in federal court the prior week; the small Montgomery law firm I'd recently joined was handling the suit. We were suing a long list of defendants: in addition to the county, we named the particular individuals who had participated, including Judge Wyatt Pickens, Sherry Grimes, Detective Stanley, and Deputy Clark. I'd heard that Molly Zimmerman and her father were receiving legal assistance from the Southern Poverty Law Center. I didn't know Opal's status. When I'd called her after Pickens's removal was announced, she hadn't responded.

As for Harold, he hadn't revealed his intentions. And I hadn't asked.

A bang and a rattle sounded outside the door. Two county employees struggled to manipulate a big industrial dolly. One of the men said, "Hey, we need to get in here."

"Right. We'll get out of your way," Harold said.

I followed Harold out of the discipline room. As soon as we exited, the men pushed the dolly inside, smacking the doorframe as they entered. Once outside, Harold started to walk away; I reached for his sleeve, to stop him.

"Just one minute?" I said.

He nodded, taking a spot beside me along the wall. We waited.

I needed to witness it, to see them remove the chair. I had to be certain that it would no longer remain inside the jail.

The chair was heavy and awkward; both men cursed and grunted as they lifted and secured it on the platform. As they rolled it out the door, one of the men said to Harold, "Can you believe it? Never thought I'd see the day that they'd do away with the Pickens chair."

Harold's jaw twitched. "How about that."

Together, we followed them all the way outside and watched them load it into a truck. As the truck drove off, Harold said, "Satisfied?"

I nodded. The retirement ceremony was complete. And I had someplace to be, people to see. We walked together around the jail to the sidewalk leading back to the courthouse.

Harold paused before heading to the courthouse entrance. "I know it was an imposition, coming over here from Montgomery. But I'm glad you came. Pleasure to see you, Martha."

"My pleasure, Harold. And it's no inconvenience. I have a couple of clients in Erva, so I'll see them while I'm here. Multitasking, you know."

He looked surprised. "Clients? Here in Erva?"

"Yeah, a couple of criminal cases. They retained me recently."

"Retained" was a slight inaccuracy. The cases were not money-makers. But my new firm was willing to let me do some pro bono work; it was part of the firm's social justice profile.

Scratching his head, Harold said, "I reckon you'll probably still represent that young man who was living with you here in town. Haven't seen him around in a while. You meeting with him today?"

"Jay Bradshaw? No, I'm not seeing him today."

In fact, I had seen Jay the prior weekend. Andy and I had met him for breakfast at a diner in Montgomery. Jay was making strides in a twelve-step program and had recently been hired as a paralegal at the ACLU. He hoped that if he kept his feet on the path, he could get his license to practice law reinstated.

Harold lingered on the sidewalk. "Can I take you somewhere, give you a lift?" Hastily, he added: "Not that I think you'll run into any trouble around here. Folks are minding their p's and q's. It's real quiet since Pickens had his set-down."

"Thanks, but no." I nodded in the direction of the public defender's office. "The new PD said I could use his office space for my appointments today. I've been helping him with the transition."

"Well, then I guess that's that." He extended his hand. "You and your boy have a nice holiday." Squinting up at the sun, he said, "Sure don't feel much like Christmas, though, not with this heat."

I grasped his gnarled hand in both of mine. "Thank you, Harold. For everything. You're my hero—you know that?"

Embarrassed, he ducked his head and turned away. As he limped toward the courthouse, I hurried down the sidewalk to the public defender's office. I was running late.

CHAPTER 70

WHEN I OPENED the door to the public defender's office, both of my clients were waiting in the reception room. They looked up as I entered, squinting against the afternoon sun.

The door swung shut behind me. "Hi, Monique, Laila. How are you ladies doing today?" I said.

The women weren't strangers to each other, or to me. We'd all been locked up together, back in June.

Laila, who still looked like a high school kid, jumped out of her chair. "Didn't you tell me two o'clock?"

"Sorry, I know I'm late. I had some important business over at the jail."

The new PD emerged from the hallway, heading for the door. He acknowledged me with a friendly nod, pausing to say, "Hey, Martha—I have to run across the street. Will you be here for a while?"

"Sure. You want me to stick around until you get back?"

"If you wouldn't mind. Feel free to use the office if you're more comfortable back there."

He stepped out, sending the blinding glare of sunlight into the reception area again. When the door shut behind him, it took a moment for my eyes to adjust. Once my vision was restored, I glanced around the room. He'd made some upgrades, hanging framed prints of landscapes. And the waiting area boasted new furniture, an arrangement of office chairs and end tables, with a rack on the wall displaying pamphlets on the criminal justice process.

But I intended to take him up on his offer and conduct conferences in the privacy of my old office—his office now. Hoisting my bag onto my shoulder, I smiled at the women.

"Who's first today?"

Monique flipped her hand in Laila's direction. "I'm not in any kind of hurry. Let Laila go ahead. Young people are always in a big old rush. I'll just sit here and rest, enjoy the cool air in here."

Laila radiated eagerness. "Yeah, I've got someplace to be. You got any news in my case?"

In fact, I did: excellent news. After Pickens's fall from power, Doug Carson had exhibited a turnaround. In our interactions, he bent over backward to be fair and accommodating. In both Laila's and Monique's misdemeanor cases, Doug had offered plea bargains that could fairly be described as sweetheart deals.

"I sure do. We'll talk about it in the office. Go on back and take a seat."

She didn't need further encouragement. Laila disappeared down the hallway, and I started to follow.

Then I heard Monique heave a sigh. Glancing back, I saw her blot the perspiration from her graying hairline with a wrinkled Kleenex. She grimaced as she eased the heel of her foot out of her worn shoe.

When she caught me watching, she made a weary chuckle. "I walked over here today, instead of taking the bus. It was a fool thing to do. I didn't count on the sun being so hot in the middle of December."

I stuck my head into my old office, telling Laila: "I'll be right back. Just a sec."

I dashed out the door and down the sidewalk to the convenience store on the corner; they would have what I needed. Inside the store, I grabbed a jumbo cup and filled it with crushed ice, then hunted the cooler for the biggest bottle of water they sold.

It only took a moment before I was back inside the office. Monique lifted a hand to shield her eyes when I entered.

Unscrewing the bottle, I poured water into the cup, filling it to the brim. When I handed the cup to Monique, her brow lifted in disbelief.

"This for me?"

"Yes, ma'am." I held out the straw.

"Bless your heart, baby. I'm just parched."

She pulled the paper from the straw and took a long pull from the cup. After she drank, she closed her eyes and sighed out with relief.

"Martha, that hit the spot. But I'm sorry to put you to the trouble."

"No trouble," I said. "Just returning the favor."

She looked up and nodded, recollection in her gaze. We both remembered.

I headed back to my old office and sat in the chair next to Laila, who had waited with poorly concealed impatience. But she chilled out as I proceeded to lay out the details of the new plea bargain: time served, costs waived.

"What do you think?" I asked her.

She broke into a wide grin. "I can't lie. I'm glad as hell they locked you up with me in June. That was a lucky day, right? You're the best damn lawyer I've ever had."

Lucky?

Was I lucky to have been locked up? Recalling the agony of the Pickens chair, I thought calling it a "lucky day" was a stretch.

But it's funny how things turn out. In retrospect, Laila had a point. My jail time had paid off with a number of unintended consequences. It had been a game changer.

Sometimes the best education a lawyer can have is a short stretch of hard time.

POWER OF ATTORNEY

PROLOGUE

AS THE SKY began to lighten over the tree line just outside the city limits of Bassville, Arkansas, Amber Lynn Travis crept across the parking lot of a convenience store. Although the temperature was as cool as it would get that August day, sweat rolled from the back of her neck and under her armpits so that her tattered flannel nightgown clung to her skin.

The sign overhead read GAS-N-GO. Amber needed to get in and out of the store without paying. She was unaccustomed to taking things that didn't belong to her, but at twenty-three, she was also an old hand at doing what had to be done. She tiptoed to the storefront on bare feet and peered inside. She could see only one person through the glass: a beefy man in his thirties behind the cash register. As she watched, he disappeared through a door behind the counter.

Amber walked through the automatic door and, taking a covert look around, sidled down one of the snack-food aisles, leaving bloody footprints on the floor tiles.

She didn't mean to dally, but the dazzling array of candy slowed her down. She snatched a Snickers from the display, tearing off the wrapper and stuffing it into her mouth. The taste sparked a distant memory of the time before Mama got sick, saying "Snickers is best" as they shared candy from Amber's trick-or-treat bag.

Next, Amber ripped into a bag of Cheez-Its. She'd meant to be as quiet as a tiny mouse but made involuntary, guttural noises of pleasure as she swallowed them by the handful.

She hadn't eaten in over twenty-four hours since she'd been on the run. The last food she'd had was some dry dog kibble, found in a dirty metal dish outside the back door of a farmhouse. She'd consumed only a small portion—it had been harder to grind between her teeth than she'd expected—before a scruffy mutt with a loud bark had chased her off the property.

When the Cheez-Its were down to crumbs, she turned around and grabbed a bottle of water from inside the coolers. Nothing had ever tasted as sweet as that cold water.

Out of the corner of her eye, Amber saw the cashier return from the back room. She ducked down between the snack-food shelves, but the man must have seen her. He shouted, "Who's back there?"

Amber made for the door, her heart racing. It was stupid to have stayed for so long. Why hadn't she grabbed the goods and gone? She rounded the end of the aisle and slammed into a display of sunglasses, knocking it to the floor. She skidded over the scattered plastic frames and fell on top of them.

The cashier approached, gripping an aluminum baseball bat with both hands. The sight of the bat filled her with horror. Sweeping the sunglasses aside, Amber scrambled to her knees, desperate to flee, but her bloody feet made the floor slick, and she slipped and fell again.

It was no use. She braced herself for the blow, lifting her forearm in defense.

The cashier raised the bat like a Little League star, but then the glare on his face transformed. His stance relaxed as he looked down at her, slack-jawed. The baseball bat hit the floor with a clatter and rolled away. Amber followed it with her eyes, calculating the danger if she tried to make a grab for it.

But then the cashier squatted on his haunches and smiled at her, shaking his head.

"I can't believe it's really you. Everybody figured you was dead."

PART I

AUGUST

CHAPTER I

THE AIR-CONDITIONING vents blew frosty air in the Cook County, Illinois, courtroom. Despite the chilly blast, as we stood to hear the verdict, perspiration beaded on my upper lip. I swiped at it with the back of my hand, chagrined by the physical evidence of my nerves. I was twenty-eight, but this wasn't my first rodeo. I was defense counsel, second banana on this case to Todd Fisher, a top litigation attorney in our Chicago law firm of Garrison, Danforth, and Shook.

The bailiff handed the verdict form to the judge for review. The plaintiff, seated in a wheelchair at the other counsel table, let out a hacking cough that cracked the silence of the courtroom. I glanced over at the plaintiff's wife, wiping phlegm from his mouth with a wad of tissues. The plaintiff couldn't do it himself. He was quadriplegic.

Todd nudged me, and I hastily switched my focus to the judge. My co-counsel didn't like me acknowledging the plaintiff's distress.

The judge pored over the paper through his bifocals, then read aloud: "'We the jury find for the plaintiff, Parker Ray, and against the defendant, Fred Myers.'"

The verdict wasn't a shock. The defendant, an Illinois state senator, had been driving drunk down Wacker Drive in the late hours when he crashed into the plaintiff's car, causing his injuries. We represented the senator's insurance company. It was our job to minimize the damages. Still, I blinked when the judge read on, naming the total amount: one million dollars.

That figure was way below even our lowest expectations. The insurance company would've been grateful for a payout of five million. And since Illinois is a comparative fault state, the damages were further cut in half when the judge announced that the jury had awarded fifty-fifty blame to both parties.

We had just won. Big time.

Todd and I stood as still as statues, careful to disguise any reaction. The plaintiff's side, however, grew noisy. Mrs. Ray burst into sobs, tears running down her cheeks. Her husband, immobile in his wheelchair, lacked the power to give the jury the finger or shake an angry fist at the defense table.

Once the jurors cleared out, Todd wrapped me in a bear hug.

"It's a miracle," he whispered into my hair. "We did it. We are gods."

When he released me, I sat down and watched the plaintiff's wife wheel her husband from the courtroom, still weeping audibly. I tried to not calculate how little half a million dollars would stretch to cover his future care, once their lawyer took the first cut.

Todd was on his cell phone, reporting the victory to the office, when Martin Drew, the plaintiff's attorney, approached our table. I rose, extending my hand.

"Good job, Martin! Congrats on your verdict." He ignored my hand, and I awkwardly stuffed it into my pocket. As a small-town transplant to Chicago, I was still disconcerted when my Arkansas niceties were rejected.

"We intend to appeal," Martin said.

I glanced over at Todd, but he'd turned his back on us, continuing to crow into the phone. I kept my tone cool. "I'll tell Todd about the appeal as soon as he gets off the call."

Martin glared at Todd for a tense moment before pivoting back to me. "It wasn't just Todd. You are responsible for this, too, Leah. This is a miscarriage of justice," he said with emotion. "You beat it like a gong, from start to finish: my client takes antidepressants and anxiety medication. Using the stigma of mental illness to insulate the damned insurance company from justly compensating my client." Martin backed away from our counsel table. "I don't know how you can sleep at night," he added before striding away, slamming the wooden gate to the courtroom gallery. The sound made me flinch.

Actually, I hadn't been sleeping very well lately.

I hadn't been sleeping at all.

CHAPTER 2

I FIDGETED AT the defense table, longing to escape the window-less courtroom. The misery we'd caused hung in the air like a funk, making it hard to breathe.

But as the underling, I couldn't depart until Todd declared that it was time to go, and he wasn't done with his telephone victory lap. Law firm associates serve at the pleasure of the partners, but at least at Garrison, Danforth, and Shook, we associates were paid handsomely for our eighty-hour workweeks.

I pulled out my own phone, which I hadn't checked since turning it off early that morning. No attorney wants to risk angering a judge with a buzzing phone. When I scanned the call log, my brow wrinkled. I'd had six successive calls from my mother. Starting at nine in the morning, she had rung me every hour for six hours straight but never left a message.

I wondered what on earth was up. Mom and I didn't chat on the phone—at all. I tried to remember the last time we'd even spoken. Maybe Christmas? Our conversation had been a strained exchange of pleasantries. She'd asked what I was doing for the holidays, and I'd told her I was working on a brief, which had been partly true. I'd done some edits on my laptop while watching Bing Crosby and Rosemary Clooney in *White Christmas*.

Next, I checked my text messages. One was from my mother:

Your daddy is sick. We need you. I AM DESPERATE. Come home.

"What the hell?" I whispered. My father, the formidable Walt Randall, was never sick. What was going on back home? I read the text again, as if it might reveal a hidden meaning.

Todd Fisher shook my shoulder and laughed at my blank expression when I looked up. "What's the matter, Leah? You look like you've seen a ghost. Let's pack up here. The big man is meeting us for a drink."

I knew who he meant. In the firm of Garrison, Danforth, and Shook, only Craig Shook was alive and kicking. The other founders had gone on to their eternal reward—or their eternal damnation, in the opinion of some legal peers. But Shook still presided over matters of importance, and if he wanted to raise a glass with Todd and me, we were in high cotton, as my dad used to say.

I put our files into their leather cases while Todd piled them onto a dolly. He couldn't keep a shit-eating grin off his face. "Since I'm the partner, and I was first chair on this case, they'll hand me all of the credit for this win," he said, generously adding, "but I want you to know, I'm sharing the glory. You were the one responsible for uncovering the medical records of his treatment for depression."

It was true, just as Martin had said. I was responsible.

Todd went on. "I might have missed that, since it had nothing to do with the injuries from the collision. It was freaking brilliant to flip the focus from the senator's negligence to the effect of the plaintiff's mental stability at the time of the incident. You spun it like an old pro."

I looked at the courtroom exit, wishing I could run away from the sound of Todd Fisher's voice.

He tipped the dolly of file boxes back on its wheels. "Didn't you tell me your father's a trial attorney? Somewhere in Arkansas? He'd sure be proud of you today."

I laughed, but it came out like a dry cackle. *Your daddy is sick.* I saw my mother's text again in my mind's eye. When Todd glanced at me side-eyed, I cleared my throat and said, "He wouldn't be. He's a plaintiff's lawyer. Solo practitioner."

Todd made a dismissive noise, blowing out his lips. "No profit in that, not in the long run. The real money is in our work, insurance defense. If I teach you nothing else, remember this: every plaintiff's case has an Achilles' heel, just like this one. You found it, Leah. And we took his golden ticket away."

He wheeled the dolly around, waiting for me to take it. "Load these boxes into your car and run them to the office. Then meet me and Shook at Gibsons."

I stared at the boxes. They represented months of labor—labor we'd devoted to shortchanging a quadriplegic man because he'd had the common misfortune of suffering from depression and anxiety.

"Leah. Wake up." Todd's fingers snapped in front of my face. "Don't stand there with your mouth hanging open, you Arkansas cracker. Move! Boxes. Car. Gibsons."

I experienced a moment of dazzling clarity.

"No," I said.

He squinted at me, not comprehending. "No? No what?"

"No, I'm not going to Gibsons. And I'm not toting your files back to the office."

Affronted, Todd drew himself up to his full height, putting me at about eye level with his meticulously folded silk pocket square. "Excuse me? Are you fucking with me?"

I lifted my own bag and pushed open the gallery gate with the same energy Martin Drew had. Its bang had a satisfying ring.

"I quit," I said. I didn't look back.

CHAPTER 3

THIRTY MILES AFTER crossing the Arkansas state line, just outside the city limits of my hometown, I pulled into the local Gas-N-Go.

I parked right in front, pausing to frown at a young hoodlum nonchalantly puffing on a cigarette while he filled the tank of his battered Chevy pickup. A Confederate flag flew from the bed of the truck. *Hello, Bassville.*

The front door of the Gas-N-Go bore a pink Missing poster that had been updated with a black marker: *FOUND!* it announced.

I walked in, heading straight for the restroom. I hadn't been back in years, but nothing at the store had changed. After washing my hands in the scummy bathroom sink, I wiped them on my jeans— more sanitary than anything in the women's restroom. When I emerged, the cashier called out to me.

"Restrooms are for customers only. You gotta buy something."

Leah, you're home, I thought, and examined the beverages in the case near the register.

"Do you have any sparkling water?" I asked.

The cashier gave me an expressionless once-over. He looked faintly familiar but was older than me. "We got club soda. It ain't cold, though."

I nodded. As I opened the cooler door and stared at the contents, I was tempted by my old favorite: Dr Pepper. I pulled out a sixteen-ounce bottle.

When I handed him my debit card, the cashier looked at it and laughed. "You're Walt Randall's girl."

"That's right."

"I ain't seen you around here in a dog's age. Didn't even recognize you. Looks like you lost a ton of weight."

A ton. People actually think it's a compliment to say that.

"Yep," I said. "You done with my card?"

He handed it back. "I heard you went up north and never come back."

"Just goes to show you," I said as I headed for the door. "You can't believe everything you hear."

I pulled out of the lot and nearly choked on a giant swallow of Dr Pepper as I passed the famous Bassville city limits sign.

WELCOME TO BASSVILLE!
HEAVEN ON EARTH!

The funniest thing about the sign wasn't just that it proclaimed my backward, narrow-minded hometown to be "heaven on earth"—the knee-slapper was that local pranksters would periodically sneak out at night and paint over the letter *B.*

Neighboring communities had adopted "Assville" as our nickname. Opposing schools would chant it in the bleachers at ball games. In my head, I'd done the same, though I learned to be careful when speaking aloud. The first time I openly referred to our town by the moniker, we were driving home from church. My dad, a flag-waving military vet, had pulled the car over and ordered me to walk the rest of the way home—just a mile or so, but it was a hot day and I was a fat kid. I'd trudged along in my church shoes, plotting my escape from Assville, Arkansas.

Eight summers later, I got out. To everyone's surprise, I was accepted into Northwestern University's Pritzker School of Law. I packed my bags, leaving behind all of my U of A Razorbacks regalia, and headed north. I lived on student loans, kept my nose to the grindstone, and landed the highest-paying job in my graduating class, as an associate for Garrison, Danforth, and Shook. I couldn't have chosen a job better designed to earn my father's disapproval.

So what the hell, I thought as I pulled into my parents' driveway, *am I doing back here?*

CHAPTER 4

I TOOK A moment to gaze at the house I'd left six years ago. It was a pretty house, a white Dutch colonial with green shutters, a sloped gambrel roof, and my mom's red crape myrtles flanking the front door—though I noticed the lawn was uncharacteristically overgrown and the paint was peeling on the shutters.

I turned the knob of the front door and let myself in. Downstairs was empty, but I heard footsteps overhead.

"Mom?" I called, walking up the staircase. "You up there?"

"Leah?"

I followed her voice up to my old bedroom, still furnished in schoolgirl aqua and white. Mom was buried in the closet, shuttling hangers. Some of my old clothes lay on top of my white four-poster bed. Others had been tossed into a heap on the floor. My mother turned to face me, reflexively running her fingers through her hair to fluff it out.

She needn't have bothered. Barb Randall—first runner-up for the title of Miss Arkansas, 1988—always looked put together. It was a gift.

Mom let out a sad-sounding laugh and came over to give me a quick embrace. I broke away hastily and nudged the pile of clothing on the floor with my toe. "What are you doing in here, Mom?"

She took a breath and sat on the edge of the bed, pushing garments out of the way.

"It's the awfulest thing. There was a murder right here in Hagar County, a farm couple shot and killed, and their house burned down."

"Wow." I was genuinely surprised. Assville was generally a sleepy community. "Anyone I'd know?"

"They were poultry farmers, kept to themselves. But they were your daddy's clients, and they had a younger cousin who lived with them. She escaped. So the ladies in our prayer circle are putting together care packages for her. Poor girl doesn't have a stitch of clothing, honey. It all burned up in the fire."

My mom started folding a church dress I'd last worn in 2013. She cut an anxious glance at me. "I didn't suppose you'd mind my giving her your old clothes, Leah. Do you?"

"No, please. Take whatever you want." I surveyed the clothes tossed around the room: old U of A garb, skirts and jeans I recognized from high school.

"That's what I thought. After all, these things don't fit you any-more." She reached out and squeezed my hand, smiling proudly. "Isn't that great?"

I didn't answer. It was still a touchy subject between us.

Mom picked up a Razorbacks hoodie, eyeing the ample garment dubiously. "I expect these things will be way too big for Amber, too. But we've started a GoFundMe account, and people are very supportive. She'll get to buy new things real soon."

I'd heard enough about my jumbo clothing. I pulled the bedroom door shut so we wouldn't be overheard.

"I want to know about Dad. You said you wanted to tell me in person. Well, I'm here. Tell me, straight out. Is it cancer?"

Mom dropped her head and closed her eyes. "Not cancer," she said. "It's worse than cancer."

I slumped onto the bed beside her. Since receiving her text, I'd prepared myself for a cancer diagnosis. I put my arm around her shoulders.

"What's worse than cancer?" I asked.

Her answer would've knocked me flat if I'd been standing.

"It's Alzheimer's. Your daddy has early-onset Alzheimer's."

CHAPTER 5

MY ARM FELL from my mother's shoulders. I jumped off the bed and faced her. "That's impossible. He's only sixty-four."

She didn't argue. Her weary eyes met mine, her face more worn than I remembered. With robotic precision, she turned and folded the nearest garment, a yellow blouse.

"This was always such a good color on you, Leah. You know, not everyone can wear it. You're lucky."

When she reached for another item, I grabbed her wrist. "Mom. How long has this been going on? Why did you hide it from me?"

With a pinched face, my mother turned on me. "How am I hiding anything from you? You don't check in, you're not around. You're the one who's hiding." She tugged out of my hold and rubbed her wrist.

I opened my mouth to contradict her, but a pang of guilt made me hush. Six years was a long time between visits home—no denying that.

She smoothed the blouse over her lap. "When his dementia first came on, I tried to make excuses. I thought, maybe that's what happens when you marry a man who's ten years older—they start slipping a little while you're still in your prime. But he changed so fast."

A sob broke from her chest. The sound alarmed me. The Randalls weren't prone to crying; we had a stiff-upper-lip ethic. I felt like everything from my youth was careening out of control.

I handed her a T-shirt from the clothing pile. She dabbed her eyes with it.

"Walt was a powerhouse in this town. Everyone looked up to him." She huffed a sad breath. "He never cared much about accumulating money, but he was a good provider. Now I can't even pay the bills."

I shook my head in disbelief. "Mom, please—you're being dramatic. You and Dad must have savings. IRAs. Mutual funds. What about disability insurance? That's the kind of thing he'd have done, just in case. I don't believe you can be that hard up."

Her eyes flashed. She jumped up and tossed the yellow blouse onto the bedspread. "You don't believe me? Fine—I'll show you."

The wooden staircase creaked as I followed her downstairs to the back of the house, where a small sunroom served as my dad's private study. The door was ajar; Mom gave it a shove and walked right up to the desk. I lingered outside the doorway, hesitant.

Dad's home office was always forbidden territory. From day one, it had been impressed upon me that the sunroom was Dad's private space, where I was not permitted. Though I never heard him order my mom to stay out, I'd only known her to cross the threshold once a week, armed with the vacuum cleaner and a dust rag.

I had rebelled against the policy just once. I had been wild to get my driver's permit, and needed my birth certificate, which I knew would be in the study. As luck would have it, Dad came home early that day and caught me looking. I always wondered whether Mom had called him to rat me out.

I wasn't permitted to take the driver's exam for another three months.

So it was jarring to see Mom now sitting at Dad's desk, jerking the top drawer open. She pulled out a handful of correspondence marked "First Community Bank of Bassville," then slapped the checking account register beside it, next to a stack of credit card bills.

I remained frozen until Mom waved me over with an impatient frown.

"This is the checking account. We're overdrawn. I got a new notice this week." She shuffled through the bills. "Here's Visa and Amex. No payments since May. Look for yourself if you don't believe me."

I couldn't. It seemed too intrusive. "What about your savings?"

From a separate drawer, she pulled out a small ledger. "The savings had only enough money in it for six months. It's all gone. And there's no income coming in."

I examined the paperwork scattered across the desk. From my cursory look, it painted a grim picture.

"What do you think you're doing in here?" Dad's rumbling bass voice, coming out of the darkened hallway, still made me shrink even after six years away. "This is my study. You know perfectly well that I don't want to be disturbed in my workplace."

I glanced at my mother. But if Mom was intimidated, she gave no sign of it. She closed the ledger and, in a pleasant voice, said, "I was just looking over the bills, Walt."

"That's not your job."

"Honey, I'm just giving you a hand like I did last month. Remember?"

Dad stepped into the sun-filled room. He was thinner by twenty pounds or more, and his clothes were too large for him. His belt, buckled on the tightest notch, sat loose on his middle, and the collar of his shirt gaped. On his feet were cheap athletic shoes fastened with Velcro.

He didn't look at me. He kept his focus on the desk, still covered with bank statements and bills. When he spoke this time, his voice had a quaver.

"I've always handled the bills. Financial matters are my department."

"Well, I'm helping you now," Mom repeated, then said brightly, "Walt, did you see? Leah's here."

I stepped away from the desk. "Hi, Dad."

Without acknowledging me, Dad walked in front of the desk and closed the checkbook register. When he bent over the desktop, the afternoon sun burned through the windowpane beside him, making his scalp shine under his thinning hair.

"I wanted to see you all, see how everyone's doing," I told him.

When my father still didn't respond, Mom piped up, "Leah's come all the way from Chicago."

That's when Dad finally looked up. His eyes sought out and bored into mine.

"Law school," he said.

I waited for the follow-up, but it didn't come. "What about law school?" I asked.

"Do you like it?"

"What?"

A wave of irritation passed over his face. Not an unfamiliar expression in our relationship. His voice was stronger when he repeated his question.

"Do you like it? Law school. How are your grades?"

Oh, no.

Mom was right. Dad didn't remember.

CHAPTER 6

I SLIPPED OUT of the house early the next morning. Mom had told me I should investigate the state of affairs in Dad's office, and after yesterday's shock, I was inclined to agree.

The Randall Law Office was a tidy one-story building located on a corner, across the town square from the historic brick courthouse. I turned the key and shoved the door with my shoulder, like my dad always had. Flipping on the overhead light, I looked around in shock.

Six years had wrought more changes inside the office than outside. Dad had kept his office orderly; in fact, he had run it with military precision. His longtime secretary, Beverly Shirk, always had joked about working for a "neatnik." But now I saw the reception area was in shambles. Files and legal documents were scattered across the floor. The trash can lay on its side, papers spilling out. Beverly's desk was piled high with armloads of files.

I glanced into the library at the back. It was also a mess. I opened the door across from Beverly's desk and entered Dad's private office. His desk was strewn with paperwork, and the drawers sat half open. I pulled the high-backed leather chair up to his desk. First tossing a handful of papers to the side, I sat in his seat and turned the computer on.

I thought of capable Beverly and picked up the landline to call her, but it was dead. I pulled out my cell to dial her number. She picked up after three rings.

"Beverly! This is Leah." I paused, one awkward beat. "Leah Randall, Walt's daughter."

Her laughter was warm. "So you're introducing yourself to me now?"

"I've been out of pocket for a while. I figured you'd have forgotten all about me."

Mock sternly, she said, "I ought to get after you, running off and leaving us all like you did. Why, you disappeared into thin air."

I cut to the chase. "Beverly, I'm back to help Dad wrap things up around here. What days do you still work for him?"

"Sweetie, Walt let me go six months ago, around Presidents' Day. When he said I shouldn't bother coming in, I thought he was just talking about the holiday—but he made it clear that I didn't need to come back to the office at all."

"Oh, Beverly. I'm so sorry."

"No, no, no! We all get older, Leah; it's just the way of things."

Another call was ringing in on my cell; I checked the screen. It was from Chicago. I let it go to voicemail.

"Beverly, could I come by and visit with you sometime soon? It would be really helpful."

"Gosh, yes. I'd be tickled to see you."

After we made a date, I focused on the office email account, crowded with unread emails. Most of them were from the circuit clerk's office. How many deadlines had Dad missed? Had he committed malpractice? The consequences could be disastrous.

I saw a recent email from Heritage Funeral Home with "Maggards" in the subject line. Curious, I clicked on it.

Hi Walt,

The sheriff's office wants to drop off Dale and Glenna Maggard's remains after they're done with them. There's not much left of the

bodies after the fire, but the sheriff says that Dale and Glenna deserve a Christian burial. I don't dispute that. But who's going to pay for it? Their next of kin is that little cousin of theirs, and she's not right in the head. I heard around town that you were their estate attorney. Did they have burial insurance? Let me know what you think!
Yours in Christ,
Jim Tucker

The email from the undertaker had to be connected to that local homicide my mom had mentioned. I wondered again what the hell I was doing back in Assville.

Swiveling in the chair, a photo on the credenza caught my eye. A framed snapshot from back when people still took pictures with film. I picked it up for a closer look. It was Dad and me latched into a bright blue seat of a Ferris wheel at the county fair. I must have been eight or so. My mouth was open wide in delight. His arm was around my shoulders. Mom had probably taken the picture. Looking at it, my eyes grew wet.

I set it back down on the dusty credenza and decided that I'd best head out of the office and go to the courthouse.

The dust in Dad's office was making my allergies act up.

CHAPTER 7

THE SECURITY LINE at the courthouse was short, but the elderly man in front of me kept setting off the metal detector.

"Did you take your keys out of your pocket?" the uniformed deputy asked.

"Yes, sir. And you've got my belt."

"Well, let's give it another try." No one appeared to be in any hurry.

A man wearing the blue uniform of the sheriff's office trotted down the stairs toward me. I did a double take.

"Danny Minton?" I broke into a smile of genuine pleasure. He'd filled out since high school, but it looked good on him. "When did you go into law enforcement? I thought you joined the army after high school."

"Leah Randall." We hugged, and he took my elbow, bypassing the security station. "When did you get back into town?"

"Just yesterday. I had no idea you're in charge of law and order around here."

"When I came home from the army, seemed like the sheriff's office might be a good fit." The sunlight from a nearby window danced off the brass badge pinned to his chest.

"I hope your mom's doing well," I said. I was prepared to lie in the event Danny inquired about my parents.

"She is, thank you. She's got a new lease on life these days. She's helping take care of the baby now that my wife's back to work."

"Wife?" I echoed. Then: "Baby?"

Before he could elaborate, his phone buzzed. As he checked the screen, I buried the brief vision I'd had of a romantic hometown interlude with Danny Minton.

Pocketing his phone, he said, "It's the sheriff. He's got everyone working overtime, trying to solve a double homicide in the county."

"Was it a couple named Maggard? And there was a fire?"

Danny grimaced. "That's right. Hell of a deal. We're sifting through ashes. Literally."

"Do you have anyone in custody?"

"We don't even have a suspect. And the only witness hasn't given us any information we can use." His phone buzzed again. "I've got to run. Good to see you, Leah."

My heels echoed on the tile as I made my way to the circuit clerk's office. Under the county seal, PHIL BENSON, CIRCUIT CLERK was painted in fresh black paint. I knew the name, but the man in the starched oxford shirt I saw was a far cry from my old disheveled classmate.

"Phil?" I said, my voice uncertain. He looked at me, his expression quizzical; he was having trouble placing me, too.

"Leah," I said. "I'm Leah Randall."

"Leah! Good to see you." Making his way to the long counter separating the public from the administrative staff, he reached across it to shake my hand. "What can I do for you?"

I lowered my voice, hoping the entire courthouse wouldn't witness our exchange. "Phil, I was hoping we could talk about my dad's cases. I saw the emails from your office."

"Oh, thank God," he said, visibly relieved. "I've tried to keep Walt abreast of things, but I haven't heard a word back." He leaned over and spoke into my ear, his voice low. "I didn't know how much longer I could go without notifying the Arkansas Bar Association."

I backed away, raising my chin with a defiant tilt. "That won't be necessary," I snapped. "I thought I would enter my appearance in his cases. Seems like the simplest way to handle it."

Phil walked around the counter. "You don't know how happy I am to hear that you'll shoulder Walt's caseload. Are you licensed to practice here?"

"Yes, actually." My former firm in Chicago liked their attorneys to have dual licenses. I'd considered a visit home when they flew me to Little Rock to take the Arkansas Bar Exam, but I had decided against it—besides, Bassville wasn't anywhere near an airport, I'd rationalized.

A man walking by the door of the circuit clerk's office stopped midstep. I recognized him as Shelby Searcy, the county prosecutor for this judicial district. From his first day on the job ten years ago, Searcy demonstrated a marked fondness for seeing his picture in the local newspaper and bragging about his trial record.

He leaned in the doorway, grasping the frame. "Are you Walt Randall's daughter?"

"Yep—I'm Leah Randall. Nice to see you." I stuck out my hand. He gave it a brief shake.

"Do you know what's going on in your father's practice?" he asked. Unlike Phil, Searcy hadn't bothered to modulate his voice. I saw three employees turn to stare.

"I'm here to find out." I didn't elaborate.

"Walt's ineptitude is causing major problems, and I don't intend to tolerate it any longer. He needs to surrender his law license."

My heartbeat accelerated. Hearing Searcy call my father inept and demanding his license in that high-handed way got my dander up.

"I don't see why this is your problem, Searcy. Dad hasn't taken criminal cases in years."

He got in my face. "It's a problem for me because I'm an officer of the court. And I have a county to run."

"Really?" I said, deadpan. "You run the whole county?"

At that, he showed his back to me and addressed the circuit clerk. "I need to see you in my office, Phil. Ten minutes."

He walked away without waiting for a reply. Phil watched him go, his eyes hooded, then turned to me. "Come back at 1:00, Leah. We'll sit in my office and go over Walt's cases, see where he stands on the docket sheets."

"Thank you, Phil. I appreciate it."

"Not a problem. Your dad is the reason I'm here."

I gave him a curious look, and he went on.

"I was in a car wreck when I was a kid—a bad one. Do you remember that? Fourth grade?"

Did I? Phil and I hadn't been close. If he'd missed school, I might not have noticed.

"Walt took my case. The settlement was substantial—a fortune in my daddy's eyes."

One of the women in the front office called out, holding the receiver of a landline phone. "Phil? It's Shelby Searcy."

"Take a message," he said. That made me smile.

Phil continued. "Walt tied it up—the money for my injuries. So that Daddy couldn't blow it. That money put me through college, paid for my degree in public administration."

"I didn't know," I said. It was true. Dad had never spoken of it.

"I'll see you after lunch," Phil said, then whispered: "If it weren't for Walt Randall, I'd be working at McDonald's."

CHAPTER 8

AMBER PEERED THROUGH the plastic blinds on her living room window. She counted a whole mess of people in the parking lot below, carrying bags and boxes.

The knock on the door made her start. She shouldn't be so jumpy; it was just a bunch of old ladies, like a brood of hens. On the other hand, Amber knew what hens were capable of. The first time Amber had seen the hens peck another chicken to death, she'd hid in the red shed and cried all afternoon long.

She opened the door a crack and peeked through. "Hello?"

A middle-aged woman with dyed blond hair and diamonds in her earlobes pushed the door open. "Amber! I'm Kate Cole. My husband, Hopp, owns this apartment complex." She walked right in, the other women following at her heels.

Kate dropped a brown grocery bag onto the kitchen counter. "We've come from Evangel Presbyterian of Bassville. When our prayer group heard your story, we knew we had to take you on as our special project."

All the eyes in the room fixed on Amber. Self-conscious, she ducked her head and looked down. "Thank you, ma'am," she whispered.

Kate turned to rummage inside her grocery bag. "Where's that cell phone? Do you have it, Barb?"

A pretty woman holding a black garbage bag looked startled. "No, Kate. I gave it to you. You said you'd present it to her." Barb clutched the plastic bag to her chest. "I have the clothes."

While Kate dug inside her purse, a stout white-headed lady said, "Can we set these groceries in the kitchen?"

"Not yet," Kate said.

"My arms are tired," the lady complained.

"Oh, for heaven's sake. Go ahead, then." Kate pulled a phone from the deepest recesses of her bag. "Here it is! Amber, we got you a cell phone. Have you ever used one?"

Amber shook her head. "No, ma'am. My cousin Dale wouldn't have one on the farm. He said the government was listening in on folks from different planets."

The ladies clucked at that. Kate took Amber by the hand and pulled her down beside her onto the couch. While Kate demonstrated the use of the phone, Amber watched the other women unpack the bags and boxes. She saw cans of pineapple and vegetables and Campbell's soup being stacked on the countertop, eggs and milk getting stowed in the refrigerator.

Kate picked up on Amber's distraction. "Do you think we got everything you need?"

"Yes, ma'am."

"Is there something special you'd like?"

Amber turned to her. "Candy?"

Kate laughed so loud it made Amber wince. And when Kate laughed, the other women laughed, too. Amber wasn't dumb; she knew what to do. She stretched her face into a wide smile and pitched her voice high, like a little old kid. "Ha, ha, ha. I like candy."

Kate's hand reached out and covered Amber's in a tight grip. "We're taking care of you, sweetheart. And that means nutritious meals. But I know that young people like sweet things. Girls, what do you say we open an account for Amber at Sunrise Donuts?"

The pretty woman knelt in front of the couch with her big black plastic bag. "Amber, I'm Barb."

"Barb," Amber repeated, thinking, *the pretty one.*

"I have a daughter who's about five years older than you. I brought lots of her old clothes for you."

Amber smiled. "Thank you, ma'am."

Barb lowered her voice. "I can tell that they'll be too big on you, but these things are just temporary. Our prayer group set up a GoFundMe for you."

She paused, and although Amber didn't know what a GoFundMe was, she knew what to say. "You all are so nice."

"Oh, honey." Barb patted Amber's knee. "So you'll be buying new clothes you can pick out for yourself soon. I hope these things of Leah's will help in the meantime."

The women had gathered in a tight circle around the coffee table in the living room. The white-headed one said, "We should pray."

Kate took Amber by the hand and pulled her into the circle. "Would you like that, Amber? We should give a prayer of gratitude for your escape from harm. And a prayer of thanks for the lives of your guardians, the Maggards."

"That'd be real nice," Amber said.

The women bowed their heads. Kate got to do all the praying out loud—that came as no surprise. It was a long prayer, and Amber's attention wavered, but when they all chorused "Amen," Amber echoed it. Then the circle broke up, the women picking their way through the parcels to get to the door.

Barb approached Amber and pulled her aside. "I want you to take this." She pressed a small card into Amber's palm. "It has my daughter's phone number on it. Now that you have a phone, you can call her."

"What for, ma'am?"

"Honey, my husband was your family's attorney," Barb answered, fluffing her hair, even though it didn't look messy. "A lawyer. You understand?" When Amber nodded, Barb looked relieved. "He wrote their wills, and there should be a copy of them at his office."

Kate called from the door. "Barb, do you want to ride with me? Because I'm leaving."

Barb glanced at Kate, then took a step in the direction of the door. To Amber, she said, "You call my daughter, Leah. She's helping out with her daddy's cases. She'll know what to do."

Amber was glad to see the door close behind the women. Looking at the card in her hand, she read aloud: "Leah Randall, Attorney at Law, Chicago, Illinois."

Then she tossed it onto the coffee table, next to the phone. Amber didn't rightly know where Chicago was. But now that she actually had a telephone, she was inclined to use it. Maybe she'd give Leah Randall a call.

CHAPTER 9

ON TUESDAY MORNING, I sat next to Dad at the breakfast table and watched him pick at his scrambled eggs. As I sipped my coffee, I mentally ran through the questions I'd been waiting to ask him. Mom believed that his mind was sharper in the a.m.

I kept my voice casual. "I saw Phil Benson yesterday."

Dad fixed his eyes on his plate. "That's nice."

"He said some really nice things about you."

At that, he looked up. "Did he? Who's that again?"

"Phil Benson. The circuit clerk."

"Where'd you run into him?"

I took another sip of coffee, toyed with the handle of the mug. "The courthouse."

"What were you doing at the courthouse?"

"Talking to Phil about some of your cases."

Dad's brows drew together, his expression guarded. "Why were you talking about my cases?"

I stood up, holding my mug. "I'm going to get more coffee. You want some?" I carried the carafe over and filled his cup too. Caffeine might help, I figured. "I was thinking I might enter my appearance, as your co-counsel."

"What for? Why would you do that?" He pushed his cup away, and coffee sloshed onto the oak tabletop.

"Oh, just to give you a hand. Since I'm in town."

"You're not licensed to practice in Arkansas."

His voice had an edge, but it was a relief to hear that he recalled my school days were in the past. "I am. I'm pretty sure I told you that. Maybe you forgot." His breath shot out in a snort, but I continued. "I'd also like to check out your bank accounts, Dad. Mom thinks it's a good idea. And I've drafted a power of attorney. Would you like to read it over?"

At that, his eyes blazed. "Funny, she never mentioned it to me."

He was getting mad. Righteous indignation seemed to light some fuses in his brain. I persevered. "Dad, do you have a disability insurance policy? I looked for it in the office yesterday, but I couldn't find the documents. Is your paperwork in a safe deposit box? One Mom doesn't know about?"

"You have a hell of a lot of nerve."

He rose abruptly, the sudden movement making his kitchen chair tip and fall on its side. I leaned over and righted it.

"Dad, it's important to get your affairs in order. I'm trying to help."

His countenance softened. He slid back into his seat. "I'm glad you're home, Leah."

That took me by surprise. "Thanks," I said.

He cleared his throat. "I've always known you were bright. And you have a good work ethic. I've always been proud of that. But you lack an essential quality."

My warm, fuzzy feelings evaporated. *Here we go,* I thought.

"What you lack is loyalty. Loyalty—and the instinct to protect. As a lawyer, you must protect your clients. You should protect your family. This should be natural for you, but I don't see it in your character."

You are impossible to please, Dad.

His voice reverberated off the walls of the kitchen. "So you need to develop it. You'll have to work on it. Do you understand me?"

Oh, hell yeah, I understand. Then it hit me: I was talking to the old dad. The pre-Alzheimer's Walt Randall. I decided to seize the moment.

I reached into my briefcase and placed the power of attorney beside his cold eggs. He shoved it back at me. I tried to keep impatience out of my voice when I said, "We can see this through together, Dad. I'm here to help." I pushed the power of attorney back by his plate. He picked it up and tossed it onto the kitchen floor.

When Mom popped into the kitchen, I wasn't sorry for the interruption.

"Leah, can you give me a ride to church?" she asked. "Terri will give me a lift home."

As I tucked the papers back into my bag, Mom kissed Dad on the cheek. "I'll be home before lunch, Walt. Don't leave the house, okay?"

He muttered an unintelligible reply.

Once we were buckled into the car, she asked how the conversation had gone.

"He seemed more lucid toward the end of the talk, so that's a good sign."

She shook her head. "It's a temporary blip. The dementia is getting worse."

I grimaced at the windshield. "Worse how?"

"He's starting to wander, honey. Sometimes at night."

"At night?" I was incredulous. They'd always gone to bed immediately after the ten o'clock news.

She nodded, whispering, "He even takes the car. That worries me to death."

"Shit," I muttered. "Shit, shit, shit. That's bad."

"Now, hush. You know I don't like to hear that kind of talk."

We drove on in silence until reaching the church, a gothic structure of white stone. Mom checked her appearance, then flipped the car mirror up and gave me a pleading look. "Come on in to the meeting and say hello for a minute, Leah. Please? The ladies are so tickled to hear that you're back."

Why not? I could spare a minute. I wasn't eager to get back home. When I returned, I'd have to try again to wrangle a POA signature from Walt Randall.

CHAPTER 10

THE CHURCH FELLOWSHIP hall smelled like coffee, the kind that percolates in large metal urns. The women of my mother's prayer group were standing in clusters, chatting over their white crockery coffee mugs.

The first person to see us was Kate Cole, who immediately grabbed me and steered me into a nearby corner. "Tell me, Leah. Do you miss Chicago?"

"I've only been in town for three days. Hard to get homesick for Chicago in that amount of time, Mrs. Cole."

"But, honey, Chicago isn't your home. Bassville is. Besides, your mama told me you quit your job." She leaned in, eyes wide, and spoke in a loud stage whisper. "Is that supposed to be a secret?"

"I haven't really made any final decisions." I was determined to dodge her interrogation.

"What about your daddy? How do you think he's getting along?" She shook her head and clucked. "I'm sure it was a shock."

My jaw locked. I gave her a silent stare, hoping my set face conveyed a message.

Another woman joined us: Terri Shelton, mother of my high school frenemy, Britney. Terri's poufy dyed hairdo, her lip liner and eyebrow liner, were all the same as they'd been for as long as I could remember.

"Leah Randall! Wait till I tell Britney you're back in town. I didn't even recognize you—Kate, did you?"

Instead of answering, Kate grabbed my arm again. "I've just got to know. Did you have bariatric surgery?"

Just then my cell phone rang. "Sorry," I said as I disengaged myself from Kate and sent out a silent thanks to the caller, whoever it turned out to be. As I walked away, I heard Kate stage whisper: "That girl's just as rude as she ever was." Terri Shelton tittered in response.

"Hello?" I said into the phone.

"Hello."

It was an unfamiliar, female voice. I waited for more, but nothing came.

"This is Leah Randall," I said, using my business voice.

"Are you in Chicago?" Her voice had a singsong lilt.

"To whom am I speaking?"

"Amber." While I was trying to place the name, she laughed and said, "This is my first phone call. *Ever*."

She sounded like a young woman, but it felt like I was talking to a child. I decided to be patient. "May I ask why you're calling, Amber?"

"Your mama told me to call you."

"My mother?" I looked across the room and caught Mom's eye. She smiled and waved.

"When the church ladies came. Your mama gave me a card with your number on it. She said I should call you because you're my lawyer."

I repeated it. "Because I'm your lawyer."

"That's what she said. And we need to get started. I don't have a speck of money. I'm wearing your old clothes."

Finally I made the connection: Amber, the girl whose family had been killed.

"When can you get here from Chicago? How long will it take?" she asked.

I wasn't sure how much I could help her, but I knew Dad was the Maggards' estate attorney. "Amber, I can meet you at Randall Law Office on the square here in Bassville tomorrow. Corner of Boone and Elm Streets. Let's say 11:00. I'll get there early, try to locate the wills for you."

"Okay," she said, and hung up abruptly.

I hurried to my mother's side. "Amber just called me."

Mom squeezed my hand. "That's wonderful!" She called out to the group. "Girls! Leah just heard from Amber."

I lowered my voice. "Why did you tell her I'm her lawyer?"

My mother whispered, "So you can handle the estate. Make some money." To the group, she cried, "Leah's going to help our little Amber with her estate."

A patchy round of applause followed the announcement. I caught sight of Kate Cole across the room; she'd ditched Terri Shelton and was making a beeline for us.

"She talks in a baby voice," I said to Mom, "and said she'd never used a phone before."

"Well, honey, she probably hasn't. They were a little, I don't know...backward on that farm."

Kate had joined us. "What did she say?"

"I can't really say. It's confidential." My words were clipped. *I'll show you rude,* I thought.

Mom jumped in, her tone placating. "Leah noticed that Amber sounded a little young for her age."

Kate looked like she'd eaten something delicious. "She's mentally deficient."

I turned to my mom. "Is she?"

"Oh, honey, I don't know. Amber was orphaned when she was young, and they sent her to live with her much older cousins on that farm. The Maggards didn't send her to school. Some of the rural people cling to those old-fashioned ways."

Kate clapped loudly. "Our prayers are being answered, ladies. Leah is home, and she is going to use her God-given gifts to help poor little Amber Travis. Now, we're running late, so we should open with a prayer. Barb, it's your turn. Will you lead us?"

When the praying started, I slipped out to my car. As good as the coffee smelled, it wasn't tempting enough for me to remain in their company for another minute.

CHAPTER 11

AMBER WASN'T ACCUSTOMED to sitting idle all day long. She'd folded and put away all of the clothes and linens the church ladies had brought. She'd cleaned the kitchen after her lunch of soup and crackers. Everything was as neat as a pin. There wasn't a speck of dust in the whole place. She would've liked to watch the television, but it wouldn't turn on when she pushed the button. No work was left to be done, so she strolled toward the town square to visit the donut shop.

The afternoon sun beat on her back. For the walk, she had donned a pair of fleece-lined gray pants with the word ARKANSAS printed down the right leg. It was a good thing they had a drawstring at the waist that she could cinch, otherwise they might've fallen clean off, they were so big. The long-sleeved gray shirt said ARKANSAS too, in bright red letters. Both the pants and shirt displayed a picture of a mean-looking wild pig with long tusks. Amber didn't know why anyone would buy clothes with ugly pigs on them, but those pigs were on nearly every piece of clothing from the pretty church woman. Amber figured that was why the lady was so eager to give them away.

The short walk took Amber past a brick building on a corner, and she noted the words RANDALL LAW OFFICE painted on the window. This was where Leah wanted to meet tomorrow.

Across the street, two women stood looking at Amber like they knew who she was. When she got closer, they gave her the same sad smiles the church ladies had yesterday. Amber stopped and asked them if there was a donut shop nearby.

"Sunrise Donuts is just a block from the courthouse, on Boone Street. Over that way." One of the women pointed.

"Thank you, ma'am," Amber said. She heard the women whispering as she walked off.

Amber found the small shop right where the woman had told her it would be. She walked in to a welcome blast of cold air-conditioning. A girl about Amber's age was kneeling in front of an empty glass case, holding a bottle of Windex and wiping the glass with a paper towel.

"We're about to close," the girl said.

Amber put her hand on the door, prepared to depart. "Oh, I didn't know. I'm sorry to be a bother. The ladies at the church said I could come."

The girl stood, examining her with interest. "Are you Amber Travis?"

"Yes, ma'am."

The girl wiped her hands on her apron. "Mrs. Cole said we're supposed to give you whatever you want."

Amber looked at the empty shelves. "Looks like you don't have nothing."

"I just put them in the back so that I can clean the case. Then I got to boxing them so we can sell the leftover donuts cheaper tomorrow. Because they're day-old."

That made sense. Stale donuts didn't taste as good.

"Tell me what you want. It's free. Really," the girl urged her.

"Do you have jelly donuts?"

"I do," the girl said. "Raspberry with white icing. How many?"

"Just one." Amber didn't want to be greedy.

Before the girl headed into the back room, she pointed out a refrigerator case. "Go ahead and get something to drink, too. It's hot out there."

Delighted, Amber studied the choices in the cooler: soda pop of all varieties, cold bottled water, orange juice, milk. Chocolate milk.

She picked the chocolate milk. This was turning out to be a good day.

The girl handed Amber a white paper bag and said, "Come back anytime you want. Mrs. Cole said so."

Amber uncapped the chocolate milk and drank it on the walk home, amazed at her good fortune. She'd never imagined that people in Bassville could be so nice. She sure never met anyone nice through cousin Dale.

A block away from her building, Amber noticed the noise. It was an ugly sound, a shrill whine. As she neared her door, the noise grew louder, and a ball of dread began to form in her stomach. She slid in the key with a trembling hand.

The front room was filled with smoke. Amber dropped the bag and ran to the kitchenette, where a heap of kitchen towels was blazing on top of the lit gas burners of her stove. She watched in shock as the flames flickered and spread to a bundle of clothing that was piled on the counter beside the stove.

While the smoke alarm shrieked, Amber grabbed the burning towels and fabric and threw them into the stainless-steel sink. She twisted the faucet full blast, then flung open a cabinet door and pulled out a container of salt. As she poured the salt on the mess of fabric to help with smothering the flames, she noticed her left sleeve was smoldering. So she ripped the shirt over her head and tossed it into the sink, too.

Panting, Amber backed away from the sink and turned off the stove burners. She felt her hand throb and looked down. The skin on her left palm was bright red and starting to blister. She hadn't felt the burn happen, but it was smarting now.

She wiped her smoke-stung eyes with her uninjured hand. With the alarm still assaulting her ears and the stench of singed fabric in her nostrils, she resolved to be on the alert.

Someone was after her.

She just didn't know who.

CHAPTER 12

I SPENT THE next morning cleaning up my dad's law office and hunting for the Maggards' file. When I couldn't find it in the metal cabinets, I collected the manila file folders scattered across the desktops and the floor and sorted through them, but nothing jumped out at me.

A few minutes before 11:00, I heard a knock on the metal frame of the glass front door. A fair-haired girl in a Razorbacks hoodie peered in at me, with sweat dampening her hairline. She was considerably overdressed for the temperature today, already in the 90s.

"You don't need to knock," I said as I opened the door for her. "I'm Leah Randall. Come on in."

The girl walked inside with a hesitant smile. "I'm Amber."

I patted the seat closest to Beverly's desk, inviting her to sit. "Amber, I understand that you have recently suffered a loss."

"Yes, ma'am."

"Please accept my deepest sympathy." My face was carefully composed in a look of professional concern. "The individuals who passed away—they were your cousins, I believe?"

"Glenna and Dale. They was my second cousins on the Maggard

side. My mama's people was Maggards, and she and Dale's daddy were cousins. My daddy's side was Travis."

"And both your parents died when you were young?"

"My daddy died right after I was born, in a bad wreck. He was DUI."

My poker face didn't crack. "I see."

"And Mama died when I was ten, but she got sick before that. She was sick for a long time. Ovary cancer."

"That's tragic. I'm sorry to hear it."

Amber slumped in the chair, stretching her legs out. I recognized the hoodie she wore. I'd bought it my freshman year; the points of the razorback's tusks had worn away from repeated laundering. She tugged at the drawstring at the neck and played with the plastic tip.

"It was bad. She'd been at the chicken processing plant for years, but when she got too sick to work, they fired her. We were awful poor then."

"So your mother's cancer treatment was unsuccessful."

"My mother didn't have no cancer treatment, ma'am." She cut her eyes at me, then went on. "After Mama was gone, the judge said I should go live with Dale and Glenna. They weren't too high on the idea. Well, not at first, anyway."

Amber dropped the drawstring and inspected her left hand. A strip of fabric was tied around her palm. As she toyed with the knot, she said, "Dale told me more than once he wanted me to have the farm when him and Glenna passed on. I believe he put it in writing, in a will. I'm pretty sure they signed it here, in your daddy's office." She stopped fiddling with the rag on her hand and shot me an expectant look. "Did you find that will?"

I shook my head. "I'm sorry, Amber, not yet. But Dad would have given the original signed wills to your cousins. I understand their home was destroyed in a fire. But do you think it's possible that they kept their wills in a safe deposit box at a bank? A lot of people do that with important documents."

Amber's mouth curved in a secretive smile. "No. Dale didn't trust banks."

I watched her try to loosen the knot of fabric binding her hand. When it wouldn't give, she lifted the edge of the cloth. Pursing her lips, she blew on the skin beneath it.

"Is your hand all right?" I asked.

She tucked the hand inside her right armpit. "I can read, you know," she said. Her voice was wooden.

I blinked. "I'm sure you can."

"I missed school when Mama was sick. She couldn't get me there in the mornings. They held me back in second grade, and again the next year. Wouldn't promote me to third." She frowned down at her hand. "I was the biggest kid in there. And the oldest. I didn't want to go back no more."

Hearing her tale made my throat tighten. I coughed to clear it. "Amber, were you homeschooled?"

"Yeah, kind of." She gave me another side-eyed glance. Amber dropped her hand into her lap, palm up. The skin that wasn't covered by the bandage looked inflamed.

"What happened to your hand?"

She huffed a regretful breath. "I burned it in a kitchen fire. It don't hurt much. What happens if we can't find that will?"

"Amber, I expect that there are two separate instruments, one for each of your cousins, signed and witnessed on the same day. That's how my dad would have handled it."

"What if it got lost somehow?"

"The short explanation is that the Maggards' estate will go to their nearest relative."

Amber was blowing on her burn again. Even from my limited view, I could see that it was a nasty one, and I grew genuinely concerned.

"Are you sure your hand's all right? Do you need to see a doctor?"

She stuck her injured hand between her thighs. "What I need is something to eat. I've been living off canned goods, and I'm hungry for some real food. Can we go get a hot lunch?"

I was certain that the burn was more painful than she was letting on. "I'll make you a deal. I'll take you out to lunch if we can run by urgent care to check out your hand."

She jumped out of the chair. "Okay. But I get to eat first."

CHAPTER 13

WE FOLLOWED THE hostess to a four-top table at the Western Roadhouse, a family-owned restaurant on the highway. She placed two glasses of ice water in front of us and set plastic menus beside our paper placemats before bustling away.

"Thank you, ma'am," Amber said in the singsong voice I'd heard over the phone. I stared at her, wondering again why she'd adopted the childish tone. "Thanks for bringing me," she then said in her usual voice. "I haven't got to come here for a while. I bet you ate here every week."

I'd been glancing over the menu. "Actually, I don't think I've ever been here before."

Her mouth dropped in astonishment. "No."

"My dad didn't like Western Roadhouse, so we always ate someplace else. We went to Chicken Mary's a lot. And Pappy's Crosstown Barbecue."

"I don't know those places. We always came here to the Roadhouse. Dale never took us no place else."

The waitress, a gaunt-faced woman with a distinct overbite, appeared at Amber's elbow. "Sorry about the wait. I'm Marcie. I'll be your server." When she looked down at us, she froze. "Amber? Oh, honey."

Amber smiled. "Hi."

Marcie dropped her notepad and pen on the table. Putting a hand on Amber's shoulder, she said, "Everybody's been talking about what happened to Dale and Glenna. I'm so sorry. Merciful heavens, what a terrible thing."

Amber's eyes drifted down. She ran her finger in a zigzag pattern over the plastic menu surface. "Folks have been real nice and helpful."

"I'm going to tell Quint you're here. I'll be right back." Marcie disappeared, leaving her pen and pad on the table.

I kept my voice low. "Amber, I can't imagine what it must have been like to witness the death of your loved ones."

Amber picked up Marcie's pen and drew a stick figure on the paper placemat. "I didn't see nothing. I was asleep."

"You slept? Through gunshots?"

"Maybe that's why I woke up. I don't know." She scribbled curly hair on the stick figure.

"Good thing you woke up when you did. You're lucky you didn't suffer smoke inhalation."

Amber didn't respond. She was drawing a long skirt on the stick figure. But I persevered. I wanted clarification.

"Do you think they knew you were in the house? Whoever killed your cousins?"

"I wasn't in the house." She scratched deep lines of ink over the stick figure and drew a rectangle beside it. "I was in the shed."

I squinted at her, perplexed. "The shed?"

"Yeah. I was sleeping outside in the shed. When I woke up and saw the fire, I ran away."

I was still puzzling this over when a loud voice boomed behind me.

"There's my little Amber!"

A short man around my father's age wrapped his arms around Amber. When he released her, he seized her injured hand and squeezed it. She winced but didn't pull her hand away.

"How are you getting along, honey?" he said.

"I'm doing all right, I reckon. Thanks for asking, Mr. Rhoades."

Quint Rhoades, proprietor of Western Roadhouse, was a squat, gray-haired man wearing a greasy apron. Though we'd never met, I knew him by sight. When I was at the University of Arkansas, Rhoades was a regular figure in the Dickson Street college bars during football season.

Marcie huddled behind Rhoades. The proprietor turned to her. "What's Amber eating today?"

"They ain't ordered yet." The waitress's voice was apologetic.

"Well, take their doggone order, Marcie. Don't stand there like a fool." Turning back, he said, "What you gonna have, Amber?"

She picked up the menu with her good hand. It bore faded color photographs of the food choices. "I'd like that one. Well done." She tapped her thumb on a picture of a sirloin steak nestled beside a foil-wrapped baked potato.

Marcie grabbed her notepad and pen from the table and scribbled it down. "How about you, honey?" she asked, glancing at me.

The photos of the food didn't excite my appetite. "I'll have a dinner salad. Ranch dressing."

"Can I have chocolate milk?" Amber asked in a piping voice.

An impatient look crossed Marcie's face. "We don't have chocolate. Just regular. It says so on the menu."

Amber sighed. "I'll drink water, then."

I was thinking about ordering a Dr Pepper with extra ice, but the waitress had already walked away.

Quint Rhoades shouted after her, "I'm comping the food, Marcie!" He turned to me with an oily grin. "The Maggards always ate for free at Western Roadhouse. Especially this little honey."

He still held Amber's left hand. When he squeezed it again, her face didn't register discomfort, though it had to hurt.

She tilted her head to look into Rhoades's face. Beaming, she spoke in a high soprano, like a kid in grade school. "The people in Bassville are the nicest people in the whole wide world!"

I watched with mounting concern as Amber continued to smile

while Quint Rhoades clenched her burned hand in his big paw. It was clear she wasn't going to speak up, so I did.

"Amber has a burn on her hand. Let go. You're hurting her."

Rhoades dropped her hand reluctantly. Amber cradled it in the crook of her right arm, staring at me like I'd sprouted a unicorn's horn in my forehead.

CHAPTER 14

AMBER WAITED FOR Leah's red car to turn the corner before opening the door to her apartment. She eyeballed the living space and sniffed before she entered. If any unhappy surprises awaited her inside, she wanted to be prepared.

But it was quiet, and the smoky smell was mostly gone. Amber had chucked the burned clothes and dish towels into the dumpster behind the apartment building, and she'd left all the apartment windows open through the night.

She dropped the bag from the urgent care clinic onto the coffee table, then went into the kitchenette and inspected the black mark that remained on the wall behind the stovetop. She didn't know what else she could do to remove it. The night before, she'd scrubbed at it with Comet cleanser until her arms ached. Briefly, Amber considered asking the church ladies for a can of white paint, but it might arouse suspicion. It was always best to keep her head down and avoid attention. She'd learned that lesson well.

Maybe she could put a picture over it. She could ask the church ladies for a picture of flowers, and they'd just think she liked pretty things.

"'That dumb Amber likes flowers. Let's give her a picture,'" she

334

said out loud, mimicking Kate Cole's bossy voice. "'Maybe it will remind her of the farm.'"

Thinking of the farm gave Amber an idea. The folks who lived at the farm next door had been taking care of the laying hens since Dale and Glenna had died. Amber knew they wanted to buy them. Maybe she could figure out how to get that money.

Amber poured herself a glass of water from the tap. The food at the Western Roadhouse had been salty, and she'd been sweating all day to boot. She pulled the gray hoodie over her head—it was sopping wet, and she sighed in relief at the feeling of the air-conditioning blowing on her bare torso. She surely did wish Leah Randall had had some lightweight old clothes.

Amber sank into the cushions of the sagging green couch and turned on the television. Through trial and error, she'd discovered that she had to push some buttons on a hand-held device to make it work. Amber liked the noise of TV; the people on the shows kept her company.

Propping her feet on the coffee table, she unwrapped the new bandage on her left hand and inspected the blisters. The nurse at the clinic had gasped when Amber showed her the burn. She'd acted like it was some kind of big deal, then gave her a tube of ointment and a warning to watch for signs of infection. Like the nurse thought Amber didn't know nothing about nothing.

Her hand throbbed, probably because of old Quint Rhoades. Amber barked a harsh laugh, just thinking about him. She'd just about fell out of her chair when Leah Randall told Quint to let go of her hand. Amber had never heard a woman talk to a man like that before, not in her whole life.

She took the tube of ointment to the bathroom. At the sink, she worked the bar of Ivory into suds, then gingerly lathered her burn. After patting it dry, she dabbed on some of that ointment, just to see if it was good for anything. While she worked on her hand, she gave some thought to that lawyer.

Leah Randall was bossy, just like the snotty church lady Kate

Cole. More than once Amber had wanted to tell Leah to shut her trap, her hand itching to slap the lawyer's smug, know-it-all face.

But Leah was Amber's best bet for getting that inheritance. God knows she'd earned it. And to get the farm without waiting around forever, she needed the will. Amber didn't believe that everything had been destroyed in the fire. Cousin Dale had probably hidden the will somewhere where he thought no one could find it.

The Maggards liked to hide things.

CHAPTER 15

JUST AS WE were sitting down to supper that evening, Hagar County sheriff Mickey Gilmore called to ask me about interviewing Amber Travis.

"Haven't you already interviewed her?" I asked. It had been over a week since the murders.

"We talked to her when we picked her up at the gas station," Sheriff Gilmore said, "but she didn't make much sense. The ER doctor said the girl was in a 'fugue state' from her traumatic experience, told me to leave her be so she could recover." He snorted into my ear. "Hell, I had to Google that."

The sheriff's frank confession was refreshing. I recalled that Dad had always liked him, back when Gilmore was a deputy.

His voice had an apologetic ring as he went on. "Leah, I know she has the mental state of a child at the best of times. We'll proceed real carefully with her. But I'm hoping she'll remember more, now that she's had a few days to sort it out. There's a killer walking around out there somewhere."

"I'd be glad to bring Amber by the office," I told him, "but, Sheriff, I'd also appreciate an opportunity to go view the farm, look at the property myself. Is that possible?"

I could hear him thinking, probably weighing the inconvenience of my request against the advantage of his access to Amber.

"All right," he said grudgingly. "I'll send a deputy to escort you first thing in the morning."

The next morning, I was relieved to see it was my old friend Danny Minton behind the wheel of the patrol car that pulled up to the curb. Our drive was short; the Maggards' farm was only about five miles outside the city limits. Soon the patrol car bumped along the gravel road leading up to where the farmhouse had been, only a fireplace and chimney still standing amid the debris.

A hundred yards away were two other structures, apparently unaffected by the fire: the narrow henhouse and a wooden shed covered in a peeling layer of red paint.

"It's kind of spooky, isn't it?" I said.

Danny nodded, his face sober. We got out of the car and walked up to the crime-scene tape skirting the ruins of the farmhouse.

"Why couldn't the fire department put it out?" I asked.

"It was the middle of the night, so nobody saw the smoke out here in the country. And whoever set it used an accelerant. These old places burn like kindling."

Staying outside the tape, Danny walked along the perimeter. I followed behind, taking pictures with my cell phone.

Danny pointed inside the tape. "That's where the kitchen was."

"How do you know?"

"We did a grid search. Sifted the debris through screens. And this was the bedroom, where we found the remains. The coroner transported them to Little Rock, to the State Medical Examiner's Office."

"I'm surprised there was anything left to find."

"Bone is harder to burn than most people realize. We found enough for the lab to determine cause of death was gunshots to the head. But we never did find bullets or shell casings."

We had reached the fireplace. Crafted of native stone, it looked indestructible.

Danny said, "This was the living room."

I surveyed the rectangle of debris and ash. "Where were the other bedrooms?"

"There was just one, apparently." He turned, nodding in the direction of the henhouse. "Are you interested in going inside? You're not going to like it."

That kind of statement always fueled my determination. Although I hadn't intended to inspect the henhouse, I said, "Of course I want to go in."

As we approached the long, low structure, I expected to hear clucking or squawking. But it was as quiet as a tomb. When we reached the side of the narrow outbuilding, Danny pulled open a screen door.

"Be my guest." His voice had a teasing note.

I took three steps inside before I realized my mistake. Though there were no hens inside, the stink was so monstrous, the air felt thick. Cussing like a sailor, I backed out as fast as I could and ran several yards to escape the smell, but it was locked inside my sinuses. My eyes began to itch, and my nose ran like a faucet.

"Oh, my God," I said, wiping my nose with the back of my hand. "I should've brought my allergy medicine."

While Danny jogged back to the squad car to get me some tissues, I walked over to the red shed, opened the door, and peeked inside. Amber had said she was in the shed when the fire started. It was a small enclosure, and there wasn't much to see. The items it contained were unremarkable: rusty garden and farm tools, a wheelbarrow, an ancient lawn mower, a wire dog cage.

Danny appeared at my elbow, holding out a wad of tissues like a peace offering. "The arson investigator thinks gasoline was used as the accelerant," he said. "We found empty gas cans here, outside the shed. They're in the evidence room."

I looked at the patch of bare dirt he indicated, but there was nothing notable from my viewpoint. Danny pushed the shed door shut. There was no lock to secure it. As we walked back to the car, I asked, "I saw that dog cage. What did you all do with the dog?"

Danny rubbed the back of his head, just like in high school. "I didn't see a dog," he said. "Guess maybe they didn't have one anymore."

CHAPTER 16

FOUR OF US gathered around a scarred table in the windowless interrogation room at the sheriff's office. Amber and I faced Sheriff Gilmore and Deputy Danny Minton. The sheriff folded his hands on the tabletop, and his weathered face creased with a smile. The eyes under his bushy brows were kind.

"Amber, are you comfortable?" he asked. "Can we get you anything? Something to drink, maybe?"

Amber bobbed her head and turned to me, as if she couldn't respond on her own.

I said, "Are you thirsty? Would you like a bottle of water?"

"Yes, ma'am," she said, her voice shy.

Danny rose from his chair. "I'll get it."

Amber pulled the long sleeves of her sweatshirt over her fingers and played with the cuffs like hand puppets.

After Danny returned with a water bottle and Amber took a long drink, the sheriff spoke.

"Amber, we're going to video this interview. That all right with you?"

I pulled my chair closer to Amber, but she answered before I could ask whether she wanted to proceed. "I just want to help out any way I can, sir," she said in that high soprano, regarding the sheriff with a trusting gaze.

The sheriff glanced at Danny, who stood and adjusted the angle of a video camera that was on a tripod in the corner of the room.

"Tell us your full name, please," the sheriff said.

Before Amber could reply, the door opened, and Shelby Searcy entered. "I told you to wait for me," he said.

The sheriff's eyes were flat. "We're just getting started. Amber, this is Mr. Searcy. He's the lawyer who handles criminal cases around here."

Amber's brows came together in a frown. "He keeps the bad people out of jail?"

When Searcy and the sheriff laughed, Amber shrank back in her chair, embarrassed.

"I put bad people *into* jail," Searcy boasted loudly. "I have the highest conviction record in the state. Nice to meet you, Miss Travis." He pulled a leather portfolio from his briefcase, slapping it onto the table. Amber flinched.

Sheriff Gilmore shot her an encouraging wink. "Your name, please, ma'am."

"Amber Lynn Travis."

"Age?"

"Twenty-three."

The sheriff's voice rumbled with sincerity as he said, "Amber, let me express my condolences for your lost loved ones. Early in August you were living on a farm outside Bassville with your cousins, Dale and Glenna Maggard, is that right?"

"Yes, sir. My second cousins. And my guardians after Mama died."

"On the day that led up to their death, do you recall anything unusual happening?"

Amber squinted her eyes and frowned, as if thinking hard. Her mouth puckered. "I dropped a basket of eggs."

Shelby Searcy barked with laughter. I shot him a hard look.

The sheriff's voice, though, was soothing when he addressed

Amber. "I meant to ask whether anything happened that day that was strange or unusual. Something out of the ordinary," he repeated, stressing the last words.

"Well, it wasn't ordinary for me to break so many. Not a whole basket. So Glenna told Dale that I done it, because she said she sure wasn't taking the blame."

The sheriff pressed on. "Did you see anyone on the property that day, or in the evening? Was anyone hanging around, maybe a stranger?"

Amber shook her head. "No. Nobody but us was around. I hadn't seen any strangers around the farm since that hobo took off."

The atmosphere in the room changed instantly.

"Hobo?" the sheriff repeated. "Tell us about the hobo."

"He came to the farm this summer. Glenna told him he better move along, but Dale said he'd give him food and a place to sleep if he could help haul hay."

"When did the man come to the farm? What was his name?"

Amber fell silent. Her hands clenched in her lap. "I don't remember," she finally responded. "It was hot. July, maybe. I don't know."

The sheriff prompted her further. "Can you describe the man? His race, age, hair color? Any unusual features or tattoos?"

She looked away, as if trying to visualize him. "White. I don't know how old. There was nothing special about him. He stunk pretty bad."

Searcy smirked. "That should make him easy to find."

Sheriff Gilmore ignored the jibe. His brow furrowed as he said, "Amber, I need you to remember a name. What did you call him? Think hard."

She ducked her head. Squeezing her eyes shut, she said, "Burry. Burry Jones."

Danny and I exchanged a look. He shrugged.

The sheriff asked, "How long did the man stay at the farm?"

"Awhile. I don't know how many days."

"Why did he leave?" The sheriff's voice was buttery, his manner nonthreatening. But Amber no longer made eye contact with him. She was growing fidgety. I wondered if she was shutting down. She reached for the water bottle and took several swigs before she answered.

"The hobo was a thief. Glenna caught him stealing money out of the cookie jar she kept in the kitchen. She caught him red-handed. And Dale come in with his shotgun and told him to get off his property. Then he chased him out of the house."

"You witnessed that? You're positive? Saw it with your own eyes? Or did someone tell you about it later?" Sheriff Gilmore asked.

Shelby Searcy murmured, "She probably doesn't recall."

Amber raised her head and fixed Searcy with piercing eyes. "I saw it and I heard it. The hobo was out by the gravel drive. He said to Dale, 'I'll come back and burn this whole place to the ground.'"

CHAPTER 17

AMBER DRAINED HER water bottle and turned to me. "I have to use the toilet," she whispered. As Amber slipped out, Sheriff Gilmore waved a hand and Danny paused the video camera.

Shelby Searcy pushed his chair back from the table and stretched his arms. Danny checked the controls on the camera. The minutes dragged. Eventually, Sheriff Gilmore sent Danny to make some coffee.

Searcy started to pace around the table. To the sheriff, he said, "I think you'll recall that I anticipated this." Sheriff Gilmore didn't respond. Searcy circled the room once again before setting his briefcase on his chair and packing his leather portfolio into it. With impatience, he said, "I told you the girl wouldn't provide any useful information. What did we learn today? She dropped some eggs. She saw a homeless man. Her description? He smelled bad."

The sheriff said, "She gave us a name."

Searcy snapped the briefcase locks shut. Hefting it, he said, "'Jones'? You think?"

Sheriff Gilmore sighed, shaking his head. "I don't know. It's something."

"I'm going back to my office. I'm pretty sure I've wasted enough time this morning listening to the ramblings of a retarded girl."

I was appalled. "Is that really how you describe your crime victim? I can't believe you would actually use that word."

"What word?" he said, playing the innocent. But his face and neck reddened.

Rising, I prepared to launch into a lecture, but the sheriff cut it off. "Leah, I'm sure Shelby didn't mean anything by it."

I wasn't fooled. Searcy had managed to toss an insult every time I encountered him. But at that moment my silenced phone gave a quiet buzz. An incoming call from Mom. When I didn't answer, the voicemail icon lit up.

Instead of blasting Searcy, I turned my back on the men and listened to my voicemail. The message was short but pleading: would I please come by Dr. Pennington's clinic when my business at the sheriff's office was done?

When I turned back around, I saw Searcy and the sheriff standing beside the table with their heads together.

"Maybe you're right, Shelby," Gilmore was saying. "And that business about the hobo, I don't know where we go with that." The sheriff shook his head with regret. "Where would we even find him?"

Searcy checked his wristwatch, then glanced in my direction. "Why don't you go check on your client."

I didn't like taking orders from the prosecutor. But it struck me that she *had* been gone for quite a spell—I hoped she hadn't run off and ditched me.

Before I walked out of the interrogation room, I had a thought. "The homeless stay in shelters, don't they? In Chicago, a homeless man was a bystander witness in one of our cases. We tracked him down through the shelters' records."

Searcy cut me a withering glance. "Bassville doesn't have a homeless shelter."

Of course Assville wouldn't. But I kept my voice measured as I replied, "Other local communities do. And I'm sure those shelters keep records, too."

Searcy's face looked like he'd been sucking on a lemon, but the sheriff was nodding.

"That's a thought," Sheriff Gilmore said. "We'll check it out."

I left the interview room and strolled down the hall, feeling cocky. When I reached the women's restroom, I pushed the door partly open, but something was blocking it. Sticking my head through the opening, I saw that Amber hadn't left the sheriff's office after all.

She was passed out on the bathroom floor.

CHAPTER 18

MY VOICE BOUNCED off the concrete-block walls as I frantically shouted for help while squeezing my way into the restroom. I knelt beside Amber and took her hand. Her eyes were closed, but her pulse was rapid.

Footsteps echoed in the hallway. "Leah?"

"In here!" I put a hand on Amber's forehead—her skin was moist, almost clammy. Her eyes fluttered open, and she focused on my face.

"Ma'am?" she said in a murmur.

Through the doorway, Sheriff Gilmore stared down at us with a troubled expression. Danny and Searcy stood behind him.

"What's going on?" the sheriff said.

"I came to check on her, and she was on the floor, unconscious." I looked down at Amber, who was gazing up at us with a confused expression. Danny squeezed by the sheriff and joined us in the small restroom. Squatting on his haunches, he helped Amber into a sitting position.

"What happened?" Danny asked, taking her pulse.

She looked chagrined. "I just got woozy. Everything went black for a minute."

Searcy's voice rang out behind the sheriff's shoulder. "I'm going back to the courthouse."

Sheriff Gilmore nodded. "That's fine, Shelby. I don't expect we'll be asking any more questions of Miss Amber today, now that she's feeling poorly."

Danny carefully inspected the back of Amber's head. "Does that hurt? I can feel a bump. You're going to have a nasty knot back there."

The sheriff frowned. "Maybe we'd best take her to the ER."

"No. No, sir. I'm fine, really," Amber said decisively.

I had a thought. "How about seeing Dr. Pennington? I'll take you. It's no trouble." I stopped short of revealing that my mother wanted me at Dr. Pennington's clinic anyway.

"I just want to go home, that's all," Amber said sharply. "I want to lie down."

The sheriff patted her shoulder and said she should go rest.

As I drove her home, I asked again whether she felt ill.

"No. I'm fine. I was just dizzy for a little bit. Probably a nervous fit."

I glanced at her, noticing a ring of perspiration under her armpit. "Do you think you were overheated? You can faint from heat exhaustion."

"I'm used to being hot. I worked on a farm. Remember?"

"Yes, but Amber, it's August, and the heat can make you sick, whether you're used to it or not. I think you should reconsider your clothing choices." Keeping my eyes on the road, I went on. "I could get you some shorts and T-shirts. You'd be much more comfortable."

Amber took a moment to reply. When she spoke, her tone was polite, though she wouldn't look my way. "I can't wear them things. But thank you very much. You sure are nice to offer."

She rolled down the passenger window, thrusting her head outside like a dog out for a ride in the car. The hot wind blew her light hair around her face.

We drove like that until I pulled up to her apartment. As she unbuckled her seat belt and grasped the latch on the car door, I tried again. "Amber, I can pick you up and take you to Walmart this afternoon. We'll get you some new clothes. All the summer stuff is on sale now."

She gave me a grim look. "I can't wear those things," she said, her childlike affect gone, "because they don't cover me up. And I wish you'd quit deviling me about it."

Defensive, I said, "I'm just trying to help."

Her eyes were hard when she replied, "If you want to help me, find that will."

She hopped out of the passenger seat, slammed the door shut, then stuck her head back through the open window. "I got to get my money so I can get out of Bassville."

CHAPTER 19

"WHAT TOOK YOU so long?" my mother whispered when the nurse waved me into Dr. Pennington's examination room. Dad sat on the examination table, his hands grasping his knees.

I dropped my briefcase by an unoccupied vinyl chair and flopped into it. "I've been babysitting Amber Travis—free of charge, by the way—because you told me to."

Mom cut a cautious glance at Dad, but he paid us no mind.

"Well, at least you're in time to see Dr. Pennington. He should be here any minute."

Reaching into my briefcase, I pulled out a legal pad where I'd jotted down a list of questions regarding Dad's condition. While I was poring over my notes, the door opened. A white lab coat brushed my knees as the doctor walked in.

"Barb, Walt, good to see you," he said.

My head shot up. The man shaking my father's hand was not the kindly old Dr. Pennington, who'd been our lifelong family physician.

It was Tripp Pennington, aka Robert William Pennington III, the golden boy of his Bassville High senior class when I was in ninth grade.

My initial impression: Tripp hadn't changed at all. The aquiline nose, the gleaming smile, the deep voice—they were all still there. The only thing different was his hair—in high school, he'd had shiny black hair that curled at his neck. Now his head was completely shaved, as bald as a baby, like Bruce Willis.

Like a *young* Bruce Willis.

"Tripp, you can brighten up a room just by walking through the door," my mom cooed.

Tripp laughed as he sat on a rolling stool beside the computer. After he glanced over the chart on the screen, he turned to me.

"And who's this?"

I blushed, which mortified me. So I made certain that my voice stayed cool. "I'm Leah Randall. Nice to meet you."

Tripp turned to my mother. "This is your daughter? The big-city lawyer?"

I didn't wait for my mother's reply. "What happened to the previous Dr. Pennington? I have some questions for him."

I flipped the pages of the legal pad and clicked my pen. I was ready to conduct a cross-examination.

"If you have any questions for my uncle, you can find him at Bull Shoals," Tripp replied. "He spends a lot of time with a fishing pole since he retired." Returning his attention to the chart, he said, "Your blood pressure's a little high, Walt."

Dad grunted. Tripp smiled as he approached Dad with a stethoscope. "So are you enjoying your daughter's visit, Walt?"

Dad nodded without much enthusiasm. Tripp listened to his chest and back. In an offhand voice, he asked whether Dad was taking his medication. Dad said he was. Mom verified it.

I intervened. "Dr. Pennington, are you inquiring about the Aricept prescription? Because it's not helping."

Tripp ignored my question; instead, he talked about Dad's eating habits, noting that he'd lost some more weight.

"Are you eating your three squares?" he asked. "Getting some exercise? It's pretty hot to get out and walk right now, but if you're an early riser—"

I interrupted, louder this time. "I don't think taking a stroll is going to help. Have you considered another medication?"

"Walt, how are your spirits? Are you feeling good?" Tripp asked, continuing to ignore me.

Dad's voice was remote. "Oh, pretty good, I guess."

My patience was exhausted. "Doctor, do you intend to ask about his memory loss? Or just chat about the weather some more?"

Tripp finally locked eyes with me. In a terse voice, he said, "I'd appreciate it if you'd let me examine your father without interruption."

"Please, Leah, settle down," Mom pleaded.

I opened my briefcase and pulled out the power of attorney file. Handing it to the doctor, I said, "If you can't find a successful treatment, can you at least help advise Dad that it's time to sign over power of attorney?"

To my surprise, Tripp opened the file and examined it, flipping through the pages.

I added a final demand: "And tell him he can no longer drive."

Tripp looked up from the document. Glancing at our faces, he focused on Dad. "Walt, are you still driving a car?"

Dad cleared his throat. His expression was stubborn when he said, "I'm licensed to drive in the state of Arkansas. And I own two cars. Yes, I drive them."

Tripp reached out and placed a hand on Dad's shoulder. "Walt, I'm siding with your daughter on that. You shouldn't be behind the wheel."

Dad's face got even stormier when Tripp pulled a pen from the pocket of his lab coat.

"I'm not a lawyer, but your daughter is. This power of attorney looks like it's in order. I'd advise you to sign it, as your doctor and your friend. It's time."

He placed the file folder on Dad's lap and put the pen in his right hand. I held my breath, hardly believing it was possible. Could Tripp persuade Dad to sign the POA when Mom and I had failed?

When I saw Dad scrawl his name, a boulder's weight dropped from my shoulders. Clearly we owed Tripp Pennington a debt.

But that didn't mean I trusted his medical judgment.

When Tripp handed the file back to me, I slipped it into my briefcase. After he wrapped up the exam, and Mom walked Dad out to the appointment desk, I lingered.

"Thank you for getting my father to sign the POA. He wouldn't do it for me."

"Glad to help," he said. He stood with his hand on the door. "If I can make a suggestion—try to be a little more understanding. It will make things easier for your parents." He swept into the hallway.

My temper flared. I followed him out. "Hey, Tripp. You know what I think? I think it would make things easier if you and my mom quit babying Dad about his dementia, acting like it's no big deal. Call it what it is, Doctor—if you've got the balls."

Tripp turned on his heel and strode back to me. "You've got a lot of nerve, Leah. You blow into town after ignoring your parents for years, then criticize your mother and question my treatment? Back off."

As Tripp stormed away, my mother appeared, looking distressed. "What was the fussing about?"

"Nothing. No big deal." I shook it off. I wanted to take the power of attorney to the bank before my father changed his mind.

As we exited the office, I saw another high school classmate hovering nearby. She'd undoubtedly witnessed the whole scene. I couldn't immediately place her, but her gleeful expression brought back unpleasant memories.

CHAPTER 20

AS WE ENTERED First Community Bank, the bank president, Hopp Cole, caught sight of us walking through the lobby. Mom turned to Dad and grabbed his hand. In a voice full of forced cheer, she said, "Honey, isn't it nice to see our good friend Hopp Cole?"

Hopp extended his right hand and Dad grasped it, repeating Mom's cue. "Hopp Cole, my good friend."

Mom prattled on. "No wonder this is the best bank in all of Arkansas! The president takes the time to come out to the lobby and greet the customers. Kate and I were supposed to meet for lunch this week, but I've been all tied up."

Hopp made some reply, but the words were lost on me. I was reeling, because it was obvious to me that although my parents had been friends with Hopp and Kate Cole for as long as I could remember, Dad didn't have a clue who Hopp was.

Mom interrupted my reverie. "Leah? Stop woolgathering and answer Hopp's question."

I gave the banker a blank look. "Beg pardon?"

He put a hand on my arm and squeezed. "I was just inquiring about the Travis girl. My wife tells me you're trying to give her a hand with some legal advice."

"Amber? She's fine," I said. I took a sideways step. His hand slipped off.

"Amber's staying in one of Hopp's apartments," Mom said to me. "Hopp, you're the picture of Christian charity."

He shook his head. "It's what any of us would have done. Bassville is a community that looks out for the welfare of those less fortunate."

I sent him a skeptical look. "So why doesn't Bassville have a homeless shelter?" I asked.

My mother chortled. "Leah, you blurt out the oddest things."

The banker sidled up to me again. "Has Amber said anything more?" He slipped an arm around my shoulders.

"She had an interview at the sheriff's office this morning. She provided some new information." I had kept it purposefully vague.

"Is that so?" Hopp kept smiling. "I have it from a good source that it was one of those random crimes you hear about when a serial killer roams from place to place."

"A serial killer?" I echoed. "That's ridiculous."

Mom and Hopp both eyeballed me. After a beat, Hopp dropped his arm and said, "Well, you all stay right here. I'll set you up with Mary in the accounts department. She'll be right with you."

After he disappeared, Mom turned on me. "What is it with you?"

"Sorry, Mom, I just don't like him."

She huffed out an indignant breath. "You can be such a pill. Sometimes I wonder whether you like anyone."

I didn't argue the point. The truth was, the list of people I disliked was long. And in Bassville, the list grew longer by the day.

CHAPTER 21

AFTER DROPPING MY parents back at home, I went to Dad's office with my mind focused on finding the wills. If I didn't locate them, Amber Travis would never give me a moment's peace.

I muddled through stacks of folders, lining them up across the carpet in alphabetical order. I found Mayfields, Martins, Marinos. But no Maggards. As I neared the end of the alphabet, I spied a skinny file with a name handwritten in faint ink: Travis.

I pulled it out and peeked inside, groaning with relief when I saw the document heading: "Last Will and Testament of Dale Maggard." Glenna Maggard's Will was paper-clipped behind it, along with some additional court papers.

I set the file on Dad's desktop, wondering if his dementia had caused him to tuck the wills away in the wrong location. Sure, Amber Travis was a likely beneficiary, but Dale and Glenna Maggard were the clients, weren't they?

A text interrupted me before I could read any further.

It was an invitation from Danny Minton:

Some people from BHS meeting for drinks tonite. Hope u come by. My wife wants to meet u. 5:00 @ Robby's Bar.

I gnawed the inside of my cheek. I was curious about Danny's wife. But an evening with my old BHS classmates? The prospect wasn't tempting.

The old wall clock—the one that hung next to a framed print of dogs playing poker, Dad's favorite decor—chimed, reminding me that I was running late for my meeting with Beverly, which she'd agreed to the day before. I slid the Maggard file—or rather, the Travis file—into my briefcase to inspect later.

When I locked the office and walked down the steps to the sidewalk, I spied a pickup circling the square, a battered black Chevy pickup with oversize tires and a Confederate flag mounted in the bed. The window on the driver's side was down, an elbow sticking out like a chicken wing in the stark afternoon sunlight. As it drove past at a snail's pace, the teenage driver swiveled his head, like he was checking me out.

I made the connection: I'd seen this kid pumping gas at the convenience store when I'd arrived in town last week. I didn't mistake the flirtatious once-over he gave me. He was a decade younger, no more than eighteen or nineteen, but he thought he was tough, and wanted me to think so, too. He was trying to intimidate me. As he passed by the courthouse, the driver revved the engine—for my benefit, I supposed.

Just a stupid kid, I thought. Walking to my car, I tried to shrug it off. I even coughed out a laugh as I tossed my briefcase into the passenger seat. But there was something unsettling about that driver that I couldn't shake.

CHAPTER 22

WHEN I PULLED up to her bungalow, Beverly Shirk was waiting for me, holding the screen door open wide. We exchanged a quick hug, and I caught her familiar scent of gardenia soap.

In the front room, she invited me to sit beside her on a velvet sofa in front of a dainty coffee table that held a flowered porcelain teapot and matching cups. As she poured, Beverly asked how Dad was getting along.

"Not too well," I replied honestly. "They have him on an Alzheimer's medicine, but it's not slowing the decline."

She shook her head. "I can imagine. It broke my heart to see it on a daily basis."

An earsplitting banging sound suddenly came from the vicinity of the kitchen. Beverly gave me a look of chagrin. "I apologize for this awful racket. I have workers in the kitchen. They should have been done by now."

"No problem," I said, though the screech of a power drill required me to raise my voice to a near shout. "I'm sorry that Dad didn't give you proper notice before shutting the office down." When the noise ceased for a moment, I added, "I've been spending a lot of time at Dad's office this week. I finally put that mess back in order."

"I didn't leave the office in a mess." She sounded hurt.

"I'm sure you left it in great shape, Beverly," I hastened to reassure her. "Dad must have been the one who tossed the files around. You know, the dementia."

She looked unconvinced. "Walt was never messy. Never." A hammer drowned out some of her words, but I caught her insistence that "Walt was the tidiest man I ever knew."

I tried to ignore the unhappy thought that raised, and the whir of the power tools making my head ache. I moved on. "Beverly, I'm worried that Dad may have new clients I don't know about or open cases he neglected. Would you know anything about that?"

"Honey, there wasn't any new business coming in." Her voice was kind, but I understood her message. *He knew he was slipping.* "We were tying up loose ends, doing referrals, closing files."

She set her teacup on the coffee table. "Since you're here, I'll confide something I haven't told a soul, not even your mother."

Her face was solemn. She glanced over her shoulder, as if she feared the workers in the kitchen might overhear, then leaned close and said, "His paranoia worried me. Have you noticed it?"

I hadn't. "How so?" I asked.

Her lips pursed, then she sighed deeply and continued. "He'd grown suspicious, seeing the worst in people. Walt was never like that before. Do you think it's a common phenomenon with Alzheimer's?"

I shook my head. "I read some articles online that talked about personality changes," I said, "but I don't know."

A man wearing dusty work boots walked into the room. "Mrs. Shirk, we're getting ready to wrap up. Want to take a look?"

Beverly rose from the sofa, smoothing the front of her skirt. "Yes, I expect so." She picked up the teapot and turned to me. "Shall I heat up more water? We can have another cup."

"No, thank you. I need to go. Let me help you with the tea things."

Following Beverly, I carried the cups and saucers. As I passed through the swinging door into her kitchen, I saw the cause of the noise and commotion.

Metal bars covered all the windows on the back of her house.

Beverly took the cups from me and set them in the sink. "I decided to install security," she explained, pulling a checkbook from a kitchen drawer to pay the workers. "I just got back from a nice long visit with my daughter and my grandsons—the cutest little guys you ever saw!—and when I walked into the house, I nearly had a heart attack." She tore out the check with a vicious rip. "Burglars had come in and trashed the place."

"Beverly, that's terrible! What did they take?"

"Not much. Mostly it was just vandalism. What kind of scoundrels would do that to an old widow? I don't know what the world's coming to."

CHAPTER 23

IT WAS JUST past five o'clock when I pulled my car into the spot facing the entrance of Robby's Bar. When I received Danny's invitation earlier in the day, I'd had little interest in the high school cocktail party. But after leaving Beverly's, my car turned toward Robby's Bar on autopilot. The prospect of another silent evening at home with my parents, staring at the television, was depressing. Maybe it would be nice to talk to people my own age.

I reconsidered my decision almost as soon as the barroom door closed behind me. But as my eyes adjusted, I made out a circle of figures around a table at the back of the room and heard Danny Minton calling my name. I headed toward them.

Danny had his arm around a woman, presumably his wife. "Cathy, this is Leah, the lawyer I was telling you about."

Cathy and I shook hands as I took the empty seat beside her. She had the most winning smile I'd ever seen. "Leah, Danny tells me you were high school buddies."

I was about to answer when someone spoke from the other side of the table. "We're all old BHS friends here."

It was the same woman from Tripp's office. Now that I saw her up close, I recognized Britney Shelton—she'd changed her hair color.

"I've been dying to talk to you, Leah," she said. "Mom told me you showed up at her prayer group." Next to Britney sat Phil Benson, the circuit clerk, who was conversing with a guy I didn't recognize.

"That's right. Nice to see you again, Britney. Been a long time."

Danny said, "Didn't you two also go to college together?"

I started to answer, but Britney spoke first. "No, I went to ASU in Jonesboro. Leah went to U of A. She's a hog. Right, Leah?"

I smiled tightly. This promised to be a long evening. "Everyone's a hog at U of A. Go Razorbacks."

"Woo! Pig! Sooie!" Britney said, pumping her fist in the air for the famous U of A chant.

The barmaid appeared at my elbow. "I'll have a vodka soda. With Absolut," I told her.

She gave me a funny look before she walked away.

Britney leaned her elbows on the table, stirring her cocktail with a straw. "Haley's here, but she's over by the bar talking to some guy. Leah, you remember Haley." She called to Haley and beckoned her with an impatient wave. Haley ignored the summons. I remembered her as painfully shy and was pleased to see she'd grown in confidence.

A burst of light flashed into the room as the door opened. Britney gasped in delight. "OMG, he actually came. Tripp! Over here!"

My muscles tensed. There was only one person by that name in Bassville, Arkansas.

Britney patted the chair beside hers. "Take Haley's chair, Tripp. She won't mind."

Tripp said, "I don't want to take her spot." He slid into the only other available seat, next to me. "Hello again, Leah."

"Hi." I scooted my chair closer to Danny's wife, Cathy, as the waitress set a glass in front of me. Two maraschino cherries floated in an inky concoction.

"What's that?" Cathy asked.

"Not really sure," I said, staring at it.

The waitress handed Cathy what looked like an iced tea and

placed a foamy mug in front of Danny. Britney said, "Tiffany, Leah says you messed up her order."

The barmaid's face was sullen. "You said you wanted vodka and soda."

Apologetic, I said, "I meant vodka and club soda."

Britney made a gagging sound. "Who ever heard of that?"

Frowning, the waitress reached for the tumbler. I stopped her. "I should've been more specific. It's fine." As she walked off, I picked up the glass and took a sip out of sheer stubbornness.

Turning to Danny and Cathy, I asked to see pictures of their baby. Cathy eagerly pulled out her phone. I was making a fuss over the baby boy's smiling face when Britney intervened.

"Leah, I saw you with your folks at Tripp's office today. I work for Tripp. In collections." She gave me a knowing look and tried to catch Tripp's eye.

Tripp cleared his throat but redirected the conversation. "So, Leah, what kind of law did you practice in Chicago?" he asked.

"Torts. Personal injury, wrongful death."

"Medical malpractice?"

"I did some med mal. On the defense side."

He relaxed. "That's a relief. Litigation against medical professionals has really harmed the profession."

My face felt hot. I didn't intend to tolerate a sermon on tort reform from Tripp Pennington. "The defense perspective gave me a bird's-eye view of the careless mistakes medical professionals make."

In the excruciating silence that followed my remark, I took another swallow of my nasty drink. I needed the vodka's medicinal effect.

Looking past me, Tripp asked Danny whether Bassville's criminal activity had been keeping him busy. When Danny laughed, the rest of the table joined in. The guy seated next to the circuit clerk claimed that Bassville didn't even have a crime rate, and Britney heartily agreed. I looked at Danny, expecting a denial. He simply shrugged.

I spoke up. "What about that double murder case you all had here recently?"

Britney said dismissively, "That was out in the country."

I wanted to ask more, but a hand on my back startled me. Looking up, I saw Hopp Cole. "Looks like this is a meeting of the in crowd," he said, smiling.

Across the table, Phil jumped up. "Can I get you a chair, Mr. Cole?"

"No, Phil, thank you. I'm meeting a friend," he said. But he made no move to depart.

Feeling claustrophobic, I pushed my chair back. "Excuse me." I darted past Hopp and hurried to the ladies' room. Once inside, I washed my hands and studied my face in the mirror, just to kill time.

By the time I left the bathroom, Hopp was no longer holding court, but I was ready to leave anyway.

I caught up with the barmaid to settle my tab. "It's been settled," she told me in a confidential tone. "Mr. Cole picked up your tab. Isn't he sweet?"

Sweet? I was infuriated. I scanned the barroom, spotting Hopp sitting near the front with another man: Quint Rhoades, from the Western Roadhouse.

"Sweet Jesus," I muttered.

I made my way over to their table and slid a twenty next to Hopp's cocktail. He looked up in surprise.

In a pleasant voice, I said, "I like to pay my own way. Thanks anyway."

Quint snorted with laughter. "I don't think she appreciates your generosity, Hopp."

Hopp stood, saying, "I'd advise you to change your attitude, miss. You're not up north anymore. You're back in Bassville now. And your family can't afford to lose any friends."

He picked up the twenty, held it out to me. I took it from his hand and dropped it into his drink.

Quint Rhoades exploded with laughter. I tore out of the bar so fast, I almost caught my foot in the closing door.

CHAPTER 24

OVER THE WEEKEND, I reviewed the Maggards' wills. As Amber had predicted, she was the sole beneficiary. The manila folder also contained a couple of older documents designating the Maggards as her legal guardians. It was just like Dad to preserve the proof of the legal relationship between the testators and the beneficiary. He was a details guy. Back in the day, that is.

I called Amber on Sunday night and left a voicemail, telling her to meet me at nine on Monday morning. When I parked outside Dad's office that morning at nine o'clock sharp, I was half surprised not to see her waiting impatiently outside the front door.

But I was more surprised by what awaited me inside.

When I turned the key and swung open the front door, I froze. Enough light filtered in through the open door for me to see desk drawers pulled out, papers and manila folders covering every surface like confetti. Beverly's phrase echoed in my head: *Burglars had come in and trashed the place.*

I stood with my hand on the doorknob, my heart racing. I wasn't sure what to do. I could walk on in, take stock of the damage, and assess what was missing. But for the first time in my life, my father's office felt like a menacing place.

I pulled out my phone, intending to call the sheriff's office and report the crime, but my hands trembled so violently, the screen wouldn't obey my commands. I backed away, locking the door with shaking fingers, and decided to make the short walk to the sheriff's office and report it in person. Before I left, I stuck a two-word note on the door, for Amber's benefit: *Back soon.*

I hustled over to the station and walked up to the uniformed woman at reception: Deputy Crystal Gaines. I'd been childhood friends with her little sister, Meg.

She scrutinized me. "Leah Randall. I heard you were back." With an approving lift of her brow, she added, "You're doing the right thing, helping your dad. Families have to stick together."

I caught my breath, winded from the jog. My agitated dash around the square seemed like an overreaction now that I stood safely across from Deputy Crystal. "Right. Deputy, I need to report—"

"Please call me Crystal."

I tried again. "Crystal, I need to report a burglary."

Her nonchalant demeanor disappeared. She swiveled in her desk chair and clicked the computer mouse. "When?"

"Just discovered it a couple of minutes ago."

Her fingers clattered on the keyboard. "Where?"

"Randall Law Office. The corner of Boone and Elm Streets."

A man's voice echoed in the hallway. "Crystal! I need a hand." She didn't answer, didn't even glance over her shoulder.

I said, "Can you send somebody over? I need to get back there. I'm supposed to meet a client."

Heavy footfalls sounded as the door behind the reception desk swung open, revealing Sheriff Gilmore. "We're out of coffee, Crystal."

"Then you ought to make another pot." She sounded unsympathetic.

"The Folgers can is empty. And I need a ham and cheese biscuit." His thundering voice softened into a wheedle. "Can't you run over to the Gas-N-Go real quick? I'll owe you one."

"I can't get your breakfast. I'm taking walk-in reports of local crime."

The sheriff snorted. "From who?"

"Ms. Randall here, for one."

He turned to me, looking perplexed. "You're here to report a crime? I figured you were here for Amber." While I puzzled over his statement, Gilmore shook a gnarled finger in Crystal's direction. "Fine. I'm getting the doggone coffee myself. There's no sex discrimination in my office."

"Sure there isn't," she murmured.

As Gilmore turned to exit, I asked, "Sheriff, is Amber in your office?"

He opened the door. Leaning against the frame, he said, "Yes, ma'am. I figured you knew. We found that vagrant panhandling the tourists, up by Branson, Missouri."

"Has he been interrogated?"

"We'll take a statement, right after Amber picks him out of a lineup." His expression was mulish as he added, "But I'm not doing it without coffee. Getting too old to keep these hours."

I put my hand on the door, intending to tell him why I was really there. But he spoke before I had the chance, saying, "Tell you the truth, I'm glad you showed up. That girl's downright twitchy this morning. Acts like she's about to jump out of her skin."

CHAPTER 25

DEPUTY CRYSTAL GAINES ushered me into the observation booth. Amber sat alone in the dark space with her head bowed, but she looked up at the sound of the door. "Where'd you come from?"

"Sheriff Gilmore told me about the lineup. Do you want me to be present for it?"

After a moment, Amber nodded, her face taut. "Yeah. It's good you're here." She toyed with her phone, nudging it with her middle finger to make it spin in a circle on the table.

Looking at her phone, I said, "Amber, I called you last night. Did you get my voicemail?"

She gave me an impatient look. "I seen I had a message, but I couldn't listen to it. I don't know how to make it give me a message. It wanted my password. If I have a password, nobody told me it."

"Well, it was good news. I found Dale's and Glenna's wills. They left everything to you."

Before she could respond, Deputy Danny Minton and Sheriff Gilmore walked in. The sheriff held a steaming cup from the Gas-N-Go.

"Amber, we'd like to get underway. Are you ready to do this?" Gilmore asked.

"I don't guess I have any choice." She sounded moody, resentful.

I bent over and spoke softly to her. "Amber, I understand how difficult it must be to see the man who threatened your family. But it will only take a minute."

Amber didn't meet my eye, just stared at the panel of one-way glass. She was wound so tightly, the tendons stood out in her neck.

The sheriff tapped my shoulder. "We've got them lined up in the hallway, ready to go."

I asked, "Aren't you doing a double-blind lineup? That's what they do in Chicago."

His mouth twitched. "This ain't Chicago."

I stood next to Amber as six men dressed in faded black-and-white-striped jailhouse scrubs filed into the space on the other side of the glass. The men had been assigned numbers on cards that hung around their necks, from one through six. They were all white men, all relatively young. When the fifth one entered and turned to face us, I stifled a gasp.

It was the teenage driver of the Chevy pickup, who'd given me the stink eye in the town square.

CHAPTER 26

AMBER SPOTTED HIM as soon as he came through the door. The sheriff didn't fool her by dressing him like the others.

This was exactly what she'd dreaded. After she'd gotten the call last night to come to the sheriff's office in the morning to view a lineup, she hadn't slept a wink. That hobo hadn't been headed to Missouri, not that she knew of. The sheriff surely had the wrong man.

But there he was: the right man, his pale blue eyes staring straight at her through the glass. Before the lineup, the sheriff had told her not to be afraid, that even though Amber could see the men as plain as day, they couldn't see into the dark little room with the folding chair.

Amber wasn't so sure.

"Take a good look at them, ma'am."

Should she say she didn't recognize him? But what if the hobo had already talked about her—wouldn't it be worse to act like she didn't remember him? It was hard to know what to do.

And how'd they find him, anyway? She'd never thought they'd run him down this fast. Inside her head, she cussed herself. She'd given too much away.

Seemed like she always gave too much away.

Amber's stomach gurgled. She'd had a pint of chocolate milk for breakfast, and it wasn't sitting right. She clenched her hands into fists, relaxed them and clenched again.

Then the words flew out of her mouth. "It's number three. He's the hobo who worked at the farm."

The sheriff kept after her. "Are you certain, ma'am?"

What she wanted was the sheriff to shut up with his questions. Amber felt like she might have a fit, start screaming or strike out at someone, if she didn't keep the panic tightly leashed.

She heard the sheriff tell the deputy to take the hobo to the interrogation room. Amber knew what that meant. They were going to ask him questions. And she knew exactly what he would say.

The shriek that she'd locked in her chest bubbled up. "You're wasting your time. That man's not going to fess up to anything! He's a liar!"

Through a blur, she saw the sheriff's bushy brows draw together. But she couldn't calm herself. She heard herself shouting, as if her voice belonged to someone else. "He's a criminal! He took money from the cookie jar and said he'd kill us all!"

The sheriff turned to Leah, who squatted beside Amber's chair and said, "It's all right, Amber. The man is in custody. He can't harm you."

"You don't know nothing. Nothing." Clutching her arms to her chest, Amber gagged and doubled over with her head between her knees. That chocolate milk was coming back up. In a muffled voice, she said, "I'm going to be sick."

CHAPTER 27

AMBER WAS GONE by the time I finished wiping vomit from my pants with damp paper towels. I returned to the lineup observation booth to find Deputy Crystal Gaines angrily wielding a mop across the tile floor. She told me that Deputy Minton had been instructed to drive Amber home.

I took a cautious step back before I spoke, intending to ask about the teenager. "Crystal, there was a young man in the lineup, a guy I've seen around town—"

"They're all from around town. Except for the one Amber picked out," she said as she wrung the mop with a vicious twist. I sidestepped just in time. "They're all creeps with arrest records." Frowning, she leaned on the mop handle. In a sarcastic voice, she said, "Did you notice who got stuck with the puke cleanup?"

I empathized. I'd done more than my share of cleanup duty at the firm in Chicago. The vomit I'd cleaned had been metaphorical, but it all stunk.

Still, I didn't linger. Crystal was clearly in no mood to answer questions, and I wanted a change of clothing before I went back to await the police at Dad's office. I hurried to my car and drove home with all my windows down.

When I pulled into the driveway, it was already occupied by another vehicle: a silver Lexus sedan. I cautiously walked inside and glimpsed Kate Cole sitting at the table in our formal dining room—a space reserved for holidays and important celebrations—and gently pushed the front door shut while remaining out of sight. Kate was talking.

"Barb, I delivered groceries to the apartment last night, and I saw something shocking."

"Was the apartment in a mess? Isn't Amber keeping it tidy?"

"I didn't pay attention to her housekeeping. Not after I saw the fire damage."

Mom gasped. "Fire? No!"

Curious, I sidled up to the French doors that flanked the dining room. Kate occupied my mother's customary seat at the end of the table, her back to me. Mom sat on Kate's left.

"She said she left a pot on the burner while she took a nap." Kate sounded like Miss Almira Gulch in *The Wizard of Oz,* complaining about Toto. "There's a terrible scorch mark, a big old black one, right over the stove top."

Obligingly, Mom gasped again. "What on earth was she thinking?"

"Hopp says we'll have to pay for repairs before we rent it to the next tenant."

Mom's voice was thoughtful. "Leah mentioned something about taking Amber to urgent care for a burn on her hand."

"Well, she'd better not try to make a claim against us for her injury. We're out of pocket for that girl as it is."

Mom sighed. "You and Hopp are so good."

I made a choking sound; I couldn't help it. Mom glanced up and caught me eavesdropping. She shot me a warning look.

But Kate hadn't noticed my intrusion. She picked up a dainty sandwich and quoted scripture in a lofty tone. "'Blessed are the merciful.'" Then she paused, sniffing. "Do you smell something?"

That was my cue to go. I tiptoed down the hall, but when I passed Dad's office en route to the laundry room, I saw his door was ajar.

Dad sat behind the desk, his head bent over an open file folder. I wondered what case he was examining. When his head nodded and he let out a slight snore, I decided to investigate. I crept up to the desk, holding my breath, and reached for the papers.

Dad's eyes popped open. Startled, I snatched my hand back as he slapped the file shut and slid it onto his lap. "What are you doing in here?"

It was the question I'd learned to fear since childhood—and like a kid, I relied on a quick distraction. "Kate Cole is here, visiting with Mom. I came in to see whether you want the door shut." I leaned over the desk, trying to glimpse a case title or client name on the file folder he held. "What are you working on?"

His hand firmly covered the tab. "You scoot on out of here. And close the door behind you." As I went to pull the door shut, he spoke again. "I need to go down and see to some things in my office."

My knee-jerk response was alarm. The sight of the vandalism would certainly agitate him. After a pause, I simply said, "We can go tomorrow."

By tomorrow, I figured he would have forgotten.

CHAPTER 28

IT WAS MONDAY afternoon when Danny pulled his squad car in front of the law office. I'd watched the clock for over an hour, feeling uneasy inside the ravaged waiting area.

When he walked through the door, I picked my way through scattered documents to meet him. "Finally," I said. "The sheriff's office took their sweet time getting over here. If the burglar was a maniac lying in wait, I'd be dead."

He laughed. "Have you been practicing that line?"

I followed him as he walked through the office, making notations on a report form and taking photos. Looking around, he gave a low whistle. "Looks like they tore up the place."

When we reached the law library at the back of the building, both of us had to watch our step. Dad's law books had been pulled from the shelves and flung onto the floor, and on the far wall, a broken window opened to the alley behind the building.

"Watch out. Don't cut yourself," Danny said, squatting down to snap a picture of glass shards lying on the rug. "You'll need to board this up if you can't get it replaced right away."

I envisioned the burglar breaking the window and crawling in.

It made me shiver, and reminded me of the barred windows in Beverly's kitchen.

"Danny, did you investigate the burglary at Beverly Shirk's house?"

He looked up, surprised. "Yeah. How'd you hear about that?"

"I saw her the other day. Beverly worked for Dad for years." I stood beside him, careful to avoid touching anything. "Do you think there's a connection?"

"Not necessarily. That was residential, not commercial. The sheriff thinks some kids broke into her place, because they didn't take anything of value."

Danny headed out of the library. I followed, and when I saw him seated behind my father's desk, it made my throat ache. I'd never seen anyone occupy that chair other than Dad.

Danny clicked his pen. "What was taken?"

I sighed. "It's such a mess, I can't tell. And I didn't want to dig around, disturb the scene, before you came. But the computers are still here. And Dad never left cash in the office."

Danny poked through the desk drawers, jotted a note on the report, and tucked his pen in the clipboard. "Well, I guess that's it. I'll file this at the office."

I was astounded to see him wrap it up so hastily. "Hey, I'm no expert, but aren't you going to dust the window for prints?"

"I can't stay here too long. I need to wrap this up."

"But you just got here. That's it?"

"Yeah. I've got to get back. Really."

Danny rose, avoiding my eye, and strode through the waiting room, but I dogged his heels.

"Before you go, I want to ask you about a guy in the lineup." He needed to know that the kid in the Chevy truck had been scoping out the office the Friday before the break-in.

Danny had his hand on the doorknob, but he paused, frowning. "I know what you're going to ask," he said. "Amber shouldn't worry."

"What makes you say that?" I kept my voice neutral, unsure why he'd brought Amber into the conversation.

Danny expelled a deep breath. "I shouldn't be talking about this. But nobody is surprised that the vagrant tried to cast blame somewhere else."

I was surprised. But I just nodded as if I understood.

"I think the physical evidence will support her," he went on. "We have the gas cans that were used in the arson. I bet they'll bear his fingerprints."

A sinking sensation washed over me. Keeping my poker face, I asked, "Danny, exactly what did the homeless man say when you all interrogated him?"

Danny pulled on the door, but it stuck in the frame and his hand fell from the knob, as if the stubborn door had convinced him to speak.

"He accused Amber of the murder. She's at the sheriff's office right now. Sheriff Gilmore is questioning her."

CHAPTER 29

I KNEW WHERE to find them. I stormed into the sheriff's office, past Deputy Gaines at the front desk, and pulled open the interrogation room door.

"What the hell is going on?" I said.

Amber twisted around in her chair to face me. She was seated across from Sheriff Gilmore. An older deputy stood beside the video camera in the far corner.

Amber wore sweats and an old top with a loose neckline I'd received for Christmas years ago. She held the excess fabric balled up in her fist, drawing the neckline tight enough to choke her.

Gilmore stood and gestured at a spare folding chair that leaned up against the cinder-block wall. "Deputy, set that chair next to Miss Travis so Miss Randall can join us."

His voice was calm, his demeanor almost courtly. I wasn't deceived.

I said, "No need to bring that chair over here. I don't intend to sit down." Glaring at the sheriff, I asked, "What's the purpose of this interrogation?"

Gilmore's face wrinkled into a benevolent smile. "We're just being thorough, Miss Randall. We're trying to clear some things up here."

Despite the sheriff's "good cop" performance, it didn't escape my notice that he no longer addressed me or my client by our first names. There had been a major shift in our status since this morning.

My voice was cold. "Exactly what are you clearing up?"

Instead of answering, Sheriff Gilmore pulled a sheet from a stack of papers that lay in front of him on the table. "This is Miss Travis's signature right here, saying she knowingly and intelligently waived her constitutional right to silence or to have counsel present."

The sheriff handed the paper to me. It contained the customary Miranda warning language. Amber's signature was underneath, in the shaky cursive scrawl of a grade school kid. The sheriff had signed off as a witness.

I said, "It's not voluntary. We dispute that it's a knowing and intelligent waiver."

Amber gave me a resentful look. She probably thought I'd insulted her intelligence. Tactically, I had.

I said, "Then this is custodial interrogation. Is Amber a suspect?"

The deputy operating the camera cleared his throat. "Sheriff, do you want this to keep rolling?"

"Yep," Gilmore said, dropping the grandfatherly demeanor. "That vagrant, he made some alarming allegations."

I locked eyes with the sheriff. "What did the man say?"

We continued our staring match. When I didn't blink, the sheriff turned to Amber. "Miss Travis, what do you think he said?"

"Don't answer that." My voice was sharp.

Gilmore pulled out a stapled document. He gazed at Amber again, before shifting his eyes back to me.

"Burry Jones said that Amber tried to hire him to kill the Maggards."

CHAPTER 30

I WAS SPEECHLESS.

By contrast, the sheriff's accusation loosened Amber's tongue.

"I didn't kill anybody!" she said, pushing back her folding chair and jumping up.

I grasped her free hand. "Hush."

"Sit back down, Miss Travis," Gilmore said. "Your lawyer wants to hear what Burry Jones told us."

She ignored the command to sit. The sheriff pulled reading glasses from his shirt pocket and made a show of flipping through the statement's pages.

I braced myself as Gilmore tapped a line on a page with his index finger.

"Here we go. The man was very specific. He told me that Amber offered cash."

The sheriff peered at me over the reading glasses, raising his eyebrows. He was waiting for me to speak.

I found my voice. "That seems unlikely."

His eyes returned to the pages he held. "It's all right here, in his own words. Jones states—this is a quote—'She said there was a lot of cash around and she knew where to get it.'"

I absorbed the information, trying to get my head around it. Gilmore kept reading.

"Question: 'What was your response?' Jones: 'I said no. No. I wasn't that guy.' Question: 'What did Amber Travis do or say when you refused?'"

The sheriff paused, looking up at me to be sure he had my attention. He did.

"Jones states: 'She offered sex. Different sex acts.'"

My heart rate accelerated. The accusation was damning.

Amber snatched her hand from my hold and backed farther away from the table. Breathing hard, she said, "I didn't kill the Maggards."

Turning to her, I used Walt Randall's most authoritarian voice. "Amber, I want you to be silent. Don't speak."

She backed up to the wall and stood there, one hand clutching the fabric of her top and holding it under her chin.

"I didn't kill them," she said again, her face flushed red. "But I tell you what, I ain't sorry they're dead. They deserved killing."

Her high soprano had disappeared. I stepped in front of Amber to create a physical barrier between her and the sheriff.

"I'm terminating this interview, Gilmore. We're being recorded, and I want to put you on notice: your attempts to continue interrogating my client over my advice and counsel are improper and unethical."

The sheriff took off his glasses and wiped them on his shirttail while watching me with a dogged look. He said, "Seems to me like Miss Travis has more she'd like to say."

I raised my voice, projecting from the diaphragm. "Is Amber Travis under arrest? Has she been charged with an offense?"

My voice bounced off the walls. The old deputy in the corner stuck a finger in his ear. Sheriff Gilmore regarded me for a long moment, narrowing his eyes. Finally, he shook his head.

"Good. Then we're free to go."

CHAPTER 31

AMBER GAPED AT the disarray in the law office. I snatched documents off the seats of two chairs in the waiting area and tossed them onto Beverly's desk.

"What happened here?" she asked.

"We had a break-in," I said. She didn't need to hear the details of the office burglary. "Amber, we need to talk about what happened at the sheriff's office. Because of the homeless man's statement, they have reason to suspect you were involved in your cousins' murders."

She rolled her eyes. "That's stupid. You're my lawyer. You fix it."

I paused to collect my thoughts. I wasn't accustomed to advising people who had no concept of the legal system. I needed to speak carefully, to make Amber understand.

"Technically, I don't represent you in a criminal case, because there's no charge against you. But, Amber, you have to listen to me when I tell you: absolutely do not make any statements to the police. And that includes Sheriff Gilmore."

She looked confused. "We have to do what the sheriff tells us. Everybody knows that."

"No. You don't have to answer the police's questions about this.

You don't have to answer any questions at all. Do you understand me?"

"I guess." She tightened her grip on her top's neckline. Earlier, I'd attributed the way she bunched up the fabric to nerves or fright, but now I wondered if it was another demonstration of her excessive modesty.

"You said you found that will. I want it," she said abruptly. When I presented her with the documents, she snatched them from my hand.

"Here's where they named you beneficiary, and here they designated you as executrix," I showed her.

"Yes," she said, placing her finger on her printed name. She smiled with satisfaction.

"Since you're executrix, you can choose to hire a lawyer to handle the estate."

"Okay, you're hired." Leaning over, she dug into her purse and pulled out a check. "Now cash this for me."

I examined it. Made out to Amber Travis, it was for almost a thousand dollars. "Where did you get this?"

"The neighbor who took over the chickens after Dale and Glenna was killed said he wanted to buy them. And I said it was fine with me."

Her face was bright. The prospect of her windfall obviously had lifted her spirits. Although I dreaded bearing bad news, I didn't have any choice.

"You can't cash this, Amber. The estate has to go through probate, over at the courthouse, before you get your inheritance."

She grabbed the check back and stuffed it deep inside her purse. "The Maggards left me everything. It's in the will."

"They did. It takes a while, that's all."

Amber hopped out of the chair and headed for the door. I followed, saying, "Don't forget what I said about the police. And you absolutely cannot tell people you're glad the Maggards are dead."

She whirled around to face me. "I'm tired of pretending. I *am* glad they're dead."

Amber jerked her purse onto her shoulder, dropping the loose neckline of her top. It gaped in front, baring her other shoulder and revealing part of her chest.

My breath caught. Her skin bore vicious weals and scars. It felt intrusive to stare, so I averted my eyes and asked gently, "Amber, how did you get those injuries?"

She didn't answer. She just snatched the neckline up again, coiling the fabric into a knot. Then she left the office, slamming the door behind her.

CHAPTER 32

BY DUSK, THE heat was so oppressive Mom stretched out on the living room sofa with an ice pack behind her neck. I joined Dad outside on the front steps, carrying two big glasses of ice water.

He accepted the water without comment and took a deep swallow. I let the silence embrace us for a moment before I broached the topic that had been troubling me.

"Dad, what did you know about the Maggards?"

He drank again. Staring out into the front yard, he said, "Not sure who you mean."

I shifted my position on the step. "The Maggards, Dale and Glenna. They were clients of yours. A childless couple who had a farm in the country, a poultry operation."

"A poultry operation," he echoed.

I wasn't getting through. By now I knew some of his tricks, like repeating information he'd been provided.

"The Maggards had a younger cousin living with them, Amber Travis. You drafted their wills. They left everything to her."

Setting his drink by his feet, he clasped his hands together. "Amber Travis. I was guardian ad litem."

That surprised me. I hadn't given the other documents in the file a close enough read. "So you were guardian ad litem in the proceeding to determine her placement, after she was orphaned? And that's when the Maggards were named her legal guardians?"

He nodded as he reached again for his water glass. "The foster care system is a hard place for children. It's a roll of the dice. It was Judge Harris's case. He always placed youngsters with blood relations, unless there was no other option. Always, without exception." Grimacing, he rubbed his hand over his face. "Some foster parents are ideal, but not all of them. There are people on this earth who shouldn't have children under their control."

"What about the Maggards, Dad? Did you have reason to oppose the placement, as guardian ad litem?"

The sky overhead was almost dark. Something rustled in the oak branches.

Dad pointed at the trees out front. "There they go."

Our old chimney was home to generations of bats. They swooped down in substantial number. Dad watched the bats settle in the trees, shaking his head with a chuckle. He finally turned his head and locked eyes with me. "Family is important. You have to protect your family, Leah."

Frustration lodged in my chest. He looked down at his hands, sitting slack in his lap. When he spoke again, I had to bend my ear close to hear what he said.

"Your mother says we need to get rid of the bats. But they eat the mosquitoes. A bat can eat a thousand mosquitoes in an hour. Most people don't appreciate that."

Silence enveloped us. Full darkness had fallen, and as we sat on the stone steps in the hot summer night, I suspected that Dad had retreated into his own twilight again.

Groaning with effort, he rose and headed to the front door. Before he entered the house, he turned and spoke to me.

"Sometimes there's no easy choice."

I couldn't be sure if he was still talking about the bats. Or about the Maggards.

CHAPTER 33

THOUGH I WANTED to unravel the mystery of Amber Travis's past, my primary goal was shutting down Dad's caseload. After I set his office to rights, I cleared out his inbox and consulted with Phil Benson and Beverly Shirk. For the handful of cases that still had loose ends, I filed my entry of appearance as co-counsel.

It was midmorning on Wednesday when I stopped to catch my breath. I needed a break and, more importantly, a reward for my labor. Locking the office, I strolled to one of my favorite girlhood haunts: Sunrise Donuts, off the square.

The interior hadn't changed—a couple of tables up front, molded plastic booths along the walls, and the delicious aroma were all just as I remembered. What I'd forgotten was that it was also a favorite stop for men of a certain age. By the time I spotted Hopp Cole presiding over a table of baby boomers, it was too late to turn around. I grabbed a bottle of Dr Pepper from the cooler and hurried to the counter, waiting behind a young mother selecting a dozen donuts while her toddlers pressed their faces to the glass case.

Hopp appeared at my elbow. "This is a stroke of luck. I was thinking about calling you this morning."

I stretched my face into a smile. "How about that."

The mother in front of me at the counter was apparently short on cash. Sounding apologetic, she said, "Can you put some of them back? Maybe the chocolate ones?"

Hopp spoke close to my ear. "Do you know what that young woman's been up to? She just waltzed up to one of my tellers, trying to cash a big old check. Why, that fool girl doesn't even have any legal ID."

One of the children wailed. "I want chocolate!"

He grasped my elbow. "I generally wouldn't use the word 'fool,' for scriptural reasons. But she's walking around with a check for almost a thousand dollars, and she's already endorsed the danged thing. Anyone could knock her on the head and cash it for themselves."

For once, Hopp and I saw eye to eye. It *was* foolish of Amber to carry around an endorsed check. But I wouldn't acknowledge it.

Red faced, the young woman ahead of me dug into her purse again. I pulled my card out and stepped up beside her at the counter. "It's on me. My treat." *Anything to get me out of here.* I set the Dr Pepper beside the debit card. "Add this to the tab."

The mother thanked me profusely, but I just wanted to ditch Hopp Cole.

He followed me to the door. "The girl's unstable. I want her out of my apartment building."

With that, he had my full attention. "You're not seriously talking about evicting her."

"What choice do I have? My wife saw fire damage in the kitchen. Amber's responsible—she admitted it. She's a danger to the other tenants. What if she burned the whole place down?"

I tried to mimic my mother's natural affability. "Mr. Cole, you're known in the community for your charity. Amber has no place to go. No resources. Her home was burned to the ground."

"And now she's trying to burn down my property."

I choked out a laugh. "Oh, come on. You don't believe that."

There was a moment's silence before Hopp spoke again. "I don't know what to think. People are starting to talk. You know how word spreads in Bassville. Maybe the best thing for Amber would be to leave town. Get a fresh start somewhere else."

A man at Hopp's table tipped his chair back onto two legs as he called to us. "Hey, Hopp! Did you tell her about that check?"

My jaw clenched. Hopp Cole was the president of a bank. He shouldn't be stooping to gossiping about his customers.

I decided there was no point in using the sweet Barb Randall treatment, because this was a man accustomed to sugar. He needed a dose of vinegar. "Have you commenced civil action?"

His eyes narrowed. "Excuse me?"

"For eviction. Tenants have rights under state law, and as a landlord, you should know the procedural requirements to remove a tenant take a while. Particularly when the tenant is represented by counsel."

"I don't have to do a damn thing. She's not my tenant since she doesn't pay rent. And if she doesn't get the hell out, I'll send the sheriff to arrest her for trespassing."

I had been blowing smoke. But from Hopp's testy reaction, it appeared I had hit the target. I struggled to keep a grin off my face. Clearly Hopp wasn't used to a fight.

I lifted my chin. "Sheriff Gilmore isn't your personal rent-a-cop. You know," I said, my voice rising as inspiration struck, "I bet local TV people would love a chance to talk to Amber. This landlord-tenant quandary would lend some drama to the local news. A story like that might get picked up in Little Rock. Who knows? It could go national. The networks love a damsel in distress."

When Hopp swallowed, I could see his neck bob. The sight sent a thrill of triumph down my spine.

He shoved his hands into his pockets and lowered his voice. "Your mother would be ashamed to see you behaving this way."

I didn't flinch, but the statement stung. Then he went a step too far.

"Tell me the truth, honey. Is your mama worried about the over-due payment on the short-term loan I made her? Is that why you're acting so ugly?"

CHAPTER 34

I TURNED ON my heel, riled by Hopp Cole's words. Out on the sidewalk, I reached for my phone. Glancing back to ensure the banker wasn't dogging my tracks, I hit Amber's number.

"Hi. Amber, I just saw Hopp Cole, and he says there's fire damage at your apartment. He's unhappy about it. He says he wants you to move out."

Amber wailed into the phone. "I ain't got no place to go!"

Now that Hopp had turned against her, I suspected the Presbyterian prayer group wouldn't provide fallback support for Amber. Hopp's wife, Kate, was the alpha of the pack.

Keeping my voice upbeat, I asked, "Who else do you know around here? What about your neighbors on the farm?"

"I don't know anybody. The neighbors wasn't our friends. Glenna didn't have no friends." She started to cry. "I don't like Dale's friends."

The mention of neighbors reminded me of another tricky issue. "Amber, Mr. Cole also said you tried to cash that check at the bank. I told you, you can't do that."

I braced myself for an argument. Instead, she jumped to a new topic. "The sheriff came and stuck a big old Q-tip in my mouth. Can he do that?"

My heart gave a thud. "What? The sheriff did what? I specifically told you not to cooperate with the sheriff."

Her soprano pitched into a shrill whine. "I thought I just wasn't supposed to talk about the hobo no more. He asked other things. Then he stuck that Q-tip in my mouth. And took my fingerprints, too. How come he done that?"

The answer was obvious to me, if not to Amber. I wasn't naive enough to believe that Sheriff Gilmore was gathering evidence to eliminate Amber as a suspect.

She had become the target of the investigation.

CHAPTER 35

WITH AN EFFORT, I worked to keep my voice calm. "Exactly what did you say when they were fingerprinting you and swabbing your cheek?"

"The sheriff wanted to know if I'd remembered more things about the night of the fire. How did it start, when did it start. Did I see anybody in the house. Things like that."

I stayed cool; it was a miracle of self-control. "What did you tell him?"

Her voice rose. "I told him I couldn't answer none of those questions."

I experienced a sliver of relief. "Because your lawyer told you to remain silent?"

"No, because the night of the fire I slept out in the shed."

Of course. Amber had mentioned that to me before. Recalling my visit to the crime scene with Danny Minton, I remembered the old wooden shed. I'd looked at the interior. It hadn't resembled a resting place in any way.

"Did you always sleep out there?" I asked.

"I usually slept inside. Either on the pull-out sofa in the main room"—her voice dropped as she added—"or in their bed."

A wave of weariness engulfed me. I could think of only one reason why Amber had shared the Maggards' bed. "Did they make you their sexual partner?"

"Not her. Him."

She sounded angry. I didn't blame her.

"So why did you sleep in the shed that night?" I asked.

Her voice was matter-of-fact. "Because that's where they kept the dog cage. When Dale was mad at me, I had to sleep in the kennel. And he was mad that day because of the eggs. I told you about the eggs, how I dropped a whole mess of them, and Glenna told on me. She didn't want him blaming her for it."

I conjured the image of the dog kennel I had seen in the Maggards' shed. The thought of Amber in there made me ill. Bile rose in my throat. I coughed and swallowed it back before I could speak.

"Amber, if you were forced into a dog cage, that's a crime. It's domestic abuse, false imprisonment."

"Dale didn't think so."

I shut my eyes and rubbed them. It struck me that Amber spoke of the confinement without emotion, as if it was an ordinary consequence. I said, "Did you ever report this mistreatment to the police?"

She sighed into the phone. "No. I knew I didn't have the right to."

"Everyone has the right to be free from abuse, Amber. Why would you think that?"

She made me wait for the answer. As seconds ticked by, I tried to anticipate her response, but when she ultimately spoke, nothing could have prepared me to hear it.

"Because I was Dale's slave."

CHAPTER 36

CAT'S OUT OF the bag, Amber thought as she tossed the phone onto the coffee table. She could see Dale's face in her mind, leaning over her and warning her: "Don't let the cat out of the bag. Don't you do it."

He must have talked about the cat a hundred times over the years.

Amber had had a real cat one time, a skinny orange stray that had wandered over to the farmhouse. The feral cat had rubbed up against her ankles and had let Amber hold it in her arms, like a baby. She'd sung it songs, like her mama used to do when she was little. She'd kept it in the shed and hadn't told a soul.

But Glenna had caught her stealing a can of tuna from the kitchen and told on her. Dale had grabbed the cat by the scruff, put it in a gunny sack, and drowned it.

Amber hadn't thought about the cat for a long time.

She rose from the sofa and tidied up, since she was expecting company. She washed a dirty cup and set it on the dish drainer by the sink, then used a dish towel to wipe dust from the coffee table and the top of the television set.

The knock at the door was loud. Amber checked the peephole,

just in case, before she opened it. The danger hadn't died with Dale.

Leah walked in, clutching that briefcase she always carried. Her face was as red as fire, like she'd been hauling hay in August.

"We have to talk about the slavery allegation," Leah said, slinging that lawyer talk around.

"Allegation?"

"Allegation—it means the same thing as 'claim.' You claim you were Dale Maggard's slave. Explain to me why you said that."

"Because it's true." Amber wondered whether Leah took her for a liar. That was the problem with sometimes speaking the truth and sometimes not. Folks never knew when to believe you, so they usually didn't. Mama had taught her that.

"You couldn't be a slave, Amber. Slavery is illegal. In the United States, slavery doesn't exist."

"Yes it does."

"No." Leah's knuckles were white. "The US Constitution outlawed slavery long, long ago."

The debate was wearing Amber out. She couldn't keep the indignation from her voice when she answered. "Well, it surely was real for me. Because of the contract Dale wrote out on my eighteenth birthday."

When Leah spoke again, her voice crackled. "You're telling me there was a contract of some kind? In writing?"

"He wrote it out himself. Dale said he was gonna give me everything: the farm, the house, the laying hens. But then after I signed it, I was stuck. I couldn't get out of it, because it was for life. The rest of my life, he said. But the way it turned out, it was for the rest of *his* life, I guess. Because him and Glenna's dead, and I ain't." When Amber thought about that, she smiled. "Lucky me."

But the smile slipped. "Whenever I tried to stop him, Dale would bring out that contract and showed me where I signed my name. He'd say, 'There it is, in black and white.'"

When Leah spoke, her voice was barely a whisper. "Stop what?"

Amber hung her head. She knew it would be hard to say it out loud. To steel herself, she thought about Dale drowning her orange cat while she stood by and watched.

"The whipping, and the electrocuting. And them other things. All of that."

CHAPTER 37

I SAT INSIDE the car, concentrating on my breathing. I hadn't felt like this since I'd flipped out right before my first jury trial. Afterward, I'd done research, learning techniques to keep panic under control.

As I took slow, deep breaths, thoughts bounced in my brain. Was it possible that Amber had actually submitted to torture at Dale Maggard's hands? Was she mentally unbalanced? Or a pathological liar, slandering a dead man for personal gain?

But someone had inflicted the scars I'd seen on Amber's bare skin; it was crucial to determine who had done it, and why.

Sheriff Gilmore was building a case against Amber, and she needed to be prepared to defend against it. If Amber had been subjected to bodily harm, she needed proof.

Squaring my shoulders, I pushed open the door of the Pennington Family Practice Clinic. I strode in, determined. When I saw Britney Shelton sitting at the front desk, I didn't even flinch.

Her eyes widened as she smiled. "Leah. What are you here for?"

"I need to make an emergency appointment." When she opened her mouth, I cut her off. "It's not for me."

"If this is an emergency, you need to dial 911," she recited by rote, adding in a whisper: "Is it your dad?"

"I need to talk with Tripp. Is he back there?"

She leaned back in her chair, looking affronted. "You can't just barge in here and demand to see Tripp."

I bent over the desk so we wouldn't be overheard. "Britney, if you don't take me to see him right now, I'm going to call your mother and tell her what really went down at your birthday sleepover in seventh grade."

Her face blanched. I pressed my advantage. "Don't think I won't. I'll call her this goddamn minute."

I'll never know whether Britney would have buckled, because Tripp walked in from the back at that moment and handed a file to her.

I smiled like a pageant queen. "Tripp! Can we chat in your office? It will just take a sec."

He gave me a dubious look but nodded. I followed him down the hallway and into his office, where I shut the door, saying, "So sorry to impose, Tripp, but it's a matter of urgency."

"I see." He sounded concerned rather than irritated. I gave him points for that. "Is it Walt?"

"No, it's not Dad. This is about my client, Amber Travis, the young woman who escaped the fire when the Maggards were murdered. She needs a complete physical. Can you do a pelvic exam here at the clinic? She needs one. And a Pap smear. And a manual breast exam."

He was quiet for a moment. "We do annual wellness exams for women at this clinic, since there's no ob-gyn in Bassville. I could probably get to it in three or four weeks, but—"

My ears rang. "No. It can't wait. It has to be soon, the next day or so." I was mortified when my voice cracked. "Tripp, you have to see her." The next words almost stuck in my throat, but I forced them out: "Please. Please do this."

Tripp made me wait for an anxious moment before he said, "Bring her in at 7:30 tomorrow morning. I'll come in early."

CHAPTER 38

I WALKED UP to our house, dragging my feet. My mother appeared at the door. "Leah! You're home early." Mom grasped my hand and tugged on it. "Let's go out to lunch."

"Nah. Not really interested in going out. Maybe I'll lie down for a minute."

She squeezed my hand in a desperate grip. "Please, honey? I need a little break from your daddy."

I paused on the landing. "Dad. I have to talk to Dad."

"Leah, no." She bolted past me and blocked the door. "He's been in a state all morning. I finally had to give him a Xanax. Let him rest."

The image of Mom sedating my father was surreal. Though after the morning I'd endured, I'd be grateful for a chill pill myself.

I agreed to lunch.

"The chicken salad here is out of this world," Mom said as we walked into Betsy's Tea Room and chose a sunny spot at the front. "Kate Cole absolutely loves this place," she continued, shaking out a cloth napkin. "There's a meeting room in the back. Sometimes we hold our prayer group there."

The mention of Kate Cole reminded me of my earlier conversation with Hopp. So much had happened since then, I'd nearly forgotten the rumble at the donut shop.

"Mom, I saw Hopp Cole this morning. He said something about you being behind on the payments for a short-term loan?"

She pursed her lips. "I can't believe Hopp would bring that up. He told me I could pay it off whenever it was convenient."

I gave my mother a dogged look. "Mom, you need to get on top of it. You don't want to be under Hopp Cole's thumb."

Mom picked up the fork and examined it critically, then wiped the tines with her napkin. "Leah, please. Kate and Hopp are loyal friends."

A young waitress appeared, smiling at Mom as she set down two tumblers of water. "Mrs. Randall, I think it's real sweet that you're having lunch with your daughter instead of with all your friends back there." The waitress pulled out a pad from her pocket. "What can I get you ladies today?"

"Give us another minute." Mom gave her a placid smile. As the waitress left, Mom pinched her lips together and shook her head.

"It could have been an oversight," I said, lying. When she still didn't respond, I leaned toward her. "Mom, don't let those church bitches hurt your feelings. Go on back there and let Kate Cole know you're onto her."

"Leah, hush."

I pushed my chair back from the table. "I'll do it."

"Don't you dare."

She was serious, and I knew it; addressing an issue head-on violated the unwritten law of Bassville. But I'd never fit the local mold, and I was poised to attack.

I noticed a white-haired woman in knit capri pants emerge from the back room and make her way to the cash register. Sheila Owens, my Sunday school teacher when I was in grade school.

"Mrs. Owens! Over here! It's me, Leah Randall," I called.

Sheila had the grace to look abashed as she shambled over to our table. "Hello, Leah. We missed you at the meeting, Barb."

My mother gave a tight smile. "Meeting?" she said.

"Kate got us together for an emergency session of the prayer group. She said a congregation in Pine Bluff is supporting a charitable mission to distribute Bibles in India, and she thinks we should join the Bible project. Instead of helping out the Travis girl."

Sheila turned and looked over her shoulder, probably fearful her coconspirators would catch her speaking out of turn. "We took a vote. The Bibles won. It was unanimous."

"I wish I could have been there," Mom said pleasantly.

Sheila's face was sober. "I thought so myself. But Kate said it would put you in a spot since Leah's tied up with the Travis girl. And she told us how you're so burdened with Walt's Alzheimer's, we can't expect you to participate in the group for a while." Sheila stepped over, placed a hand on Mom's shoulder, and whispered, "I'll be praying for you, Barb."

After Sheila left, I tried to touch Mom's hand, but she scooted out of reach. "Let's go. I'll meet you in the car," she said.

Mom tore out of the restaurant before I could get the keys out of my bag. We drove home in silence while I contemplated how the real target of the Bassville community's ire wasn't my mother.

It was Amber.

CHAPTER 39

AFTER I TOOK my mother home, I went to get wood at the lumberyard so I could board up the broken window at Dad's office, since the cardboard I'd originally used provided little protection. I wasn't an expert do-it-yourselfer, but it had to be done, and there was no one else to do it. While I worked, I kept hydrated with a six-pack of Coors Light I'd picked up at the Gas-N-Go.

By the time I finished, it was dusk. I walked out into the back alley to evaluate my labor, pounding on the boards with a closed fist.

A circle of light blinded me. A man's voice barked, "Freeze!" Gravel crunched as the figure approached. "What the hell are you doing, skulking around in the alley?"

Danny Minton. My shoulders sagged in relief. I knocked on the wooden planks. "Testing out my security system."

He followed me inside and inspected my work, nodding with approval. "Not bad. You did this without any help?"

I felt a warm surge of pride. "My dad was super handy around the house. Maybe I inherited that gene."

I popped the tab on my third beer and offered Danny a Dr Pepper from the fridge. It was a treat to have company. I joined him at the library table, ready to shoot the breeze for a while.

It surprised me when Danny asked, "You want to tell me what's wrong, Leah? You're all wound up."

I barked out a guttural laugh. "You should've seen me a few hours ago."

"You want to talk about it?" he said again.

"Oh, Danny. Wish I could." It would have been a tremendous relief to unburden myself. But Danny was law enforcement, so Amber's story couldn't be shared. And we weren't tight enough for me to confide my family's woes. Still, the beer had loosened my tongue.

"You're the best friend I've got in Bassville." I pulled a face. "Most of the people who live here are such assholes."

"Not all of them," he said.

"Name ten people in Bassville who aren't total shits. Just ten."

Danny rubbed the back of his head with a rueful expression. "I'd probably prefer to keep my list a secret."

"That's the problem with Bassville. Too many damn secrets!" I complained.

"Okay, I'll tell you one of mine." Danny dropped his voice to a whisper. "One time, when I was sixteen, I sneaked out at night and painted over the *B* on the Bassville sign."

I shrieked with delight. "I did it twice!"

"Sounds like Amber Travis has some dark secrets," he said, changing direction so quickly it caught me off guard.

I stared at him as the friendly glow dissipated. "You know I can't talk about Amber with you."

"Fine. That's fine. I get that," Danny said. "Just trying to be a friend. You know, any association with the Travis girl is going to hurt you, Leah."

Feeling injured, I said, "Is that why you came in here tonight? To scare me off Amber?"

His expression held no remorse. "It wouldn't be a bad idea."

I was suddenly overcome with weariness. "Why don't you head on out, Danny. I'm going to lock up."

He looked at me askance. "How are you getting home?"

"Uber or Lyft." When he started to speak, I flipped my hand to cut him off. "Joke. I'll call Mom. I guarantee, she's stone-cold sober."

My personal head count of trusted friends in Bassville had dropped from one to none.

CHAPTER 40

THE NEXT MORNING, I dropped Amber off at her 7:30 appointment at the clinic. As I watched her walk off with Tripp, my eyes misted. I knew the examination would be difficult for her.

An hour or so later, I was scrolling through Arkansas's eviction cases when the law office door rattled, and Tripp Pennington entered.

I rose, but before I could speak, he slammed the door shut behind him.

"Who did that to her? I want a name."

I pointed him to a chair across the desk and kept my voice even. "You can talk to me about the exam, since I'm her attorney."

With a shaking hand, Tripp pulled the chair up to the desk and faced me. "Yes. We also had her sign a waiver giving consent for me to share all her medical information with you."

"Okay, then." I braced myself. "Tell me about the examination."

A sheen of sweat glistened on his forehead. He swiped at it with the back of his hand. "From just visual observation, I saw a lot of injuries. Some relatively recent, others inflicted further back in time." Tripp shut his eyes. When he opened them, he continued. "Starting at the top: she has marks circling her neck."

I thought of the hooded sweatshirts Amber had endured in the August heat. "What do the marks represent? In your opinion?"

"They're consistent with strangulation. She confirmed that. Lower down were scars, mostly on her back and buttocks, some on her chest. Made with an instrument like a whip." He looked at me.

I confirmed, "Amber said something to me yesterday about being whipped."

He focused on the wall opposite. "And there were burns consistent with electrocution."

Bile rose in my throat. "She mentioned electrocution too. But the only burn I saw was on her hand. She said it came from a kitchen fire."

"I'm not talking about that. The electrical burns I observed are on her sexual organs."

"Jesus," I said, horrified at the atrocities Amber had suffered. But it was my responsibility to listen.

Tripp was wiping tears from his face. He had borne witness to torture, seen with his own eyes the horror and cruelty inflicted upon her. I gave him a moment to collect himself before asking, "Were you able to do a Pap smear? Or check for STDs?"

He started to answer, then paused and didn't meet my eye. "I did. After I removed the stitches. Someone sewed her—"

"Stop." I didn't want to know, didn't want to hear about it, not even secondhand. I turned to the wall, trying to collect myself. "Stop. Give me a minute."

After I regained a scrap of composure, I took a deep breath and turned to face Tripp. His eyes met mine, with a haunted look. I said, "Where is she? Did Amber go home?"

"I told her to go directly to the sheriff's office. To make a report to Sheriff Gilmore."

The word "sheriff" sent a shot of adrenaline through me like a bolt of lightning.

"Oh, hell no," I said, jumping up.

Tripp blocked my way. "She said you told her she couldn't go to the police. What's up with that? I feel ethically bound to report her abuse to the police. Don't you?" His eyes pinned me with an accusatory glare.

I didn't blink. "You're a smart guy. You can surely figure this out," I said more calmly than I felt. "You said the marks on Amber's body were inflicted over time."

He nodded.

I continued, "Everyone knows her history. She's been stuck out on that chicken farm with her cousins for years. So who's your perpetrator?"

He didn't answer.

I nudged his shoulder. It felt good to give him a shove. "Dead guy, maybe?" I said. "This is a trickier situation than you realize. Gilmore is looking for a murder suspect."

Understanding dawned on Tripp's face. "Amber's the target of the criminal case? Shit."

"She hasn't actually been charged," I said.

He added the word I'd left unspoken: "Yet."

We stood in silence until the wall clock chimed.

"I've got to get back. People are waiting on me," Tripp said with a sigh. Instead of heading for the door, though, he first strolled up to examine the tacky framed picture that hung next to the clock.

He tapped the glass, looking amused. "Dogs playing poker. Damn. Haven't seen one of those since we sold Grandpa's house."

I dug deep for a clever reply but came up blank. As soon as the door shut behind him, I grabbed the picture frame, determined to retire the beer-drinking canines. I didn't want anyone to think I approved of the wall art. Especially Tripp Pennington.

The picture was harder to remove than I had expected. When I finally wrenched it free, I understood why Dad had hung it so securely.

Behind it, a locked wooden cabinet was built into the wall.

CHAPTER 41

AMBER WAS FROZEN with indecision. The doctor had said she should tell the sheriff about Dale. But the lawyer woman had said she wasn't to tell the sheriff nothing about nothing.

Amber wasn't used to deciding important things for herself; she was accustomed to doing what she was told. But when people told her two opposite things, who should she pay mind to? Mama had never offered any helpful wisdom for this kind of situation. She'd have to figure it out on her own.

She pulled the hood of the sweatshirt over her head. The impulse to cover up was rooted too deep to break, even though it made her hot. As she grew warmer, Amber had a hankering for chocolate milk. She was thirsty, and she hadn't had a bite of food for breakfast.

When she entered Sunrise Donuts, it was crowded. People stood in line at the counter, and Amber had to wait her turn. Peeking around the person ahead of her, Amber was glad to see the regular girl at the cash register. She knew what Amber liked.

As she waited, she saw two women seated in a booth along the wall. They both wore plastic name tags that read FIRST COMMUNITY BANK. Amber saw the women give her the side-eye and huddle together, talking in whispers. She got the feeling they were talking about her.

Amber was relieved when her turn to order finally came. "I'll have a chocolate milk and one of them jelly donuts," she told the cashier.

The cashier jabbed the buttons on the cash register. "That'll be two dollars and forty-one cents," she said. She didn't sound a bit friendly.

"I got an account here. Remember?" Amber glanced at the booth by the wall. The women from the bank were watching.

"The prayer group closed your account," the cashier said. "Mrs. Cole called yesterday."

Amber tried to think of something to say as she stood there, looking the fool. Her throat was tight as she choked out, "I'd best move on."

She backed away from the counter and hurried out of the shop. Outside, a passing pickup laid on its horn, making her jump. As it rolled toward the intersection, Amber studied the truck through narrowed eyes. She'd seen that same pickup with the flag flying in the bed too many times for comfort. Seemed like it popped up everywhere she turned in Bassville.

It was time. She needed help. And she knew better than to seek it from the church ladies or the sheriff. She pulled out her cell phone and checked the screen. It still worked. The prayer group hadn't cut it off yet.

This call couldn't wait.

CHAPTER 42

I JUST COULDN'T leave it alone.

The hidden cabinet captured my imagination. I'd confiscated Dad's keys after Tripp forbade him to drive, and now I tried them all, jamming in each key. But the cabinet remained closed.

In the law library, my eyes fell on the hammer I'd used to board up the window. The landline rang just as I was considering whether to bash through the wooden cabinet door.

I didn't pick up the call until the robot-voiced caller ID announced, "County prosecutor's office."

"Is Walt there?" a woman asked when I answered.

"No, he isn't in the office. This is his daughter, Leah."

"When will he be in?"

Surely everyone at the courthouse in Bassville knows Dad's not occupying his office anymore. "He's on a leave of absence. I'm helping with the caseload. Is there an unresolved case with your office? I'm closing his old files."

"No. It's a new case. Shelby Searcy just filed the murder charge against Amber Travis. The criminal complaint is already in the circuit clerk's office, though as a courtesy they'll hold the warrant if Walt brings her in for arraignment," the woman said, adding,

"Shelby said to remind Walt that the judge goes home at 4:30, so he'll need to do it before then."

I absorbed the message. The news was distressing, though I'd seen it coming. But what did it have to do with Dad?

In a chilly voice, I said, "I'll be sure to tell my father about the prosecutor's action, but I'm certain there's been a mix-up. Walt Randall doesn't represent Amber Travis in a criminal case."

"Yes, he does. He entered his appearance today."

CHAPTER 43

I'D CHERISHED A faint hope that the prosecutor's office had contacted me in error, but Phil Benson saw me coming into the circuit clerk's office and had the entry of appearance in hand. He'd graciously made me a copy of the handwritten document, bearing my dad's distinctive signature.

I left the courthouse and hustled straight home with the entry of appearance wadded in my fist.

As always, the house was unlocked, as if Bassville was Mayberry. Crossing the threshold, I called out for Dad.

"I'm in here," he said from the living room. I found him stretched out on his recliner with the television remote control in his hand. He pushed the Mute button. I walked up to his chair and loomed over him.

"How did this happen?" I thrust the wrinkled entry of appearance in front of his eyes.

He took the paper and glanced at it before setting it on the armrest. "I filed it at the courthouse today," he said.

"I see that. I want to know what possessed you to do such a thing."

Grunting, he pushed the footrest of the recliner down to move him into a sitting position. Then he gave me a bemused look and said, "Not hard to explain. Miss Travis called and asked me for help."

"Amber called you? How did she have your phone number?"

"Looked it up, I reckon." He began to smooth the wrinkles out of the paper with the palm of his hand, an expression of satisfaction on his face. "She called on the landline. I recognized the name, so I picked it up."

I flopped onto the couch, befuddled.

"Dad, did Amber know she was being charged with murder? I was with her first thing this morning. She didn't say a word about it to me."

"Nope, I don't think so. I found out about the charge when I went to the courthouse."

A troubling thought intruded. "How did you get over to the courthouse, Dad?"

"Your mother gave me a lift."

Mom hovered in the living room doorway, and I turned to her, throwing my hands up. "You drove him to the courthouse? Jesus Christ."

Dad's voice rumbled like thunder. "No one takes the Lord's name in vain under my roof."

Behind his back, Mom gave an apologetic grimace. "Leah, I had to. He was going to call a cab. Just think how that would look."

I said firmly, "Dad, you can't do this."

Adjusting his spectacles, he met my eye. "It felt good to get out today. Good to be back in the courthouse."

He was as sharp as I'd seen him since returning to Bassville. His funk had lifted. It was painful to dash his spirits into the dirt.

"Dad, you can't take on Amber's case just because you enjoyed going back to the courthouse. They won't appoint the public defender until you withdraw. And you are in no position to assist her."

The words sounded harsh, even to my ears. But Dad was unbothered.

He said, "Sometimes you have to help people in distress, even when it's difficult. Haven't you learned that, Leah?" Under his breath, he added, "Guess you didn't pick up on that in Chicago."

His comment stung. Because he was right; the firm in Chicago had never directed me to aid the underdog.

With a defeated sigh, I stood and said, "If you want to do this, we need to move. We have to get Amber to court before 4:30."

CHAPTER 44

WHEN I PULLED open the courtroom door, Mom led the way, keeping a tight hold on Dad's hand. Amber followed, pulling up the hood of her sweatshirt.

I snatched at her arm. "Pull that down, Amber," I whispered.

She looked at me with wide eyes. "I like it."

"Believe me, it's not a good look for court. You want to make a positive impression, and that hood doesn't help."

Ignoring me, Amber sat in a chair beside Dad at the counsel table. I followed, taking the seat on her other side, still determined to make her listen to me. "Please pull your hood down. It looks like you're hiding something."

She turned from me and faced Dad. "Mr. Randall, is it bad for me to cover my head in here?"

He had been rotating a pen in his hands, but when she spoke to him, the movement stopped. "Are you cold, Amber?"

She shook her head.

"Then you should remove the hood. The bailiffs require men to remove their hats in court. Although historically ladies were permitted to wear dress hats, you should remove your hood, as a sign of respect."

"That makes sense. Thanks, Mr. Randall," Amber said, immediately pulling the hood down.

I leaned over and tapped Dad on the wrist. "When the judge takes the bench, I'll do the talking."

He straightened in his chair, giving me a look of disbelief. "You're barely out of school. How many times have you appeared in court?"

"You'd be surprised." I was prepared to elaborate—my courtroom experience was considerable for a lawyer three years out— but Shelby Searcy had joined us in the courtroom, and I suspected he was eavesdropping.

Judge Parson emerged from chambers. I remembered him as a ruddy, barrel-chested man, but his face looked pale and gaunt under the fluorescent courtroom lights.

The bailiff said, "All rise."

"Everyone stands up when the judge comes into court," I whispered to Amber. Obediently, she stood, an angelic smile spreading over her face.

"Be seated," the judge said, adjusting the laptop on the bench. "Let the record show that in the case of *State of Arkansas v. Amber Lynn Travis,* the defendant appears in person and by counsel, Walt Randall." He gave Dad a curious glance before he fixed his gaze on me. Squinting through his glasses, he said, "Please identify yourself for the record, ma'am."

Amber started to rise. "I'm Amber," she said, in her piping soprano.

As I stood, I put my hand on her shoulder and pushed her back down. "I'm Leah Randall, Your Honor, also appearing on the defendant's behalf for the purpose of this hearing."

The judge cleared his throat. "Are you licensed to practice in Arkansas, Ms. Randall?"

"I am, Your Honor."

Judge Parson opened the hard file that rested on the bench. "Miss Travis has been charged with the offense of capital murder, in violation of section 5-10-101 of the Arkansas Criminal Code."

Amber's smile had disappeared, replaced by a blank expression.

I spoke up. "Your Honor, we waive the reading of the charge and enter a plea of not guilty."

The judge nodded at his clerk, and she tapped on her keyboard. He said, "The record will so reflect."

I heard a chair scrape across the floor, followed by my dad's booming voice. "The defense respectfully requests that the court set a reasonable bond."

My head swung to face him. I caught his eye and whispered, "Sit down."

But he remained on his feet, so I continued his request. "Your Honor, Amber doesn't pose a danger to the community and is no flight risk. She's a young woman without family or connections, and she has no funds. She has no money to support a run and nowhere to go."

I glanced over at the prosecutor. Shelby Searcy stood and said, "Ms. Randall's partly correct. The defendant has no place to go because she burned her home to the ground. And since then, while living on the charity of our local citizens, she attempted to burn her apartment down, too. She's no longer welcome there precisely because she poses a danger. And a woman without a roof over her head is the epitome of a flight risk. We request that she be held without bond."

"The prosecutor is making baseless allegations," I replied. "Ms. Travis has not been accused of committing arson in her apartment, and no eviction proceedings have commenced under state law. We request a bond amount of fifty thousand dollars—a reasonable figure in this case."

My stomach sank when Judge Parson said, "The prosecutor makes a convincing argument. Defendant will be held without bond. Her preliminary hearing will be held on September third." He slapped the file shut. "Court is adjourned."

When the deputies descended on our counsel table, all hell broke loose. Amber fought the handcuffs, shrieking as she was forcibly cuffed. I reached out to calm her and caught an elbow in my ribs.

As the deputies dragged Amber out of court, she protested, "Let me go! I ain't done nothing!" When she disappeared through the door that led to the holding cell, her voice still echoed through the courtroom.

CHAPTER 45

I TURNED, GRABBING the table for support, and noticed my dad. He was seated again, with his head bowed; his chest heaved with violent sobs. Tears dropped onto the legal pad in front of him, blurring the ink on the page.

I had never seen him cry before.

I caught my mother's eye and said, "Mom. Get him out of here."

She sprang into action, sweeping up to the counsel table. "Walt, honey," she said. "Walt, everything's going to be fine. Let's go home."

She bent and whispered in his ear. I couldn't hear the words, but I saw Dad collect himself, nodding his head. He rose from his seat, and Mom slipped her arm through his.

Watching them go, I stepped away from the table and collided with Shelby Searcy. He started to speak, but I beat him to the punch. "What the hell is going on, Searcy? You've done a total turnaround. When did Amber Travis become the villain of this drama?"

He made a mournful face. "Bizarre, isn't it? The vagrant, Burry Jones, has an alibi for the night of the murders. He was staying at a shelter across the state line. And we got those gas cans from the farm tested. They bear Amber's fingerprints."

I attempted a show of bravado. "You're going to base a double murder case on a vagrant and some gas cans that Amber could have handled at any time? Pretty thin case to make against a young woman with no criminal history."

"Well, there's also the motive. Ms. Travis hasn't shut up about her inheritance since she was discovered at the Gas-N-Go." Searcy snickered and gave me a confiding look as he leaned against the counsel table. "Leah, please believe me—I don't want to prosecute the wrong person for the crime. If you have any conflicting evidence, I'd like to hear it. Do you have any mitigating circumstances to share, something that might cast a different light on Amber's actions?"

I almost spoke, before my better judgment silenced me. The wisest course would be to keep Amber's abuse allegations close to the chest. One lesson the sharks at my Chicago firm had taught me: timing is everything.

I bent down to pick up my briefcase, thinking fast. "The sheriff made it clear that he considers Amber to be 'mentally deficient.' That's a quote, by the way. And here's another one: you yourself described Amber as 'retarded.'"

His face hardened. "I have no recollection of that."

My face heated up in response to his blatant lie. "I was there when you said it, Searcy. Our firm will file a motion contesting Amber's ability to understand the proceedings against her."

He rolled his eyes like a teenage drama queen. As he gathered his paperwork, he said, "Go right ahead. We'll have a battle of the shrinks. It will be a novel competency hearing, that's for certain. The record will show that the criminal defendant is more competent than her attorney."

I gasped. He'd gone too far, insulting my father. "You worthless sack of shit. Walt Randall could outmaneuver you from his deathbed. And I will personally kick your ass all over Hagar County."

His mouth twitched in amusement. "You'll be a dream team, no question about that. Your father has forgotten all the law he ever knew. And the jury's going to love that Yankee accent you brought back from Chicago."

He hefted an accordion file, balancing it on his hip. "See you in court."

CHAPTER 46

WALKING OUT OF the courthouse, one thought pounded my head like a boxer's right hook:

What the hell am I doing?

I'd just wanted to help my parents by wrapping up loose ends. But the loose end I'd picked up known as Amber Travis was a fuse connected to explosives.

Mom drove Dad home, and I crossed the town square to the law office to put the new hard file, *State of Arkansas v. Amber Travis,* into the file cabinet. When I pulled out my phone, I saw a text from Tripp Pennington had come in while I was in court:

Can we get together and talk? Robby's @ 5:00?

I stared at the screen, then responded:

Sure. See you there.

Dr. Touchdown wasn't asking me on a hot date. He wanted to talk about our joint client-patient. Nevertheless, I touched up my hair and makeup, and chewed two breath mints as I walked the short blocks to Robby's Bar.

Once inside the dim interior, I spotted Tripp instantly. With a sinking sensation, I also recognized Britney Shelton. If Hopp Cole or Shelby Searcy happened to drop by, I could claim a biblical experience: being seated at a table of my enemies.

Tripp waved me over, saying, "I have a corner booth for us."

Britney grabbed his arm and clung to it. "Absolutely not! Tripp, we *all* want to talk to Leah."

With an affable nod, he pulled out a chair for me. We were a tight squeeze. Tripp and I sat knee to knee.

Phil Benson came up from the bar with Haley and set a tall tumbler in front of me. He said, "Vodka and club soda, on me. If anyone needs a drink today, I'm thinking it's you, Leah."

I looked up at him in grateful surprise. Phil had remembered my order from last time. I took a sip and let out a satisfied sigh. "Thanks, Phil. You're a lifesaver."

Britney pounced, her eyes glimmering with curiosity. "Come on, Leah. Spill. Phil told us about the murder charge, but we want to hear it from the horse's mouth."

Looking around, I found myself the target of the table's rapt attention. But instead of responding, I took another deep swig of my cocktail.

Britney moistened her lips. "Did she do it?"

Phil said, "Britney, Leah's not in a position to tell you that."

She turned on him. "Shut up, Phil. Haley, go to the bar and get me a whiskey sour. The waitress is taking too long."

Obediently, Haley stood, casting a glance in my direction. "I don't want to miss anything."

"I'll fill you in later—go. It's after five. You should get two for one."

Danny appeared, dressed in his civvies. "Can I join y'all?" He pulled a tall stool up to the table and sat directly over my shoulder. I felt trapped.

Britney said, "Leah was about to tell us about Amber Travis killing her cousins."

He looked down at me, quizzical. "Is that right?"

"No, it's not. I didn't say anything." I lifted the glass again and drained it, feeling the burn when the vodka hit my stomach. When I set the empty glass down, it was magically replaced by a fresh one.

Tripp said, "Has anyone checked out the SEC schedule? The first game of the season is coming up."

I shot him a thankful look. If anything could change the direction of the conversation, it was college football.

Haley was back with the whiskey sours. "First game, we play a cream puff. But then we're up against Alabama."

Britney took a bite of her maraschino cherry. "We'll beat the cream puff and lose to Alabama."

Phil and Danny jumped in with an assessment of Alabama's defense. Thank heaven for the Crimson Tide. I pretended to be absorbed in the football talk while I polished off my second drink.

Tripp nudged my elbow. "Someone snagged our booth." Bending to speak in my ear, he said, "I don't think we can have a private conversation here after all. Let's talk some other time. Do you want another drink?"

After polishing off two large glasses of diluted vodka, I was buzzed, too buzzed for a conversation about Amber. "I don't need any more to drink."

He stood and said, "Can I give you a lift home?"

Tripp Pennington, giving me a ride? This would never have happened to high school me. But I felt more than ever like a teenager when I saw Mom waiting for me on the front porch as we pulled into the driveway.

CHAPTER 47

THE NEXT MORNING, I sat on a plastic chair in the inmate interview room at the county jail, waiting for Amber to appear. My morning was off to a rocky start. The prior night's vodka had left me with a sour stomach and a bad taste in my mouth. It was unusual for me to have gotten intoxicated twice within a week: first at the office with Danny and last night at Robby's Bar. Strong drink had never been my weakness. Soft drinks, yeah. Food, definitely. But alcohol had never held any dangerous allure.

With a thunk, the metal security door opened. A big woman in an ill-fitting uniform, her hair plaited into two long braids streaked with gray, stood with her hands on her hips. "You here for Amber Travis?"

"Yes. I'm Leah Randall."

Looking me up and down, she said, "Well, look who's back."

I met the jailer's gaze. She wasn't particularly familiar, just a woman in her late forties with the north Arkansas twang. I glanced at her name tag: ROSE HICKOCK. Smiling, I said, "Nice to see you, Rose."

She nodded without returning the greeting. "I'll get her. She's been asking for you."

Within minutes, the jailer returned and ushered Amber into the interview room. The sight of her black-and-white-striped jail scrubs made me flinch. She slid into the chair across from me, and I waited until the jailer pulled the door shut before I spoke.

"Amber, how are you? I've been worried about you in here."

The V-neck of her top clearly exposed the strangulation marks. Amber caught me staring and grasped the fabric, then appeared to catch herself. Folding her hands before her on the table, she said brightly, "I'm okay."

"I'm relieved to hear that." I pulled a copy of the criminal charge from the file and pushed it across the table to her. "This is the criminal complaint, describing the crime you're charged with."

She cast a quick glance at the murder charge before returning her focus to me. "Where's your dad? Why didn't he come?"

Choosing my words with care, I said, "I know you wanted him to represent you, but he's not himself these days."

Cocking her head, she said, "Not himself? What do you mean? I like him." She smiled at me. "You can help him out, Leah. I mean, he is your daddy."

"You know, Amber, the state will provide a lawyer for you, free of charge. The public defender's office has attorneys on staff with a lot of experience handling murder cases. You might want to consider it."

Blinking, she stared at me for a long moment, looking as if she didn't comprehend. "I don't need a free lawyer. I've got money, the money for the hens."

"I'm just saying you should think about it."

"I don't want to."

Swallowing back a sigh, I said, "Then we should talk about some preliminary matters. I want to file a motion contesting your ability to understand the case against you. Before the hearing, you'll need to have an examination."

Frowning, she shook her head, and I hastily explained, "I'm not talking about another physical exam. I mean an examination where a doctor asks you questions. You just talk. That kind of thing."

"I can keep on my clothes?"

"Absolutely. I guarantee it."

Amber relaxed. In a pleasant tone, she said, "What else you thinking?"

The distress she'd exhibited in the courtroom seemed to have disappeared. Cautiously, I said, "Amber, you seem to be feeling better today. I'm glad. I know it's got to be hard, being held in jail."

Her shoulders lifted with a philosophical shrug. "It's not so bad. There's coffee in the morning, and free food. And they give me these clothes to wear that are lots cooler than your pig clothes. And I can't hardly believe this—they got cable TV!" She looked delighted. "I never got to see no TV at the farm. There was nothing to watch at Dale and Glenna's but them DVDs, and I sure didn't like those."

Abruptly, she stopped. She pinched her lips together and looked away.

"DVDs?" I prompted. "What kind of DVDs?"

Amber's body language was easy to read. She was hiding something from me. At length, she said, "Not anything you'd want to watch."

There was growing tension in the room, but I didn't let up. "What is it that's worrying you? Dale Maggard's dead, Amber. You don't have to be afraid of a dead man."

She hummed tunelessly. The sound sent a chill down me, as if someone was walking across my grave. Finally, she met my eye. In her childlike soprano, she said, "There's scary people in Bassville."

I whispered urgently, "Tell me. Tell me who frightens you."

Looking down, she brushed a piece of lint from her scrubs and smoothed the fabric over her abdomen. "I'm wearing zebra clothes, so I'm in the zoo. It's funny. I like zebras."

"Amber," I pleaded. "If you want me to be your attorney, you have to tell me what's going on."

In a singsong voice, she repeated, "I'm in the zoo."

I remained in the room for another half hour, but she wouldn't talk. When the jailer entered to escort her back to her cell, Amber hopped up eagerly, looking grateful for an escape.

CHAPTER 48

AT THE LAW office, my cell phone rang as I proofread the documents for my entry of appearance as counsel for the defendant, and a motion for psychiatric evaluation. I hit the speaker button with barely a glance.

The voice on the line said, "Are you bored yet?"

I sighed, wishing I'd let the call go to voicemail. I was in no mood to duel with Todd Fisher from my old Chicago office.

But it was too late. I said, "Hi, Todd. What do you want? I'm busy."

His voice was as smooth as butter in a hot kitchen. "I want to give you another chance. We'll pretend your sudden departure was unexpected family leave. If you're back in the office by Monday, all will be forgiven."

Dad's wall cabinet caught my eye. Its secrets, whatever they were, remained locked behind the door. "Sorry, Todd. I have my hands full right now."

There was a protracted silence. Todd sounded testy when he finally spoke. "Okay, here's my best offer. We'll increase your salary by 25 percent."

Momentarily tempted, I turned the offer over in my head. My salary had already been above average. Would I be better able to help my family by returning to Chicago and increasing my earning power? My parents' loan at First Community Bank was hanging over their heads.

I swiveled back and forth in the chair, weighing my options. "Todd, I can't get back by Monday. Can't be that soon."

The phone exploded with his mocking laugh. "'*Cain't*'? Did you actually say 'cain't'? Two weeks back in Arkansas and you already sound like a hick again. I thought we broke you of that."

His derision made me recall Searcy's snarky comment—the prosecutor had accused me of sounding like a Northerner, while Todd said I talked like a hick. I wondered where on earth I might actually fit. In some ways, I was as much of an outsider as Amber Travis.

"Oops—got another call coming in." I tapped the screen with my finger. Hanging up on Todd Fisher gave me a powerful rush of satisfaction.

I turned back to the computer and e-filed the motions, grateful for the timing of Todd's call. Together, he and Searcy had provided the push I needed.

I recalled one of my mother's favorite sayings: In for a penny, in for a pound.

She generally recited it like a dirge, before confronting a task she dreaded. I hoped I could put a new spin on the adage.

When I walked to my car, I saw the battered pickup driven by the scrawny young man that I'd seen in the lineup and in the square. As I approached, I shouted, "Hey! I want to talk to you!"

He turned his head to look at me out the open window, holding a cigarette in his left hand. When I got close, he revved the engine, but the truck didn't move.

"Why are you stalking my office?" I yelled over the engine.

Instead of answering, he pulled away, flinging the lit cigarette at me. It missed, but the Confederate flag on his truck whipped up as he passed, catching me in the eye.

Cursing, I covered my eye with one hand and used the other to give him the one-finger salute. "You should be ashamed to fly that flag!"

CHAPTER 49

EVEN DRIVING WITH one eye shut, I reached the Maggard farm in fifteen minutes. As my tires bumped over the gravel drive, I wavered. The ruins of the farmhouse were still barricaded with tape spelling out a clear warning: CRIME SCENE—DO NOT CROSS.

My hesitation was short-lived. As her defense lawyer, I had a clear responsibility to Amber. Ducking under the yellow tape, I stepped carefully through the rubble of the farmhouse.

Pretty much all that was left standing was the stone fireplace. Resting on the hearth, I surveyed the distant henhouse, recalling my prior visit. I reached into my bag, shook out an allergy pill, and dry-swallowed it. Resolutely, I approached the henhouse, opened the door, and looked inside.

The screened windows were shuttered. I couldn't see much in the gloom, save the rows of nesting boxes inside the coop. But the air was still thick with the stench of old chicken droppings. Backing away, I resolved to save an in-depth investigation of the henhouse for another occasion. I trotted away, headed for the red shed.

Nothing had been disturbed since my last visit. The rusty gardening tools and farm implements rested in place, surrounded by dust motes.

I felt a pang in my chest as I squatted down on the floor to examine the dog cage in the corner to the right of the door. The knowledge that Amber had been made to sleep inside the crate gave it a sinister aspect. I observed dark brown stains clinging to the metal wires. When I realized the dried substance might be Amber's blood, my stomach heaved.

Then it struck me: the kennel was a DNA gold mine for Amber. It provided powerful evidence of her abuse. I pulled out my phone to photograph the cage from different angles, taking care to check that the close shots of the stains came through in clear focus. When I was satisfied with the photos, I called the sheriff's office.

Deputy Crystal Gaines answered. "Hey, Leah. What can I do for you?"

"I need to talk to Sheriff Gilmore."

She paused before answering. "He's tied up. Can I take a message?"

I wanted Gilmore to hear about the evidence directly from me, but I couldn't force him to take the call. I opted for plan B.

"Is Danny around?"

"Nope. He's off today." Her voice was brisk, all business.

My impatience mounted, but I held back a sharp reply. Surveying the cage, I briefly considered loading it into my car, before discarding the notion—from an evidentiary standpoint, the cage needed to be taken from the shed legally as evidence.

I decided to lay out my cards. At least some of them. "Crystal, I'm at the Maggard farm. I want the sheriff to know there's important physical evidence out here. He needs to take custody of it."

It sounded like she covered the receiver of the phone. When she replied, her voice was sharp. "What evidence?"

"A dog kennel. I want the sheriff to collect it and send it to the state lab for testing."

"Leah, Sheriff Gilmore isn't going to be happy that you're out there contaminating a crime scene."

"Tell him if he doesn't bring it in, I'll come back for it myself."

Crystal said, "Does the prosecutor know you're out there, messing around? Because if he doesn't, I'm going to have to call Shelby right after we hang up."

"You do that," I said. "And remind Mr. Searcy that it's his duty to provide the defense with exculpatory evidence. Tell him Leah Randall said so. The judge understands the Brady Rule. I'm going to file a motion with the court."

It was no empty threat; I intended to get that kennel to the lab, one way or another.

CHAPTER 50

DRIVING BACK TO town, I pulled into the Sonic Drive-In for a large Dr Pepper with crushed ice. While I waited for the carhop, my cell phone buzzed; the caller was Beverly Shirk. Curious, I picked up.

She said, "Honey, how are you doing?"

"Fine, Beverly."

"I'm glad to hear it." She didn't sound convinced. "I'm just calling to check in. I heard about Walt in court yesterday."

It was no surprise to hear that the Travis-Randall courtroom tale was making the rounds. I said, "Yeah, it got pretty wild in court."

"That's what I heard. Is Walt all right?"

"He's okay. Mom got him calmed down." The Sonic waitress walked up to the car, bearing a huge foam cup on her red plastic tray. When I reached into my bag for my wallet, I felt Dad's key ring. "Hey, Beverly. Did you know Dad had a locked cabinet in his office? Behind that picture you hated?"

Beverly chuckled in my ear. "Oh, my word, those silly dogs. Yes, honey, I knew."

"What did he keep in there?"

I could tell that I'd wounded her dignity. "Goodness gracious. I can't even guess. It was private. I never disturbed it."

Unlike Beverly, I was determined to disturb it. "Any idea where he kept the key?"

She breathed out deeply, engaged in an internal debate. At length, she said, "I hope I'm not betraying Walt's confidence. He always kept it in the desk drawer. The lower one, on the right-hand side."

Disappointed, I said, "I checked the desk. Didn't find anything."

"Did you look under the false bottom? The right-hand drawer—the deep one—has a compartment, under the hanging files. Walt kept important papers there. Personal things. And that key."

False bottom drawers? Secret cabinets? What was Dad up to?

I thanked Beverly for calling and started up the car. When the phone rang again, I let it go to voicemail but played the message when I stopped at a red light.

It was Tripp.

He said he was disappointed that we hadn't gotten to talk at Robby's and wondered whether I was free that evening to meet him for dinner at the Western Roadhouse.

After the message played, I pulled my sun visor down to look at myself in the mirror. As I feared, the reflection was frightening. I needed a cleanup; I did not intend to show up for dinner looking like a chimney sweep.

Dad's wall cabinet would have to wait.

CHAPTER 51

I RECOGNIZED MARCIE, the waitress who filled my water glass, as the same gaunt woman who'd waited on me and Amber. Smiling, I thanked her and took a sip, leaving a bright red print from my lipstick smeared on the rim of my water glass. I rubbed it off with my thumb.

I picked up my phone and checked the time again: 7:04. It was my own fault for arriving early. Just then, Tripp walked in and spied me. "Am I late?" he asked, joining me at the table.

"No, not at all. I got here early." I picked up the plastic menu. Keeping my voice noncommittal, I said, "So you're a fan of the Western Roadhouse?"

Glancing around, he lowered his voice. "It's not long on atmosphere, I know. But Quint Rhoades serves the best ribeye in the area. If you're going to eat steak, this is the place to do it."

Marcie appeared at his elbow. "Dr. Pennington, it sure is good to see you. Can I get you something to drink?"

He looked over at me, brow raised. I shook my head. "Just water," I said.

"I'll have a Diet Coke," he told her, then said to me, "I'm on call." I nodded, doubly glad I hadn't ordered a big glass of vodka.

His face grew sober. "How's Amber?"

I hesitated to discuss her in a public setting, but the restaurant was noisy with the hum of conversation and the clatter of dishes. "She's in better spirits than I expected. But I don't think she fully comprehends the gravity of her situation."

He folded his arms on the table, listening closely.

"I think the first legal matter is to attack her fitness to stand trial. But if I raise the issue, I'll have to present evidence to prove it. Evidence of her mental incapacity. I need a doctor."

Tripp gave a slight frown. "She has a better chance with an independent examiner, someone who's not an employee of the state. I'll send you the contact information for a med school friend of mine."

A boulder rolled off my shoulders. The notion that I had an ally was more intoxicating than the prior night's vodka.

But the high was short-lived. Quint Rhoades barreled through the swinging door of the kitchen and strode up to us, grinning broadly. He slapped Tripp on the back. "I heard we had Bassville royalty eating in here tonight."

Tripp made a comic face. "Show me where they're sitting, Quint. I've never seen royalty before."

Quint brayed with laughter, then pinned his eyes on me. "Well, if it isn't the Randall girl. You're the talk of the town."

I offered a bland smile, determined to skirt controversy. "Tripp says the ribeye here is spectacular. I can't wait to try it," I said.

"Best in the state of Arkansas. I bet you worked up an appetite, nosing around over at the Maggard place today."

How does Quint Rhoades know I was at the farm?

Tripp stepped in. "Quint, we'll need a minute to look over the menu."

"All right. I'll leave you to it." Quint shot me a broad wink before he left us.

Tripp gave a sympathetic look. "You probably forgot what small towns are like when you lived in Chicago. Now that you're back, you're in the goldfish bowl, Leah."

"Doesn't it drive you crazy?" I asked. "After your residency, you could have gone anywhere. Why did you come back?"

"It's home. My family's been in Bassville for a long time."

"But as a place to live, there's nothing to recommend it. No arts, no culture. And you can't swing a dead cat without hitting a small-minded bigot."

"I think you're being too hard on it. The people here are good folks at heart. And small towns need doctors. There's a health-care shortage in towns this size."

As if on cue, his cell phone rang. "Excuse me," he said, standing up and leaving the table.

Marcie brought Tripp's Diet Coke and set it down. "Are you all about ready to order?" She'd dropped the effusive manner she'd shown earlier.

"Not yet," I said, glancing over at where Tripp stood in the vestibule, talking intently into the phone.

The waitress sidled up close to me. "They say Amber's in jail. She better be careful."

"Careful about what?"

But Marcie was already scuttling off to another table.

Tripp slid back into his seat with an apologetic grimace. "That was one of my patients. I'm sorry to do this, but I have to meet him over at Memorial Hospital." He reached out and took my hand. "Can I have a rain check?"

"Of course. I hope everything's okay."

We walked out together, and I gave Tripp a wave as I pulled away. Though I regretted that our conversation had been cut short, I wasn't sorry to leave the Western Roadhouse behind. Sixteen ounces of ribeye steak could not compensate for the bad vibes that pervaded that place. No wonder Dad had never taken us there.

CHAPTER 52

IT WAS BARELY 7:30—too early to go home and field Mom's questions about Tripp. I decided to swing by the office instead. Maybe, with Beverly's counsel, I'd finally find that key.

After the blinds were drawn and I was shielded from prying eyes, I settled into Dad's leather chair and pulled open the deep right-hand drawer. The scent of peppermint wafted up. Dad's fondness for Altoids was legendary. He'd always had tins of the mints tucked away in his desk.

I removed the hanging files and surveyed the false bottom Beverly had mentioned. It was cleverly done; unless you knew the secret, you wouldn't guess there was a hiding space. I had to use my claw hammer to dislodge the board, but once I lifted it, I hit pay dirt. The shallow compartment held a file on top, marked PERSONAL. The first thing I beheld was Mom and Dad's marriage certificate. I set the file on the desktop, intending to review it before I left.

Underneath the personal file, I saw a few other folders and manila envelopes—and a small brass key, wedged into the far corner of the compartment.

I dug the key out and hurried to the cabinet. The key fit neatly into the lock. With anticipation humming in my veins, I pulled the door open.

The cabinet was empty.

My spirits flagged. I reached inside and felt around the space, but there was nothing to be found, just a faint acrid odor that assaulted my nose. I relocked the cabinet, but instead of rehanging the poker-playing dogs, I took a portrait from Dad's office—a posed family photo from when I was thirteen, Mom with a happy smile, Dad and I looking grim—and hung it over the cabinet door.

I went back to Dad's desk and flipped through the items in the personal file. Underneath the marriage certificate, I found their wills; two expired passports from their fifteenth wedding anniversary trip to London; Dad's service records from the US Army; and a sheaf of insurance policies covering life, household, and disability.

I jumped into reading the policy from beginning to end, including the fine print, hardly daring to hope that it was still in full force and effect. When I saw that it was paid up to his sixty-fifth birthday—still five weeks away—I wanted to fling confetti in the air.

I looked up the instructions to apply for benefits. Dad was a veteran and entitled to Social Security disability as well. While I was at it, I should move forward with his Medicare application.

By the time I wrapped up my research, it was nearly ten o'clock. The rest of the items from the hidden drawer would have to wait for another time. I covered it with the wooden panel and replaced the hanging files, eager to get home and tell my mother the good news.

CHAPTER 53

WHEN I PULLED into the driveway, I saw the flicker of the TV screen through the living room windows. Dad was up watching the local news. But my mother was positioned in the entry hall when I came through the door. She pounced before I had a chance to speak.

"You must have had a successful evening." Her face was positively gleeful.

"It *was* a successful evening, no question," I said.

Mom followed me into the dining room. "What did you and Tripp eat?"

"Didn't eat, actually. He was called away to the hospital."

Her face fell, the good cheer seeping out of her like air from a balloon. "But you just said you had a nice evening."

"A *successful* evening," I said, opening my briefcase. Pulling out the papers, I spread them across the dining room table. "Mom, I found Dad's disability policy."

A furrow appeared between her brows as she examined the document. "Where did you find this? I've been searching for months all over the house."

I dropped my voice so Dad couldn't hear me over the TV. "Dad had a hidden drawer in his desk at the office. And did you know he had a hidden locked cabinet, behind that stupid dog picture? The key was in the drawer, but the cabinet was empty when I unlocked it. Do you know what he kept in there?"

Mom shook her head. "He never said anything about a hidden cabinet." Her eyes narrowed. "How did you learn about the drawer and the cabinet?"

"Beverly told me about it, thank God."

My mother's mouth tightened into a thin line. "So he let Beverly in on his secrets. But not me. Not his wife."

She bolted into the living room, her hands clenched, and marched up to Dad's recliner.

"Why didn't you tell me about the cabinet, Walt?" she asked. "Leah found an insurance policy hidden in your desk. Why didn't you let me know? Do you have any idea how we have been struggling?"

Dad's eyes remained fixed on the television set. He didn't respond, didn't even look at her. He pointed his finger at the television screen.

"Walt, are you listening to me?"

He remained focused on the screen. His arm outstretched, he began to mouth words but made no sound.

Mom turned to face the TV and let out a shriek. I saw the cause of the commotion: a live report showed the local fire department responding to a fire. But when I saw the stone chimney, illuminated by the flames, I didn't need the newscaster to provide the location.

The Maggard farm was on fire—again.

CHAPTER 54

AMBER HUNCHED OVER the folding table in the interview room, a pencil clenched in her fist. She tried to concentrate on the paper in front of her, but her thoughts kept returning to her recent loss.

She looked up at Dr. Barnes. "Did you hear about my farm? What they done to it?"

The doctor nodded, but she couldn't tell what he was thinking. She was a fair hand at reading people, but it was harder to do when they had a beard like the doctor.

"Somebody burned down the henhouse and the shed. Somebody burned up all the buildings, and the bank won't cash my check for the hens."

The doctor adjusted his black-framed glasses. They were so thick, his eyes looked tiny.

"Concentrate on these questions, Amber."

She blew out a long breath that ruffled the papers on the tabletop.

"I can read—I told you so. But I don't know some of those words. And a lot of it just don't make sense."

"Do your best, Amber."

She bent over the papers again. It took some time, but she finally came to the end. Sighing with relief, she pushed the papers away and set down the pencil. When he handed her yet another test booklet, Amber picked up the pencil and buckled down.

At length, she finished. "I guess we're all done now," she said.

"Not yet." Dr. Barnes smiled at her. "I'm going to quote you a proverb, an old expression. You tell me what it means: A bird in the hand is worth two in the bush."

Amber thought it over. "Well, seems like it's better to have one to hold on to. If they're in the bush, you might not catch them before they fly away."

He was writing fast with a pen, even though he was also recording on his phone. When he looked up from his notebook, he said, "Don't cry over spilled milk."

Looking up at the ceiling, Amber squinted her eyes. That one was tricky, because it reminded her of the eggs. Finally, she said, "Can't say I'd go along with that. Sometimes, when something's spilled or broke, people get real mean about it. I can just see that milk, hear somebody getting after me. Might be bad enough to cry over."

She looked over at the doctor. Dr. Barnes was scribbling again.

He gave her another one: "Rome wasn't built in a day."

Amber thought hard. But no matter how she turned it over in her head, she couldn't make any sense of it. "I don't know what you mean."

"Shall I repeat it?"

"It don't make any difference if you do or not. I don't get it." Amber was trying to cooperate. But he wasn't making sense.

The doctor's voice was soft when he said, "Rome, Amber. Think about it. Rome wasn't built in a day."

"What's Rome?"

He started writing again. Amber shifted her weight. She'd been sitting in that plastic chair for hours.

Dr. Barnes reached into his bag and pulled out a folder. Opening it, he said, "Amber, this is an inkblot test. I want you to look at these pictures and tell me what you think they look like." He paused, holding a stack of cards facedown.

Amber didn't know what he was talking about, but she smiled anyway. "Okay," she said.

He turned over a card. "What do you see?"

The doctor let Amber hold the card. At first, she didn't see anything. It was just a blob on a white background. Then it seemed like it shifted, taking shape. Amber stared down at it.

"That's a woman. I see her dress, but she don't have a head. And I see that man's face there. He's laughing, but it's a mean laugh."

She pushed the card away. The doctor handed her another one. "What might this be?"

The card had red ink mixed with the black. Amber shuddered as she studied it.

Finally, she said, "Somebody's making a girl bleed, and she's trying to make it stop."

Dr. Barnes showed her a third card. When Amber saw it, she began to tremble.

"They're burning the girl. And he brought someone in to watch it." Her hands shook so hard she dropped the card. "I don't want to see no more of them pictures," she whispered, squeezing her arms tightly against her chest. "They're too scary."

"Does the inkblot remind you of something? Something that frightened you? Maybe something you witnessed, happening to someone."

Amber knew when it was safest to keep her mouth shut. For a while, she didn't utter another word. When she talked again, she was careful. She knew the doctor was trying to draw her into dangerous territory, but she was too smart to let him do it. She didn't say anything about burns and blood and pain. And she never said one word about Dale Maggard.

CHAPTER 55

I SLAMMED THE landline receiver into the cradle. I wanted information about the fire at the Maggard farm, but Sheriff Gilmore was refusing to take my calls.

Distracted, the sound of the front door opening startled me. A bearded man with glasses stepped into the lobby. "I'm looking for Ms. Randall."

I guessed this to be Dr. Barnes, Tripp's medical school friend, who'd promised to stop by the office once he left the jail. "Dr. Barnes? I'm Leah."

He nodded, adjusting his eyeglasses. "I've just come from my meeting with Ms. Travis. Our interview didn't last as long as I had hoped. But I'd be glad to discuss it with you. Or if you prefer, you can wait to read my written report."

I gestured toward Dad's office. "Please, come in. I'm anxious to hear your thoughts."

I held my tongue as Dr. Barnes sorted through his notes, though I wanted to pepper him with questions.

Finally, he looked up at me and smiled. "Your client is a very interesting young woman."

"No question about that." But I didn't want to chat about Amber's quirky nature. I was ready to get down to brass tacks: intelligence. "How did the IQ test come out?"

"Yes, IQ. Interesting story on that, actually."

No stories, please, I thought. Though my interactions with Amber had raised my opinion of her, for legal reasons she needed a low score. *Make it low. Please.*

"I'd say that Amber demonstrates average intelligence. Arguably, above average."

I tossed my legal pad onto the desktop in frustration. "Dr. Barnes, the woman has a second-grade education."

"That's true. I took her history."

"She was held back twice in elementary school." I leaned toward him, holding his eye. "The woman can barely spell 'cat.' Sometimes she acts like she's from another planet."

His face lit up. "Exactly! That's why the Wechsler is an inexact measure of her ability, because it relies on language skill, you see. Ms. Travis is a classic example of the bias inherent in certain IQ tests. But I also tried another test."

He beamed. My own face didn't reflect his happy expression.

"When I used Raven's Progressive Matrices, her achievement showed marked improvement," Dr. Barnes said in a jubilant voice. "Raven's utilizes visual designs and shapes, so it minimizes educational biases and cultural environment. Her cognitive abilities to analyze information were entirely satisfactory."

Retrieving my legal pad from the desk, I scanned the questions I'd prepared to ask him. I said, "You surely understand why the results are unsettling, from a defense perspective. Did you observe any disorders that would interfere with Amber's fitness to stand trial and her ability to participate in her own defense?"

His face grew sober. "In my opinion, she shows distinct characteristics of emotional disturbance." He lowered his voice, though we were alone. "She exhibited intense psychological distress during the testing. I observed detachment, fear, high anxiety. She has an exaggerated startle response. I saw evidence of hypervigilance."

"What does that all mean, in your opinion?"

"Post-traumatic stress disorder. She has suffered severe trauma, likely on multiple occasions. From her responses to the Rorschach test, in particular, I suspect that she's been exposed to serious injury and sexual violation."

I nodded emphatically.

"But she denies it," he said.

I dropped my head into my hands, realizing that if asked, Dr. Barnes would have to admit Amber's denial under oath. She had poisoned her own witness.

So far, it seemed to me that Amber Travis was her own worst enemy.

CHAPTER 56

DAMAGE CONTROL.

Walking up the varnished wooden staircase to the main floor of the courthouse, I tried to pump myself up. It was time to utilize my persuasive skills. Shelby Searcy needed to go back to viewing Amber as a victim, rather than as a criminal.

"You can do this," I whispered aloud, pulling open the door to the county prosecutor's office.

The receptionist looked up from her computer. I pointed to Searcy's office door, which was ajar. "He's in," I said. It wasn't a question.

I walked into the office without waiting to be announced and pushed the door shut. "Let's talk."

Searcy gave me a suspicious glare as I sat in the chair facing his desk.

"You know I filed a motion contesting Amber's fitness to stand trial," I said.

The prosecutor looked smug. "I've already scheduled her exam with the state's expert. He's seeing her this week." Searcy added: "He's never found any defendant incompetent to assist at trial in all the years I've worked with him. But who knows? Maybe Ms. Travis will be the exception."

Obviously Amber couldn't rely on assistance from the expert Searcy had cherry-picked. I needed to appeal to the prosecutor's sympathies. "Shelby, Amber has been examined by an independent expert, who will testify that in his professional opinion Amber has suffered abuse."

I waited. He didn't respond, didn't reveal that my words had any impact whatsoever.

I tried again, saying, "I think we can show that the abuse constituted torture. And because of that, Amber suffers from PTSD."

He rolled his eyes. "PTSD? That's it? Every bullied child claims PTSD. You know what I think? Those false claims are disrespectful to military personnel and first responders who have suffered actual trauma."

My heart began to pound. "Believe me, Amber suffered actual trauma when she lived with the Maggards. I'm prepared to produce evidence of—"

He sneered. "Evidence? What kind? The word of your hired shrink?"

"Physical evidence," I said with emphasis. "I'm in a position to make an offer of proof. But if I do, I want you to assure me that you'll consider it as mitigation. To dismiss the case or at the very least reduce the charge."

"What's your physical evidence?"

I thought of Tripp's physical exam of Amber. "Scars. Bodily scars."

"That's it?" Searcy snorted. "Everyone has scars. They usually come from accidental injury."

My throat was tight. "This was no accident."

"Then you'll have to prove it. And that the deceased inflicted it. The Maggards were well thought of around here, a respectable couple in a God-fearing community. Salt of the earth."

Doggedly, I reached into my bag for my phone, which held the photos I had taken inside the red shed.

"If the Maggards were such fine people, why did they force Amber to sleep in a dog cage?"

"Oh, please. If Amber wants to deflect criminal responsibility, you'll need to do a better job. Caging her? That's a pretty convenient claim, now the farm has been destroyed. You'd best advise your client to plead guilty and throw herself on the mercy of the court. That will get her a life sentence."

Searcy stood up, as if our conversation had reached its conclusion, but I remained in the chair.

"The shed contained exculpatory evidence. The state should have taken custody of it when I contacted the sheriff. You violated the Brady Rule."

He was edging toward the door. "You've got nothing, Leah. If your fallback is a claim of self-defense, it won't fly. The Maggards' remains show that they were shot as they lay in their bed. I don't know what you learned in Illinois, but in Arkansas, deadly force can only be used in self-defense, when there's an imminent risk of death or serious physical harm."

He twisted the knob and pulled the door open. "Glad you came by, Leah. I'll have Judge Parson schedule our pretrial hearing on the defendant's competency next week, if he's got an afternoon free. Once that's out of the way, we can move forward to a jury trial, where your client will have the opportunity to spin her tale of woe."

I stood and made my way over to him. "We'll make a case that will rock the whole state of Arkansas. This case will make you famous, Shelby. But not in a good way."

"You may not be aware of my trial record, since you ran out of town years ago. But it's the highest conviction rate in any district in the state." He regarded me with exaggerated patience. "You can leave now. If you won't go voluntarily, I'll get the sheriff's office to escort you."

I stalked past the reception desk and made it out of the courthouse before the physical shakes overtook me. Sinking onto a concrete bench, I clenched my hands together.

Searcy's words echoed in my head, and I couldn't block them out. Because I feared that everything he had said was true.

I didn't have a prayer. No one in Bassville would listen to me. I would lose this case. His perfect trial record would continue, unblemished.

An ugly voice in my head taunted me: I was about to go down in flames, and I would take Amber Travis with me.

CHAPTER 57

WITHIN A WEEK, we sat in the Hagar County courtroom, embroiled in a "battle of the shrinks," just as Shelby Searcy had predicted.

After our witness, Dr. Barnes, testified, the county prosecutor called his guy: Dr. Price. I scratched notes on my legal pad, fretting over the direction of the testimony. We'd had to proceed first in this hearing because I was the one who'd raised the issue of Amber's fitness to stand trial. Dr. Barnes had made a credible showing for us, laying out Amber's verbal deficits and expounding on her anxiety. We had a shot—unless the prosecution witness was more convincing than our expert.

As Searcy and Price methodically walked through the expert testimony, I sat with my eyes fixed on the witness stand, staring down the prosecution witness. Between him and Searcy, they were doing their best to destroy the slim foundation that Dr. Barnes had laid in support of our motion.

Searcy said, "Dr. Price, what is cognition?"

The witness, a fleshy man with a thick neck, adjusted his necktie before answering. "Cognition is the ability to think, to solve problems."

"And what is reasoning?"

"Thinking through problems. Solving problems adaptively."

Shelby Searcy glanced over at our counsel table, giving Amber a casual inspection, before turning back to his witness.

"Doctor, what tests did you conduct during your evaluation?"

The doctor took a breath. "The MMPI. The Thematic Apperception Test. Wechsler's Adult Intelligence Scale."

Searcy continued. "From your evaluation, does the defendant have a mental disease or defect that renders her unable to understand the proceedings against her and assist in her defense?"

"In my opinion, no. Ms. Travis has the ability to understand the proceedings. And there is no medical reason why she can't assist her counsel in the case."

"Thank you, Doctor." Searcy glanced down at the notepad resting before him on the podium. In a deceptively nonchalant voice, he asked, "Do you have an opinion whether the defendant lacked capacity to appreciate the wrongfulness of her conduct or conform it to requirements of law—"

"Objection!" I jumped out of my chair. "Irrelevant, Your Honor. And outside the scope of this hearing. My client has not entered an insanity plea; she pled not guilty to the charges. Criminal responsibility isn't an issue unless and until the defendant pleads not guilty by reason of mental disease or defect."

Searcy waved a hand in surrender. "I'll withdraw the question. Your Honor, I have no further questions."

But as he passed me on the way to his seat, Searcy shot me a knowing look. If Amber tried to raise an insanity defense when the case went to jury trial, his expert was prepared to refute it.

Judge Parson said, "Ms. Randall, you may cross-examine."

As I approached the podium, the doctor tugged at his necktie again. A nervous tic, I suspected—but I'm no shrink.

"Dr. Price, when you examined Amber, did you observe any signs or symptoms of emotional or mental disturbance?"

His face creased with a frown, as if giving the question some thought. "I would say she exhibited anxiety."

My tension eased slightly. "What specifically did you observe?"

"Her affect during the interview, and in certain responses during testing. But to some extent, that's to be expected. The defendant is charged with murder. If she didn't exhibit some anxiety, it would be odd."

That wasn't the response I wanted. I forged ahead.

"You testified that you administered the Wechsler IQ test."

He looked wary. "I did," he said.

"Tell us about the results of the Wechsler test."

His hand reached for the tie but froze midway. With a dogged look, he crossed his arms on his chest. "It's not simple to answer that. The results were mixed."

I stepped out from behind the podium and moved closer to the witness stand. "I see. Let's restrict it to the area of function involving language. How did Amber perform regarding verbal ability?"

He cut his eyes away. Glancing into the empty jury box, he said, "It was not her strongest area."

"Be specific, Doctor. And remember you're under oath."

His complexion grew ruddy, which didn't surprise me. He looked to see whether the prosecutor would jump to his defense, but Searcy remained in his seat.

"Her verbal function is low," he said.

I wanted to hammer the nail further. "And what did you observe about Amber's verbal acuity during your interview?"

His eyes were calculating. "She spoke in simple sentences. But she's entirely capable of making herself understood."

I looked over to make sure the judge was paying attention. I was gratified to see that he was listening closely, with his chair turned toward us. "But did she always understand you, Doctor? Or did you have to rephrase questions and substitute or define words in order to communicate with her?"

He didn't answer immediately. A drop of sweat trickled down the side of his neck.

"Ms. Travis sometimes claimed that she did not understand me."

The aha moment was just outside my reach. I pressed forward, asking, "From her inability to understand language, what might you conclude about Amber's competence to follow and comprehend court proceedings?"

His mouth formed a rueful, upside-down smile. "I'm not certain. I have to take the MMPI findings into account, too. And the defendant's results showed she was 'faking' to make herself look good." He turned to the judge. "That means she was deceptive. The MMPI is designed to distinguish honest responses from deceptive ones." The doctor swiped at the perspiration on his jaw. Looking back at me, he said, "So according to the personality test, your client is a liar."

My heart flopped in my chest. I'd walked straight into the trap, by doing one thing no smart lawyer ever does: ask an open-ended question on cross-examination.

I tried to recover, but he'd regained his confidence; though I hammered away at him, I made no headway. Finally, I returned to the counsel table and sat down.

At the bench, Judge Parson adjusted his glasses and examined his computer monitor. Amber tugged on the sleeve of my jacket. She twisted in the wooden chair to look behind her, as if she was afraid of what she might find. Then she whispered directly into my ear. "I don't want to be in jail no more. It scares me."

The judge cleared his throat. "In the case of *State of Arkansas v. Amber Lynn Travis,* I'm prepared to rule on defendant's motion. I've reviewed the psychiatric reports, and we've heard evidence from experts for both sides." He picked up the hard file, containing my motion and the experts' reports. Judge Parson fixed his eyes on Amber. "I've concluded that the defendant is competent to stand trial. Defendant's motion is overruled."

The wisp of hope I had harbored evaporated. I opened my own file to jot down the judge's ruling. As I wrote, I heard a rattling noise; it came from Amber as she stood, raising her shackled hands to catch the judge's attention.

"Excuse me, sir? I don't like the jail. I want to go back to my apartment."

A shadow of annoyance passed over the judge's face. Ignoring Amber, he studied his computer screen. "I've reviewed my upcoming jury docket for the calendar year. I have a two-week opening, beginning nine weeks from next Monday. Jury trial in this case will commence on that date."

Amber remained on her feet. I stood and grasped her arm, urging her to sit back down.

Her volume increased as she made a shrill plea: "There's scary people in jail. Get me out of there!"

CHAPTER 58

AFTER JUDGE PARSON shut himself in his chambers, I prevailed upon the bailiff to bring Amber to the holding cell that adjoined the courtroom, so my client and I could talk.

Inside the holding cell, Amber was seated on the opposite side of a Formica counter, separated by a metal screen reinforced with chicken wire. The irony of the poultry parallel struck me, but I shrugged it off. We had important matters to discuss.

However, no discussion could take place with the bailiff standing at Amber's elbow. I gave him a stern look, like an old schoolmarm. "I need to speak privately with my client." He left without argument, though I suspected he stayed right outside the door.

I said to Amber, "We'll need to whisper."

Looking frightened, she nodded, and started to tear up. "I don't want to be in jail anymore. What was the judge talking about nine weeks for?"

"He's set your case for jury trial. It will start nine weeks from Monday."

"That's too far off. I got to get out of here before that."

"Amber, it's an incredibly speedy setting for a case like yours. We need to buckle down and get to work on your defense. It's time to focus on strategy. Both of your doctors, Dr. Pennington and Dr. Barnes, believe you've been abused and assaulted."

Amber hung her head.

A wave of sympathy washed over me, and I softened my voice. "You confided in me when you told me about the contract, and how you suffered from Dale's treatment. But you didn't share those facts with your doctors. It's time to come clean about all of it, everything that happened at the farm."

Her hands disappeared into her lap.

Taking care to keep my voice low, I continued. "It's crucial to your defense, Amber. Very, very important."

She looked around cautiously. "But if I tell, will I still get the farm?"

I closed my eyes for a moment, grasping for patience. "The probate case is not your primary concern, Amber. You need to focus on the criminal case."

The pitch of her voice rose. "That property belongs to me. I earned it. Dale made money off me, and I don't mean the chickens neither." When I didn't respond immediately, she added with emphasis, "Some people liked to watch when Dale hurt me."

Aghast, it took a moment before I could frame the words. "People paid to watch you get tortured? Who would do such a thing?"

With a grimace, Amber raised her shoulders. "I don't know. Dale always put a hood over my head. He always said not a soul would believe me. But if you find the DVDs Dale made, they'll have to believe it."

I recalled our earlier conversation, when Amber had mentioned distasteful DVDs at the Maggard farm—it was sickening to imagine what had been on them. Still, she was right that if the DVDs were found, they could be her ticket to freedom.

But it was impossible. Every building on the farm had been destroyed.

Trying to sound upbeat, I said, "Even without the DVDs, you can testify about what happened. If we can't get an acquittal, we'll hope for a lighter sentence."

She squinted at me, clearly not comprehending my words. "Why would they blame me? I never hurt nobody."

My knee started jiggling under the counter. Trying to remain cool, I uttered the words every attorney needs to speak. "I just want you to tell the truth."

Amber's eyes shifted—not an encouraging sign.

I said, "At trial, you have the right to remain silent. But if you take the witness stand, you'll be under oath. And in this case, I expect the jury will need to hear from you."

"Hear what? Maybe the hobo done it. Maybe Dale done it himself. Maybe he shot Glenna and then shot himself. You never know what awful thing Dale might think up."

My jaw was tight. "And then he set the place on fire? After he shot himself?"

"I don't know." Looking at me, she said it again, forcefully. *"I don't know."*

Moments ticked by as I stared at her without speaking.

Her face crumpled and her voice broke. "You're supposed to help me. I never have nobody on my side." Amber lifted her shackled hands to swipe at the tears streaming down her face. Wiping her nose on her forearm, she whispered a desperate plea. "Help me."

God, I wanted to. But her best defense involved an admission she refused to make. I wanted to bury my face in my hands and howl, but I didn't permit myself the luxury.

I was all she had. No one else was on her side. The sheriff, the prosecutor, the church, the town—they had all turned on her. During the hearing, the judge hadn't demonstrated any sympathy. He couldn't be counted on for leniency.

The outlook was grim, and I had no time to waste.

CHAPTER 59

IT HAD BEEN a mighty long day.

At supper, some of her fellow inmates pestered Amber about the court hearing, their eyes beady with curiosity like the chickens on the farm. She stayed mum, shaking her head, no matter how much they plagued her.

Before lights out, she had her turn in the showers. The water was tepid and the shower smelled of mildew, but she gritted her teeth and scrubbed with the bar of soap the county jail had provided. She heard the jailer's voice and saw a flurry of activity through the side gap of the ragged vinyl curtain: women running from the showers dripping wet, covering themselves with frayed towels.

Amber held her breath while she waited. When she heard the curtain of her stall rustle as the plastic rings skittered across the bar, she tensed.

A hand grabbed Amber from behind, twisting a hank of her wet hair. Amber could feel one of Rose Hickock's long braids pressing into her naked back.

"I heard you told the judge today that you don't like our jail."

Amber didn't say anything. She stared at the wet wall, concentrating on the patterns made by streaks of black mold.

"They say you talked to your lawyer today, right after court. What did you tell her?"

Amber's brain was working a mile a minute, trying to figure out how to answer without getting into trouble. She could smell danger, overwhelming the moldy scent of the shower.

"I don't tell her much. She does all the talking."

The grip on Amber's hair tightened.

In a whisper, she said, "You're hurting my head."

"You like it."

Amber's heartbeat stuttered in her chest. She never, ever liked it.

The woman jailer said, "What about the videos, those DVDs? Does she know about that?"

Amber reached out, supporting herself against the slimy shower wall. "They all burned up in the fire."

The jailer gave her a hard shove, and Amber's forehead cracked against the concrete wall. She didn't make a sound, though the pain ricocheted through her skull. Rose Hickock's breath blew hot into Amber's ear. "You'll want to keep your mouth shut or you'll be sorry."

A moment of silence followed. Amber knew the woman was waiting for an answer.

"I won't say nothing."

Amber waited until she heard the footsteps retreat and the door bang shut. Then she slid down the wet wall and huddled on the floor, trying to think. There were people in Bassville who knew Dale's dirty business, and they still wanted to hurt her, even with Dale and Glenna dead and gone.

With a groan, she crawled out of the shower stall. Staring into the dim bathhouse mirror, she saw an angry lump already taking shape on her forehead. As she wrapped herself in a thin towel, Amber wondered whether she'd manage to stay alive until the trial.

Nine whole weeks seemed a long way off.

PART II

NOVEMBER

CHAPTER 60

IT WAS THE end of the second day of the trial. In a grueling jury selection, we'd whittled down our crowded courtroom to a group of thirteen: the jury plus an alternate. As Judge Parson called out names, the jurors who would decide Amber's fate stepped up and took their seats in the jury box.

Amber's eyes darted around the courtroom. I'd outfitted her for trial in a high-necked cream wool sweater and gray pants. The long sleeves conveniently covered the manacles that chained her wrists, and the pant cuffs concealed from the jury her ankle restraints.

At first glance, she looked unremarkable: a conservatively dressed young woman with her hair neatly secured by a plastic barrette. Only a closer inspection would reveal the tension in her shoulders and her hands clenched tightly on the counsel table.

I scrutinized the parade of jurors: ten women, two men, plus one male alternate. The gender makeup was intentional. Before the voir dire process had begun, Amber had insisted that she didn't want any men deciding her fate. I had tried to convince her that we shouldn't eliminate jurors without getting a feel for them during jury selection, but she had been adamant. She didn't trust the men in Bassville. She'd rather cast her lot with the women—a direct quote.

There was one woman, however, I'd had to remove. Jury selection had started off with a bang when Kate Cole strutted into the court-room as the panel assembled. She was easy to spot, dressed to the nines in a bright print sheath with a teal cardigan draped over her shoulders. She even looked like she'd had her hair freshly high-lighted. I watched from the corner of my eye as Kate whispered and giggled with the people seated near her in the gallery. I knew the moment Amber recognized her, because she choked out a gasp and clutched my sleeve.

When Amber began to protest in my ear, I cut her off. "Don't worry. I'll get rid of her."

I bided my time, waiting until I could approach the bench with a challenge for cause. Once I had Judge Parson's ear, I made short work of it. When the judge dismissed Kate Cole from the court-room, her injured expression had given me a moment of deep satisfaction.

But now, as I surveyed the jury settling into the box, I felt ambivalent. I was seized by a panicky regret for all those grandfa-therly panelists I'd intentionally booted out of court. I'd resigned myself to Amber's gender mandate, because conventional trial wis-dom corroborated it; women were traditionally more inclined to acquit in criminal cases than men. But maybe a more balanced panel would have been preferable in our particular case. We would never know.

The double row of jurors shifted in their chairs, looking uncom-fortable. When Judge Parson instructed them to raise their right hands to be sworn in, one woman hesitated, as if she couldn't commit to the job.

As the judge continued to address them, Amber inched close to me, whispering in my ear, "Them women don't like me."

Without changing my focus, I wrote *Shhh!* in giant letters on my legal pad and nudged it in front of her. She ignored my message.

"They don't like me. I can tell by looking at them."

I turned to her and spoke sternly. "Hush. The judge is talking."

But I understood what Amber meant. The ten women seated in the box represented a broad range of ages, from thirties to seventies, but they wore a similar expression. As they listened to the judge, I studied their set, uncompromising faces, searching for a sign of compassion.

I couldn't detect any.

Leaning forward in my seat, I tried to make a silent bond with one of them, plant a seed of connection that could grow into a not guilty vote. My spirits lifted when one of the three men briefly fixed his eyes on Amber. His mouth twitched—with pity, I discerned. As he looked away, I grabbed my jury notes to identify him.

He was the alternate.

We couldn't catch a damned break.

CHAPTER 61

JUDGE PARSON CLEARED his throat. To the jury, he said, "Ladies and gentlemen, we'll begin tomorrow at nine o'clock sharp." When he closed his file and left the bench, we rose to our feet.

The bailiff shuttled the jurors outside to a waiting van, which would convey them to a motel on the highway. The jury would be sequestered for trial, at my insistence.

They had scarcely marched past us when Amber clutched my arm again.

"I don't like that jury. Get me a new one."

I glanced around, hoping the jurors hadn't overheard. "Amber, it's done. We're going to have to live with the people we've got."

"Easy for you to say," she muttered as the deputies approached our counsel table.

One of the uniformed men was Danny Minton. He avoided my eye, but his tone was not unkind when he spoke to Amber. "It's time to take you back to jail. Do you need another minute with your lawyer?"

"No, sir," she said, stepping away from her chair at the table with a dejected air. As I watched her walk off, flanked by Danny and the gray-haired deputy, my chest grew tight.

I walked through the courthouse like the Invisible Woman. No one spoke to me, but I kept my chin up as I made my way out the door and down the stone steps to the sidewalk. The silent treatment came as no surprise. No one ever claimed that criminal defense attorneys were heralded as community heroes.

My parents' finances were in order, at last. Now that they were receiving their monthly stipends, they were no longer a step away from bankruptcy. I, on the other hand, had been living on a very inconsistent income. I'd taken on some clients—mostly family law cases that no one else in the area wanted—but I no longer had the luxury of a steady paycheck. And though I lived on a shoestring, still bunking with my parents and eating at their table, those law school loans demanded to be paid on time.

So I was delighted to find a sizeable check from my former landlord in Chicago in that day's mail when I unlocked Dad's office. The old pirate had finally refunded my security deposit. I gave the landlord's big fat check a light kiss as I pulled a cold can of Dr Pepper from the twelve-pack I'd stashed in the refrigerator. I could deposit the check immediately, but I'd been thinking of opening a new account, in a bank that wasn't run by Hopp Cole.

With that in mind, I was inclined to hide my treasure. I decided to tuck the check away in one of my dad's secret spots, to keep it safe. Opening the right-hand drawer of his desk, I pulled out the hanging files and slid out the false bottom. The brass key to his locked cabinet lay on top of the various contents, including a bulky manila envelope that, in my earnestness to convey my parents' personal documents to them those few months ago, I had forgotten was in there.

I pulled the big envelope out and inspected the contents. It was an old property abstract, encased in a thick leather-bound cover, with pages that had yellowed with age. I skimmed a legal description of a sixty-acre tract of land in Hagar County. Pieces of the tract had been parceled off over the years. Toward the back, a familiar name caught my attention: a quitclaim deed to Dale Maggard.

It didn't surprise me that Dad would've consulted Dale Maggard's abstract for an accurate description of the real property when he drafted Dale's and Glenna's wills. But why had he hidden it? The abstract should've been returned to the Maggards, or filed away with the probate records.

A folded piece of ruled notebook paper fell out of the document as I rifled the pages.

I stared at the paper on the floor for a protracted moment, then bent over to retrieve it, a buzzing noise in my ears. Something about that innocuous-looking slip of paper made my senses tingle.

As I unfolded it and glanced over the handwritten contents, my pulse began to pound and the buzz in my ears became a roar.

At the top of the page, a word was handwritten in ink: *CONTRACT*.

I sat back in the office chair as I read the rest.

> *I, Amber Lynn Travis, agree to accept Dale Edward Maggard as my master. I consent to do his bidding and be under his ownership, from this day forward. In exchange, I will receive by inheritance all of Dale and Glenna Maggard's property. I understand this is a binding contract and can't be broken except by death.*

The handwriting on the page was unfamiliar to me, until I came to the signature line. Amber's childish scrawl was recognizable on sight.

Underneath her name, Dale and Glenna had both signed as witnesses. The contract also bore a date. I didn't need a pen to do the math. It would have been Amber's eighteenth birthday.

CHAPTER 62

LATE IN THE afternoon, I was so anxious to share the news of my discovery, I sought Amber out at the county jail.

The jailer who delivered her to the interview room was a familiar figure: the middle-aged woman who wore her hair in braids, like a schoolgirl. "Thirty minutes," she said, shutting the door without waiting for me to agree to the time limitation.

Amber sank into the seat opposite mine. It looked like I'd dragged her out of bed. Her hair hung in limp strands along her face, and she wore the striped jailhouse uniform. The cuffs of her scrubs almost covered the dirty flip-flops she wore on her feet.

I scooted my plastic chair up to the table and gave her a wink. "I have some good news: I found it. The contract."

Amber's head gave an involuntary jerk. Hastily, she looked over her shoulder, then said, "Sweet Jesus—don't talk so loud."

"It's a miracle, really. The contract was hidden away, just as you suspected—but not on the farm. Dale apparently stuck it inside a property abstract, and it ended up in Dad's office. Dad probably asked Dale to deliver the abstract to him when he was drafting the wills, so he could get the property description right."

As I spoke, Amber began to tremble violently. I reached out and placed a reassuring hand over hers. Her fingers were ice-cold.

"I know it's a shock, after all this time. It's still hard to believe." Triumph made my voice rise. "We have the contract!"

Amber's eyes widened as she uttered a harsh whisper. "*Quiet.* Didn't I tell you? You got to be still."

The rebuff finally registered. In a more businesslike tone, I said, "You don't realize the opportunity this newly discovered evidence creates. It's a lucky break. When I inform the judge about it, he'll have to grant us a continuance. We can delay the trial."

She sucked air through her teeth. "No, no, no, you can't tell nobody. No delay."

My sunny mood disappeared. "What did you tell me yesterday? You said you wanted a new jury. Guess what—because of the contract, you're going to get one."

Amber jumped out of her chair. She looked wild, with tangled hair framing her fierce eyes. "How many times do I have to tell you not to say that word out loud?"

I stared at her in bewilderment as I reached into my brief-case and pulled out the file marked MOTION FOR CONTINUANCE. I flipped it open to show a copy of the handwritten contract between Dale Maggard and Amber Travis. "The original is safe, back at the office."

Leaning close to my ear, she said, "You think? Maybe they'll burn your office down."

A chill went down my spine. "We need to have the document— the handwriting on it, I mean—evaluated by an expert, Amber. That takes time. That's why I need to ask the judge for a continuance. Do you understand?"

She exhaled slowly. "I ain't got no time. As soon as this gets out, I'm as good as dead. You understand that?"

I wanted to accuse her of overreacting, being dramatic and fanciful. But staring into those hazel eyes, it was clear that she was serious. Dead serious.

As a final attempt to reason with her, I said, "Sitting on the contract means you'll be rolling the dice with the jury that was seated yesterday. You understand the stakes, Amber, don't you? You're facing prison. The real deal, not this little county jail. *Prison*— maybe for the rest of your life."

"There's worse things than prison." Amber's voice was barely audible when she added, "And them bad things is right here. In Bassville."

CHAPTER 63

THE NEXT MORNING of the trial proceeded in such typical fashion, no one would've suspected that an evidentiary bomb ticked in my briefcase.

After opening statements, Judge Parson nodded at Shelby Searcy. "You may call your first witness."

Searcy stood, buttoning the jacket of his navy suit. "The state calls Rupert Forrest."

Forrest was the regional fire chief who had responded to the fire at the Maggard farm the night they were killed. The fire chief was a big, ruddy-faced man whose powerful build was not disguised by his dress uniform. He balanced a dress hat on his knee with a hand that sported a Bassville High class ring. As Rupert Forrest recounted the fire department's futile struggle to battle the blaze that consumed the farmhouse, I kept to my seat, letting his testimony proceed without objection. At the same time, my mind lingered on that unfiled motion for continuance, and worried that Amber had talked me into another terrible mistake. How had I become a lawyer who let her client run the show?

When Searcy said, "No further questions," however, I popped up to cross-examine. It's never too early to remind the jury that the defense will have its own points to make.

"Chief Forrest, your testimony relates to the fire that occurred on the Maggard farm in Hagar County on August second—is that correct?"

"It is."

In a pleasant voice, I said, "You testified that gas cans were collected at the scene, is that right?"

"Yes, ma'am. But we didn't take custody of them. They were collected by the sheriff's department after they arrived."

"I see. But you testified that the cans were taken as evidence due to suspicion that accelerants were used at the fire on August second, correct?"

"Correct." Turning to face the jury box, Forrest said, "In my opinion, the accelerant was gasoline." He faced me again and said, "That's what I testified. The record will show it."

"I expect it will." I flashed a smile at him, to remind the jury that I wasn't attacking a first responder. "And at the fire approximately three weeks later at the Maggard farm, on August twentieth—in your opinion, was gasoline used to accelerate that fire also?"

"Objection!" As I'd anticipated, Searcy was on his feet. "Irrelevant."

I stepped over to the jury box and rested my hand on the wooden railing. "Your Honor, I think the second fire at the Maggard property is entirely relevant to this case."

Searcy made a run for the bench. "May we approach, Your Honor?"

I remained by the jury box, as if my feet were glued to the floor. "I don't believe that's necessary. Why does the prosecution want to discuss the Maggard fire on August twentieth outside the hearing of the jury?"

"Ms. Randall," the judge said, frowning. At that point, I was obliged to join Searcy at the bench. But I gave the jurors an expressive look before I walked away.

At the bench, Searcy spoke in a confident whisper. "Your Honor,

Ms. Randall's question is clearly outside the scope of direct examination. I didn't ask the fire chief about the second fire."

"He opened the door, Your Honor," I replied.

"I did not," Searcy snapped.

Keeping my voice low, I said, "Of course the second fire is relevant. It occurred shortly after the incident the witness testified to, in precisely the same location." I refrained from adding *while my client was in jail,* but Searcy knew where I was headed.

Searcy loosened his tie. "Ms. Randall knows the question is improper. I ask that the jury be instructed to disregard."

"You sure about that, Mr. Searcy? Because that'll really excite the jury's interest when I produce evidence regarding the second fire in the defendant's case." I gave him a cocky look, which he answered with an audible scoff.

Judge Parson spoke up, settling the matter. "The objection is sustained. Ms. Randall, you will confine your questions to matters covered in direct examination. Mr. Searcy, I don't believe the question is sufficiently inflammatory to require an instruction to disregard."

As we stepped away from the bench, I said, "I have no further questions of this witness at this time, Your Honor."

"Redirect?" the judge said.

"No, Your Honor," Searcy said.

Judge Parson asked, "May this witness be released?"

Before Searcy could answer, I shot out: "No, Your Honor. I'll be calling the fire chief to testify for the defense." Swinging by the jury box, I gave the jurors a triumphant look.

Amber caught my eye as I returned to the counsel table and rewarded me with the ghost of a smile.

CHAPTER 64

THE GRAY-HAIRED deputy was up next: Jim Rust, the first person from the sheriff's office to appear at the scene. Shelby Searcy used Deputy Rust to establish the chain of custody for the gas cans, which had been sent on to the Arkansas State Crime Lab. He then had the deputy authenticate a series of photos of the crime scene, displaying them on a large screen erected between the witness stand and the jury box.

After the deputy swore that the photos were fair and accurate representations of the scene, Searcy said, "Your Honor, I offer the photographs, state's exhibits 3 through 13, into evidence."

"No objection," I said. When I stood up for cross-examination, I strolled to the witness stand and said, "Deputy Rust, I'd like to direct your attention to state's exhibit number 9."

The photo was a long shot of the farm, taken in the morning, with the smoking ruins of the farmhouse in the foreground and, in the distance, the red shed.

The pointer Searcy had used during his direct examination lay on the prosecutor's table. I would have preferred to use my own pen, but I feared that my arm wouldn't reach high enough on the screen. I stepped up and said, "May I?" in a voice so sweet, butter wouldn't melt.

Standing near the screen, I tapped the image of the shed and said, "Deputy, do you recall this red shed on the property?"

"I do. The shed didn't catch fire that night. Henhouse was still standing, too."

"Did you have occasion to inspect the interior of the shed on that day?"

"We did." He glanced over at Searcy, then back at me. "A basic inspection, as we secured the scene."

"And would you recognize it if you saw it again?"

The deputy cleared his throat. "It's not there anymore."

Searcy rose to a half stand. "Objection. Nonresponsive."

I aimed the pointer at Deputy Rust. "He's your witness, Mr. Searcy."

Judge Parson leaned over to the deputy. "Just answer the question."

Rust's face betrayed uncertainty. "Could she repeat it?"

The court reporter looked up at the judge. "Do you want me to read it back, Judge?"

I waved the pointer. "Your Honor, permit me to rephrase the question." When he nodded, I said, "Deputy, if you saw another picture of the shed, do you think you'd recognize it?"

He looked relieved. "I reckon so."

Walking back to the defense table, I picked up an enlargement of a picture I'd taken with my phone. Passing it to the deputy, I said, "I hand you defendant's exhibit number 1 and ask if you can tell me what it is."

He frowned, studying it. "Looks to be a picture of the inside of that shed."

"The shed you inspected on the Maggard property when you secured the crime scene on August second?"

"Yes, ma'am."

"Does the shed appear to be in the same condition as it was on August second of this year?"

"I think so, yes."

"Is anything depicted in defendant's exhibit number 1 different from what you saw that day?"

He grimaced at the picture, like he was looking for the trick in the question, then finally said, "Not that I know of."

I tapped the dog cage in the bottom corner of the picture with the handle of the pointer. "Was that item there on that day?"

Searcy was on his feet again. "What is the defense talking about? I object, Your Honor; the question isn't clear."

As cool as a chilled glass of sweet tea, I said, "Certainly, Your Honor. I'll rephrase." With exaggerated enunciation, I said, "Deputy, I'm referring to the cage. Was the dog kennel present in the shed on August second?"

"Objection. Irrelevant," Searcy interrupted.

Judge Parson squinted through his glasses, considering. "Overruled."

Deputy Rust looked confused, so I prompted him. "You may answer, Deputy."

"Seems like it. Seems like it was there. I think so," Rust said, shooting an apologetic glance at Searcy, as if he feared he'd spoken out of turn. I took the exhibit from his hands and addressed the court with a flashy show of self-assurance.

"No further questions."

CHAPTER 65

"THE STATE CALLS Buck Ritter," Searcy said.

Surprised, I twisted around in my seat in time to see the Gas-N-Go clerk walk into the courtroom. I'd expected more law enforcement figures to testify first, before Ritter was called.

Then it struck me: Ritter was being brought in to supply an in-court identification of Amber. Searcy wanted to tie her to the testimony sooner rather than later.

Amber elbowed me. She was focused on Ritter as he walked to the witness stand. Ritter wore a bright red shirt with the Gas-N-Go logo embroidered in blue thread. The shirt was a poor fit, and he yanked at the hem to make it cover his belly. As a child, I'd adopted the same habit. On occasion, I still unconsciously tugged on my shirt when I was nervous.

"Be careful of that one," Amber said to me.

I inclined my head to hers. "What do you mean?"

"Just you be careful when you shop for goods in his store. He keeps a baseball bat under the counter in there. He almost whacked me with it."

I flipped through my files, hunting for the notes on Ritter that I'd gleaned from the police report. In the local newspaper, he had been proud to discover Amber that August morning. For weeks after the fact, he had held himself up as her rescuer. I hadn't anticipated any trouble from him on the stand, but Amber's concern and the aggressive set of his jaw as he was sworn in put me on guard.

"Please state your name, sir," Searcy said.

"Buck Roy Ritter."

"What is your occupation?"

"I clerk at the Gas-N-Go on the highway."

"How long have you been working in that capacity?"

Ritter stopped to think, squinting with the effort. "Five years, near about."

"Directing your attention to the early-morning hours of this past August fourth, were you working on that date?"

"I was. Yes, sir."

"And what, if anything, occurred at Gas-N-Go at approximately 5:30 a.m. on that date?"

"A woman sneaked into the store and stole merchandise."

Amber tapped my arm. "That ain't right. He's talking like I stole a whole mess of stuff. It was just a Snickers. And some crackers."

I acknowledged her correction with a nod, my attention trained on the witness. He'd changed his tune since August. Obviously Buck Ritter no longer regarded himself as Amber's savior.

Searcy said, "And then what happened?"

Ritter glanced over at our counsel table. "I saw she was trying to sneak around and run out of there, and I stopped her because she was a shoplifter. When I got a good look at her, I seen she was the girl on the Missing poster they'd put up after the Maggards got murdered. So I called the sheriff. They came right out to the store and got her."

"Is the shoplifter who tried to flee your store on August fourth in the courtroom today?"

"Yes, sir."

"Point her out for the jury, please."

Ritter stretched his arm full length to point at Amber. She shrank back in her seat. "She's sitting right over there, next to that woman lawyer."

"Your Honor, may the record reflect that the witness identified the defendant, Amber Lynn Travis?"

The judge inclined his head. "It shall."

"No further questions." Searcy returned to his seat. I suspected he thought he'd pulled off a coup, characterizing Amber as a criminal from her first mention in trial testimony.

I took my time, giving the Gas-N-Go clerk a couple of moments to worry about what he might expect from "that woman lawyer." After I set my notes on the podium, I pinned him with a stare and asked, "Did you mention this shoplifting allegation to the sheriff's deputies when they arrived?"

A shadow of confusion crossed his face. "I don't know. Probably. I might have."

"'I don't know'? 'Probably'? 'I might have'? Those are three inconsistent responses, wouldn't you agree?"

He shrugged his shoulders.

"Mr. Ritter, you'll have to speak words when you respond to questions, so the court reporter can get your sworn testimony on the record. Did you accuse Amber of shoplifting when law enforcement arrived? Yes or no."

He looked mulish. "Maybe."

Shaking my head, I looked at my notes, making a point of pulling out the police report and studying it. "And if the officer's report makes no mention of shoplifting, then would the deputy be lying?"

Searcy's voice rang out behind me. "Objection, calls for speculation."

"Sustained," the judge said.

"Mr. Ritter, isn't it true that you neither asked for payment nor gave Amber an opportunity to offer to pay for," I emphasized, "the Snickers candy bar?"

"She was going to run," he insisted.

I counted to five in my head before I spoke again. "Mr. Ritter, do you keep a baseball bat under the counter at Gas-N-Go?"

"Sure I do. For protection."

"For protection," I repeated. I walked back to the counsel table and said under my breath, "Amber, stand up."

Though I was only five foot six, Amber was so petite she looked childlike next to me. "And you needed 'protection' from this woman, so you threatened her with the bat?"

He looked wary. "I never touched her with it."

To Amber, I said, "Please be seated." I picked up an exhibit from a small stack of mounted photographs on the table and ambled up to the witness stand.

"Mr. Ritter, please describe Amber's appearance when you saw her at the Gas-N-Go on August fourth."

He paused, as if trying to anticipate a trap. "She was wearing a nightgown."

I gave him a tight smile. "Describe the condition of the nightgown."

"Just an old nightgown." Leaning back in his seat, he added, "Had some blood on it."

I was ready for that. The lab reports verified that it was Amber's own blood, but I needed to blow away the smoke of suspicion that Searcy had already created through the clerk. "What was she wearing on her feet?"

"She was barefoot, seems like."

"And her feet were bleeding, isn't that right?"

"Yeah. Her feet made the floor at the Gas-N-Go bloody. I had to clean it up later."

"And when you threatened her with the baseball bat and she fell on the floor, that's when the blood got on the back of her night-gown, isn't that right?"

"I don't know how it got there."

"Okay, what else did you notice about the nightgown Amber wore into the store?"

He looked puzzled. "Nothing."

"Did you see splatters of blood or gore on the front of the gown?"

"Nope."

"Was the nightgown burned or singed?"

"I don't know."

"You don't know?" I made a point of looking at my photo exhibit, while keeping it from his view. "If you saw a girl in the Gas-N-Go before dawn in a nightgown with visible burns, wouldn't you recall that?"

"I might. I don't know."

I drew close to the stand. "What did the nightgown smell like?"

"I don't remember."

"Did it smell like smoke? Did it smell like gasoline?"

He shifted in the chair, rubbing his neck with the palm of his hand. "How would I know?"

I gave my head a small shake. "You are employed at Gas-N-Go, Mr. Ritter. Are you familiar with the odor of gasoline?"

His eyes were hard. "Yep."

"Well, did Amber Travis's nightgown smell like gasoline?"

He looked up at the ceiling. "No."

Someone in the jury box snickered. It was a sound like the sweetest music.

I continued. "Thank you, sir. I hand you what's been marked as defendant's exhibit number 2. What is it?"

He looked down at the photo the sheriff's department had taken when they rescued Amber at the Gas-N-Go. The photo was part of the prosecution's file, provided to me through the discovery process.

"It's a picture of the girl at the Gas-N-Go."

"And is Amber wearing the nightgown, which you've informed the jury had no odor of gasoline, that you saw when she came into the store on August fourth?"

"Looks like it."

I handed him a Sharpie. "Please circle any evidence of blood, burns, or scorch marks that you see on the front of the gown Amber is wearing."

"Can't," said Buck Ritter. "Don't see none."

"Thank you, sir. No further questions."

Walking past Searcy's counsel table, I couldn't resist giving him a look that said: *Don't mess with me.*

CHAPTER 66

WHEN I WALKED into my parents' house, I felt bone tired but upbeat. I'd made some progress over the course of the day. Amber's plight didn't seem quite so hopeless.

"Leah, I kept a plate warm for you," Mom's voice called from the kitchen.

The smell of pot roast made my stomach growl. I'd skipped lunch to prep for cross-examination.

"How did it go today?" Mom asked, her face bright with interest, handing me a full plate, with roasted carrots and potatoes too.

"Not bad. Not too bad at all. We scored a couple of points in the morning: small victories, but it felt really good, believe me." I paused to take several massive bites.

"Well, what were they? What happened?"

"I got the state's witnesses to establish some matters we'll be pounding in the defense case. And I slapped down that jerk who works at Gas-N-Go. He tried to characterize Amber as a shoplifter in court."

Mom clucked with disapproval. "What else?"

I was distracted when my phone pinged. I pulled it from my pocket and saw a text from Tripp Pennington:

Call me.

I stared at the phone, trying to read some layers into the two-word message. Tripp and I had been getting together on a fairly regular basis over the past two months. Our growing friendship had provided much-needed support at a lonely and difficult time.

Mom interrupted my thoughts. "What will happen tomorrow?"

With my fork in midair, I said, "You're awfully interested."

She waved a dish towel, saying, "It's not me so much. Kate's really disappointed that she didn't get to sit on the jury. Two of her friends made it, but she can't get them to answer the phone. I'm supposed to call her tonight and fill her in."

I dropped the fork with a clatter. "Don't you dare."

She looked hurt. "What? Kate is my friend."

"Mom, this is a murder trial. Thank God I got that jury sequestered, so Kate can't stick her nose into it. Amber's case is not fodder for the Bassville gossip circle."

The Assville gossip circle, I thought, then turned on my mother with a baleful eye. "Nothing I say about Amber's case leaves this house. Do you understand me?"

"Yes, I hear you. Goodness sakes, you sound just like your daddy," she huffed. "Why don't you go find him and leave me be. I don't want to put up with one of your moods."

Returning to my briefcase, I pulled out the Maggard file, walked down the hall, and knocked on the study door. "Dad?"

I opened the door and saw him dozing in the high-backed chair. I hated to disturb him, but the mystery of the Maggard abstract had nagged at me since I'd discovered it.

"Sorry to wake you, Dad," I said, leaning against the edge of the desk and giving his shoulder a gentle shake.

His eyes popped open. "What time is it?"

"Around eight o'clock, I think. Hey, Dad, I need to ask you about something I found in your office last night."

He looked from side to side, as if trying to determine where he was. "This office?"

"No, the law office. I found a big envelope hidden in the bottom of your desk drawer. It contained an abstract for the Dale Maggard farm."

"An abstract."

Patiently, I repeated, "For the Maggard farm."

"Maggard farm," he echoed.

I picked up his hand and gave it a squeeze. "Dad, there was a piece of paper inside that abstract, a signed contract between Amber Travis and Dale Maggard. It's a contract for involuntary servitude."

He gave me a blank look.

I opened the file containing the motion for continuance and turned to the attachment. "Dad, did you ever see this piece of paper? Is that why you hid the abstract?"

He adjusted his glasses and studied the handwritten page. Shaking his head, he said, "I don't understand. Involuntary servitude is slavery. This is illegal. It's an illegal contract. One of the elements of a valid contract is that it must be for a legal purpose." He shoved the paper across his desk. "I didn't draft it."

"Of course you didn't, Dad. But have you seen it before?"

"That's not mine," he said, his voice gaining strength.

My phone buzzed. When I saw it was Tripp, I stepped into the hall. "Hi, Tripp," I said.

"Hey, Leah." I heard him pause and take a deep breath. "I need to talk to you. About the trial."

He sounded like he was wound up tighter than a spring. I tried to counter it by sounding upbeat. "Sure thing. Do you need an idea of the day you'll be taking the stand? Because it's a little early to make the call, but I know your schedule is busy, you have your patients to consider. I should have a better idea tomorrow. Maybe we can talk then? Over dinner?"

"Right. My patients: I do have to consider them," he said and then paused. An uneasy feeling crept up my neck. Tripp continued. "Leah, I'm rethinking the wisdom of testifying in Amber's case."

My knees suddenly felt weak. I backed up to the wall, leaning against it for support. My voice shook. "You're kidding me, right?"

He sighed. "No."

I heard myself speaking forcefully. "Tripp, we don't have a case without you. We need you to give validity to Amber's testimony."

"You still have my written report of her examination. I was thinking you could submit that instead of calling me as a witness."

"No, I can't do that. There's something called the hearsay rule." I was so angry, my vision was graying out. "Where is this even coming from? You've been my ally in this case. My only ally, by the way," I added.

He sighed into the phone. "I didn't want to worry you, but I think I'd better let you know. Somebody called a bomb threat into my office today and blamed it on the Amber Travis case. We had to evacuate the office."

I was speechless. Tripp went on. "Don't you see the bind this puts me in? This changes everything. I can't risk the safety of my patients and my staff. Surely the judge will understand."

I finally found my voice. "This changes nothing. You are under subpoena. If you don't show up to testify, I'll ask the judge to send the sheriff to bring you into court."

He sounded stunned. "Are you kidding? I thought we were friends."

I scoffed, "Yeah, you're a real friend, that's for sure. I guess I should be grateful you finally showed me that you're just like everyone else in Bassville."

Then I hung up on him, because there was nothing left to say.

CHAPTER 67

WITH A STRING of experts imported from Little Rock, the state's case proceeded swiftly on Thursday. One witness described the Maggards' grisly remains and established gunshots to the head as the cause of death; another identified gasoline as the accelerant used in the farmhouse fire; a third testified that Amber's fingerprints were on gas cans collected at the scene.

Despite the prosecutor's emphasis on the print evidence, on cross-examination I demonstrated that Amber's were not the *only* fingerprints found. I was prepared to argue that the gas cans were routinely handled by Dale and Glenna too, and shouldn't convict Amber beyond a reasonable doubt.

At the end of the afternoon, Shelby Searcy called Sheriff Gilmore to the witness stand. I studied the sheriff as he stood with his right hand raised. Would the sheriff actually drag Tripp into court for failing to comply with the subpoena? As Gilmore took his seat on the witness stand, I asked myself the next question. Would I really put Tripp in that position? A muscle in my jaw knotted up, and I massaged it as my brain provided a definitive answer: *Yes.*

I would do whatever my job required, regardless of the personal cost. I had to protect my client.

Searcy's direct examination of the sheriff was brief and to the point.

"Sheriff Gilmore, did you have occasion to see Amber Lynn Travis on the thirteenth day of August?"

"I did."

"For what purpose?"

"We questioned her in connection with the investigation of the murders of Dale and Glenna Maggard. The defendant lived on the farm with them at the time of their deaths. We didn't have any leads. Not then, anyway."

The jurors listened with rapt attention, several even leaning forward in their seats, as the sheriff described his interview with Amber and how she'd told them about the homeless man who'd stayed with them.

"The defendant stated that the homeless man stole from the Maggards," Gilmore said, "and threatened to burn the place down." Under Searcy's direction, the sheriff continued. "We brought her in again, after we had the homeless man in custody, to clear matters up regarding some statements he'd made."

"During your interview on the sixteenth of August, did you have occasion to advise the defendant of her rights before questioning her?"

"I did."

With a flourish, Searcy handed the sheriff a sheet of paper encased in protective plastic. "I show you what's been marked state's exhibit number 33. Can you tell us what it is?"

The sheriff glanced down at the sheet, nodding. "It's the Miranda waiver, signed by Amber Travis."

"How do you recognize it?"

"I recognize her signature. It's distinctive. And my signature also appears, as a witness."

"Has the exhibit been altered in any way since it was signed on August sixteenth?"

"It has not."

Searcy walked up to our table, giving me an opportunity to

inspect the document as he said to Judge Parson, "The state offers exhibit number 33 into evidence, Your Honor."

I rose. "The defense objects, Your Honor, for reasons that have already been stated and are part of the record."

Prior to trial, I'd attempted to keep Amber's statements out of evidence by filing a motion in limine. In a brief and unsuccessful hearing, my impassioned plea that Amber's waiver was not knowing, educated, or voluntary within the meaning of *Miranda v. Arizona,* and that her statements were not admissible against her, had fallen on deaf ears.

Judge Parson reclined in his high-backed chair. "Your objection is noted, and overruled. The exhibit shall be received."

Searcy stood behind his seat at the prosecution table and said, "Sheriff, after the defendant signed the waiver, what statements, if any, did she make about the demise of her cousins, Dale and Glenna Maggard?"

Grasping the arms of the witness chair, Gilmore hefted his bulk to the edge of the seat and said, "The defendant said she wasn't sorry they were dead. That they deserved killing."

At that revelation, two women in the jury box gasped. One clasped a hand to her chest.

Searcy crossed his arms against his chest and lowered his head. In a voice that rumbled like an angry god, he said, "Is the woman who made those statements sitting in the courtroom today?"

When Sheriff Gilmore pointed a finger at Amber, half the jurors refused to look at her, and the ones who did condemned her with their eyes.

CHAPTER 68

WHY WASN'T THE prosecution simply playing the video of Amber's interrogation?

They were playing games with Amber's out-of-court statements. When I stood up for cross-examination, I jumped on the issue.

"Sheriff, isn't it true that when you interrogated Amber, she denied killing the Maggards?"

"She said that. At first."

I continued, saying, "Sheriff, was a video made of the interrogation you conducted on August thirteenth?"

A shade crossed his face. "There was."

"Have you seen and reviewed the video of the interrogation?"

His expression was unreadable. "I have."

"Is the video a fair and accurate representation of the interrogation that occurred on that date?"

"It is. Well, it was."

What is he playing at? I swung around to face Searcy. "Your Honor, I request that the prosecution produce the video of the interrogation for the purpose of cross-examination."

Searcy's face was pinched. "Judge, may we approach?" At the bench, he stated, "It's been destroyed, Your Honor. Something went wrong with it. I'm not a tech geek, I don't know. Maybe a deputy erased it accidently, or maybe some glitch occurred. But the video doesn't exist."

My face started to heat up, along with my temper. "This is unacceptable, Your Honor—for multiple reasons. Why wasn't I informed? The prosecution's failure to disclose the disappearance of the evidence is a violation of the prosecutor's discovery obligations under Rule 17."

Parson raised a brow at Searcy, who had the grace to look apologetic as he said, "I didn't know about the problem with the video, Judge, until I was preparing for the trial. If I'd had any idea that the defense intended to use the video, I would've told Ms. Randall. But it's news to me, all the way around."

I took a breath and said, "You have an ethical obligation—"

The judge cut me off. In a weary voice, he said, "What relief do you seek, Ms. Randall?"

I hesitated. Under ordinary circumstances, I'd ask for a mistrial—but my client didn't want more delay, so I tempered my demand. "I ask that the sheriff's testimony regarding the defendant's statements be struck from the record."

Judge Parson cast a swift glance at Sheriff Gilmore, who watched us covertly from the witness stand. "Your request is overruled."

With a wave of his hand, the judge dismissed us from the bench. As I walked back to the podium and straightened my back, an idea struck.

Stepping up to the counsel table, I fished inside my briefcase. The prosecution had tripped me up—but I would give them a surprise of my own, as payback.

I turned back to Sheriff Gilmore with a smile on my face. "Sheriff, when you identified state's exhibit number 33, the Miranda rights waiver, you stated that you recognized Amber's signature, correct?"

"Yes, ma'am."

"Because her signature is distinctive. Right?"

"Yes."

I opened my file, removing the copy of Amber's contract, and handed it to the court reporter. After she marked it, I folded the paper so that only the signature lines were visible.

Then I stalked up to the witness stand, feeling more daring with each step. "I hand you what's been marked defendant's exhibit number 4. Can you see the first signature?"

He frowned slightly. "I can."

"Have you ever seen it before?"

His head was bowed over the paper. "I think so."

"You think so?" I parroted. "Have you or haven't you, Sheriff? Can you identify the signature?"

He scratched his ear. "I believe it's the defendant's."

"It's the same signature you just identified in state's exhibit number 33, isn't that right?"

"It appears to be." He tried to hand the folded sheet of paper back to me. When I didn't take it, he rested it on his knee.

Searcy jumped up. "I object to this line of questioning, Your Honor. It's not clear to anyone what we're talking about here."

I said loudly, "I'll clear that right up, Your Honor. Sheriff, please read the document aloud, so we all know what the exhibit contains."

A strangled noise of protest came from Amber at the defense table. I knew she wouldn't like the step I had taken. But it was high time for me to start acting as the attorney in charge of the defense, rather than deferring to Amber's strategic plan—whatever that was.

Keeping my eyes focused on the witness stand, I took a step forward.

"Read it," I repeated. "Aloud."

CHAPTER 69

SHERIFF GILMORE SQUINTED at the sheet of paper, as if he needed bifocals. After a moment of silent reading, his weathered face seemed to blanch, and his mouth twisted.

He turned to the judge. "Your Honor, I never saw—"

"Sheriff Gilmore," I said, my voice snapping like a whip. "You've been instructed to read the exhibit aloud."

In a halting voice, the sheriff read, "'I, Amber Lynn Travis, agree to accept Dale Edward Maggard as my master. I consent to do his bidding—'"

Searcy launched out of his seat and bounded around the counsel table, shouting, "Stop!"

Talking fast, I said to the witness, "Sheriff, what comes after 'consent to do his bidding'?"

"Objection, Your Honor! I request a recess so we can confer in chambers."

I swung around to face him. "Oh, please—I object to this interruption. Your Honor, please instruct the prosecutor to sit down and let me finish. I permitted the state's evidence to be identified. I demand that the prosecutor extend me the same courtesy."

"What you are doing is impermissible," Searcy chided.

I scoffed. "I am trying to lay a foundation for my defendant's exhibit. I'm not finished yet, and I won't be until the sheriff reads it in its entirety. The jury deserves to know that my client was being held as Dale Maggard's sex slave."

There—I did it, I thought, as the courtroom buzzed.

Judge Parson slammed the gavel. "Ms. Randall, approach the bench," he said in a stern voice. I didn't care. My adrenaline was pumping, and I was ready for a fight.

Searcy launched into a harangue, accusing me of so many breaches I couldn't keep count of the particulars. I waited until he stopped to draw breath, then spoke to the judge.

"Your Honor, my exhibit is material to the defense we're raising, and I'm using the sheriff's expertise to demonstrate its validity."

"You can't do that, you absolutely cannot," Searcy huffed.

"Actually, I can, because you opened the door in direct when you had the witness testify to his familiarity with Amber's signature."

Searcy started to contradict me, but the judge raised a hand to silence him. To me, he said, "Let me take a look at this exhibit."

Stepping over to the sheriff, I politely asked him to hand the paper to me. Before I returned to the bench, I stopped to scan the contents while standing close enough to the jury box to excite their curiosity.

The judge scrutinized the contract, eyes narrowing as he read. Looking up, he asked, "Is this some kind of joke?"

"Judge Parson," I said flatly, "there is nothing funny about that document, I assure you."

He sighed. "I may permit this document to be received into evidence when the defense presents its case, if you can prove that it's material to the defense and produce evidence as to the identity of the rest of the handwriting and the validity of the instrument."

Searcy spoke up. "It's highly inflammatory, Your Honor."

"That's true," the judge agreed. "And it purports to bear the handwriting of three different individuals. I will not admit it into evidence at this time."

"Instruct the jury to disregard," Searcy demanded.

Judge Parson sat in silence, tapping the paper with his forefinger. At length, he said, "Are you certain that's what you want, Mr. Searcy?"

I understood the subtext. Presuming the contract *was* later admitted into evidence, it would take on heightened significance because of the prosecutor's attempt to hide it.

Searcy's eyes burned. "Instruct the jury to disregard, Judge," he said again.

I returned to my seat beside Amber and listened to the judge address the jury, feeling determined.

That contract would be in the jury's hands before long.

CHAPTER 70

IN A HIGH-PITCHED whisper, Amber said, "What are you trying to do to me?"

Her fingers were painfully digging into my thigh. I grabbed her hand and jerked it up, banging my knuckles on the underside of the counsel table.

"Not now," I whispered.

Searcy said, "Your Honor, for our next witness, the state calls Burry Jones."

Judge Parson said, "Hold up," and made a show of pulling up the sleeve of his black robe and checking his wristwatch. He grimaced. "It's already past 4:00, and you've provided a lot of information for our jurors to absorb." He cast a benevolent smile upon the group in the jury box, then added, "I'm adjourning for the day. Court will convene at 9:00 tomorrow morning."

As the judge disappeared into chambers and the jury filed out of the courtroom, Amber tugged on my jacket, her face puckered with distress.

"I never meant you to show the sheriff that paper Dale had me sign. I told you, it's dangerous." She stepped closer, standing on tiptoe to whisper in my ear. "That paper will make trouble for me at the jail."

"Why would the contract create a problem at the jail?"

It was clear that Amber was worried. Her chin began to tremble. "Can't say."

I caught a strong whiff of stale perspiration coming off her. "Are they letting you shower? You're supposed to shower every night while you're in trial."

"Don't want to," she said, refusing to meet my eye. She tucked a lank lock of hair behind one ear.

I turned around to peer through the glass of the courtroom door. I needed to catch Burry Jones before he left the courthouse, and I was anxious that I might miss my chance. "Do you have enough soap and toiletries? Should I bring some for you?" I asked, shoving my files into the briefcase. "You be sure to let me know. I'll be by the jail tonight, to drop something off for you."

She let go of my sleeve. "What are you bringing?"

"It's a sweater set. I want you to wear it tomorrow." I'd decided to give her a black cotton sweater set I'd splurged on at Marshall Field's back in my deep-pocket days in Chicago.

She tugged at the wool sweater I'd provided for the first days of trial. "What's a sweater set?"

"It's two sweaters. You wear one over the other."

Looking stubborn, she shook her head. "Too hot."

I sat back down. "You won't be hot. The one under the cardigan is sleeveless."

"What's a cardigan?"

I paused, wondering how any responsible psychiatrist could've concluded Amber had the ability to understand legal proceedings given her limited vocabulary.

With a smile that disguised my desire to depart, I said, "A cardigan is a long-sleeved sweater that buttons all the way up the front. But I only want you to do the top button."

I patted her hand and stood, clutching my briefcase. But Amber wasn't finished with me. "If it's got all them buttons, why do I only use one?"

I glanced around. The bailiff and deputy lingered nearby, waiting to escort Amber back to jail. Bending down, I whispered in her ear, "To make it fast and easy when you take it off in court."

She opened her mouth to protest, but there was no reason to debate it. The hitch would be convincing the judge to leave off the handcuffs first.

We were going to give the jury something to think about, by God.

CHAPTER 71

JUST BEFORE 9:00 on Friday morning, the bailiff and a deputy marched Amber into court. The twinset was too large on her, but she'd followed my instructions, securing the cardigan by the top button. At my request, Amber entered and exited the courtroom without the jury's presence. I didn't want them to see her shuffling across the floor in shackles, like a dangerous creature kept in chains for the safety of others.

Searcy was already on his feet as soon as the jury was settled into the jury box. "The state calls Burry Jones."

Burry Jones appeared in the doorway. Searcy had cleaned him up; he sported a fresh haircut, and his stiff denim jeans and tan cowboy shirt were so new they bore creases.

Amber watched Jones with a furrow between her brows. "I thought drifters just moved around. Why's that guy still here?"

I nudged her with my elbow. "Don't worry about it. I finally managed to grab a word with Burry Jones last night. He's got some interesting information."

She spoke again, but I shushed her. Searcy was starting his questioning. I listened serenely, even when the testimony entered precarious territory.

"When you were staying on the Maggard farm in the summer, did the defendant ever ask you to harm her cousins, Dale and Glenna Maggard?" Searcy asked his witness.

Objection—leading, my head whispered, but I remained silent.

"Yes, sir," Jones was saying. "She said she'd pay me to knock them off. That there was cash money on the farm, and she'd find it."

"What was your response?"

Jones looked alarmed. "I said no!"

"What, if anything, did the defendant offer you at that point?"

"Sex," Jones said.

Searcy waited, obviously expecting the man to elaborate. When no details were forthcoming, he prompted him. "Exactly what did she say, to the best of your recollection?"

"She said she'd have sex with me."

Jones fell silent again, so Searcy continued, "Can you tell us what kind of sex acts the defendant offered?"

That got me out of my chair. "Objection, Your Honor. Asked and answered." I shot Searcy a haughty glance, to imply to the jury that his inquiry was sordid.

"Sustained," the judge said.

Searcy snatched his legal pad off the podium. "No further questions."

I stood at the podium facing the witness stand and took a moment to establish eye contact with Jones. "Mr. Jones," I began, "you stayed at the Maggard farm for a period of two weeks, correct?"

"Yes, ma'am."

"During the time you were staying there, where did you sleep at night?"

"I got a tent and a sleeping bag with my gear. I set it up behind the house a ways."

"Do you recall a red-painted shed on the property?"

"Yes, ma'am."

"Did you observe whether Amber ever spent the night in that shed?"

"Yes, ma'am. A couple of times."

A chair squeaked across the floor behind me. I could sense Searcy's tension mounting.

"Do you recall the circumstances that led to Amber sleeping in the shed?"

Searcy's voice boomed behind me. "Objection. Irrelevant."

"I'll allow it," the judge said.

I gave a nod of encouragement. Jones answered, "Dale was put out with her about something. So she had to spend the night in there."

"Did you have occasion to see the inside of the shed?"

"Oh, yeah. Sure."

I handed him my mounted photograph of the shed's interior. "Mr. Jones, I hand you what's been marked defendant's exhibit number 1. Tell us what it is."

"It's a picture of the shed. The inside of it."

I continued. "Is defendant's exhibit number 1 a fair and accurate representation of the interior of the shed that stood on the Maggards' property?"

"Yes, ma'am."

"The shed where Dale Maggard made Amber sleep on occasion, correct?"

"Yes."

"Can you tell the jury where Dale Maggard made Amber sleep inside the shed? If you know," I added.

He knew.

"That dog cage there, in the corner. He'd stick her in the kennel overnight, hunkered down like a dog."

A shocked murmur came from the jury box. I wanted to look over but didn't dare break my stride.

"And you saw Dale do that to Amber with your own eyes?"

"Yes, ma'am."

I took the exhibit from his hand but remained close to the witness stand. "Mr. Jones, aside from imprisoning her in a dog cage, did you ever observe Dale Maggard mistreat Amber in any other way?"

"I seen him beat her once," Jones said.

"Describe the beating, please."

Searcy's voice was belligerent. "Objection. Irrelevant. Request to approach the bench."

I opened my mouth to protest, but Judge Parson was already shaking his head. "Overruled. You may answer, sir."

Jones said, "He threw her to the ground and whaled on her with a whip. A horsewhip."

I snuck a look at the jury. They were frozen in their seats, waiting to hear what would come next.

"Did you ever see a horse on the Maggard property, Mr. Jones?"

"A horse? No, ma'am," he said. "Just chickens."

Stepping away from the witness stand, I approached the jury box and leaned on the railing. "Mr. Jones, why did Dale Maggard beat Amber?"

Burry Jones shrugged and gazed down at his feet. When he lifted his head to answer, he grimaced, saying, "He was one of them dudes that gets off on hurting women."

I nodded solemnly and then looked up at Judge Parson.

"No further questions, Your Honor."

CHAPTER 72

SHELBY SEARCY WAS out of his chair before the judge had the chance to invite him.

"Mr. Jones—Burry," he amended, as a reminder of whose side the witness was supposed to be on. "In your time at the farm, did you have occasion to observe Glenna Maggard?"

"Yes, sir."

"How often?"

"Every day I was staying there. She never left the farm, I don't think."

Searcy glanced at the jurors before asking, "Did you ever see Glenna Maggard abuse Amber Travis?"

Burry Jones cocked his head and squinted one eye. "How do you mean?"

"Did you ever observe Glenna engage in abusive treatment of the defendant?"

"I heard her give the girl the rough side of her tongue."

Searcy waved his hand impatiently. "I'm talking about physical abuse. Did you ever see Glenna strike or use physical force on Amber?"

After a pause, Jones said, "No, sir."

"Ever see Glenna beat the defendant or cage her?"

"I didn't. But I never saw her do nothing to stop it neither."

I enjoyed watching Searcy's complexion darken, hearing the pitch of his voice rise in frustration. Amber listened intently, too. I felt her nudge me, and I leaned close so she could speak in my ear.

"Will you get another chance with that guy?" she asked.

I nodded. She said, "Ask him how come Glenna didn't stop Dale."

I glanced at her, to see whether she wanted to elaborate, but she'd returned her focus to the witness stand.

Searcy's attempts to rehabilitate the witness's description of the deceased couple fell flat. After making no headway, he abruptly ended the examination.

I stood up at the counsel table. "Mr. Jones, you stated that Glenna Maggard never interfered with Dale Maggard's abuse of Amber, correct?"

"That's right."

"You never saw her intervene to defend Amber or stop the abuse?"

"No, ma'am, she never did."

Reaching out, I rested my hand on Amber's shoulder. "Mr. Jones—Burry," I said, stealing my adversary's thunder, "do you know why Glenna didn't do anything to help Amber?"

He hesitated, casting a nervous glance at the prosecution table before a determined expression crossed his face, and he said, "Glenna told me that if Dale wasn't whaling on Amber, he'd go back to doing it to her. 'Better her than me,' she said."

My heart was pounding. I wanted the jury to hear his answer again for good measure. I prompted, "Is that a quote, Burry? To the best of your recollection, what exactly did she say?"

"'Better her than me.' Them was her words."

"Thank you, Burry. No further questions, Your Honor."

As Jones left the witness stand and walked past the counsel tables, I caught the furious glare Shelby Searcy directed at the homeless man. A trickle of unease ran across the back of my neck.

I hoped Burry Jones had the good sense to get out of Bassville as fast as his feet could take him.

CHAPTER 73

SHELBY SEARCY ROSE. "Judge, this would be a good time for a recess. We need to confer in chambers."

Judge Parson pushed back from the bench. "Court will be in recess for fifteen minutes. Counsel, meet me in chambers."

Amber clutched my arm as I prepared to leave. "What's going on?"

In a whisper, I said, "The judge gave the jurors a break. And Searcy wants to talk to the judge."

"What about?"

"I don't know. As soon as I find out, I'll tell you. Okay?" I patted the hand that clutched my arm. Before I left, I told her, "Don't worry. Things are coming along just fine."

I meant it. The trial was proceeding in a positive direction for the defense. Maybe the prosecutor should have anticipated that a homeless man might ultimately sympathize with the accused rather than law enforcement.

Inside chambers, Searcy drummed his fingers on the wooden arm of his chair. "Judge, I have a complication. A small one, really. A witness has fallen sick—she can't testify."

"Oh, that's too bad," I said with mock regret. Searcy gave me the evil eye.

"Shelby, it's not like you to excuse a witness from her obligation. How sick is she?"

"She has laryngitis. Her nephew called me this morning."

"Ah," the judge said, frowning. "Well, these things happen, Shelby. Who's the witness?"

"Her name is Marcie Hickock," replied the prosecutor.

I recognized the name from Searcy's list of trial witnesses. Marcie was the waitress I'd met at Quint Rhoades's restaurant.

Searcy explained that the waitress would testify that Amber had never attempted to escape from the Maggards, despite dining at the restaurant over the years.

I rolled my eyes. "Not relevant," I snapped.

Searcy's tone was defensive. "It's obvious that the defense is mounting a smear campaign on the murder victims. If the Maggards subjected the defendant to such vile treatment, why wouldn't Amber have run off when she had the chance?"

I started to respond, but the judge lifted a hand, saying, "I think it's relevant, in light of the testimony given by the prior witness. But it's moot if the woman is unavailable."

Searcy edged forward in his seat. "Your Honor, if I may, I'd like to propose an alternative. Marcie's nephew, Michael Hickock, is also a busboy at the restaurant. He could testify to essentially the same facts."

There was a note of disapproval in the judge's voice when he asked, "You want to put the Hickock boy on the witness stand?"

It sounded like an unspoken message, but I had my own agenda. I leaned forward, grasping the edge of the judge's desk. "Has this nephew been endorsed? I don't recall the prosecution providing his name during discovery. Searcy can't call witnesses whom he failed to identify through discovery. It's a clear violation of Rule 17. I've never had the opportunity to contact this man, never talked to him."

Judge Parson swiveled in his chair, making a quarter turn. He fingered the corner of the Arkansas state flag that hung beside the window as he considered the matter. After a moment, he turned back to face us. "Defendant's objection is sustained. The court will not permit the state to call a witness who was not named prior to trial."

"That's fine, Judge," Searcy said, remaining cool. "We'll call him as a rebuttal witness, after the defendant's case."

"I may allow that, if he's a true rebuttal witness. We'll see what the evidence shows." The judge checked his watch; our fifteen-minute recess was running long. "Who's up next, Shelby?"

Searcy stretched his legs out. "If I can't call my restaurant witness, the state will rest." He grinned at me, like the wolf wearing the grandmother's nightgown.

My heart started to beat faster. It had never occurred to me that the state's case would take less than a week. My voice rose as I said, "It's a murder case. I never dreamed that the prosecutor would rest by Friday of the first week of trial. I didn't subpoena the defense witnesses to appear until next Monday."

The judge cocked his head, as if he didn't understand me. "Next Monday?"

"Your Honor, sir," I said, stammering over the s sound, "I respectfully request that we adjourn until Monday morning."

"Monday?" he repeated, his voice rising. "Ms. Randall, you are the one who demanded a sequestered jury. At your insistence, thirteen citizens are locked in a motel on the highway, separated from their homes and families."

"I realize that, but—"

"I don't want to hear any excuses. I intend for this trial to proceed this afternoon. And you should be advised that I may, in my discretion, decide to hold court tomorrow as well."

My voice wavered. "But tomorrow is Saturday."

The judge rose from his chair and bent over a small refrigerator to pull out a plastic-wrapped sandwich and a carton of milk. He placed them on the desk and unzipped his robe.

"In light of these developments, I'll instruct the bailiff to give the jury an early lunch break. Mr. Searcy, Ms. Randall, I'll see you in court at 1:00 this afternoon. The defense will call its first witness after the prosecution rests."

In stunned silence, I followed Searcy out of chambers and back into the courtroom, mentally flipping through possibilities. The handwriting expert I'd contacted was from a university on the eastern end of the state, and she hadn't provided me with her conclusions yet; we had a phone conference set for Saturday. And I knew Tripp Pennington wasn't sitting in the hallway, waiting for the bailiff to call out his name. I doubted I could even get the local fire chief over here on such short notice.

A desperate thought took hold: I could appeal to Searcy. Maybe he didn't like the idea of rushing the trial either. If we presented a united front to Judge Parson, maybe we could persuade him to adjourn until Monday.

With that plan in mind, I chased after Searcy as he headed into the tiled lobby of the courthouse. I started to call his name, but the sound died in my throat when I saw the young man at his side.

It was the teenage pickup driver.

CHAPTER 74

I HAD NO time to ponder the unexpected appearance of the driver. It would be preferable to have ended the defense case with Amber's testimony rather than open with it, but we were painted into a corner. My client was bound for the witness stand.

After we reconvened following lunch, and before the jury had returned, Judge Parson said he'd instruct the deputy to remove Amber's handcuffs, but I wanted the leg shackles off, too.

"Forcing Amber to walk to the witness stand with her feet chained together will prejudice the jury against her," I said.

"No way, Judge," Searcy argued. "As the head law enforcement official in Hagar County, I can't sanction it. She's a danger."

I wheeled on him, barely managing to keep my tone civil. "It's not your call, Searcy. This is the judge's decision." I appealed to Judge Parson. "Look at her, Judge. She's barely five feet tall, one hundred pounds soaking wet. Where's the danger?"

At that, all three of us looked over at Amber. She sat at the defense table, her fair head bent over a legal pad, doodling. She wore her hair in a high ponytail, which brushed her left shoulder.

Judge Parson cleared his throat. "I'm granting defense counsel's request—only for the purpose of testimony." He directed Deputy

Danny Minton to remove Amber's restraints, then cast a warning look at me. "Ms. Randall, you'd be wise to advise your client to behave herself. One misstep, and I'll order the deputy to shackle her. That is not an empty threat."

"I understand. Thank you, Your Honor."

After the restraints were removed, Amber rubbed her wrists. I could see red marks on her skin where the cuffs had been secured too tightly.

I bent my head close to her. "Amber, the jury will be coming into court any minute. Are you ready?"

Her eyes filled with dread. "I don't know as I have any choice. Ready or not, like they say."

She was right. I heard the door open and the footfalls of the jurors as they trooped in.

In a whisper, I said, "Remember to remain calm. Tell it just like we practiced. And when Searcy cross-examines you, don't let him get under your skin. The jury doesn't like to see people lose their temper." *Particularly people charged with murder.*

There was no time to offer any additional advice. The jury was seated, and Searcy was on his feet. "Your Honor, the state rests."

We stepped up to the bench, where the judge made short work of my motion for judgment of acquittal, denying it without further comment. As we stepped away, he said, "Ms. Randall, you may call your first witness."

I waited for the prosecutor to sit down, so that he wouldn't obscure the jury's view. "The defense calls Amber Travis to the witness stand."

She stood carefully.

I spotted Quint Rhoades and Hopp Cole sitting in the back row of the spectators' gallery, but I focused my attention on Amber. With trembling hands, she undid the top button of the cardigan and removed it, turning her back to the jury as she draped it neatly over the arm of her chair. The sleeveless shell underneath had a scooped back and neckline; on Amber's small frame, it showed enough skin to display scars on her back and chest, marks on her arms, and the circle around her neck formed by years of repeated strangulation.

As Amber made her way to the witness stand, my eyes slid to the jury box. The jurors were shifting in their seats. Some of them looked distinctly uncomfortable: a good sign, I thought. When I saw a young woman juror exchange a glance with the male alternate, I knew Amber had scored at least one new supporter.

After she was sworn in, Amber sat in the witness chair, grasping both arms of the chair so tightly that tendons stood out in her hands. I smiled at her, mentally urging her to relax.

"Please state your name," I said, my voice carrying the same note of respect I would offer to the Duchess of Cambridge, Kate Middleton.

"Amber Travis. Amber Lynn Travis," she amended, giving the judge an anxious glance, as if she feared he would upbraid her for making an incomplete response.

"How old are you, Amber?"

"Twenty-three."

"Where were you born?"

"I was born in Pocahontas. But after my daddy died, me and Mama moved to Russellville, Arkansas. I've lived in Arkansas all my life."

"How long did you live in Russellville, Amber?"

"Until I was ten, when my mama died of cancer."

I paused for a moment, to let the jurors envision a ten-year-old orphan watching her mother waste away.

"After your mother died of cancer, where did you go?"

"I moved up here, to live with the Maggards, Dale and Glenna."

"And exactly where did you live with Dale and Glenna?"

"On their farm. Just outside of Bassville." She released the arms of the chair and twisted her hands together in her lap. She was wound up tight.

"Is that farm in Hagar County, Arkansas?"

"Yes, ma'am."

"What was your relationship to the Maggards?"

"They was my second cousins. The only relatives I had. A judge made them my guardians because I was little. They was supposed to take care of me."

She had emphasized the word "supposed." I glanced at the jury, hoping they'd caught it.

"Did they take care of you?"

Amber paused and bowed her head. When she lifted it and spoke, her voice had an edge. "I lived on the farm and ate their food. They gave me clothes to wear."

"What kind of clothes?"

"Glenna's. I wore Glenna's old clothes." Amber looked up to the judge, as if she thought he might require additional explanation. "She showed me how to do some sewing, so I could make them smaller."

I didn't want Amber to direct her communications to Judge Parson; she needed to appeal to the jury. So I walked over to the jury box and propped my hip against the far corner, determined to redirect her focus.

"Were the Maggards kind guardians, Amber? Were they good to you?"

Her face hardened, aging it dramatically. "No, ma'am. I don't think they were good."

In my right hand, I held an exhibit: the contract.

"Amber, directing your attention to your eighteenth birthday, what happened on that date?"

A flush mounted up her neck, suffusing her face. "That was the day Dale had me sign that paper."

"What paper, Amber?" I asked, glancing down at the exhibit.

"He wrote out a paper, saying I would agree to be his slave. And if I signed it—"

Searcy's booming voice cut her off. "Objection, Your Honor. Request permission to approach the bench."

Judge Parson peered at Searcy over his glasses. "Grounds?"

Searcy was already trotting to the bench. "Irrelevant, immaterial."

"Overruled." The judge gave him a warning look. "Ms. Travis, you may answer."

After a moment's hesitation, Amber said, "If I signed it, I was supposed to get his and Glenna's property when they died."

Again she emphasized the word "supposed," but this time it worried me. *Dear God, don't let her start harping on her inheritance in front of the jury.*

I strode to the stand and handed her the contract, instructing her to read it aloud. As she did, some jurors registered shock; others looked skeptical. Several revealed no reaction at all.

So I wrinkled my forehead and asked Amber the question I assumed they were turning over in their minds.

"Amber, are you telling the court that you actually believed you were a slave?"

"Yes, ma'am."

"Why did you believe that?"

"Because of the contract."

"But, Amber, aren't you aware that the Constitution makes slavery illegal?"

"I don't know what that is."

Someone in the jury box snorted. Steeling myself, I kept my gaze on Amber, though I wanted to turn a scathing eye on the scoffer.

"Why didn't you learn about the Constitution in school?"

"I never went to school. Not much."

"Why not?"

I chanced a glance at the judge. He watched Amber with a curious air.

"I just got through second grade. Mama couldn't get me there, because she was so sick, and so they held me back a time or two. Then when I lived with Dale and Glenna, I didn't go to school."

"Did they teach you at home?"

"They taught me to work with the laying hens." Someone in the courtroom chuckled. When Amber looked over at the jury box, the sound swiftly converted to a cough.

"You never went to school in Bassville?"

Searcy stood. "Judge Parson—"

Parson interrupted, admonishing me with a look of reproof. "Ms. Randall?"

I changed course. "Amber, why did you sign that contract?"

Sighing, she said, "Well, I thought I was pretty much doing whatever they wanted anyway. They had me working on the farm every day since I was a little old kid and didn't pay me nothing. So I thought, if I signed my name, maybe someday I'd get something for all the work I done."

I stood close to the witness stand. "Amber, tell us what happened after you signed the contract."

Her voice was flat. "That's when Dale started hurting me. First it was beatings. Then he thought up them other things to do."

"What other things?"

Her hand went to her throat, where the ring around her neck was clearly visible. "He'd put a cord or a rope around my neck, so I couldn't breathe. Sometimes a plastic bag."

"What else, Amber?"

"He'd shock me, electrocute me. It burned."

"Where on your body did he inflict the electric shock?"

It took effort, but she managed to get the words out. "My privates. Lady parts."

An involuntary grunt of disgust came from either the jury box or the spectators' gallery, but I concentrated on Amber. I hoped she would provide one more revelation.

"Did he do anything else to your private parts, Amber, that hurt you?"

Her face was scarlet. She cut her eyes away and pinched her lips together, the muscles of her jaw working. Her eyes slid to the jury box and then squeezed shut.

Finally, she whispered, "I can't say it out loud."

I was afraid if I pushed her, she might shut down entirely. Moving to less perilous territory, I said, "Did Dale Maggard ever force you to have sex with him?"

Her breathing relaxed a bit. "Yeah, there was that, too. After I signed the paper, all that started."

"Amber, why did Dale Maggard abuse you physically? Including but not limited to suffocation, beating, and electrocution?"

Again, Searcy's voice rang out. "Objection. Calls for speculation."

Judge Parson didn't pause to consider. "Overruled."

Amber looked confused, so I prompted her. "Why, Amber?"

"Because he liked it," she said, her voice rising on the last word. Then, as if it was an afterthought, she added, "And he made money off it."

CHAPTER 75

A QUICK GLANCE into the jury box revealed that we had the group's attention, though not everyone looked convinced.

"Objection. Request to approach." When the judge nodded, Searcy made a run for the bench. I joined them, irritated that Searcy was interfering with the flow of Amber's testimony.

He whispered to the judge, "How long will defense counsel be permitted to continue this line of questioning? It has no connection to the circumstances of the victims' deaths, serves no purpose other than to demean the character of two people who can't speak up to defend themselves against vile accusations."

Looking thoughtful, Judge Parson said, "I'm inclined to agree with the prosecutor, Ms. Randall. I've been lenient, but you need to move on to testimony related to the offense with which the defendant is charged."

"Exactly my point." Searcy's voice had a triumphant lilt.

Had I taken too long to reach the crucial point? We needed to address the basis for Amber's subjection to Dale. "Understood, Your Honor. We'll focus on the day of the Maggards' demise."

The judge gave me a dour look, magnified through his eyeglasses. "I'll hold you to that, Ms. Randall."

As I returned to my position in front of Amber, I observed that she'd grown antsy during the bench conference; she held the neck of her sweater twisted in her fist. I stared at it silently for a moment, until she picked up the message. She released the fabric and dropped her hand into her lap.

I nodded. "Amber, directing your attention to August second, where did you sleep on that date?"

"I slept inside the red shed, in the dog kennel."

"Why did you sleep in a dog kennel that night?"

"Dale made me. He was mad at me because I dropped a mess of eggs and broke them."

I showed her the photo of the interior of the shed, instructed her to mark the cage. After she handed the exhibit back to me, I said, "Did you fall asleep in the cage depicted in this photo?"

"Yeah. It's not easy to sleep all cramped up like that, but you get used to it."

At that point, an elderly man on the jury shook his head, but I couldn't discern whether it was an expression of sympathy or disbelief.

"What happened in the night?"

"Well, I woke up and it was still dark, but I could see light shining in the window of the shed."

"What else did you observe or notice?"

"Smoke. I smelled smoke."

"What did you do?"

"I undid that latch and crawled out of the cage. I was pretty stiff, so it took me a minute to stand up. Then I went outside of the shed and that's when I saw it."

"What did you see?"

"I saw the farmhouse was on fire."

"What did you do?"

"I ran off."

"Why?"

Amber clenched her teeth and grimaced. "It just popped into my head. That I could finally get out of there. Not have to put up with Dale no more."

"Where did you go?"

"I went through the fields, down country roads. It was hard because I wasn't wearing no shoes, just my nightgown is all. And I got lost for a whole day, didn't know where I was until I got onto the highway and seen the Gas-N-Go store."

"Amber, did you kill Dale and Glenna Maggard?"

She looked startled. "No! No, ma'am."

"Did you set their house on fire?"

"No, ma'am, I didn't."

"Did you ever see gas cans on the property?"

"Yes, ma'am. Dale kept gasoline for the generator and the mower and such."

"Did you ever handle them?"

"Sure I did. Any kind of work there was, Dale had me do it. I probably handled everything on that farm."

"Thank you, Amber. No further questions."

Amber had held up well, better than I had dared to hope. But something about Shelby Searcy's face as he passed me on the way to the witness stand plucked a string of apprehension in my brain.

CHAPTER 76

WHEN AMBER SAW that prosecutor coming for her, she grabbed the arms of her chair and held on for dear life. There was something in the man's eyes that made the sweat bead up in her armpits and roll down her skin. Amber knew she stunk to high heaven, and she was stinking up the sweater her lawyer had given her to wear. But she had known better than to set foot in the jailhouse shower last night. The jailer woman was gunning for her.

The prosecutor stopped just inches away from her. Instinctively, she scooted backward in her seat.

"Did you run for help?" he asked.

"Sir?" She'd been so lost inside her own head, Amber hadn't paid attention to the question.

"Help. When you saw the fire, did you try to get help? Call 911?"

Confused, she said, "Well, I don't know how I would've done that. There wasn't no telephone in the shed, where I was at."

"Did you try to rescue your cousins, Dale and Glenna?"

"No." A defensive reaction bloomed in her chest. "The house was burning. There was fire everywhere. I couldn't do nothing."

"Did you run to the nearest neighbor to report the fire?"

"No, sir."

"But you could have done that, couldn't you?"

"I guess." The sweat was getting heavier.

"You guess?" He shook his head, like he didn't understand the words. "Could you or couldn't you? Yes or no?"

"I could've," she said. "But I didn't." Amber lowered her head, squinting at him through narrowed eyes. She knew what he was up to: making her look bad, making her out to be a coward. She heard Leah's voice whisper in her head: *Don't let him get under your skin.*

"So you knew that the people who took you in as a child, when you had nowhere to go, who fed and clothed you and put a roof over your head, were burning up in that house. But you did nothing. Correct?"

"I ran."

The lawyer stared at Amber, a snotty look on his face. Then he turned around and walked over by where the jury sat. Amber breathed out in relief. She was grateful for the distance.

When he spoke again, he sounded sneaky, like he wanted to trick her. "As your guardians when you were a minor, the Maggards were responsible for your upbringing and had the right to punish you when you misbehaved. Wouldn't you agree?"

Amber had her guard up. "I behaved myself just fine."

"Were you angry that Dale Maggard would discipline you when you did something wrong?"

"I didn't do nothing." It was a trick. She knew it was a trick.

"Never?" He sounded amazed, like she was a big fibber. "Nothing at all?"

"Nothing bad enough for Dale to do what he done to me after I turned eighteen."

The lawyer made a funny face, rubbing the back of his head. "When you were older and Dale disciplined you"—he stopped and stared at her hard before he finished the question—"did you enjoy it?"

Speechless, Amber's jaw dropped, and she gaped at him. But she didn't get a chance to answer him, because Leah flew out of her chair like a shot.

"Objection! How dare you?"

CHAPTER 77

FURIOUS, I STUMBLED over my words.

"Your Honor, that's badgering! He's badgering the witness and I strenuously object—improper!"

Unruffled, Searcy said, "Your Honor, I'm just following up on the line of questioning the defense introduced in testimony on direct."

"That's preposterous. It's argumentative and demeaning."

Searcy gave me a smile so cold it lowered the temperature of the room. "Permit me to respond without interruption, Ms. Randall. This topic was also raised by the defense in the cross-examination of the state's witness, Burry Jones. Ms. Randall opened the door, Your Honor."

I waited impatiently for Judge Parson to speak, to support my objection, and was shocked when he said, "Overruled. Mr. Searcy, you may proceed."

Searcy said smugly, "I'll repeat the question for the defendant. Did you enjoy it?"

Amber's face was like granite. "No."

"Never? Not even a little bit?"

Her head jerked, as if he'd slapped her. "No."

"Ms. Travis, have you heard of a book entitled *Fifty Shades of Grey*?"

Out of my chair again, I snapped, "Irrelevant and immaterial."

"Overruled." The judge's eyes were fixed on his gavel.

"There's a book—also a movie—called *Fifty Shades of Grey*. Have you heard of it?"

Amber's face twitched. "Yes. I heard about it at the jail. A woman tried to give it to me. I didn't read it."

"Not even a peek?"

"No. She told me about the story in it, though."

"So you've heard the story. Did you like it?" Searcy prodded her. "What did you think? A lot of women like the story. Did you think it was interesting?"

Amber laughed with a sound so devoid of humor, I shivered.

I wasn't conscious of leaving my chair. "Your Honor, please. This is preposterous. I thought *In Cold Blood* by Truman Capote was interesting; that doesn't mean I want someone to kill me."

Judge Parson looked up. "Counsel, please approach."

At the bench, I spoke in a heated whisper. "Your Honor, the prosecutor is browbeating my client with an improper line of questioning. It's beyond offensive, it's—"

The judge shook his head. "Ms. Randall, you opened this Pandora's box. We'll have to see it through. Your objection is overruled."

Searcy said, "Judge, that wisecrack she made about Truman Capote? I object to *that*. She made a speaking objection. Defense counsel is attempting to testify."

"I did not—" I began, but Parson interrupted.

"No speeches, Ms. Randall." He sat up straight and raised his voice to its normal pitch. "The court reporter will read the last question."

I watched Amber listen as the reporter reread the question. Her face was splotched with patches of red, and her fingers dug into the seat of her chair when she responded.

"I told Ms. Hickock, thank you very much, but I didn't like the story and I didn't want to read her book. Because it was stupid, it wasn't real. I know what it feels like when it's real."

I scrawled *Hickock?* on the legal pad in giant letters. Was this a relative of Marcie Hickock, the Western Roadhouse waitress?

Searcy inched closer to the witness stand. "Ms. Travis, you claim that Dale Maggard beat you and hurt you. You've testified that you didn't believe you deserved it. So why didn't you walk away?"

There was a long silence before she responded. "I couldn't walk away."

"You couldn't? You're not a child. You're an adult, Ms. Travis. Why couldn't you leave?"

"He would've stopped me."

"How? How would he stop you?"

"I was trapped. I was trapped on the farm." Amber was starting to lose control. I could see red blotches on her neck, like a bad case of hives.

"But you weren't always on the farm, were you? What about the times you came into Bassville with the Maggards? Did Dale ever take you to dine at the Western Roadhouse?"

"We'd eat at the Roadhouse sometimes. Maybe once a year or something like that."

I checked over my shoulder. Quint Rhoades still sat in the back of the courtroom. When I turned back around, Searcy had moved closer to Amber.

"Did you ever tell anyone at the restaurant that you were being abused?"

"No."

"Did you ever try to use the phone at the restaurant to call the sheriff and report the abuse?"

"No."

"Did you ever try to escape from the Maggards when you went to the restaurant?" Searcy was setting the stage for his rebuttal witness. I made a note that he was clearly intending to put the Confederate-sympathizing busboy on the witness stand.

"No."

"Why not?"

"How was I gonna do it—just walk out? Where would I go then?" I watched Amber's face as she spoke. She looked like an animal who'd been cornered. Turning to the jury, she repeated the question, her voice rising. "Where would I go?"

Oh, God, no, I thought. *Amber, don't let him make you mad.*

Searcy looked like the cat with the canary. "Let me get this straight. When you had the opportunity, you didn't walk away. And when the alleged abuse was occurring, you didn't fight it."

She panted for breath. "I couldn't fight it."

"Why not? You're an able-bodied adult."

"If I fought back, he'd have done it double. He made the rules, he was in charge, because of the contract."

She'd become so agitated that the word "contract" had come out in a shriek.

"The abuse made you angry, didn't it?" asked Searcy.

"Yes!"

"You're still angry, aren't you?"

"Yes, I am!"

"You sound like you're angry right here, as you sit in this courtroom."

I stood to object, but Amber was yelling, "I'm mad because nobody helped me!" She looked from the judge to the jury. "Nobody in this town lifted a finger to save me!"

"Request to approach, Your Honor," I said, my voice booming.

Searcy ignored me. He loomed over Amber and said, "So you killed them."

Her face twisted with anguish. In a voice that cracked, she said, "Somebody needed to."

"So you admit it?"

"No!" she wailed. She jumped out of her chair. Searcy blocked the exit to the witness stand as the judge banged his gavel, calling for order.

Amber flung her leg over the front of the stand and hoisted her body across it, dropping onto the floor. I heard a juror squeal as I ran up to intervene.

But Danny reached Amber first, wrestling her to the ground. Her eyes were wild as he held her arms behind her back and fumbled for the cuffs.

I stood helplessly by, watching as they shackled her hands and feet, one frantic thought drumming through my head.

We're screwed.

CHAPTER 78

"WE'LL ADJOURN UNTIL Monday morning," Judge Parson said. As the jury shuffled out, murmuring, Parson beckoned us to the bench. His customary stoic demeanor had cracked during Amber and Danny's scuffle.

I cast a burning look at Amber before I left the counsel table. "Wait for me in the holding cell." When Danny walked up, I snapped at him. "Holding cell. Don't take her back to jail yet."

At the bench, the judge watched the last juror file out of the courtroom.

"Ms. Randall, I've decided to adjourn for the weekend, as an accommodation to the defense. I recommend," he began, removing his glasses and focusing on them as he polished the lenses with a tissue, "that you utilize the time to get your client under control."

"Yes, Your Honor." Privately, I wondered whether giving the jurors two days to reflect on Amber's cross-examination hysteria, and ponder what it signified, would help or hurt us.

"Mr. Searcy, I'll give you the opportunity to finish cross-examination on Monday."

"Oh, I think I'm done with cross-ex of the defendant, Your Honor." His mouth twitched, and I had to stifle the urge to headbutt him.

"Then the defense will have the opportunity for redirect. If Ms. Randall thinks it's wise." Judge Parson replaced his glasses and adjusted them, giving me a warning look. "I expect to hear that your other witnesses are ready to go on Monday, Ms. Randall."

I nodded without comment. I hoped Tripp would reconsider, especially when he learned about Amber's breakdown on the stand. He might know about it already—the story had probably reached every corner of Bassville within minutes.

I made my way to the holding cell, where Danny stood with Amber. When I took my seat on the opposite side of the counter, he said, "I'll give you some privacy," and slipped out, shutting the door behind him.

Amber slumped in the chair, her head lowered, looking like a sulky kid.

"So. About your testimony."

She pressed her lips together and looked away. Her rebellious expression infuriated me, and I spoke more harshly than I'd intended.

"It was a disaster out there. You know that, right? Jurors don't like it when the defendant lashes out on the stand. What was up with you shouting at the judge and jury? Are you trying to make them hate you?"

Squeezing her eyes shut, she shook her head back and forth but didn't offer a verbal reply.

"What possessed you to try to climb out of the witness stand?" I continued scolding. "I warned you that Searcy would try to make you mad, told you not to fall into the trap. You were supposed to make the jury like you. That was your job."

Her eyes popped open with a glare that startled me. "You do *your* job," she said.

"Excuse me?" My face twisted in disbelief. I'd been fighting like a madwoman on her behalf.

Her voice rose to a shrill pitch. "Do your job! Why don't you find those DVDs Dale hid?"

The knot of frustration in my chest tightened. "Amber, everything on the Maggard farm was burned to the ground. It doesn't matter whether Dale hid them in the house or the shed or the damned chicken coop—everything's gone."

She stared at me resentfully but didn't argue the point. I tempered my voice, hoping to decrease the tension that simmered in the cell.

"On Monday, we'll present our evidence. I'll call Dr. Pennington, and he'll bolster your credibility when he describes your injuries and offers his medical opinion. That will help the jury to understand that you've been telling the truth." Keeping my manner encouraging, I said, "When the handwriting expert authenticates Dale's and Glenna's signatures based on their signatures on the wills they signed in my dad's office, we can get the contract into evidence. It shouldn't be a problem."

Amber gave a slight nod.

I smiled, relieved. "The contract will be a key piece of evidence, because it also supports your testimony, your version of events."

"Contract," she muttered, like she was uttering a curse.

I hesitated before adding, "And you will have to get back on the stand."

Her eyes widened as she shrank back in her chair. "No."

"Amber, you have to go back to the stand. You left the distinct impression that you condoned the Maggards' murders."

"I did not."

"You did. When Searcy asked if you killed them and you said, 'Someone needed to.' Remember that?"

"Somebody did need to."

I expelled a sigh. The back of my head throbbed, and I rubbed it. "That's the problem, Amber. The jury won't forget when you say things like that."

"I don't like that jury. There's a bunch of mean women on there." She looked down, tugged at the black cardigan, and began to button it all the way up the front.

"It's not too late to enter a guilty plea," I said.

Once the words were out of my mouth, I regretted them. Her hands stilled on a black button she had pressed halfway through its buttonhole, and she looked up at me, glowering. "I can't do that because it's a lie. I didn't kill nobody."

"You could enter an Alford plea. Say: I didn't do it, but I acknowledge there's enough evidence against me to convict. Then the sentence would be in the judge's hands, rather than the jury's. It's an option."

"I don't want to do that. I want you to get on out of here and go to the farm and get those DVDs. They're out there, I'm telling you. He hid them in a safe."

I thought I might have misheard her, but she repeated, her voice insistent.

"You go on out to the farm."

I stood and snatched my briefcase off the floor. I walked out, so angry I couldn't look back at her.

"You're crazy," I said under my breath.

CHAPTER 79

"I'M CRAZY," I muttered, my car bouncing up the gravel drive to the Maggard farm. A jumbo-size Dr Pepper from Sonic rode shotgun. I grabbed the cup and took a long sip, for medicinal purposes.

After leaving Amber, I'd spent two restless hours in my office poring over Tripp's medical report. Yet I couldn't stop obsessing over Amber's unfeasible demand that I somehow find Dale Maggard's stash of DVDs.

I pulled up to the farm. Staring at the burned shells of the farmhouse and outbuildings, I heaved a weary sigh. There was no rational hope of finding anything in the ruins of the farm. But I wouldn't be able to silence Amber's shrill voice in my head unless I gave it a shot.

The sun was sinking toward the horizon, and the notion of digging through the ashes in the dark, all alone, sent a tremor through me. My cell phone's charge was low, but I didn't need to rely on it for light. Opening the trunk, I grabbed a sturdy aluminum flashlight from my emergency kit. Walt Randall had raised me to anticipate disaster. Sometimes it was a handy trait.

Back in the office, I'd had a revelation: maybe the Maggards had a storm shelter on the farm. Though I hadn't seen one when I toured the property with Danny, it would make sense; Bassville was in tornado country, and many local homes had underground shelters for violent weather. A storm cellar could provide a hiding place for Dale's stash of ugly secrets, and it wouldn't necessarily have been destroyed by a house fire.

Aiming the beam of light along the ground, I circled the remains of the farmhouse, looking for a cellar entrance built into the ground. When I couldn't find one, I stepped over the crime-scene tape. Danny had pointed out the kitchen area to me, and now I crawled along the space on my hands and knees, trying to find a hole in the ground.

With a groan, I pulled myself out of the ashes, wiping my dirty hands on the seat of my pants. I moved over to where the red shed had stood, prior to the second fire. The destruction was less devastating than the farmhouse fire. My flashlight picked out shards of metal inside the cavity of the structure. But I found no hiding place for DVDs.

A rustling noise over by the farmhouse chimney spooked me. I hoped my presence hadn't attracted any company. I waved the flashlight beam with wild aim, but it didn't provide sufficient light to illuminate anything. Doggedly, I returned to the car. As I sat behind the wheel, I burned to throw it into reverse and head for home. Instead, I aimed the headlights at the chimney and went back to inspect it.

Feeling my way along the charred stones, I pushed at them with the palm of my hand, but they didn't give. I felt foolish—a fireplace that could stand for a century and weather a massive fire would not crumble under my efforts. I walked behind the chimney, flashing the beam of light back and forth along the stones. When I pointed the flashlight at eye level on the far corner of the chimney, a flurry of bats spewed out, brushing my face in their flight.

Screeching, I dropped to my knees and covered my head with my hands. My heart racing, I thought of my mother's antipathy to bats. "Rabies," I whispered.

I picked myself up off the ground and turned to go. The Maggard farm had totally creeped me out. And though I didn't really think I'd been bitten by a bat, I wanted to check my face in the car mirror, just to be sure.

Then the question occurred to me: *Where did the bats come from?*

At my parents' house, the bats emerged at night from the top of the chimney. For these bats to have flown straight into my face, there must be an opening in the Maggards' stone fireplace. So I returned to the fireplace and ran my hand along where the bats had materialized. When I shoved it, the stone shifted.

The rough surface scraped my fingertips, but I persisted, putting down the flashlight and pulling at the stone until I was able to grasp it with both hands. Giving a mighty tug, the rock came out, and I tossed it to the ground. Then I picked up the flashlight and peered inside.

Under a layer of bat guano, a metal box was wedged into the mortar.

CHAPTER 80

THE HAND I was using to hold the flashlight began to tremble, making the beam flicker across the stone as I trained the light into the recessed space.

I slid my other hand inside, trying to nudge the box from its hiding place. It didn't move easily. I returned to the trunk of my car for a lug wrench. Using the wrench as a pry bar, I got the box to shift close enough for me to grasp it.

I pulled with all my strength—and when the box suddenly emerged, I dropped it onto the ground, narrowly missing my feet. Though it was roughly the size of a boot box, it was much heavier than it appeared, and I grunted like a weight lifter as I hefted it up and stumbled along the rocky ground, carrying my burden to the car.

I inspected the box under the dome light. It had to be the safe Amber had told me about. The realization that I might have possession of the long-sought evidence made my adrenaline spike. I didn't even consider contacting the sheriff's office. When I'd asked them to take custody of the dog cage in the shed, they'd ignored my request, to the detriment of my client.

I was wild to open up the safe. But it wasn't going to be easy. The metal box was secured with a formidable combination lock.

Running my finger across it, I tried to imagine what Dale Maggard might use as a numerical combination.

In general, people used codes that were easy to recall. My mother liked to rely on her birth date, despite my dad's disapproval. He had warned her that her birth date was easy for scammers to access, which made her accounts easy targets for fraud. Mom was stubborn about it, though. She said she couldn't remember all the different passwords and codes she was supposed to keep. When Dad told her to write them down and store them in a secure spot, she had just laughed.

That was the old dad, the pre-Alzheimer's Walt. Over the past months, my father's decline had accelerated; at this point, he might have trouble recalling his own date of birth.

Pushing aside the depressing thought, I sifted through the files in my briefcase and pulled out the police reports on the Maggard murder case. The first page, which identified the victims, provided Dale's date of birth. Taking care to push the right buttons, I entered the six-digit combination of his birth date. No dice.

With mounting impatience, I plugged in Glenna's birth date, also without success. I tried Amber's DOB, but the lock remained shut. Tossing the reports onto the floorboard, I seized the aluminum flashlight and used it to beat on the lock. The assault dented the flashlight but had no impact on the safe.

Frustration buzzed up my spine. My discovery of—but inability to access—what could be crucial evidence in my possession, shattered what remained of my composure. Tears began to trickle down my face. I dashed them off my cheeks with my wrist, chagrined by the display, even though no one was present to witness it.

"Pull yourself together, Leah," I said to myself in the rearview mirror. "What if Dad could see you now?"

I was hit with a wave of profound longing: if only I could spend a few minutes with the person he had been. The old Walt Randall would know how to handle this problem. But that man had slipped away. Mom was my ally, but Barb was no safecracker.

That left only one person to whom I might possibly turn. With a grimace, I put the car in gear.

I was halfway to Tripp Pennington's house when I remembered that I hadn't replaced the stone that had disguised the box's hiding place in the chimney. I hit the brakes and considered turning the car around. Then I changed my mind.

"To hell with it," I said aloud.

CHAPTER 81

TRIPP'S FRONT PORCH light was on, but he didn't answer his doorbell. I peered through his living room window, cupping my hands around my eyes, and saw the room was unoccupied and the television was off, but a tableside lamp was glowing.

Growing frantic, I returned to the door and pounded on it with my fist, making a racket that he couldn't possibly ignore. Finally, the door opened, and Tripp appeared, wearing workout clothes and mopping his face with a towel. He looked surprised to see me standing on his doorstep.

"Hi. Got a minute?" I said. I attempted a smile that felt like a grisly baring of teeth.

Tripp stared down at my clothing, covered in ash and mud. I expected that he'd ask why I was so dirty, but instead he said, "Is this a citizen's arrest?" Before I could respond, he continued, "Because it's not necessary, Leah. I intend to comply with the subpoena on Monday."

"Oh, yeah—Monday. Thanks, Tripp. That's great. I knew you'd come through."

He tossed the towel around his neck and gave me a wary look. "So what are you doing here?"

When I tried to answer, a ragged sob escaped. The sound mortified me. I turned away and instead pointed at the gray metal box, which sat beside the welcome mat.

When I got my voice under control, I said, "I need help. Do you have a sledgehammer?"

Squatting down on his haunches, Tripp studied the box. "What is this?"

I took a deep breath and said, "Oh, I think it's what you'd call a smoking gun. At least I hope so. Can you help me open it?"

He lifted it far more easily than I had and carried it into the kitchen, where he set it on his kitchen table and turned to face me. "Leah, are you all right? You look like you've had a rough night. Can I get you anything?"

I was too wired to sit. Instead, I stripped off my dusty jacket and dropped it over the back of a chair. "What I'd really like is to get into that safe. Do you have some kind of implement we can use to pry it open?"

He pointed at the lock. "You need the code to open it."

"But I don't know what the combination is. Can't we bust it open?"

Frowning thoughtfully, he took a seat. While he toyed with the lock, he said, "We can't just break into it. This looks like the same kind of reinforced, fireproof safe I've got at the office, and they are tough. Where did you find this?"

"At the Maggard farm, hidden in the chimney."

Our eyes met. "No shit?" he said.

"No shit." When my knees began to tremble, I dropped onto the chair beside him.

"Have you tried any number combinations to open the safe? Like a birthday. Maybe you can—"

"I tried those already," I interrupted. I beat on the lock with my fist, until Tripp stopped me by covering my hand with his.

"What about addresses, then? Their farm road number, maybe, with the zip code?"

Together, we tried. We made all manner of combinations,

everything we could think of. We used Dale's and Glenna's dates of birth again, their wedding anniversary, possible high school graduations. We punched in the date of Amber's eighteenth birthday, when the slavery contract was signed.

With a surge of infuriation, I angrily jabbed: 1 1 1 1 1 1.

The lock clicked open.

"No way," Tripp said as my mouth dropped open in astonishment.

I seized the small door. When the safe opened, a large quantity of cash fell out, mostly hundred-dollar bills. I removed the currency and laid it on the table. Behind the money, the safe held at least a dozen DVDs.

"Oh, my God," I whispered. With my eyes glued to the DVD cases, I asked Tripp whether he had a DVD player in the house.

"Leah, nobody has one of those things anymore."

The tightness in my chest loosened a bit. "That's not quite true. Can you help me get all this back to my car? I need to go home."

Tripp looked at me in disbelief. "You're kidding me. You have a DVD player?"

I nodded. "My dad does. He's never thrown away anything in his life."

Our eyes locked again. I reached out and grasped his hand, and he pulled me in for a hug. When he released me, my body began to shake. "Are you all right?" he asked again.

I just nodded, unable to explain my jumble of conflicting reactions: triumph at the discovery, remorse that it had taken so long, and fear of what I'd find on those DVDs. Though I needed to see what evidence they provided, I also shuddered at the prospect. I suspected that I might never be able to block the images from my mind.

CHAPTER 82

MONDAY MORNING I hunched over an old laptop on my counsel table, checking to ensure it was connected to the courtroom monitor. My witnesses were lined up on the bench outside the courtroom, and when I heard the door creak open, I wheeled around to see if one of them had a question for me. When I saw that it was Shelby Searcy, I turned my back. The county prosecutor walked up and dropped his briefcase on the prosecution table.

Ignoring Searcy, I focused on my client. Amber looked as fresh as a daisy in a bright floral print with cap sleeves. There were no hand-me-downs for Amber today. Mom had helped me pick out the dress at JCPenney, shuffling hangers until she had pulled it out with a note of triumph. "There!" she had said. "This is just the thing."

Amber had been delighted when I told her the pretty dress was hers to keep. "This is my first new dress in the longest time!" she'd exclaimed.

Her hair was still slightly damp, but it was pulled back neatly off her face. She smelled of soap and shampoo, because I had stormed the jail early that morning to ensure she'd have an opportunity to shower, and with my most forbidding air, I'd stood in the jail-house waiting room while she'd been given the chance to clean up.

Hopefully this would be the last time Amber would have cause to be frightened of the jailhouse showers. Over the weekend, I'd planted a seed for her protection that should bear fruit.

Per my instructions, she wore no makeup. I wanted Amber to look as young and vulnerable as possible. In her new frock, she could pass for a teenager dressed for church—except, of course, for the cuffs that shackled her hands and feet.

The door to Judge Parson's chambers opened. "Counsel, are we ready?" he asked.

"Yes, Your Honor," I said calmly.

"I'll tell the bailiff to bring the jury in," he said, and he disappeared behind the door again.

As the jury took their seats, I bent my head down to Amber and whispered, "You'll be fine."

With her eyes fixed on the jury box, she nodded, but she looked unconvinced.

"All rise," the bailiff called, and we stood as Judge Parson took the bench. Settling into his chair, he said, "You may be seated. In the case of *State of Arkansas v. Amber Lynn Travis*, we adjourned on Friday during the cross-examination of the defendant. Mr. Searcy, do you have further questions?"

"No, Your Honor."

"Ms. Randall, redirect?"

I stood. "Yes, Your Honor." I ignored the pounding in my ears.

The judge looked down at Amber as if he didn't quite know what to make of her. Maybe it was the Sunday-school dress. "Ms. Travis, you'll return to the witness stand. You are still under oath."

Amber stood and shuffled slowly across the floor, the restraints rattling on her ankles. Her hands were cuffed in front of her, and she clasped them together as she advanced to the stand.

Before she sat, Judge Parson said, "Permit me to warn you, Ms. Travis: if you don't conduct yourself properly, you will be held in contempt. Do you understand?"

Sliding into the chair, she offered a meek, "Yes, sir."

I opened my briefcase. The exhibits were already marked; I'd pounced on the court reporter that morning, barely giving her a chance to walk through the door. Plucking a DVD case out of the briefcase, I walked up to Amber and held it out to her.

I held my breath, sending up a heartfelt prayer on Amber's behalf that she'd have the strength to endure this part of the trial. It was abject cruelty to subject her to the DVD, but I'd explained to her that it was absolutely necessary. If she didn't authenticate the exhibits, they wouldn't be received into evidence. "Amber, I'm handing you defendant's exhibit number 6. Can you tell me what it is?"

She fumbled with the plastic case, then managed to pop it open. She looked at the disc for a moment before she held it up and replied, "This is a DVD movie. One of them that Dale made."

"By 'Dale,' are you referring to the deceased, Dale Maggard?"

"Yes, ma'am."

"How can you identify it?"

"He wrote on it with a marker. It says 'Amber number 1 July.'"

Searcy was on his feet, storming to the bench. "Objection. May we approach?"

Parson shot him a disgruntled glance. "Grounds?"

"Irrelevant. Inflammatory. Prejudicial."

I said, "Your Honor, it's entirely relevant. The exhibit refutes issues that the prosecution raised on Friday during cross-examination."

Searcy's eye was twitching violently. "Your Honor, I renew my strenuous objection and request a recess."

The judge leaned back in his chair. "Mr. Searcy, sit down. Your objection is premature. The evidence is still being identified. You may continue, Ms. Randall."

I went on. "Amber, who is the subject of this video?"

"Me."

I took the disc from her and slid it into my laptop, adjusting the volume to ensure it would provide maximum effect. After I pushed Play, I crossed my arms and gripped my elbows to brace myself.

I stared at the big overhead screen between the witness stand and the jury box.

And I waited.

The DVD whirred in the laptop as the disc began to play, showing Dale Maggard strapping Amber's naked body to a long wooden table in the farmhouse kitchen. As he clamped metal devices to her genitals, and then to her toes, Amber lifted her head off the table, weeping and begging.

"Please, Dale, I can't stand it. Please, don't. I'll do anything."

Dale ignored her as he checked the wires that ran from the clamps to an innocuous-looking crank phone that sat on the kitchen counter. When he grasped the crank, I grew queasy and averted my eyes from the screen. I'd already seen what Dale did to her.

Glancing at the witness stand, I saw that Amber's head was bowed and her shoulders hunched. At the bench, Judge Parson stared at the screen with a look of dread, wiping his face with a cloth handkerchief. It occurred to me that he probably knew the purpose of the apparatus in the video. The judge was old enough to remember the scandalous abuses at Arkansas's Tucker prison farm, and the infamous Tucker Telephone, a crank phone that had been used to shock inmates.

On the screen, Dale Maggard turned the crank, and Amber's pleas became inarticulate shrieks as her body convulsed in agony. As Maggard relentlessly electrocuted her on-screen, I clutched my arms more tightly, pinching the skin above my elbows to keep from crying out.

The jurors' faces were contorted with horror. As the recording played on, some of the jurors tried to cover their eyes. An elderly woman in the front row made a keening sound, but it was drowned out by Amber's recorded screams. The alternate juror, Amber's supporter, wept audibly, wiping tears from his face.

When the video ended, I cleared my throat and said, "Your Honor, I'd like to offer defendant's exhibit number 6 into evidence. And if it please the court"—reaching into the briefcase, it required both hands to seize the remaining plastic cases—"I have thirteen more DVDs to introduce."

CHAPTER 83

AFTER THE VIDEO evidence was presented, I called my other witnesses. Searcy didn't bother to contest the testimony, so we made quick progress to closing arguments. When the jury retired to deliberate, Deputy Danny Minton escorted Amber to the holding cell to await the verdict.

As the courtroom emptied out, I collapsed into my chair while Searcy grabbed his briefcase and a handful of notes he had used in his closing argument and walked out without a word. It was common practice for opposing counsel to shake hands after the jury retired, to congratulate each other on a job well done. I was relieved when he didn't make the gesture.

God knows I wasn't interested in any kind of friendly exchange with him, and I had no inclination to make physical contact.

I gathered my scattered papers and file folders and stacked them together, along with pens and legal pads. When someone tapped my shoulder, I whirled around to see the bailiff standing behind the railing.

I let out a nervous laugh, embarrassed by my skittishness.

He said, "I didn't mean to scare you."

"Sorry, I'm all wound up. Quite a day."

"It was something, that's for certain—and I've seen a lot of trials over the years. Judge Parson wanted me to make sure we can get in touch with you if the jury has a question. You'll let me know if you step out, okay?"

The prospect of a steaming cup of hot coffee was tempting, but I wavered. Although I expected the jury probably wouldn't return a verdict for hours, they could have questions, or Amber might need something. "I'd best stick around," I told the bailiff.

As if we'd conjured it, a knock sounded on the door of the jury room. The bailiff hurried to the door and stuck his head into the room. He returned quickly, and I stood up, wondering whether the jury's question related to the exhibits or maybe the jury instructions.

"They've got a verdict," he said.

I dropped into my chair, stunned. They'd been deliberating for only twenty minutes.

CHAPTER 84

WHEN WORD CIRCULATED that the jury's decision was imminent, Shelby Searcy returned to the prosecution table as people quickly flocked back into the courtroom.

One of the first people to reenter was the alternate juror. Although Judge Parson had dismissed him right before the jury retired to deliberate, the young man must've stayed at the courthouse. He strode to the front row, taking a seat right behind the defense counsel table. *Friend of the bride,* I thought.

Amber emerged from the holding cell, flanked by deputies Danny Minton and Crystal Gaines. I'd anticipated that Amber would be nervous, possibly hysterical, as we awaited the verdict, but she was composed as she shuffled into court. With a look of fierce determination, she scooted behind the counsel table and into her chair. She gave me a jerky nod but didn't speak.

Behind the railing, the alternate juror rose from his seat. Grasping the wooden rail, he leaned toward Amber and spoke in a fervent voice. "I'm praying for you, Miss Travis. I believe you," he said.

She turned around in her seat, met his eyes, and gave him the ghost of a smile. "You're awful nice. Thank you."

Inclining his head, he started to say more, but Judge Parson's chamber door opened, and we all rose to our feet. I watched the jury file into the box with my heart in my throat; I couldn't summon Amber's fatalistic calm.

Judge Parson asked whether the jury had reached its verdict.

A silver-haired lady in the front row held the verdict form in her hands. The old woman's voice was hoarse, but her answer was audible: "We have, Your Honor."

I quailed inwardly, then pushed away concerns that this woman had not been one of Amber's clear supporters during the trial. Folding my hands to still any telltale tremors, I concentrated on presenting a stoic facade.

The woman handed the paper verdict to the bailiff, who carried it up to the bench. As the judge scanned the paper, I caught a grim flash of satisfaction crossing his face.

He confirmed it was the verdict of the jury, then read aloud: "We, the jury, find Amber Lynn Travis"—he paused for a moment, glancing up at the people assembled in the courtroom—"not guilty."

Amber bent over at the waist with a guttural moan of relief. I threw my arm around her as I absorbed the outcome: she was free. Really free, for the first time since childhood. Free from incarceration, from servitude, from torture.

Parson said, "Would either side wish to have the jury polled?"

"No, Your Honor," I said as Searcy shook his head. Then I turned back to Amber, who tucked her head onto my shoulder and began to sob. I patted her back, making the soothing noises that my mom had made when I was a kid. When she recovered sufficiently to stand upright, she tried to wipe her eyes, but the metal handcuffs poked into her face.

After he had dismissed the jury, I called out to the judge, "Your Honor, please instruct the deputy to release my client from the restraints."

Judge Parson nodded, looking remorseful. "Deputy, remove the cuffs. Miss Travis, you are free to go."

Sheriff Gilmore must have come in to witness the verdict. As he took the key from Danny's hand and came toward us, Amber looked at me with trepidation.

"Is he taking me back to the jail?"

"No, he's taking off your cuffs. The judge said you're free to go, Amber. Didn't you hear him?"

"I thought maybe they might change their mind."

Sheriff Gilmore gave me a glance under his bushy brows as he unlocked the cuffs. "Leah, you did quite a job for your client. Kind of puts me in mind of your daddy, back in the day."

"Thanks, Sheriff. That's high praise." Although I struggled to sound polite, my voice was frosty. I wasn't quite ready to forgive and forget how he had treated my client.

Amber also seemed dubious. "Leah says I'm not going back to the jail, Sheriff. She says the judge decided I can get on out of here." She had spoken as if she expected him to dispute it.

He fastened the handcuffs onto his belt. "Well, the jury has spoken, so you can do whatever you please. On the other hand, the verdict puts me back in the hot seat. I've still got an unresolved murder."

As Gilmore freed her feet, I said, "Sheriff, you should be aware that there's a personnel problem at the county jail. Amber tells me she's been physically harassed and assaulted."

His face was grave. "And you never reported it?"

"I did report it," I told him. "This weekend."

"Funny, nobody mentioned it to me," he said, skeptical.

"I reported it to the Arkansas Attorney General's office. It's my understanding that it's being handled by the Arkansas State Police."

As the crowd filtered out of the courtroom, two people remained: a man in the blue uniform of the Arkansas State Police, accompanying a young woman in business attire, who lifted a hand in greeting when I caught her eye.

The tension in my shoulders eased as I prepared to hand off the baton.

CHAPTER 85

PUSHING THROUGH THE wooden gate, I left Amber and Sheriff Gilmore and hurried up the aisle to grasp the young woman's hand—an old classmate of mine from U of A, now an assistant in the Arkansas Attorney General's office. "Melissa, thanks so much for coming up here today."

"I appreciated your trip to Little Rock this weekend," she said. "I've shared the evidence you brought with the state police, and Lieutenant Wilson here has notified the FBI. A special agent should be here this afternoon. We all want to talk to your client."

The trooper was eyeing Amber with professional interest. He said, "Ms. Randall, will you introduce us to Ms. Travis?"

We returned to the defense table. When I made the introductions, Amber took a step back, hiding her hands behind her as if she feared the trooper would snap cuffs around them again. Giving me a pleading look, she said, "But the judge says I'm free to go. He said so, just now."

The trooper said, "Ms. Travis, we're not looking to charge you. We're investigating the human trafficking activity that happened on your cousin's farm in Hagar County. The videos your lawyer shared are shocking."

The sheriff spoke up, frowning. "Trooper, why hasn't anyone filled me in on this?"

"The investigation has just commenced," the trooper acknowledged.

Melissa broke in. "Lieutenant Wilson and I served on the state task force on human trafficking, so we'll be heading it up. But we hope we can join forces with local law enforcement as well."

Searcy stepped into the circle, nudging me out of the way. "So you seriously intend to investigate the defendant's claims of her abuse at the hands of Dale Maggard?" His voice rang with incredulity. "The man who committed the assaults is dead." He turned to Melissa, addressing her. "What's the point?"

Edging away from Searcy, Melissa said, "The point is, it's a violation of the Arkansas Human Trafficking Act. This isn't a case of simple assault. And the FBI is interested in possible violations of federal law."

Sheriff Gilmore shook his head, dumbfounded. "The Feds? Investigating the Maggards?"

Searcy thrust both hands into his pockets, scoffing, "But the Maggards are dead. You can't prosecute the deceased."

I stood watching the county prosecutor with clinical detachment as I waited for the Little Rock bomb to drop.

The trooper said, "We think Dale Maggard was part of a commercial sex-trafficking conspiracy. I'd like to ask you some questions about it, Mr. Searcy. But before we begin, I must inform you of the following: You have the right to remain silent."

As the trooper recited the rest of the Miranda warning, Searcy blanched and backed away, waving an arm in dismissal. "I know my rights, and I have no intention of participating in this absurdity. The man who assaulted the girl is dead. This has nothing to do with me."

As Searcy fled the courtroom, the trooper followed. Sheriff Gilmore turned to me. "This doesn't make a lick of sense. Why is Amber's mistreatment the prosecutor's fault?"

"Because Dale Maggard didn't torture Amber for only his own kicks. He made money from customers who paid to watch or participate in her torture. That makes it a human-trafficking conspiracy, and the customers are criminally liable."

I glanced down at Amber, concerned that the discussion might be distressing to her, but her head was bent over her dress as she traced the flowers on the fabric.

Impatient, Gilmore said, "I'm an officer of the law. You don't need to explain conspiracy to me. But why are they interrogating Shelby?"

"Sheriff, I didn't bring all of the DVDs to court. I left one in Little Rock," I said. "On that video, Amber is hooded, but a man's voice can be heard participating in her torture." The recollection nauseated me. "You'd recognize his voice if you heard it, Sheriff."

Gilmore's face contorted. "No. No, that's crazy, that just can't be." He seemed to shrink inside his uniform, and he sank into my chair, as if his knees had suddenly given way. Looking up at me, he said, "Your dad tried to tell me some wild suspicions a while back, Leah. I just wrote it off, figured it was the dementia. Everyone knew he was losing it."

I wasn't surprised to hear that Dad had reached out. And it was no shock that, in Bassville, his concerns had fallen on deaf ears.

Shaking his head ruefully, Sheriff Gilmore rose from the chair and turned to go, but before he departed, he looked back. Doggedly, he said, "It doesn't seem possible. I can't believe a man like Shelby Searcy would do such a thing."

I explained it in a way I hoped the sheriff would understand. "Remember your own witness, that homeless guy? He nailed it: Searcy's one of those dudes who likes to hurt women."

CHAPTER 86

WHEN AMBER WAS little, her mama used to say that things could turn on a dime. She'd never understood what Mama meant until it happened to her.

After the jury set her free, the whole town of Bassville turned on a dime. Everybody wanted to be her friend and lend a hand. Even Kate Cole chased her down and flat begged her to move back into that apartment.

But Leah didn't like the idea. She told Amber that the state police were investigating Hopp Cole and some other people in town, too. And that Amber couldn't eat at Western Roadhouse anymore.

So Amber moved to a different town, one where people welcomed her—churches, clubs, businesses. Leah told her it was a smart move, because the streets of that community were paved with Walmart gold. Amber knew the streets didn't really have gold on them, but she saw shiny new buildings and fancy stores and restaurants. And she had a new place to live, called an Airbnb. It was the prettiest little house she'd ever seen, with cozy furniture to sit on and pink sheets on the bed. And a women's group was letting her stay for free while she helped with research on domestic violence and worked with the Arkansas Human Trafficking Task

Force. Because as it turned out, Amber was a kind of expert about that.

One sunny afternoon, Amber sat at her kitchen table, surrounded by schoolbooks and papers. Some old schoolteachers were determined to see Amber get a high school diploma called a GED, and Amber was grateful to them, most of the time. Today, she felt plumb wore out.

As she shuffled through her homework papers, her cell phone rang. When she glanced at where it came from, she giggled.

Los Angeles, CA

Amber let the call go to voicemail. It was best to let her lawyer do the talking with those Hollywood people. If they wanted to make a miniseries based on her life, they'd have to win the bidding war. That's what Leah said, anyway.

Maybe it was time to give Leah a call.

CHAPTER 87

MY CELL PHONE buzzed as I sat at my desk on a Thursday afternoon. When I picked up, Amber spoke before I had the chance to say hello.

"Those California people called me again. They left a message."

"Just forward it to me. I'll get back with them," I said. "How are you doing?"

She groaned into my ear. "Those schoolteachers just left. I'm lying down. My head hurts."

I was glad she couldn't see me grin. The retired teachers in Rogers, Arkansas, must be formidable, to make Amber hit the books.

"Remember to thank them. They're donating their time to help you. Have you heard anything new from the attorney general's office? Or the US attorney?"

"No, not lately. Just what we already been told. About the Hickocks and the breaking in and that."

The investigation had led to the teenage pickup driver, Michael Hickock, and his mother, Rose, the jailer. Searcy had placed the boy on deferred prosecution for petty theft, then had used the threat of prosecution as a tool to coerce him to commit crimes. The kid had confessed to burglarizing both Dad's office and Beverly's home, in efforts to unearth Amber's slavery contract. He'd also copped to setting the fire in Amber's apartment and the second arson at the Maggard farm that had destroyed the henhouse and shed. Rose had said Searcy also had blackmailed her to keep Amber under wraps at the county jail. But neither mother nor son claimed to have any involvement or knowledge regarding the murders of Dale and Glenna.

"Have they told you when they'll need further testimony?" I asked. Amber had testified before a grand jury, which had led to multiple indictments against Searcy for conspiracy to commit human trafficking, but the investigation was ongoing.

"No, they said they'll be in touch." Her voice brightened. "Can I sell the farm yet?"

"Not yet. Soon." Since Amber's not guilty verdict, the stalled probate action was moving with lightning speed.

"Good. I've been thinking of some things I need to get with that money," she said. "Well, I got to go. The Methodists are having a picnic tonight, and they want me to be there."

"You're the toast of the town, Amber."

She sighed, as if the celebrity was a weighty burden. "Yeah, I reckon so. Bye."

The door to my office opened, and I caught a whiff of gardenia scent as Beverly said, "You told me to remind you that you need to leave at 3:00 today, Leah."

"Thanks, Beverly. You head on out, too. I'll lock up."

When I left shortly after, I turned the key beneath the glass panel in the front door that still bore Dad's name in shiny black letters. Beverly had posted a temporary sign underneath: LEAH RANDALL, ATTORNEY AT LAW. I made a mental note to contact the window painter to make it permanent.

Across the square, I saw the newly installed interim prosecutor exit the courthouse. "Good luck," I whispered. He would need it. The new district prosecutor was a kid, even younger than I was. They'd asked every attorney in the district to take the post—except me. My mother was indignant on my behalf, especially when Britney's mother, Terri Shelton, had reported that people thought I was "too contrary" and that some folks in town had called me a bitch.

It didn't sting. It was the truth.

"I'm the bitch who's putting the B back in Bassville, Mom," I'd said, laughing, when she'd repeated the news.

In addition to taking over Dad's office, I still resided in my parents' green-and-white house. Mom had asked me to stay at least until we got Dad settled into a new living situation; but she'd seen and rejected four assisted-living facilities with memory units so far, unwilling to sentence Dad to an inferior nursing home. So the search continued.

Mom conducted her care-facility inspections on the sly, fearing Dad would flip out if he suspected what she was planning for his future. When I arrived home, she headed out to tour a fifth one while I headed into the garage. I'd promised to deliver Dad's seven-year-old Buick La Crosse sedan to the dealer that afternoon. I hoped my folks would get a good return on it. Armed with a plastic trash bag, I emptied the trunk and dug around in the seats and under the floor mats, but there wasn't much litter to collect. Dad was always, as Beverly used to say, a neatnik.

I slid into the front passenger seat. When I pushed the button on the glove compartment, I was surprised to find it locked up tight. But I used my dad's key ring, and after a couple of tries, the door fell open.

My nose wrinkled as an unpleasant odor assaulted me—a smell of solvent, like WD-40, mixed with Dad's signature minty smell. Behind the proof-of-insurance cards and owner's manual, and a tin of Altoids, I found an object wrapped in a white pillowcase.

Handling it gingerly, I pulled the object from the glove box, nestled in one of the cross-stitched monogrammed pillowcases my mother had embroidered.

It was a large revolver.

I slid the gun back into the pillowcase, wrapping the excess fabric around it, then exited the Buick. In my rush to get back into the house, I nearly tripped over a few empty metal gas cans.

I found Dad in the living room, flipping through channels with the television remote.

When I entered the room, he looked up with a frown. "It's time for the news, isn't it? I can't find the news."

"No, Dad. The news doesn't come on until five."

He tossed the remote onto the side table, shaking his head in disgust. "A hundred channels of nothing."

I set the pillowcase on the coffee table, then reached inside. I placed the revolver out of his grasp on the table. "Dad, I found this in your car."

"I'm not driving. You took my keys." His face was resentful.

"I know that. But what is this doing in the glove box?"

Dad stared at it for a long moment while I tried to keep feelings of panic at bay. "Dad?" I prompted him.

"I believe that's my handgun," he said eventually. He leaned forward in his chair and made a move to grab it, but I snatched it away. "What are you doing with it, Leah?"

I drew a shuddering breath. "I found it in your car."

"Well, that's not right. I keep it locked up, in my office."

The statement sparked a recollection: the smell in the empty cabinet at Dad's office. It had smelled like the gun on the table, with that distinctive odor of oil.

Dad looked up. At length, he said, "I need to get rid of it."

My shoulders started to shake. "Why, Dad?"

His brow furrowed, and he set his hands on his knees. "That girl. I can't think of her name. She was a little bitty thing. I was her guardian ad litem."

"Amber Travis," I said.

He grimaced. "Could be. The judge put her with some cousins. I had a gut feeling—I didn't like it. I opposed the placement, but I didn't have grounds."

Tears welled up in my eyes, but I blinked them back. "It's not your fault, Dad. You couldn't have known."

He cleared his throat. "Sometimes in a small town like Bassville, you hear things." He met my eyes, adding, "And sometimes you find out the truth behind those whispers. It was my duty to look out for the girl's welfare."

"Dad, what did you do?" I whispered.

"I've always maintained that you have to protect the people who are entrusted to your care. Do you remember that? I taught you that, Leah, didn't I?"

He looked away, as if trying to recall. Shaking his head with frustration, his eye caught the remote.

Pointing it at the TV, he said, "Have I missed the news? I like Tom Brokaw. He's a good journalist, for a liberal."

"It's Lester..." I started, before I fell silent. It didn't matter.

He gave me a curious glance. "Where do you live now?"

"What?" I was still living upstairs, in the aqua bedroom.

"Do you live close to the Wrigley Building? I walked right by it when I took your mother on a trip one time." He shook his head again and said, "Can't remember the year. Seems like it was quite a while ago."

I made my decision. Wrapping the fabric back around the gun, I walked away. But I glanced into the living room again before I left. Dad was still struggling with the TV, trying to find Tom Brokaw.

"See you in a little bit, Dad."

"Right," he said.

I was dry-eyed as I drove off with the weapon that had been used to execute Dale and Glenna Maggard. When I pulled into the town square, Sheriff Gilmore drove by in his squad car, and I gave him a friendly wave.

When he saw me, he stopped and rolled down his window. "Hey, Leah. Have you heard anything new about the investigation?"

I gripped the steering wheel but lifted my shoulders in a casual shrug. "Nothing new. Not that I've heard."

When I reentered the office, I closed the blinds before I removed the dated family portrait that hung over the hidden wall cabinet. After I returned the gun to its original resting place inside the cabinet, I replaced the photo and nudged the frame to ensure it hung perfectly straight. I focused on the faces in the photograph. Dad and I looked identical, staring into the camera with grim expressions.

Dad had always thought I didn't listen to his lectures. He'd preached to me nonstop about duty: duty to family, to clients, to the underdog. To protecting the people in my care.

I remembered it all.

I gave the photo one last look before I turned away, shaking my head over the irony.

Turns out, I am my father's daughter.

ACKNOWLEDGMENTS

Several attorneys provided valuable assistance as we shaped the court cases and legal issues our characters encountered. Special thanks go to John Appelquist for his knowledge of criminal law and procedure; Donald Bacon for his aid on Arkansas legal practices; and the late Susan Appelquist, former vice chairperson of the Missouri Supreme Court Advisory Committee, for her expertise on professional ethics and disciplinary proceedings.

ABOUT THE AUTHORS

James Patterson is one of the best-known and biggest-selling writers of all time. His books have sold in excess of 400 million copies worldwide. He is the author of some of the most popular series of the past two decades – the Alex Cross, Women's Murder Club, Detective Michael Bennett and Private novels – and he has written many other number one bestsellers including non-fiction and stand-alone thrillers.

James is passionate about encouraging children to read. Inspired by his own son who was a reluctant reader, he also writes a range of books for young readers including the Middle School, Dog Diaries, Treasure Hunters and Max Einstein series. James has donated millions in grants to independent bookshops and has been the most borrowed author in UK libraries for the past thirteen years in a row. He lives in Florida with his family.

Nancy Allen practiced law for fifteen years in her native Ozarks and served as a law instructor at Missouri State University for sixteen years. Nancy is co-author with James Patterson of *Juror No. 3*. She is also the author of the Ozarks Mystery series.

Also by James Patterson

ALEX CROSS NOVELS

Along Came a Spider • Kiss the Girls • Jack and Jill • Cat and Mouse • Pop Goes the Weasel • Roses are Red • Violets are Blue • Four Blind Mice • The Big Bad Wolf • London Bridges • Mary, Mary • Cross • Double Cross • Cross Country • Alex Cross's Trial (*with Richard DiLallo*) • I, Alex Cross • Cross Fire • Kill Alex Cross • Merry Christmas, Alex Cross • Alex Cross, Run • Cross My Heart • Hope to Die • Cross Justice • Cross the Line • The People vs. Alex Cross • Target: Alex Cross • Criss Cross • Deadly Cross

THE WOMEN'S MURDER CLUB SERIES

1st to Die • 2nd Chance (*with Andrew Gross*) • 3rd Degree (*with Andrew Gross*) • 4th of July (*with Maxine Paetro*) • The 5th Horseman (*with Maxine Paetro*) • The 6th Target (*with Maxine Paetro*) • 7th Heaven (*with Maxine Paetro*) • 8th Confession (*with Maxine Paetro*) • 9th Judgement (*with Maxine Paetro*) • 10th Anniversary (*with Maxine Paetro*) • 11th Hour (*with Maxine Paetro*) • 12th of Never (*with Maxine Paetro*) • Unlucky 13 (*with Maxine Paetro*) • 14th Deadly Sin (*with Maxine Paetro*) • 15th Affair (*with Maxine Paetro*) • 16th Seduction (*with Maxine Paetro*) • 17th Suspect (*with Maxine Paetro*) • 18th Abduction (*with Maxine Paetro*) • 19th Christmas (*with Maxine Paetro*) • 20th Victim (*with Maxine Paetro*) • 21st Birthday (*with Maxine Paetro*)

DETECTIVE MICHAEL BENNETT SERIES

Step on a Crack (*with Michael Ledwidge*) • Run for Your Life (*with Michael Ledwidge*) • Worst Case (*with Michael Ledwidge*) • Tick Tock (*with Michael Ledwidge*) • I, Michael Bennett (*with Michael Ledwidge*) • Gone (*with Michael Ledwidge*) • Burn (*with Michael Ledwidge*) • Alert (*with Michael Ledwidge*) • Bullseye (*with Michael Ledwidge*) • Haunted (*with James O. Born*) • Ambush (*with James O. Born*) • Blindside (*with James O. Born*) • The Russian (*with James O. Born*)

PRIVATE NOVELS

Private (*with Maxine Paetro*) • Private London (*with Mark Pearson*) • Private Games (*with Mark Sullivan*) • Private: No. 1 Suspect (*with Maxine Paetro*) • Private Berlin (*with Mark Sullivan*) • Private Down Under (*with Michael White*) • Private L.A. (*with Mark Sullivan*) • Private India (*with Ashwin Sanghi*) • Private Vegas (*with Maxine Paetro*) • Private Sydney (*with Kathryn Fox*) • Private Paris (*with Mark Sullivan*) • The Games (*with Mark Sullivan*) • Private Delhi (*with Ashwin Sanghi*) • Private Princess (*with Rees Jones*) • Private Moscow (*with Adam Hamdy*) • Private Rogue (*with Adam Hamdy*)

NYPD RED SERIES

NYPD Red (*with Marshall Karp*) • NYPD Red 2 (*with Marshall Karp*) • NYPD Red 3 (*with Marshall Karp*) • NYPD Red 4 (*with Marshall Karp*) • NYPD Red 5 (*with Marshall Karp*) • NYPD Red 6 (*with Marshall Karp*)

DETECTIVE HARRIET BLUE SERIES

Never Never (*with Candice Fox*) • Fifty Fifty (*with Candice Fox*) • Liar Liar (*with Candice Fox*) • Hush Hush (*with Candice Fox*)

INSTINCT SERIES

Instinct (*with Howard Roughan, previously published as* Murder Games) • Killer Instinct (*with Howard Roughan*)

THE BLACK BOOK SERIES

The Black Book (*with David Ellis*) • The Red Book (*with David Ellis*)

STAND-ALONE THRILLERS

The Thomas Berryman Number • Hide and Seek • Black Market • The Midnight Club • Sail (*with Howard Roughan*) • Swimsuit (*with Maxine Paetro*) • Don't Blink (*with Howard*

Roughan) • Postcard Killers (*with Liza Marklund*) • Toys (*with Neil McMahon*) • Now You See Her (*with Michael Ledwidge*) • Kill Me If you Can (*with Marshall Karp*) • Guilty Wives (*with David Ellis*) • Zoo (*with Michael Ledwidge*) • Second Honeymoon (*with Howard Roughan*) • Mistress (*with David Ellis*) • Invisible (*with David Ellis*) • Truth or Die (*with Howard Roughan*) • Murder House (*with David Ellis*) • The Store (*with Richard DiLallo*) • Texas Ranger (*with Andrew Bourelle*) • The President is Missing (*with Bill Clinton*) • Revenge (*with Andrew Holmes*) • Juror No. 3 (*with Nancy Allen*) • The First Lady (*with Brendan DuBois*) • The Chef (*with Max DiLallo*) • Out of Sight (*with Brendan DuBois*) • Unsolved (*with David Ellis*) • The Inn (*with Candice Fox*) • Lost (*with James O. Born*) • Texas Outlaw (*with Andrew Bourelle*) • The Summer House (*with Brendan DuBois*) • 1st Case (*with Chris Tebbetts*) • Cajun Justice (*with Tucker Axum*) • The Midwife Murders (*with Richard DiLallo*) • The Coast-to-Coast Murders (*with J.D. Barker*) • Three Women Disappear (*with Shan Serafin*) • The President's Daughter (*with Bill Clinton*) • The Shadow (*with Brian Sitts*)

NON-FICTION

Torn Apart (*with Hal and Cory Friedman*) • The Murder of King Tut (*with Martin Dugard*) • All-American Murder (*with Alex Abramovich and Mike Harvkey*) • The Kennedy Curse (*with Cynthia Fagen*) • The Last Days of John Lennon (*with Casey Sherman and Dave Wedge*) • Walk in My Combat Boots (*with Matt Eversmann and Chris Mooney*)

MURDER IS FOREVER TRUE CRIME

Murder, Interrupted • Home Sweet Murder • Murder Beyond the Grave • Murder Thy Neighbour • Murder of Innocence • Till Murder Do Us Part

COLLECTIONS

Triple Threat • Kill or Be Killed • The Moores are Missing • The Family Lawyer • Murder in Paradise • The House Next Door • 13-Minute Murder • The River Murders • The Palm Beach Murders

For more information about James Patterson's novels, visit www.penguin.co.uk